SONS OF SCRAPYARD

PART 1 OF 2

CHILDREN OF AUREUM SERIES

BY CAMERON LISAMA

Sons of Scrapyard Pocket Edition

Contact info:
Website: https://www.sonsofscrapyard.com
Youtube: https://www.youtube.com/@cameronlisama
Email: sonsofscrapyard@gmail.com

Credits:
Critiqued, Coached, and Edited by Makayla Julianna Lisama

Concept art by Nolan Lu:
https://www.artstation.com/nolan192
https://www.instagram.com/billowypillow/
https://x.com/billowypillow

Map brought to life on Inkarnate.com
Formatted on Adobe InDesign
ISBN: 978-1-968430-01-6

First Edition: 2025
10 9 8 7 6 5 4 3 2 1

For Makayla,
Sweet girl...

And for our son, who will know
not but the love he deserves and the
worlds we build for him...

CONTENTS

AUREUM
THE GOLDEN WORLD

AL AND MEEKO
I

'DON'T BE AFRAID.........' He awoke to these words with a jolt, escaping from a nightmare he couldn't remember. Gasping for breath like it was his first, he choked on the earth that accompanied the air as he struggled to lift his face from the dirt.

The silhouette of a young forest surrounded him. Sun either just setting or about to rise, as gray light filled the cracks between the tall shadows. The air was cool and still, wet against the back of his neck. A steady trickle of water could be heard not far off. Mouth dry with the taste of blood and dust. *Tastes like a fight.*

Stuck, face down, in a crumpled pile. Attempting to move proved far more difficult than he had hoped. Like one of Bali's bad ideas that gets crushed into a little paper ball and tossed in with the kindling. The numbing fog of death slowly thinned and through it, he could make out the familiar throbbing of his own broken neck. *Well, that's no good.* The only thing in his view was red dirt and his right hand, the palm of which was tucked flat between his wrist and the ground. Like a hand sandwich. *A Handwich.* It was less of a laugh and more of a cough that escaped his chest.

Breathing was limited at the moment, but he filled his lungs as best he could and, without dwelling on the thought, flung his arm forward. His wrist exploded. A growl crawled up his throat and morphed into a groaning tearful chuckle. *Sink my ass... That fuckin' hurt...*

He had yet to look, but he was very much expecting his hand to no longer be his. Maybe thrown several feet away, gaining its own sentience, and fleeing his cursed body on weird little finger legs. He wondered if it would scurry off on all fives like a spider or try running upright on two fingers, like a little hand person. Either thought was equally amusing, but more importantly, distracting. At least enough for the pain to fade.

Peeking with one eye, his hand had successfully flopped back into a more natural position. Soon after the bones realigned, their throbbing pain was replaced by the buzz of pins and needles. He always imagined an army of tiny spiders sewing his body back together, like Sarah mending another tear in his jacket. The sensation made him squirm, but in those few uncomfortable minutes, he'd remember the smell of that dirty sling Fordo had to wear for several weeks after their tumble down the aqueducts.

One by one, he located the still broken bones and groaned them back into place until he was able to finally sit upright. Wrist, collar bone, ribs, and a lot more spine than he was comfortable with. *A new record.* He usually awoke just as the final wound was healing. Whatever had killed him this time tried a lot harder than its predecessors.

After wiping away the tears that followed the uncoiling of his neck, he inspected himself. Jacket worn with age and adventure, but no new holes or rips, as far as he could tell.

Dozens of scars and stitches in the leather exposed the gray flesh of it, darkened by the dampness of the dirt and the dew of the morning. His calloused hands were patched with blood and grime, fingernails bordered black. His wooden prosthetic ring-finger had twisted itself around, mud filled the small spaces between the hand carved joints. He screwed it back into position and ran his thumb along the twin purple scars that circled his half healed wrists. His light brown skin camouflaged them well enough that he often forgot they were there. He wondered when that memory would come out of hiding. *One death, one scar at a time*, he reminded himself.

He was littered with shallow cuts and scratches, he could feel the itch of his skin nitting back together. The needles faded and soreness crept into his neck, back and shoulders. His head was split with a piercing ache. Sometimes he wished he was able to die just to avoid the hangover.

Slowly the world grew brighter. *Sunrise.* Shapes transformed back into things and he found himself at the edge of a small clearing. A near perfect circle of red leafed trees looked down at the half broken creature that had fallen at their feet, patiently waiting with cautious concern. A shallow stream slithered through the center of the clearing. Across it lay other dark shapes he could only squint at in the gray. *Have I been here before?*

What he guessed was his pack had been flung near the creek, its contents spilled about. On the other side of the stream lay what appeared to be the body of his slayer. He couldn't make out the true shape of it from where he rested, but just the crumpled pile was far larger than him. Probably a Bot, too many trees for a Wyrm. Maybe a bear. He really hoped for a bear. Apart from the deer, rabbits, crows, and occasional dog, he had only met so many earth-born monsters, and always wanted to see where Bali got his title.

He picked himself up and retaught himself how to walk, hobbling towards his things. Most of them seemed to be in attendance. Rope still strapped and bundled on the side of the pack. Wyrms teeth, whetstone, fire starter, and other various tools and treasures were all in their place or found near. On his person, however, he was missing quite a lot. His knife was absent from its sheath just as his hatchet from its holster, both of which he rarely used in a fight. He almost always preferred to use his sword, whose scabbard lay empty beside his pack. The familiar soreness in his limbs that often followed an extended battle was missing, this fight had been brief. *They'll turn up.* After gathering his scattered whatevers, he went to meet the sleeping giant.

Pink sunlight began to pour in from between the trees, signaling the end of twilight and lifting the blanket of shadows from the clearing. The "giant" was indeed a giant. A hulking humanoid robot swallowed up by the earth, its lower half and left arm planted firmly in the ground. Orange and purple moss bordered where the rusted metal met the dirt. His missing sword was found, stuck deep in the articulated neck of the beast. Al placed a hand upon the metal, layered so thick with moss and rust the bot could have been made of stone. It felt ancient......older than any other bot he'd seen, older than the forest around them.

"Oy, what happened to you, big guy? You look like absolute glass..." He smiled, plucking off some of the dried roots growing out from between the armored plates and flicking them right into the monster's one big empty eye socket in the center of its 'face'. Moss dangled from the opening like eternal tears. Al's smile faded to a frown finally recognizing the bot's design. "Aw, man......"

He sighed and plucked away the teary moss, gently knocking on the side of its head, "You're a Gardener......" Al kissed his own hand and pressed it back against the sunken scrap. "I didn't know......I'd say I'm sorry I killed you, but.........you probably started it......Rest easy, friend......I'll send some folks to find you soon, I promise."

Hopping onto its back the metal screeched as he unsheathed his sword from the creature. He sat on its shoulders, running his eyes along the length of the short, black, diamond shaped blade, checking for dullness or damage. There were no cracks, no new chips, and the double edges were still sharp enough for at least one more fight. Hopping down and walking back to his things, he sheathed his blade, packed his pack, and whistled loud and sharp. "Meeko!"

Within moments, his ears were filled with the pad of paws and buzz of gears. A smile sprouted and grew as the sound drew nearer. Paws rolled like a drum as a handsome black and silver shepherd dog burst through the bushes and tackled Alexander back to the ground, unleashing a hail of wet kisses on the face of his brother. His one metal paw digging into Al's still healing ribs.

"Alright, alright, ya big baby…" Al laughed, trying to fend off the onslaught of affection, "What, you miss me or somethin'?" Meeko yelped and cried, maneuvering through Al's defenses for some additional damage.

Alexander held Meeko's face to calm the frenzy of cries and kisses, "Hey, hey I'm alright, buddy, promise…" He pressed their foreheads together and scratched Meeko's neck and back until his shaking stilled. "What are you crying for? I always come back, buddy. We always come back…" He held his boy down with a hug until the pins stopped buzzing. "How you doin', Meeks?" Meeko whined and licked where his fur met the prosthetic paw. *Pawsthetic.* The metal frame was slightly bent and twisted. "Yeah, me too…" Scrap got the better of them both, it seemed. Alexander studied the damaged paw for a moment. Apparently Meeko could still sprint on it, but Al could sense some pain. "Looks like we're heading back home. Can't have you limping all the way to Julia."

Meeko cocked his head and stared at his brother. His eyes were two different colors. Both hazel, but the left more red and the right, almost gold. Whenever Al looked into them, he could see the intelligence behind them. He often wished Meeko could speak. *There's wisdom in you, boy.* Meeko's fur, usually sleek and shiny, was now matted and filthy from however many days he had to wait for Alexander to return to the world of the living.

I hate sending you away…

Al knew he could trust Meeko in a fight, but not against a metal giant with no flesh to bite. Even though they both healed the same, he'd rather die alone and spare his boy some suffering.

He turned and knelt by the creek, leaning over to see his reflection in the now yellow light. His dark hair was longer than he remembered and in a similar state as Meeko's coat, covered in mud and tangled to oblivion, the back of his head completely caked in dried blood. The gray bags that hung under his light brown eyes made him wonder if he wasn't really such a young man. *You'd think that for someone who's been Dead asleep for who knows how long, you'd look more rested.* Shoving his dirt and blood covered face into the cold water he scrubbed the grime away. "What are you waiting for, Meek? You look like something Brash pulled out of the gutters." Without hesitation, Meeko hopped in and rolled himself in the refreshing stream. *Filthy animal.* Al watched his old friend and smiled to himself.

Once the water cleared, he dipped his hands into the stream and drank his fill. He relished the feeling of quenched thirst. It cleared his head and reminded him he was alive again. A less filthy Meeko lay drying in the warm sunlight, resting his eyes for the first time in who knows how long without worry for his brother's safety. Al wondered at the worry. *I'll always come back, buddy. We always come back.* Al let him rest a while and wandered the clearing, trying to recall the fight.

Using the rising sun to get his bearings, he walked back to the western end of the clearing and reentered. The body of the beast was the only notable thing about the place and from behind it looked even more derelict. He kicked a rock at the bot with a dull clang. Deja vu kicked in and his memory returned:

Walking into the clearing he found Meeko already there, sniffing the sunken giant. "Meeko, get back!" Meeko obliged and ran to Al's side. Al drew his sword and stepped toward the beast. Resting the blade on his shoulder, he waited a moment. If it was alive it should have noticed them by now. He kicked a rock at the bot with a dull clang. Nothing. He took a breath and went to sheath his sword. "Good find, Meek...Mee..."

With no warning, the urge to sneeze overtook him. He tried to fight it, but just as his eyes closed and his face exploded, the massive arm of the monster slammed into them both. Meeko cried out as he was flung back into the forest. Alexander was knocked back several yards, landing on the ground gasping and coughing. You gotta be fucking kidding me. "Meeko... Run!" He shouted when he could. The beast's arm still swinging wildly, like it was swatting at an invisible swarm of insects. It reared its head, the decaying metal shrieked and roared as it rubbed together, moving for the first time in ages, tearing off its own trapped appendage in the struggle.

Alexander held his chest, coughing up warm salty blood into his mouth and down his chin. The bot was completely sunk and Al was launched beyond its reach. Most folks would've left the trapped monster for someone else to deal with, but Al knew someone else might come along who was far less capable and far less healy than he was, and he refused to accept the possible pain of those distant strangers. More personally, however, he now had a few more broken ribs than he would have liked to and wasn't about to let that go.

He unslung his pack and raised it like a shield, retrieved his sword and took a breath, trying to time out the beast's flailing.

Left...Right...Left...Now!

Al sprinted forward, breathing heavy. He launched his pack toward the monster only to be swatted away. Al dove over the arm as it swept back, rolling onto his feet. He was in front of it now, circling around the armless shoulder and ducking under the attempted grab, he reached the monster's back and raised his sword. Gotchya.

Letting out a triumphant roar, Al plunged his sword deep into the back of the monster's neck. "Hit my dog again you rusty cu-Ahh!" As a final act, the monster reached back and grabbed Alexander by the head. Uh oh. Launching his glass body through the air, across the clearing, sending him crashing into the trunk of a tree. He heard the wet crack of his own bones shattering before blacking out into oblivion...

"Don't be afraid..." Al mumbled to himself, staring at the black stained trunk of the tree. He fiddled with something in his pocket a moment before the flashback was interrupted by a curious Meeko. As he knelt, Meeko sniffed at his empty belt. "I'm not sure," Al scratched behind Meeko's ears, "Wanna give it a shot?" Meeko licked his own nose and wandered off in search of Al's lost items.

Pulling his unfinished map from his inside jacket pocket, Al charted their course. The hand drawn 'map' was pathetic by any standard. A crooked line of six triangle mountains, bundle of four half circle hills, with a single dot between for Scrapyard village. They weren't more than two days north of where their journey originated. "Hm..." He stared blankly through the map. Meeko trotted back with Alexander's ax between his teeth.

"Meek, how long was I-oh, thank you, by the way. How long was I out for?" Meeko paused a moment and pawed at the ground in front of him three times. Al returned his ax to his belt. His face and shoulders dropped, "Three days??" He tapped his fingers on Meeko's head. "I'm sorry, buddy, I didn't mean to leave you alone for that long..." Meeko twisted his head to lick Al's hand. "No, it's not okay. I'll be more careful."

"Two days up, three days out, and two days down..." They'll be returning from what was potentially a year long journey, in little more than a week. If it weren't for Meeko's repairs, they'd probably continue on their quest, leaving this little detour behind them. Ba*li's gonna kill me if he finds out I died again.* "Just sink me now, Meeks..."Al sighed

He stood and gathered his everything, starting toward the trees, waving one last goodbye to the lonely giant. Meeko barked, digging near where Alexander had awoken. "What is it, buddy?" The sunlight flickered off of something metal hiding in the leaves. Meeko stared back at him blankly. Al smirked, "Don't look at me like that."

Walking back, he scooped up his knife. A dirt covered, wyrm tooth dagger, engraved with the words: "Don't Lose This One" on the steel handle. Al sheathed it and coughed out a quick "Thanks..." Meeko shook his head and waddled off into the brush. "Let's get out of here."

II

SONS OF SCRAPYARD

FORDO

I

"Fuckin' glass..." Cursed Carth, a tall, broad, olive skinned, young man with dark eyes and a goofy smile, accidentally putting his hand in something gray and slimy on the cave wall. "I don't know how much more cave I can take, Fordo."

"I have to find her, Carthy," Replied Fordo, a smaller, thinner, younger man with paler skin, sharper features, and deep gray eyes.

Gotta make this trip worth it...

"Riverwood's got plenty of little girls, they can spare one," Carth said, trying in vain to fling the goo off his hand.

"And you can spare one day in the dark with a little slime," Kira chimed in, almost invisible with his dark skin, save for his bright blue eyes. "Someone's kid is missing and you're worried about getting your hands dirty."

"Then you lead the way, Kira, you know all about getting slimed in the dark," Benji laughed, nudging his twin brother, Jacks. They were nearly identical with their red hair and green eyes, but Jacks kept a tidier beard and Benji had a few more scars on his cheeks.

"Sink that, Benji, Kira's right," Fordo said, without looking back, "I made a promise and we're going to keep it. I'm not leaving this place without her."

The air grew thicker, the deeper they went. That was the only real evidence that they were closing any distance at all. Even with five torches, they could only see a few paces ahead of themselves. Just a wall of darkness and the slight shine of torchlight on the slime covered walls. There wasn't a single sound that they didn't make, just shuffling boots, shifting gear, creasing leather, and torch torn air. No dripping water, not even an echo, just a stale, unnatural stillness.

There should be an echo.

Everyone marched with a raised torch and a hand resting ready on their holstered warhammers. *I think I hate this place.* Fordo thought. "I think I hate this place," Carth said, tugging nervously at the straps on his pack. Fordo glanced at his friend, comforted by their mutual discomfort.

"What do you think this is?" Jacks asked, using the spike on his warhammer to scrape at the gray goo. "It kinda smells like the forest, but doesn't seem like a fungus or really anything that grows."

"This is an old Wyrm route, right?" Carth asked, "Maybe the slime's how they slip through the rocks so fast."

"Girl at the Sleeping Giant mentioned a drill dragon came outta here," Fordo said, "We've seen plenty of those and never seen this glass."

"Maybe my wife came in here and the place creamed itself," Benji laughed

"Mmm...Gross. That doesn't even make sense," Kira shook his head as Carth and Jacks chuckled.

As glad as he was that the boys didn't seem as scared as he was, Fordo couldn't hear himself think, "Whatever shat this out, let's hope it's busier than we are," Fordo said, "Now can we focus up? We're on a fuckin' rescue mission. Can we find this little girl and stop talking about creaming our pants or whatever?"

"Sorry Ford, trying not to let it get to me," Benji nodded, "I've been swallowed by things with bellies cozier than this place."

Carth looked back and forth at either wall, "Bugging me how straight this tunnel is, it's not natural. I feel like we've been walking the same twenty feet for-" Fordo's arm shot back, blocking Carth's path.

"...Ah Sink my ass," Carth exhaled.

They all stopped in their tracks with just enough light to see the end of the tunnel. Three more steps and there'd be no more floor, no more ceiling, just a yawning black nothingness. They all held their breath. *Think it heard you, Carthy.*

"Find me a new torch with a heavier head," Fordo said, still holding Carth back. Everyone but Fordo stood back as Kira pulled a fresh torch from his pack and handed it to him. Fordo traded his for the heavy and set it alight with a sizzling crack. Taking a deep breath, he wound up as far back as he could and launched the torch whirling end over end into the darkness.

Their eyes all widened at how far it flew, and how far it fell. Its brief trail of light revealed a vast open cavern littered with stalactites tall and thick as trees. Slime shimmered on everything touched by torchlight. There was no sign of a ceiling. The flame finally landed, so far that they couldn't hear the collision.

"That's gotta be a sixty yard throw," Jacks said to himself. Fordo blinked the fear from his eyes before turning back to his friends. He reached his hand out to Kira, who returned his original torch. Fordo traced the edge of the drop with the light and tossed it over the edge, revealing not the sheer jagged cliff he imagined, but a smooth steep bank. The torch rolled to a stop at the bottom, it couldn't be more than a thirty foot slope. No one spoke, maybe hoping if they don't acknowledge that they have to go down there, then maybe they won't.

Fordo cleared his throat and gripped the head of his hammer to keep his hands from shaking. "How many more torches do we have?" He asked, his friends quickly rifling through their bags and counting.

"Fifteen, altogether," Jacks replied. *Not enough.*

Fordo took another deep breath. "That's plenty," He said, tapping his hammer, "Kira, light two and secure them on either side of this opening. I wanna be able to see the way home at all times. Jacks, Benji, hammer some stakes back from the ledge a bit to get a rope secure. Carth, get some knots in the rope, give us some grip in this goo, and check every inch of it, make sure it's not gonna break on us when we need it. We're gonna go down there, we're gonna find this girl, and we're never going into another fucking cave ever again. Prime?"

"Prime..."

"No crows today, boys."

"No crows."

"Let's get to work." They all nod, scrambling to their tasks.

Keep 'em busy, keep 'em brave. Kneeling over the edge, twisting his mother's black ring around his finger, Fordo squinted at the far away light, praying that the probably dead girl would save them some trouble and reveal herself.

The villagers said her favorite hunting dog ran in here after an elk. *Little dramatic to charge in yourself, girly. I like dogs as much as anyone, but I don't know anyone who'd kill themselves looking for one.*

Well, I guess that's not true. I do know one guy. I miss you, Al, you smug bastard. Hope you're in a worse place than I am. Next time you disappear on a guy, could at least have the decency to leave a trail. Meeko could've been in and out of this cave in five minutes with the girl on his back.

"Rope secure, Fordy?"

Both of his knees popped as he stood, "You ready, boys?"

"Ready to go home," Benji laughed

"Yeah, me neither," Fordo said, hopping off the ledge and sliding down the bank. Carth and Kira shook hands before leaping off after him. Jacks and Benji stared at each other then down at the rope and proceeded to climb down like civilized humans.

"What took you guys so long?" Carth laughed, covered head to toe in gray.

"What are we, animals? I'm not getting that glass all over me," Jacks said, shuffling down the last few feet.

"You got a little on your hand earlier and freaked out. Now you're fuckin' bathing in it," Benji said

"Hey man, if you're underwater, are you really wet?" Kira asked, extending a gooey hand towards Benji.

"Hey man, if you're covered in glass, are you really disgusting? Yeah, asshole. Don't touch me." Carth and Kira laughed as Benji dodged past them.

"Come here, my big strong man," Kira moved to pull in Jacks for a kiss, but Jacks ducked underneath.

"Nuh uh, that slime ain't gettin' me," Jacks smiled.

"Not yet," Kira laughed.

Fordo was busy trying to figure out what all the long lumps in the floor were, like a web of tree roots under all the slime. For a moment, he feared they were alive, maybe grubs of some kind, but he noticed no movement as he held his breath. *Thank the gods...*

"Jacks," Fordo called out.

"Yes sir?"

"Yeth thir?" Benji mocked.

"Plant a torch by the rope and then every twenty yards or so as we go. We're not getting lost down here."

"Aye, sir"

"Everyone else, spread out, comb forward, keep a light in sight at all times, and call out if you find anything."

Nothing but long lumps, stone spikes, and porous boulders as they crept through the cavern. The spongy slime left no tracks to follow. No trail, no sign that they weren't the first people stupid enough to come into this disgusting place. Fordo looked back, relieved to see Jacks busy lighting their way home.

Something scraped his boot in his distracted steps. A small metal lantern, like he'd seen hanging from Riverwood's porches, sat glass cracked and half sunk in the goo. "Lantern here!" He called out.

"So she is real," Benji said as he jogged up with the others.

"She just might be," Fordo breathed as he kneeled over the lantern.

"It's not a lot to go on," Kira said, looking all around.

"Well, if this was her only light source, how far do you think she could really wander in the dark?" Jacks asked. Almost immediately Carth closed his eyes and dropped to his hands and knees.

"You alright, Carthy?" Fordo laughed.

"I'm following the trail," Carth grunted, blindly feeling his way along the mushy floor. He crawled his way towards a pillar and tried to stand, feeling his way up.

"You don't gotta do all that man," Fordo laughed, impressed by the commitment.

"A true tracker must put himself in the mind of the tracked," Carth said, reaching out with both hands for another pillar in vain, feeling with his foot like a walking stick.

"Come on, Carth, we don't have time to-"

Carth tripped and fell almost flat on his face to the group's amusement.

"Are you done?" Fordo chuckled.

"I landed on my hammer..." Carth groaned. Slowly pulling his arms out of the slime, they emerged with a long, black, braided cord. "But I found this"

"No way!" Kira exclaimed

"She was chasing her dog, right?" Benji asked.

"I think this dumbass found the leash," Carth groaned, victoriously. Picking himself up and tugging the cord, it emerged from the slime, leading into the darkness ahead. "Come on."

"That's our boy," Fordo shrugged and they all followed. The leash pulled taut the whole way, only fifty feet or so before they found the end, wedged tight underneath a large porous boulder at the base of a stalactite, along with two small unmoving paws.

"Oh, Sink my ass..." Carth cursed

"You think it fell on the guy?" Benji asked

"Round boulder at the base of a spike, should've definitely rolled a bit," Jacks said

"And there's no blood..." Kira said, "Falling rock that size could crack a pillboy shell, he should be mush."

Carth got in position to push, "Maybe if we try rolling it off we can get a better-Ahhhh!" Carth's arms sank straight into what they thought was a boulder. The rest of him followed, slimy gray mass folding around him. They all screamed. Fordo scrambled to grab Carth's pack to pull him out. "Get it off! Get it off!" Carth screamed as he was pulled free. Fordo and Carth both fell on their backs, kicking to slide away from the thing.

It started to move. They all froze in place. Half of the sticky gray mass peeled itself from the floor and slowly floated upright, swaying back and forth like it was underwater.

"Ford...?"

"I don't know, Carthy..."

Several thick, vine-like legs unfolded from underneath it. The group retreated further. It stood, revealing the shriveled gray corpse of the girl's dog and four black, talon-like pincers. They all stared in horror as it unleashed a deafening screech and launched itself with a heavy whoosh up into the darkness above.

"Time to go!" Jacks and Benji yelled in unison, pulling Carth and Fordo to their feet. Kira backed himself against another pillar, staring in the direction of the monster. Without warning, tiny gray arms shot out from behind the pillar and wrapped around his leg. He screamed and fell, struggling to retrieve his hammer. The more he struggled, the tighter they gripped. The others rushed to his aid.

Benji lunged to stick the arms with his torch before he was stopped by Carth. "Wait!"

A little black haired girl, covered head to toe in slime, started to cry, squeezing Kira's leg with all her might. "Mira!" The little gray girl latched onto Fordo's chest as he pried her off of his friend, "We gotta go, girly. Your family's waiting for us."

Another screech sounded high above them, then another, then another. They all stared up at the disembodied sound, "How come the echo got louder?" Carth asked

The sound grew and multiplied, spreading in every direction. "That's not an echo..." Jacks whispered

Fuckin' glass...

"Move! Move! Run to the rope!" Fordo shoved his friends forward all sprinting toward the trail of torches. Fordo held Mira's head, running as hard as he could. Even with the girl, he ran ahead of both Jacks and Carth.

Through his heaving lungs and Mira's cries, he noticed a new noise coming from above. Like a flag flapping faster and faster until a meteor of a monster crashed in front of them, barely missing Benji, an explosive spray of slime shooting out from the holes in it's body. His friends scattered. Fordo fell and slid to a stop, shielding Mira with his body, rolling as another monster flapped and crashed beside them.

Carth jumped straight over them, yelling and slamming his warhammer into the gray mass, its flesh folding unharmed around the hammer like fighting an impenetrable bag of water. Carth cursed and pulled Fordo to his feet as the monsters stretched their legs to uproot their pincers from the ground.

Cries and creatures rained down all around them as they ran and dodged, keeping the torches in sight. Benji dropped his pack and sprinted like a madman only ever a pace ahead of the creatures trying to crush him. Throwing his torch and leaping towards the bank as soon as the rope was in sight. He scraped and scrambled his way to the top, rolling exhausted onto the tunnel floor. "I made it..." He cried.

He made it! Fordo thought.

Kira reached the rope and began to climb. Benji pulled from the top to lift him faster.

That's two!

Fordo was almost there himself. *Can't climb with one hand.*

"Sorry, sweetheart..." Fordo whispered before yelling, "Take her!" Picking up speed, he sprinted halfway up the bank and tossed Mira up to his companions without waiting for an answer. She screamed even after she was caught by Kira. "Get her out of here now!" Fordo ordered as he slid back down the bank.

"But I can't-"

"Now, Kira! GO!"

Kira nodded and took off down the tunnel.

We did it! We really-

"Fordo!"

Carth tackled him to the ground as a monster crashed into the bank right where he was standing, rolling onto the torches below. It screeched and flailed as it touched the flames, a black vine swinging to put them out.

Hearing more flapping right above them, Fordo pulled and pinned Carth to a stalactite, hugging the stone spike and praying as a shower of slime drenched them once more, black vines dangled limply down from the dark above. *I'm gonna say that was on purpose.*

The burning creature finally rolled upright and leapt back into the black sky. An exhausted Carth crawled for the rope, but collapsed against the slope.

"Oh no you don't, up you go!" Fordo kicked him in the ass and pushed on Carth's pack until he started climbing. Benji helped haul them both up to sanctuary. "Where's Jacks?" Fordo asked, between pants

"Taking his sweet fuckin' time," Benji muttered, eyes darting around for his brother, "Jacks! Move your ass!"

Fordo looked back to see a single torch sprinting through the maze below. The road to the rope only had a few lights left and Jacks had run himself far from them. *Oh Fuck, he's lost his way...* "Make some noise!" Fordo ordered, "He can't see the trail!"

"Damnit...Jacks! We're over here, you fucking idiot!" Benji screamed, cupping his hands around his mouth. Jacks' torch turned in their direction as it dodged and weaved through the labyrinth of stone spikes, a new monster screaming out of the black above him nearly every second.

"Come on, boy! Over here! Over here!" Carth and Fordo both screamed, lighting and waving new lights in the air. Jacks was heading the right way, but his pace was slowing. *He's getting tired.*

"Don't You Stop Running, You Son Of A Bitch!" Benji screamed, eyes desperate, spit flying from his mouth, "You're not Fuckin' dying down here! I'm not telling Daisy you were sunk by flying balls with legs!" Jacks' regained speed, he was in sight of the rope, so close they could hear him gasping for breath. *Come on, Jacks, you're almost there!*

"You're Never Gonna See Kira's Sweet Ass Again, If You Don---Jackson, No!"

They all gasped watching him trip and fall. A screaming monster shot out of the sky, crushing him underneath it, sending his torch flying through the air, the light snuffing as it landed. They heard his muffled screams from beneath the beast going silent then still. "No..." They all stood and stared, mouths gaping, as the dark filled with more and more screeching cries.

"NOOO!" Benji roared, eyes filled with tears and rage. He shoved past Carth and Fordo, leaping off the ledge with a torch and hammer drawn. "Benji, don't!" Fordo caught Benji's leg, pulling them both, head first, over the slope. Carth grabbed the rope and hugged Fordo's ankle to anchor them.

"Let me go!" Benji cried, trying to claw his way down the slope.

"There's nothing we can do!" Fordo yelled

"Let Me GO!" Benji boot stomped Fordo's nose with a wet crunch, releasing his leg and sending him sliding down the slope.

"Benji, wait!" Carth cried

"That's my twin fucking brother!" Benji scrambled to his feet and took off running through the darkness. Fordo held his throbbing face, warm blood wet his hand.

"Benji..." *Come back!* Still hanging over the slope as he watched Benji's flame fade further and further, revealing a writhing mass of piled monsters. Benji jabbed and stabbed his torch into the pile until it too was snuffed out by a flash of falling fangs. "No, damnit, why??" Tears joined the blood. Carth dragged Fordo back from the ledge as more monsters slammed against the slope.

"We gotta go..." Carth said, through tears of his own. Fordo was still on the ground shaking his head, covering his ears, digging his nails into the back of his head.

I'm sorry. I'm sorry. I'm sorry. I'm sorry.

"Hey!" Carth shook Fordo until he'd look him in the eyes. "We gotta go, now!" Fordo gave him a shaky nod and let Carth pull him to his feet. Leaning on each other's shoulders, they silently shambled back through the tunnel, chased by monstrous shrieks and muffled screams.

I'm sorry......

THE NURU BROTHERS

A lanky, dark skinned, young man fiddled with a wooden lock box atop a high stone wall. He pressed it against his ear, slowly twisting the combination dial, listening for a click or any sort of indication that he was making progress.

Cursing the wind that whipped his ears, he shook the box and pulled on the lid until his fingers hurt. After doing everything short of using his teeth, he contemplated simply tossing it off the wall into the cobblestone courtyard below and scraping together whatever burst out of it.

In his defeat, he looked for patterns in the blue moonlit prairie that stretched between Hilltop Fortress and the mountain lined horizon. As much as he tried to avoid it, his eyes always landed back on the jagged shadow of The Great Wreck. It was the only gap in the Dragon's Teeth Mountains, like one of them had died and left behind a skeleton. He thought he should be used to seeing it by now. One full lap around the known territories a month, for eight years, and the sight of the massive derelict space station still gave him the creeps.

Even the high, stone, ballista lined walls of the fortress didn't give him as much comfort as they were probably supposed to. With no upkeep, he'd seen floating villages less rickety. He swore, even the great bell tower looked like it was leaning.

"You're getting quicker, brother..." A familiar voice called up from the steps behind him.

"Or you're getting slower," He smiled towards a bright eyed face that looked an older version of his own.

"Gathii," The young man raised a hand out.

"Natori, my brother…" Their palms met with a satisfying clap. They pulled each other in for a hug, their fists thumping each other's backs. "Cut your hair all you want, won't make you faster than me, Little Bird," Gathii said as Natori ducked under an attempted pet.

"What's your excuse this time, old man?" Natori laughed.

"Young lady in Gateway needed a little special attention with her delivery."

"Do tell, do tell?"

"Her Scrapyard boyfriend told me to give her his love, but I gave her some of mine instead."

Natori smiled and shook his head, "That glass's gonna catch up to you, one of these days."

"We're the fastest men on Aureum, Little Bird, ain't nothin' catching up to us. Besides, Beans can take the heat on his way around." Gathii leaned his long arms against the wall and stretched his back.

Natori twirled the box between his palms, "Speakin' of Beans, he gave this to me our last pass, I can't figure it out."

"He say what it's for?" Gathii took it from Natori, examining every inch.

"Bet me I couldn't open it before our next lap."

"What's the wager?"

"If I don't, he'll tell my girl over in Julia that my name's not Alhaadi," Natori laughed.

"You guys are still pullin' that sharing shit?" Gathii laughed and shook his head.

"Hey, man, if you can share blame with your twin, I can share love with mine."

"Just seems weird, brother's grubs sharing the same burrow."

"Basically the same grub, if you think about it."

"I've got better glass to think about," Gathii laughed

"If you say so, brother"

Natori quickly frowned as he looked back out towards the mountains. An eerie fog formed low over the field below. Thick and pale, it crept across, devouring all in its path, like an eraser wiping away the painterly view.

"Any news from the north?" Gathii distracted Natori. He was too busy cracking his bare, dust covered toes to notice the grim mist.

"Milo's 'War' is gettin' weirder...He's tryna turn the whole of Gray Quarter against Julia Proper. Start a full on Warphan Revolt."

"Just noisy kids, man...Runnin' around alone too long in their painted city. Most've grown up, you'd think they'da moved on by now."

"A lot graduated to full on Blackwyrm, itchin' for a Real fight in that colosseum. But the gangs are all turnin' second generation...The angry kids raisin' even angrier kids...I don't know, man, it was rough last I ran through."

"Maybe next lap they'll have finally killed each other... and Julia will be nothin' left but artsy soft boys and lonely women."

"Your two favorite things," Natori smirked, "Oh, speakin' of angry kids...Fordo Balison's lookin' to make a name for himself in the northern territories. Passed him heading into Riverwood with young Carth. Said to spread the word: Anyone who needs a helping hammer, they can come to him."

"Fordo north? I figured he was off huntin' Wyrms on my last pass...He's still pissed at pops, huh?"

"Pissed enough to leave that cozy cabin out in Scrapyard behind, that and his fine ass step mom."

"Mm mm mm" Gathii rubbed his palms together, "South's been real quiet, nothin' crazy."

"Southern boys stay busy," Natori said, still staring at the ever-creeping fog.

"Somethin' interesting maybe, few Coward Clan Hunters came up through Silkpool, 'bout a week ago."

"Coward Clan..." Natori shook his head, "What those bastards want?"

"They say they got some kinda spooky monster problem, down south of the Daisies."

"Hm..." Natori grunted, "Well they ran from our last spooky monster problem, so long as it stays down there, they're on their own."

"'That's none of our business.' Seemed to be the general consensus around the port."

"Speakin' of spooky, are you seein' this, man?" Natori pointed down towards the fog. It had closed more than half the distance between the mountains and the fortress in minutes. The whole horizon was covered in white.

"Hm..." The brothers squinted into the mist. "That's a first for me..." Gathii said, Natori nodding.

It took a gust of wind threatening to push him over the wall for Natori to realize, "Oy, that's moving against the wind..." Neither man moved for several minutes. It was close now, approaching the base of the hill the fortress sat upon.

A dark silhouette appeared through the veil. Both of their eyes widened at the sight. "No way..." Humanoid in shape, but far too large to really be, a single, dark armored giant stood motionless upon the cloud. Natori squinted to see its face only to realize it had none. A smooth featureless surface, pointing straight up towards the twins, like someone had sanded off the eyes, nose, and mouth of a metallic human skull. Dozens of smaller man-sized shadows followed close behind, similarly silent, faceless, keeping pace with the mist, all glowing the sickly blue of moonlit metal. "No Way!" The little wooden box slipped through Natori's fingers, over the edge of the wall, and tumbled down the steep hillside.

"Oy, that can't be...That's-"

Bong.........Bong.........Bong!

Natori was cut off by the deep clang of the bell tower and the panicked shouts of the fortress guards above. *They're back...* The brothers looked up towards the tower, at each other, then back toward the shadows below.

Mist swept over the wooden box and crashed against the foot of the hill like a wave. The dense cloud surrounded Hilltop fortress, making it feel like they were standing in the sky. It might have been beautiful if not for the metal monsters marching out of the mist.

Bong.............Bong.............Bong!

The Great Bell shook the fortress with each boom. Clouds of decade old dust caught the moonlight as it swung for the second time since it had been hung, fourteen years prior.

"What's happening? A wyrm sighting?" asked a young woman, rubbing her eyes, a thin wool blanket clutched tight around her shoulders, "I've never heard the bell before..." Her hands shot to her mouth, staring eyes wide at the approaching horde.

Bong.............Bong.............Bong!

"What's wrong? What's happening?" More voices called from below as torches and people trickled into the courtyard and climbed the walls to see for themselves. Filthy folks of all shapes and sizes, tourists, traders, and wanderers from every corner of the continent gathered atop the walls, squinting into the mist. Some people screamed. Some ran for the gates. But most stood in silent awe, holding themselves or their loved ones staring at the metal wave like a tornado, or a drill dragon, or any other encroaching natural disaster too close to escape.

As more and more people lined the walls, more and more shadows emerged from the fog. Dozens became hundreds, hundreds became thousands, and any hope they had that this was merely a sad remnant of the first robot menace became the world changing nightmare that it was happening all over again. The bell banged on. Babies cried. Even so, the world felt still, like a held breath on a hard sprint.

Bong...............Bong...............Bong!

Clang!

A new sound rang out from atop the castle keep. All turned to see the wide silhouette of Brother Ingram Iron-cast, looming like a gargoyle at the peak of the keep, pounding his iron gauntlets against the stone walls.

"People of Aureum!" His heavy voice boomed out over them, strong and deep, "The day we've feared for fourteen years has come at last...And we are the lucky few who get to face it!"

You could hear them now, the marching metal, thousands of feet shuffling through the grass.

"For fourteen years we feared this day and we put that fear to work! We did not run south like those Coward Clan bastards! We pushed back metal with sticks and stones! We built walls! We built weapons! We dared them to try again, now here they are!"

Bong...............Bong...............Bong!

"Raid the armories! Load the batteries! Light the signal fire! And send these monsters off to Scrapyard!"

Maybe half the men cheered, but everyone scrambled around the brothers to either hide or arm themselves. The too old and very young all shuffled into the keep while everyone in between holstered warped warhammers or passed down dusty crossbows with rusted bolts from the ancient unkempt armories. The brothers didn't move, watching intently, knowing full well their role as messengers, taking in every detail they could as the army approached, nearly at the base of the hill.

The rusted joints on the ballistas groaned, awakened from their decade long slumber as metal, man-sized harpoons were loaded into place.

"We're safe right? They can't climb the walls?" Gathii asked nervously.

Natori couldn't take his eyes off of the large bot, standing, staring like the gears were turning in its brain. Natori recalled an endless march, an aimless, relentless wandering, he had never seen a bot stand so still. Somehow that scared him more.

"I don't know, man, this feels...different..."

The large bot cocked its head, slowly raising its hand into the air and in a single wordless moment, the thousands of smaller bots all came to a halt.

Bong..............Bong..............Bong!

Every man and woman working on the wall stopped what they were doing to stare wide eyed at the frozen forces.

"That's new..." Gathii whispered.

"That's worse..." Natori answered, a pit forming in his stomach. They had no leaders before, no orders, no organization, just a mindless marching wave of slow angry metal. A leader means they can take orders, plan strategies, adapt, get angry. A leader means we have no idea what the fuck we're fighting.

"Now!" Ingram shouted from behind. The ballistas launched their massive missiles towards the army of silent shadows with a heavy snapping wave of whooshes. Some of the old batteries splintered and crumbled under the release of their own tension. Not a single bot flinched as a storm of spears large enough to shred a dragon came raining down, impaling or shattering dozens where they stood with a thunderous crash of metal on metal. While one spear that was destined for the leader was caught midair in its four fingered fist.

.............Bong............

"Oh fuck..." The brothers cursed in unison.

A dreadful silence swept across the castle walls.

.............Bong............

The beast looked up, slowly twirled the harpoon around in its fist and wound back... **"OH Fuck!"**

Whoosh!

They both ducked as the bot hurled the bolt towards the wall like a javelin!

CRASH!!!

Everyone screamed atop the wall as the ballista closest to the brothers exploded on impact. Gathii shielded his brother with his body as splinters rained about them, a half dozen people catching wooden shards to their eyes or face, tumbling bloody to the ground or over the edge of the wall, the metal spear itself lodged deep into the stone walled keep.

As the brothers peaked over the wall once more, the large bot pointed towards the fortress and the smaller shadows silently went from frozen to sprinting up the hill, moving almost as one. Natori thought he was going to throw up. The men began to scream and panic, struggling to load new bolts with shaky hands. They never ran before. If they could learn to run, could they learn to climb? Men rained volleys of bolts down upon them, but few fell and none slowed, merely trampling the dead and shoving past the slow.

"We have to go!" Gathii shouted

"We can't leave yet!" Natori shouted back over the panic, against his own instincts, "We're the messengers, we have to warn the barons!"

"The signal fires will warn the barons!"

"But the fires can't tell them what's happened, what's different! The world will only know what we do! We can't leave 'til we know what we're dealing with!"

Gathii cursed, unable to argue.

Shadows leapt and clawed at the base of the wall, but none could get a grip on the smooth stone. Natori thanked the gods. *We're safe for now.*

Brother Ingram boomed over the battlefield, "See how they break upon our walls! Now wash this filth away with a razor rain!" The men cheered, firing at will into the mindless horde of writhing metal. Natori watched in awe and relief that their preparations all those years ago paid off, that neglected decade old weapons and fortifications may be enough to keep this nightmare at bay.

But new fears arose as he watched. Dozens of bots fell with every volley, but thousands still poured out of the mist. All silent, all sprinting, inching their way closer and closer to the tops of the wall as they climbed upon their dead. *Could they...? No, impossible...* The walls stood forty feet at least, there's no way they could pile that high.

Something drew his attention back to the large bot, the leader they shouldn't have. Natori's eyes widened as the giant grabbed a passing shadow, plucking it up with one hand like picking up a toy. The leader cocked its head and held the bot a moment before turning it in its hand like it had the ballista bolt. "Gathii…" Natori felt his stomach turn over as he realized what he was seeing, "Gathii!" The giant wound up and launched the small bot hurtling through the air, its body flailing like a doll as it flew and crashed into the screaming crowd atop the wall.

The bot emerged from the panicking pile of bodies, grabbed the face of the nearest man with a four fingered hand and crushed his head against the stones, splattering them purple in the blue moonlight. The crowd of defenders screamed and scrambled away, tripping over themselves. The bot dove straight into the pile of people shoving and throwing anyone in its reach over the edge of the forty foot walls. Those who fell were immediately swarmed by metal hands and dragged screaming down the hill, vanishing into the mist.

"They're not killing them…" Natori said, petrified.

"They're taking them," Gathii said

A brave man drew his warhammer and swung on the beast to knock it off the wall, caving in the side of its head. The bot caught the man's arm on impact and pulled him over the edge with it.

The defenders all turned in horror to see more and more bots flying and crashing upon the wall. Defenders ran, stampeding away from the bots, blocking the brother's view of them.

Bong...............Bong...............Bong!

"The fire! Light the signal fire! Warn the world!" Brother Ingram called over the chaos, pointing up at the pile of dried wood, stacked high at the top of the bell tower.

"With me!" Natori heard a man with a torch yell from across the courtyard. The brothers watched from afar as the man sprinted for the bell tower followed by two others and a woman. Just as the group disappeared into the stairwell, a bot was thrown, crashing through the wooden guard rails and into the bell above, scrambling down the stairs to intercept them.

Natori held his hands to his head, "Oh fuck, fuck, no..."

Two of the men crashed and fell through the window, halfway up the tower, blood staining the shattered glass. Natori's heart pounded. The woman emerged from the top, wielding the torch, the bot right on her tail, arms outstretched. She dodged the still swinging bell and leapt up the final steps towards the ladder. The third man followed and tackled the bot just in time, sending them both thrashing through the splintered guard rail and sailing off the six story tower, vanishing into the metal sea below.

"She made it!" Natori yelled. The woman called and cried to her falling friend. Visibly shaken as she turned and climbed the ladder to the perch of the signal fire.

"She made it..." Gathii sighed. They watched her yank a chain that dropped a bucket of oil that was who knows how old on top of the dried wood. And the moment she raised the torch to light the flame-

Her devastated wail broke their hearts as a ballista bolt javelin impaled and carried her away, still clutching the torch.

"No! No! That's not..." Natori's heart sank. He tracked her flight off of the tower like a shooting star, with tear filled eyes, as she disappeared beyond the wall.

"Damnit! Damnit! How did-?" The brothers were reminded of their immediate danger when a bot flew right over their heads, overshooting the wall and landing in the courtyard below. The moment it hit the ground, it rolled, scrambled and sprinted to shove its metal arm straight through the chest of the nearest person.

"Alright, let's go, Little Bird!" Gathii pulled Natori to his feet. The brothers pushed through the panicking crowd and down the stairs to the yard. Men and bots alike tumbled over the wall in the struggle. A bot fell out of the sky and landed on their backs, knocking them down the stairs.

Natori landed flat on his stomach, the cobblestones grating the left side of his face. Before he could rise and find his brother, something heavy fell upon his back. Metal arms wrapped around his head and neck, choking the air from his lungs. Natori struggled, but the weight was too great and his strength too little. *Brother!* He mouthed, his eyes filling up with water as he tried to cry out.

Just as he thought he was going to pass out, he felt something slam into the bot, releasing Natori. He coughed and scrambled away from it, turning to find Brother Ingram standing over him wielding his iron gauntlets in a boxer's stance. The bot launched itself up at the large, dark skinned man, aiming to drive its fist straight through the wide scar across Ingram's bare chest only to be clobbered with a clang back to the ground.

Natori crawled out of the way of their fight looking all around for Gathii, who he found rubbing a deep cut on his forehead.

"Are you alright?"

"Dizzy...But breathing"

Ingram's fists hit as hard as any warhammer, soon leaving a dented wet crater where the bot's head was moments before, oily black and red liquid dripping from his iron gauntlets. "Are you two Nuru?"

"Yes, sir..."

A group of guards, battered and bloodied, rushed out of the keep, hammers dripping with black bot's blood. "They're already in the keep, sir, what the fuck do we do??"

"We get these boys out, whatever it takes! If we can't reach the tower, they're the only one's fast enough to warn the barons! No matter what happens, they need to make it, do you hear me?"

His men nodded.

Ingram dropped a gauntlet and picked up Natori with one hand, pulling him to his feet, "Can you walk?"

"Yes, sir..."

Ingram picked up Gathii, "Can you run??"

"Aye, sir..."

"Then start running! Find Warren and Balian, tell them whatever this is, the people aren't prepared! Run as long as you have to, as hard as you can! If you don't make it, Everyone Dies! You understand?"

Natori swallowed, nodding with his brother.

"We'll cover you as best we can! No matter what happens, we're getting you out! No matter what happens, you don't stop! Now G-Ahhhh!"

BWRRRRRRRRRRRRRRRRRRRRR RRRRRRRRRRRRRRRRRRRRRRR!!!

A deep, deafening, hornlike blast, pulsated from beyond the wall. They all grabbed their ears at once, pressing as hard as they could. The noise grew and grew, threatening to melt their brains through their skulls, until-

....

....

Silence......Not distant......not muffled......but absolute, nauseating, mind numbing silence. He touched his own face and slapped the sides of his head, nothing. He screamed and yelled, with a hand on his throat to feel the vibrations, but he heard no sound. Even the banging bell was silent, though he still felt its shaking through the ground.

mmmmmmmm...............mmmmmmmm...............mmmmmmmm

He looked up to see Gathii testing his ears the same way. Ingram and the guards looked just as disoriented. *Can you hear me?* He mouthed to Ingram, gesturing from his mouth to his ears. Ingram shook his head in reply and pointed toward the main gate, about a hundred yards away. He looked back at his men left upon the walls all holding their ears and screaming in silence as bots rained down, pulling them over the edge, over a dozen monsters hurling their bodies down the stairs sprinting right for Ingram and the brothers.

"You start running and you don't stop until you're safe..."

Natori heard his mother's voice from over fourteen years ago, sending him and his brothers away from the village when the bots first attacked. "Your brother falls, you pick him up, but you don't stop, understand? You never stop running...I'll catch up to you...Now go...Go!"

Go! Ingram mouthed as he shoved his fist back into his gauntlet and slammed it into the closest monster, black oil clinging to the knuckles. Natori dug his toes between the cobblestones and launched himself like a ballista bolt hurtling towards the gate, Gathii right at his side. Hearing nothing, Natori felt everything; The stinging cold, the scraping stones, his pounding heart ready to burst at any moment, the wind of a bot sailing right above their heads crashing violently into the road ahead.

Gathii jumped straight over the monster while Natori tripped and dove to the side of it, scraping his shoulders on the ground, two of the guards throwing their bodies on top of the monster before it could grab Natori.

The brothers kept running, leaping over bots and bodies, past choking women with bots on their backs, past the people fighting for their lives, past their overturned delivery carts, almost slipping on the pile of countless letters, packages and obligations from all around the continent. Natori grit his teeth at the sight, he'd never once failed a delivery.

A hundred yards turned to fifty, fifty turned to twenty, twenty turned into a shut gate. *No, Fuck!* Natori punched the fifteen foot, cast iron grate that stood between them and the rest of the world. Gathii pulled him towards two men already struggling to turn the manual crank, the brothers instantly joined them on the other side, yanking the chains, turning the four foot pulley with all their might, the ancient rusted mechanism barely cooperating, relinquishing mere inches each turn. *Come on! Come On!*

Natori glanced back to see their guards fall bloody to the ground as bots unsheathed their arms from their bodies, Brother Ingram now the only thing standing between the brothers and the clamoring wave of silent swarming monsters. Dodging, bashing, crushing, he broke through their armor like tin cans, their fists bouncing off his bloody cheeks and ribs like he was the one made of metal. But for every bot he beat, two more would charge around the corner or crash into the courtyard.

Sons of Scrapyard

Gathii pulled Natori towards the gate, panic in his eyes, spit spraying from his silent shouts, Natori turning Just in time to see a bot materialize in his peripheral vision, charging on all fours, lunging straight into the other two men helping them with the gate, tearing them apart, the brothers diving, crawling, pulling themselves under the two foot opening they'd created.

Dozens of bots poured into the courtyard just as the brothers slipped through. Blood, sweat, and oil sprayed with every swing of Ingram's gauntlets until he was finally swarmed, tackled, and buried under the pile of metal monsters.

The bridge was held...

Not one could pass...

Through Brother Ingram Iron-Cast...

The heavy gate slowly dropped back closed behind them, a dozen metal creatures throwing their bodies against it, denting the metal, their angry arms swinging, clawing, reaching for the brothers in vain through the iron bars while they took off down the hillside as quick as the wind, away from the fortress, gravity propelling them like the hands of Aure. The fog covered all but the dirt road, like invisible walls were keeping it at bay.

Natori's brain kept screaming for him to look back, the entire world behind him disappearing with every turn of his head, he expected the worst, but found they weren't followed. They flew down the hill as fast as they could. As soon as they outran the edge of the fog, sound swept over them like suddenly emerging from deep underwater. Natori felt like he could breathe again. He screamed and slapped the sides of his head, overjoyed by the painful pop of his palm against his ear.

"I can hear!" Natori shouted, still sprinting.

"Me too!" Gathii gasped, "What the fuck was that?"

They both looked back without stopping.

"I can't...I can't hear the battle..."

"I couldn't either..."

"No, I mean Right Now...No screaming, fighting, nothing!"

"Me...Me neither.........What the fuck does that mean?"

"I don't know..." The fog had closed around the road, "That's some...dark magic, that..." Natori shook his head, "I can't believe...they're back..."

"We're so fuckin' sunk...This is so much worse...than before..." Gathii panted.

"They weren't just...killing everybody like before."

"That doesn't make it better...At least that made... more sense...I don't even wanna think about what they could be doing." They reached the first fork in the road, "I can't believe we made it out..."

"I can't believe we left them all behind..."

"They stayed behind For us, Little Bird..."

They slid to a stop at a wooden post standing in the fork with an arrow pointing in either direction. *Riverwood-North. Gateway-East.* "Come here..." They clasped hands and hugged once more, "Better bring my brother home to Julia," Gathii said into Natori's shoulder.

"Only if you bring mine..." Natori thumped his brother's back.

"Get Gateway locked down, then straight to Scrapyard..."

Natori nodded.

"Get Warren to evacuate...And find Fordo, he should still be near Riverwood!" Gathii nodded.

"I love you, brother..." Natori squeezed him tighter, "I'll find you in Julia."

"Fly, Little Bird..."

They both sprinted off their separate ways, Gathii toward Riverwood, Natori toward Gateway. Natori looked over his shoulder once more. Though he could still see the bell swinging in the tower, he could not hear it.

Dark magic...

Sons of Scrapyard

Al and Meeko

2

"Did you get fatter while I was dead?" Al grunted with every passing branch. They were almost at the top now.

Meeko poked his head out of Al's pack and shot a warm sarcastic bark down the back of his neck.

"And you didn't leave any for me? Carth would've dragged my ass there and saved me a bite."

He felt a single lick.

"It's okay, buddy, it's just my feelings."

Stopping just short of where the branches thinned, Al hung Meeko up by the straps of his pack. Weaving a web of rope between the two sturdiest branches, he made a comfy little perch to enjoy the view. *'Seat in the sky'* Sarah liked to call it. Tying the final knot, Al flopped comfortably against the trunk, opening his arms wide like it would help him take in more of the view.

Every cloud, every tree was a work of art. A whole wide world wrapped around him like a whirlpool of light and sound and color. The red glow of the leaves as the forests played catch with the afternoon light. The music as the breeze bowed and bashed the blades of the golden grass that hugs the road and blankets the rolling hills of the Yellow Sea. The higher they climbed, the more accurate the name became; Golden grass stretched from road to horizon, rising and falling like waves in the wind. The sky towering bright and blue like a tsunami come to douse the fiery reds and yellows of the flora.

"Look at that, that's the prettiest thing you've ever seen!" Al almost shouted

Meeko barked an objection.

Al laughed and bounced a crumpled red leaf off of Meeko's nose, "Don't make me blush."

Wind and Tree slow danced together, swaying gently to the melody of the Yellow Sea. A herd of pillboys grazed in the fields, sunlight glistening off of their round armored shells, all beautiful blues, browns, and grays. Crows cawed in the distance, Al squinting to see a line of hundreds shoot out of the grass in a wave of their own as something disturbed them from below.

Al grinned, "Look, Meeks" Al followed the crows until the ground churned where they once rested, the great maw of a breaching wyrm bursting from the dirt, its countless tusks and teeth twisting like the bit of Aure's drill, scales red as realwood glistening in the sunlight as it arched and plunged back into the depths with a distant rumble Al could feel reverberate through their tree.

"You know, they're kind of beautiful from far away."

Meeko barked in agreement.

"Yeah, I'm sure they're a lot scarier on the inside," Al yawned, tucking himself into the blanket of sunlight. He smiled to himself as the grass played them a melody. *Life is good, Meeks.*

From so high, the fluffy forest reminded Al of the red velvet cake he watched Daisy bake for the twin's birthday. *Soft and sweet.* Though it seems someone had already taken a piece. A near perfect circle was cut right from the center. "Look Meeks, that must be where we woke up!"

"That's gotta be!" The sparkly line that was the distant creek seemed evidence enough. "That's crazy, Meeks! It's so far away!" Meeko didn't seem nearly as excited as Al. "Took us more than half the day to get back to the road! How did we even end up......?" Al's voice wavered, his grin fading to an unfocused stare. *I see......* "We've been up here before, huh?" Meeko stayed quiet, avoiding Al's eye. *Happened again......I hate when I forget...... I swear I don't mean to......*

"Well......" Al rubbed his wrist and squeezed his eyes shut, "Just means we got to see this view with fresh eyes twice, right?" He said through a sad smile. That cheered Meeko up a bit. Al reached up and gave him a good scratch, "Time to go, bubby."

***

Al unwove his web and watched a shrinking Meeko in his descent to the world below. Meeko started barking uncharacteristically, like Al had ever dropped him more than once. Aiming near his pile of whatnots at the base of the trunk, Al tried to ease the rope at a comfortable pace. The barking continued. "You're almost there, you big baby," Al said under his breath.

Though he grew farther, his barking grew louder. Meek was almost at the ground now. *Something's wrong.*

Jumping down to a lower branch, Al swiftly hoisted Meeko back up to a safer height. He re-tethered the rope to a branch and listened for danger, doing his best to block out the barks. He couldn't see or hear anything unusual. Just a dangling Meeko, Al's pile of things, and a kart on the road. *A kart on the road!* Al scanned the everything below, searching for the owner through the tangle of leaves and branches.

A pair of bare feet stepped forward and planted themselves right below an angry Meeko. *Go away.* Al pulled the rope, raising Meeko even higher. The feet stepped back, appearing startled. *That's right, fear the mysterious floating dog.* Two steps forward and a dirty hand joined them, reaching up towards Meeko whose angry barks turned to frightened cries. "No!" Al yelled, leaping off his perch and dropping straight down at their assailant.

Branches beat and whipped him all along the far fall, punishing him for his carelessness and putting Meeko in danger again so soon. Al yelled the whole way down, both from fear of falling and hope to scare off the phantom feet. Al burst through the canopy and hit the ground with a crack. Retrieving his sword expertly from his pile of things and rolling to face his opponent.

Looking down at him was a tall brown man and a still dangling Meeko. They looked at each other and then back at Al in the dirt, looking just as concerned and confused as the other. The biggest, whitest smile Al had ever seen, spread across the man's goofy face as his eyes went from sword to dog to Al.

Everything about the man was big. He wore a strange beige coat, too large for his already lanky frame, and looked to be a whole head taller than Al. His wide nose and ears seemed too large for his face, like he was wearing them over his real ones, and his hair a perfectly circular puff, like Sarah's blackberry bush. Upon the plump pink lips that framed his smile sat a thin black mustache. The laugh that emerged was deep and whimsical. "Is he like your puppy puppet?" The man asked

Al didn't know what he expected the stranger to say, but that wasn't it. "You kind of look like a puppet yourself." Al panted, still out of breath from the falling and the screaming.

"There's a little puppet on my mom's side, I've got buttons for nipples, want me to get your dog down for you?" Al strained to keep a straight face.

"Uh No thanks, I think I got it."

"That's a pretty tall tree, Ely loves trees, climbs them all the time, is your leg supposed to bend that way?" Al looked back at his, not one, but two broken legs. One of which was hyperextended far past the knee.

"I don't think so, no."

Without missing a beat, "I'm Andre!" The man reached out and shook the blade of Al's still extended sword like a hand, "What's your dog's name?"

"That's Meeko."

Meeko barked his hello.

"And what's his dog's name?"

"I......What?"

"Oo You like music?" Andre half skipped, half tripped back towards his kart. As soon as his back was turned, Al scrambled to realign his throbbing legs. A flood of pins and needles washed away the pain, but of the many tears he was holding back, one escaped and ran down his cheek. Quickly wiping it before it could fall to freedom, Al recomposed and raised his sword again, just in time for Andre to turn his smile back in their direction.

"I think so. I've only ever heard my friend's piano," Al didn't think Andre's smile could get any bigger. Andre yanked the blanket that covered his kart and flung it into the air, raising his arms in a presentory stance. The kart was piled high with what looked to be all sorts of instruments and musical contraption, most of which Al was unfamiliar. Al remained silent, unsure of what to say.

"Which one do you want?" Andre asked

"Want? I'm not really sure what they are," Al's sword arm was tired and lowered almost to the ground.

"Music! Here!" Andre tossed something long and wooden towards Al, but it landed short and rolled beyond the reach of his two working arms and two still broken legs. Al and Meeko both looked at the whatever and then at each other.

"How 'bout this one, that one's glass anyway."

Al caught a small, rectangular, metal bar with a line of narrow square holes along the side.

"How does......what do I do?" Al laughed

"You blow into it and it goes Bzz Bahzz zz."

Pleasantly perplexed, Al blew into the holes, creating a bright hum. Moving along the line, he found the hum was brighter on one side and deeper on the other. Al smiled and laughed to himself. The noise was silly to him and the buzz tickled his lips and hand.

"So how do you play?"

"Play what?"

"Play this......"

"No, you play."

"No, I don't know how, you ghoul."

"What is going on with you? You sound insane." A look of strained concentration overtook Andre as he reached shoulder deep into his pile of musical whatnots. Meeko whispered a confused yelp.

"I don't know, Meeks, didn't know what else to call him."

Al waited patiently for Andre to find whatever he was looking for. The longer Andre was distracted, the more time Al's legs had to heal, and the quicker they could-

"I've got it!" Andre's arm emerged with a short curved something, "This is perfect for you." He ran over to Al like an excited child, wielding a polished wyrm's tooth, beautifully carved into a Sienan Drill Dragon, every tooth and scale expertly detailed.

"Whoa......" Al's eyes widened in awe of the craftsmanship. At a glance, with a little dirt, one could mistake it for a living grub.

Meeko barked, seemingly impressed.

"It really is, Meeks......"

Andre held it out to Al, who dropped his sword completely to accept the gift, "Where'd you find something like this?" Al cradled the tooth like a baby, tracing the scales with his fingertips.

"Made it," Andre boasted, rocking back and forth on his heels, "Made all of them, even the kart. Ely helped a little, sang while I designed and built and put all the pieces together."

Al couldn't help but smile, "So why's this perfect for me?"

"Only makes one loud noise, so even a weirdo like you can figure it out."

Al and Meeko laughed, "You're not much of a teacher, huh?"

"Oh My Ely's the teacher, I just like buildin' things for her."

"Where is Ely? I'm sure Meeko'd love to meet her."

"I don't......I don't know," Andre immediately looked lost, "Where is Ely......?" His smile faded for the first time since Al fell out of the tree.

"You didn't build her too, did you?" Al laughed

Andre's grin returned, "If I could build a girl, I'd build Ely," He laughed while he returned the thrown instruments to the cart, tucking them in with the blanket once more.

"You sure I can keep this?" Al asked, still cradling the wyrm's tooth.

"Ely wants us to spread as many of these out as we can."

"But you can't even tell people how they work," Al laughed.

"Well, how does anything work?" Andre raised his arms in a dramatic shrug.

Al shook his head and smiled as he got to his feet and removed his sheathed dagger from his belt, handing it to Andre, "Here, work for work, I insist," Al smiled

"ooo What noise does this make?" Andre tossed it in his hands excitedly.

"Makes other things go 'Ow'"

"I love it," Andre tucked the blade under the blanket, picked up the handles of his kart and started rolling down the road, "See you round, weirdos." After a few steps, he stopped and turned around, "Hey, aren't your legs broken?" Al paused and panicked, then raised his arms in Andre's same dramatic shrug. Andre just smiled and nodded like: *You're right* and went humming on his way.

"The hell was that? Did he care about my legs or not?" Al shook his head and laughed to himself as he got Meeko down from the tree. Meeko hopped out of the pack and stretched his back. "Let's get us home."

***

As the road shortened beneath their feet, the air slowly filled with the welcoming smell of fire and the rhythmic singing of metal striking metal. Rounding the bend of the last hill, they were greeted by the glorious sight of Scrapyard village, a cluster of small brown buildings nestled between a giant rock and a literal pile of trash. Meeko's mouth hung open in a puppet-like grin as he panted. Al took a deep breath and smiled. "Welcome home, buddy."

Sons of Scrapyard

Fordo

2

Sunlight called to them as they limped out of the cold and the dark. Fordo welcomed the warmth, his sore feet instantly relieved as the ground turned from gray stone to red dirt and purple moss. They were greeted by the towering, brown-barked trees of The Realwood Forest. Living giants stretching half as tall as the mountains they leaned on, reminding Fordo just how small he really was. "We made it…" Carth whispered to himself.

Before any gratitude could manifest, a faint ringing in Fordo's ears built and grew into a scream. The sun appeared to grow as well, drenching everything in a blinding white. Fordo dropped to one knee, covering his ears with his hands and squeezing his eyes shut as tight as he could. Every light was too bright, every noise was too loud. "Fordo?" Carth called, dropping down to hold Fordo steady. Fordo couldn't hear him over the pounding in his heart and the screaming in his head. "Oy, Fordo, stay with me!" Carth dragged him to the shade of the trees.

Fordo shook his head, breathing hard and heavy until the sun shrank and the ringing faded. He reached up and grabbed Carth's shoulder, "I'm alright, Carthy…" He said through a shaky breath, "I just need a minute."

"We need a couple minutes…" Carth slumped down against the trunk of the tree. Fordo heard him sigh, then he heard him cry. "Both of them, man…" Fordo could hear Carth bringing his fist down on the moss covered ground, tearing off a chunk, and throwing it to the side.

"Both of them…" Fordo's lip began to quiver, but he choked down the tears as best he could, "Save some of those tears, man." Carth looked up at Fordo as he stood and held out his hand. "We still have to tell Kira…"

Carth cursed as Fordo pulled him to his feet.

"It's gonna kill him."

Fordo shook his head, "I'm not losing three friends today." Fordo leaned down and rubbed his throbbing ankle, it must have gotten twisted when Carth caught it. He sighed, stood, and limped into the forest.

***

They found Kira and Mira munching on sticks of elk jerky on a mossy boulder, not far from the cave. Two wetskins lay empty at Mira's feet.

Kira threw up his hands and cheered when he saw them limp around the bend. "You made it, thank Gah!" He jumped up and ran to greet them, almost knocking them down with a hug. "You guys took so long, I was so scared that…" Kira's voice trailed off as he stepped back and searched the path behind them, "Where are the twins?" He looked to Carth. Kira's smile melted when Carth couldn't meet his eye. Fordo could, but his were full of tears. "No…no…they can't…" Kira heard faint footsteps behind him. "Oh That's not fucking funny, you pieces of-" He spun around with a fist raised and flinched, expecting the twins to be sneaking up behind him, but he found Mira instead, walking up to take his hand. He took hers slowly and squatted down to her level. "Both of them?"

"I'm so sorry, Kira..." Fordo said. Kira's head and shoulders dropped as he broke down in tears, crying into Mira's tiny hand. Mira hugged his drooping, sobbing head.

"How?" Kira croaked, his tone twisted by grief.

"Jacks lost his way...Got tripped up once he found it."

"Why...?" Kira fell back onto his ass, twisting the simple silver wedding ring on his right hand, "Jackson...My boy." He shook his head and cried into his hands. "But Benji pulled me up, he was safe!"

"Benji jumped back down when he saw Jacks fall. They got Benji before he reached him."

Kira mumbled something through his sobs.

"What was that?" Fordo asked

"Why didn't you help him?"

"Well..." Fordo stammered, "There was nothing we could do, Benji nearly broke my nose when we tried to stop him."

"You tried to STOP him?" Kira stood and turned abruptly. "From saving my Jacks??" His eyes red with tears.

"There was nothing we could do, Kira..."

"Did you even try??" Kira raised his voice and Mira fled behind the boulder. Fordo was stunned, mouth gaping.

"Stop, Kira, that's enough," Carth chimed in.

"This is all on you..." Kira stabbed a dagger of a finger into Fordo's chest.

"Oh Yeah, how's that?" Fordo asked, not budging from the jab.

"You're the one who dragged them there, why didn't you drag them out?" Kira shoved Fordo back.

"Enough!" Carth stepped in between them.

"Oh, I didn't know you had all the answers, Kira? Tell me, what was I supposed to do??" Fordo pushed past Carth and got into Kira's face.

"You were supposed to bring them back, not use them as bait!" Fordo felt his fist clenching as specks of spit flew into his face.

"Hey! That's not fair and you know it, they were his friends!" Carth wedged between them once more.

"They were My Family! They were His Pawns! And so are we! Nothing but fodder for the mighty Fordo Balison, destined for greatness! How long until we're all sunk on another one of his missions just so he can keep pretending to be a big fucking hero??" Fordo's hand shot over Carth's shoulder and grabbed Kira by the collar. Fordo pulled him forward, and drove his forehead into Kira's nose, knocking him to the ground. It happened so fast that Kira was on the ground before Carth could react.

"Oh Fuck!" Carth cursed, unsure if he could keep an angry Fordo at bay while he looked down at Kira clutching his bloody, swollen nose.

Fordo fell back and sat on the ground with his hands over his eyes as he began to cry once more. Kira sat up slowly, sniffling, still holding his nose. He looked over at Fordo with softer eyes and sighed. "I'm sorry, man..."

Fordo didn't answer.

"I didn't look back once..." Kira began to rock in place, "I was too scared. I left him down there just as much as you did." Fordo wouldn't look at him. "You didn't deserve all that," Kira said.

"We didn't deserve any of this," Carth grumbled, falling to the mossy ground himself. They all sat in silence for a long while until the sniffling stopped and their breathing steadied.

Fordo rubbed the wet from his eyes and sighed, "Let's get the fuck out of here."

"Are you okay, Mira?" Carth called. Mira stuck her head out from behind her little boulder with more jerky in her mouth. "Let's get her home, boys."

"Fordo..." Kira started, but Fordo pulled Kira up to his feet without looking at him. Kira opened his mouth to say something, but stopped himself.

"There's a little creek just off the path before the lumberyard. Can we wash this glass off before heading in?" Carth suggested, raising his gray covered arms.

"No..." Fordo said sullenly. Carth and Kira both looked at him. "I need them to see."

***

"She's back-"

"Fordo found her-"

"Mira's back-" Fordo heard the grunted observations of sweaty Woodwyrms as they returned through the busy lumberyard. Lumber johns and Janes alike stopped their chopping and sawing and singing to wipe their foreheads and stare at the passing party. They all had thick clothes and thicker beards, even some of the Janes. Leather suspenders crossed behind their shoulders and latched onto their heavy belts, an ax holstered on every hip. Reminded him of Al, that smug bastard. *They'd still be here if you were...*

Mira waved shyly to the cutters as they passed, who smiled in return, but there was no clapping, no cheering, no dropping of logs and rushing to greet them, no offers to carry them the rest of the way to the village on their shoulders, none of the reactions Fordo had fantasized their return would bring when they first passed through. The best they got was maybe a cheerful indifference. *My friends died for this...* Fordo's stoic demeanor fell to a frown as soon as they reached the edge of the lumberyard. He tried not to squeeze Mira too tight as he carried her, but his blood was boiling.

The Realwood trees towered over them like drill dragons as they reentered the forest. Red-barked monoliths of wood that hurt fordo's neck to try and see the tops, their tallest branches scraping the sky. *Al's probably up in that canopy, somewhere, napping with his beast. When are you gonna come down and help my ass?*

They walked silently up the wide dirt trail. The grunting came from above now. Fordo looked up at the bearded faces peeking over the railing of suspended wooden platforms that hugged high on and between the trunks of the Realwoods. The closer they got to Riverwood's gates, the higher, more intricate its levels became, until the network of platforms and rope bridges was as thickly woven together above them as the roof of branches itself. A floating city of wood and rope that climbed to the very tops of the mighty trees that supported it. Fordo imagined it took a thousand years to build such a vast network of structures. *What are you, an idiot?* He winced as his father's voice blasted in his head, remembering humans have only been on Aureum for a little less than a hundred.

Fordo limped a little harder as they approached the west gate, trying to look even more miserable than he already felt. The wall consisted of sections of felled, twenty foot tall, Realwood logs, wedged between the trunks of living others, like a tree had grown sideways along the ground and skewered its brethren. A huge archway had been bored through where the road met the log, housing the large metal gate which cut through the center of the arch's tunnel.

Shouting voices came from above the wall as they approached. The metal gate split down the middle and receded into either end of the great log as they passed under the arch to enter the city. A smooth glossy finish covered the whole length of the hollowed log tunnel, like the realwoods were secretly made of black glass beneath their bark. Fordo glanced over his shoulder to see Carth dragging his hand along the smooth wall. The gates closed behind them as they entered the courtyard.

Riverwood was the only settlement who's security hadn't laxed in the decade and a half since the First War. The baron's paranoia saw to that. Even Hilltop had let their ballista's rust and they're only a few leagues from The Great Wreck. Though very few survived Hilltop's fall, its current population consists of those with no memory of the slaughter. But

Riverwood remembers. They were hit harder than anyone, being the only other settlement on the continent without the Siena River between them and the monsters. Warren Den seemed to have made good on his promise of "Never again."

Buildings were sparse on the ground. Most of the various shops and homes seemed to have migrated up the trunks, in the years since Fordo's last visit. Many rectangular, house sized imprints were scattered throughout the courtyard like missing puzzle pieces, as if the buildings were lifted by their very foundations to join the rest of the floating city above. Fordo noticed that it was mostly Blacksmiths, Smokehouses, and other fire friendly buildings left on the forest floor, the heat from their ovens and forges carried up through filtered vents to warm the rest of the windy city.

They approached one of the many lifts up to Riverwood Proper, a square, roofed, wooden platform with railing all around the edge, that resembled a wooden lantern. Wrought iron chains, with links as thick as Fordo's arms, almost thick enough to support Daisy's mountains, hung down from the city above and attached to each corner of the slanted roof.

"Oy!" Shouted a square, stocky man with a red beard and redder cheeks who jogged over to intercept them at the lift. A heavy chain belt jangled as he jogged, a rectangular metal box, lined with handles of what looked to be knives, slapped against his thigh. His brown, leather apron was splattered with red and black stains.

Fordo instinctively dropped a hand to his hammer and angled himself between the man and little Mira. But she leaned and reached her hand out towards him like she wanted the man to carry her.

"Mira!" The man cried, holding out his arms, tears streaming down his rosy cheeks. Fordo looked between them then decided to hand her over. Mira leapt from Fordo's arms and into the stranger's. The tiny girl disappeared into his beefy arms as he kneeled all the way to the ground to embrace her at her level. The man sobbed. Fordo had never seen such a large man cry, apart from poor Brash. The scene created a lump in Fordo's throat that he pushed down to ignore.

"Oh Little One..." The man said, when he could, "You brave, brave, stupid girl. I'm so glad you're okay." He leaned back, wiped his eyes, then put his hands on her shoulders. "Did-did you find him?" Mira's lips quivered as she nodded.

"I'm sorry..." Mira spoke in a tiny voice, breaking into tears. Fordo realized those were the first words she's spoken since they found her. New tears welled in the man's eyes as he shook his head and embraced her once more.

"No, I'm sorry. I'm the one who let him run off."

"Does this girl belong to you?" Fordo asked the man when he finally stood.

"No, Vigilance belonged to me..." The man replied, still wiping his eyes.

"The puppy?" Carth asked

"Aye..." The man nodded his head, "A true friend...I wasn't brave enough to follow him down into that sunken place, but she was." He patted Mira on the shoulder, who had her face buried in his pant leg. "Thank you, strangers. If I had lost them both, I never could forgive myself. I am forever in your debt..." The man stuck out his meaty hand, "They call me Chop."

"They call me Fordo," Fordo clasped the man's hand. Rough with calluses and nearly twice the thickness of his own, like Fordo's father.

"Fordo Balison?" Chop's eyebrows raised and a smile blossomed despite the tears, "I knew your father well during the war, saved me more than once. I'm glad to see his son picked up the same hobby."

Fordo suppressed a twitch as he nodded in reply, "That there is Carth and Kira."

"Fordo, Carth, and Kira. I will remember your names."

"Remember Jackson and Benjamin, as well," Kira said over Fordo's shoulder, "They never left the cave..."

Chop's eyes widened.

"Monsters," Fordo spoke like a stone, "You were right not to follow."

"Mm..." Chop grunted gravely, "Damn those blasted caverns. I'll gather folks to seal the entrance tomorrow." They all nodded in agreement.

"We need to get this one home," Fordo looked down at Mira. "Do you know where her family is?" Chop twisted his face like Fordo had just insulted him.

"Her mother lives up on the eighth level, far west off the main trunk, but she's probably lurking somewhere near the Dark Market." Mira made a small sound and squeezed Chop's leg even tighter. Chop put a heavy hand over Mira's exposed ear. "But you should find her somewhere better to leave her."

"Shouldn't she be with her mother?" Fordo asked

"Some mothers shouldn't be..." Chop answered calmly, but sternly.

Fordo grimaced, unsure what that's supposed to mean. "She can stay with you then? Seems to trust you well enough."

Chop shook his head and put his hands up. "No, no, her mother sent Grifters after me last time I tried to...interfere. As much as I love her, I can't risk a brand like that."

"Grifters?" Carth exclaimed, "That's pretty serious."

"She started telling tales to them after our last 'disagreement', saying I'm a little more than just friendly with the kids, evil Splint..." Chop scowled.

"Glass, she tried to have you killed, man," Kira said, "That's no light charge."

"Everyone knows me and my business, I was always gonna beat the brand, but the less reason Grifters have to look, the less likely they'll find an excuse, so I still gotta keep my distance."

Chop patted Mira on the back, "I'll let you run along now," He knelt down to her, "Take care, Little One. No more running off for a while." Mira nodded and hugged him. He turned back to fordo, "Take care of her and come to me anytime you need food for your journeys." Chop tapped the metal box of knives and walked back to his shop with the jangle of chains.

Fordo looked to Carth, hoping for some thoughts, but Carth made a slight shrug, pressed his lips together, and gestured up the lift chains with his head. Fordo scooped up Mira as they all stepped onto the wooden platform. Kira pulled on a red handled chord that hung in his corner and the platform began to rise at a slow, steady pace.

***

Fordo daydreamed of how fun it must be to grow up in this place as they drifted slowly up through the levels of the city. He imagined a dozen children in a game of chase, leaping fearlessly from platform to platform, swinging down the web of ropes and ziplines, cornering each other on a bridge only to dive over the edge at the last second onto the giant safety nets that stretched between each level, rolling off onto someone's roof.

They heard something small land on and scamper across the roof of their lift as they rose. Fordo thought it part of the daydream, but both Carth and Kira looked up. Fordo spotted the fuzzy purple shape of a flying moss spider, slightly larger than a cat, gliding off their lift towards the nearest tree trunk.

By the time they arrived on the eighth level, the wooden walkways had grown considerably darker. Fordo guessed sunlight could only travel so far through the trees and buildings. Lit mostly by hanging lanterns and Candle Leaf vines, everything had a warm, orange and yellow hue. Fordo wished he could take the glowing candle leaves back to Scrapyard, green glowing plants created by their spacewalking forefathers, but Scrapyard's dry climate didn't suit them.

Most folks stayed busy in the lumber yards until the sun went down, leaving the walkways quiet and empty, save for gaggles of children running around, unsupervised. Fordo waited for one of the groups to notice Mira and run up excitedly, wondering where their friend had gone. But those who did notice merely pointed and whispered.

One rather filthy looking boy frowned and stuck his tongue out at Mira, who buried herself in Fordo's shoulder. His hair was long and stringy, his body not much different. He kind of looked to Fordo as if Al had a kid brother who was locked in a cupboard his entire life. Fordo focused an evil look at the boy, hoping he'd run away scared, but he just flashed a crooked yellow smile before moving along. *You're not the most popular kid, huh girly?*

Carth asked Mira if they were headed the right way and she nodded into Fordo's shoulder. They walked and walked. Mira shook her head every few houses they passed when Carth would ask "This one?" until they reached a lampless, leafless, shadowed corner at the end of the walkway, the very last house. The place had the same wooden frame as all the others, but it was the only house that didn't look like a home. There were no decorations, no personal touches. The other houses had welcome mats, little signs, carvings, planter gardens, some kind of paint or stain that personalized each one. But this one just felt blank and cold and lonely, nothing on the porch but a single metal hook where a lantern used to hang. "This one?" Carth asked in a hesitant tone. Mira nodded, squeezing Fordo's shoulder tight.

Fordo considered Chop's warning. "Is this where you live?" Fordo asked her in a soft, hushed voice. She nodded again. "Is this where you want to?" Mira shook her head without hesitation. "Is there any other safe place that will take you?" Mira paused then shook her head once more, squeezing his shoulder even tighter. Fordo sighed and rubbed her back. "We'll find you a better place soon." He promised. She nodded and whispered a tiny "Thank you..."

Fordo knocked on the door. It sounded hollow, like the door led to an empty room. There was no answer. Fordo knocked again, a little harder. They heard a stirring, the rustling of sheets or blankets through the thin door. "Who is it?" A drowsy woman's voice came through the door.

"My name's Fordo. I have something that belongs to you." The rustling grew more frantic. Something hard and heavy crashed and rolled on the floor and they heard the woman curse.

"You son of a bitch, where is it?" They heard her struggle with the apparently many locks on the front door. "I knew somebody stole my flowers! You think I won't-" The door swung half open and she stopped her shouting as soon as she saw who they were holding. Warm, musty air spilled out from the doorway, reminiscent of the cave.

She was older than Fordo, maybe in her early thirties, wearing a robe that looked like it was stitched together from an old blanket. She looked shocked and frightened for a moment, then a slow grin spread across her face when she looked at Mira. "You're back!" She exclaimed. She tossed something heavy from her hand behind the door before holding out her arms to hold Mira. Mira didn't move.

"Oh give your mother a hug, I was...worried sick about you." She said, glancing nervously at Fordo. Her grin was warm, but her eyes were cold. Fordo pat Mira's back and she reached for her mother, who kissed her long and hard on the cheek then let her slide to the ground. "Oh You're filthy!" She said, grabbing a hold of Mira's wrist, "Where did she run off to this time?" The woman turned to Fordo with an innocent look.

"Nowhere nice," Fordo said, stone-faced, unsure of what to make of this woman.

The woman looked him up and down and smiled, "Oh you're filthy too," She laughed, "Would you boys like to come in and take a nice hot bath? It's the least I could do for bringing me back my sweet little sap." She leaned against the doorway, her hand fiddling with the tie on her rope.

She kind of looked like Fordo's step mom, Sarah, the more he looked at her, but less healthy, less warm. Her eyes were green and colder, her smile less bright, he didn't trust her. "No ma'am, that won't be necessary. We're just happy she's safe." Fordo said, eyeing her up and down. She seemed to notice his gaze.

"Do I look like a ma'am to you?" She giggled, "Call me Helena," She rested a hand on his chest, grabbing a hold of his ruined jacket.

Fordo nodded, "We really must be going, ma'am." He looked down to Mira whose eyes were sad and empty, "Take care of yourself, Little One. We'll come visit soon." Mira nodded and rocked in place.

"You can come visit me anytime," Helena said, "If there's anything I can do for my young heroes, *Anything...*" She hugged Fordo longer and tighter than she did her own missing daughter. "...Stop by and let me know," She whispered in his ear.

"Yes ma'am," Fordo said, halfheartedly returning

her hug. She smiled and kissed him right under the chin before backing into the house and quickly closing the door. Fordo caught a glimpse of Mira's sad eyes right before the door closed and the many locks were clicked into place. Fordo didn't move, he listened for voices, for movement, for a sign that the woman had any love or worry for her child, but they heard nothing, which meant she was listening right back at them. Fordo looked back at Carth and Kira. All three of them shook their heads and exhaled through their noses before walking back to the lift.

They didn't say a word until they were almost to the lift, far out of earshot. "We can't leave her there," Kira said

"She barely even reacted," Carth said

"That smile was so fake and weird and off…" Kira shook his head, "We can't leave her there…"

"She was holding her wrist too tight," Carth squeezed his own wrist just as tight.

"Did you see in the house?" Kira asked, "It was so empty, just a pile of blankets on the floor."

"What was she holding when she first opened the door?" Carth asked

"I couldn't see, but I heard that too," Kira replied.

"It smelt just like the cave," Fordo said somberly. Carth and Kira both looked at him. "The house smelt just like the cave…" Fordo shook his head, "We didn't save her from monsters just to give her back to one. We'll come back for Mira tonight, but for now…" They stepped onto the lift, "…We have more stops to make."

AL AND MEEKO

3

Smoke and brick, wood and sweat, fire and metal; Al couldn't help but smell and smile as the duo made their way through Scrapyard's bustling streets. The roads themselves were paved with metal. Countless nuts, bolts, screws, and parts all lost, dropped, and stomped flat into the dirt like cobblestones. If Riverwood was a tangle of vines wrapping up and around the Realwood Forest, Scrapyard was a patch of moss, creeping and clinging flat against the stones in the shadow of Daisy's Mountains.

A clustered shantytown of brown shops and homes, each as unique as their individual owners. Some several stories high with beautifully odd architecture and intricately angled rooftops, shingled with black and gray solar panels. While others could be two large pieces of corrugated sheet metal, leaning haphazardly against one another. In a world where you only own what you can build, Al liked to think Scrapyard embodied that best.

Few thoughts were as awesome to Al as:

People built this place. Every nail and screw in every plank and beam, deliberately crafted and placed with the purpose of creating a home. A home where the bright eyed and fuzzy faced can tinker and craft and invent freely. Use good ideas to transform bad memories into a slightly better world.

Or at least one slightly more prime.

Less like a factory and more like a fireplace, the village was filled with shooting sparks and puffs of smoke. A symphony of hammers pinged, panged, and pounded through all hours of the day. Countless chimneys cast a cozy gray canvas over the village. *Even the clouds are man made.*

Meeko loved to run through the crowds, dodging carts full of metal, pulled by bodies full of odor. Weaving through the leather booted legs of Limb Smiths and Grub Farmers, trading food for tools, work for work. A trail of startled and delighted faces always marked Meeko's path.

'Bright eyed and fuzzy faced' Sarah liked to call Scrapyard's everyone. Metal limbed mechanics, smiths, and engineers alike. Hundreds of botsthetic arms and legs hauling piles of scrapped rusted robots back to their forges and benches to tinker with their hopes and dreams. Mustache wielding, pipe puffing, First War refugees, journeyed from far and wide in search of new hands and a new home. *And Bali gave them both.*

Al's eyes followed the human trail all the way to Scrapyard's scrapyard, a mountain of robot husks looming over the northern hills. An unfathomably large pile of both immense pain and endless opportunity. *"One of the few places on Aureum where the past and the future meet,"* Daisy once said. Al squinted at the twisted pile. As often as the thought crossed his mind, he measured to see if the mountain had shrunk by even an inch from the endless flow of give and take.

"They took your hands, now take them back!" Exclaimed a quote on the metal muraled walls surrounding the mountain. Embossed with First War scenes of the glories and horrors of

men against machines, they told the tale of Scrapyard's origins. Each scene fading into the next, from Hilltop's Horde, The Stand at Julia, all the way through Bali's Fist and the founding of Scrapyard. Al's Favorite scene was near the end; A man who had lost his arm, standing at the peak of the pile of dead robots, triumphantly raising a robot's arm above his head, while an army cheers below.

They took your hands, now take them back.

Minus the many children, maybe three in ten people had all four of their original limbs. The rest were branded with botsthetic replacements, a generous gift from Scrapyard's grumpy and gracious founder.

Al stepped through the curtain of the crowd and onto the welcoming porch of The Green Grub Inn, whose cozy red bricks and green trimmings shone bright like a flower in gravel against the rest of the town. The sweet scent of freshly baked bread cut through the cloud of sweat and dust. Daisy's howling laugh overpowered all the clashing and clanking of metal.

He stepped inside the swinging doors to find Meeko sprinting excitedly all around an ancient woman. Knocking over wooden chairs and metal mugs, diving under her flowy black dress and out the back. "He's everywhere!" She hollered and howled through her toothless gums, "Hoo Hoo I'm gonna getch ya!" She knocked over just as many chairs and tables herself, swinging and swiveling a wooden serving cart which supported her unreasonably large breasts. Al's laughter grew with the chaos. Soon he was doubled over in the doorway, unable to breathe.

"There you are, young man!" Al wiped his eyes and greeted the woman with a grin. "Well get over here! Give Daisy a hug!" Al dropped his pack and hugged his old friend.

"Hey you," he croaked out as she squeezed the air from his lungs.

"So good to see you boys, was worried you'd never come back!"

"You miss us that much? It's barely been a week!" Al laughed

"Hoo Hoo Don't tease me! I miss you boys whenever you step out that door. Thought you'd see the rest of the world and forget all about little ol' Daisy, just like the twins."

"You'd have to sink them to forget you, girly."

"Well what brings you back 'so soon', then? Oo Did you find her? Tell me all about it!"

"We didn't get as far as we hoped. Just came back for some repairs, Meeko hurt his leg."

She looked around at the destroyed inn and the still sprinting Meeko. "Are you sure?" she laughed

"His Pawsthetic's a little bent, we came home to be safe."

"If you were being safe, it wouldn't be bent," she teased

"When did you upgrade to a cart?"

"Oh, Brash made it for me when my poor walker finally broke, snapped right in two. Cracked the floorboards when these puppies fell."

Al and Meeko burst into uncontrollable laughter, "I can't believe we missed that."

"Ya miss a lot of things when you're gone so long."

"Well you tell us about them tomorrow, we're just stopping by. Gotta get to Bali before sunset or he'll be too grumpy."

"Oh, He's always grumpy."

"Want some help cleaning up?"

"No, no, gives me an excuse to wake Brash, sweet boy." Daisy picked up a metal tankard and tossed it with a clang into the little nook under the wooden staircase. A mound of a man rolled out from his den, rubbing his small sleepy eyes. Brash was the only man who could rival Balian in sheer size, and arguably creativity, but he had the build, the brain, and the bald of a giant baby, which thoroughly amused Al.

"Brash, look what you did sleepwalking again!" Daisy winked at Al.

"Sorry, Miss Daisy..." Brash yawned, waddling to turn tables and chairs back on their feet.

"Love you boys! And tell Sarah to come by tomorrow, when you see her!"

"Love you too, Daisy. We'll be back."

***

"Bah Roh Cah Doh Deh Fen Doh Roh! Bah Roh Cah Doh Deh Fen Doh Roh!"

A wide grin spread across Al's face as they cut behind the Green Grub to hear the distant chant of Fordo's legacy. The grunts and clash and excited yells of a brawl echoed up the alley ways. The dull knocks of wooden weapons against wooden shields sent Al into an eager jog towards the action.

Whistling for Meeko to run ahead, he tossed his pack without care behind him, picked up speed, kicked off of the brick wall, and caught a thin pipe sticking out the side of the building. Shimmying his way up to the slanted roof top, he followed his ears leaping from roof to roof, chimney to chimney until he spotted other kids with the same idea, legs dangling from the shingles watching the game from above.

"Jasper!" Al called to one of the younger boys.

"Al! When did you get back? It's been like-!"

"I know, I know, I don't wanna talk about it," Al hopped on over, plopping down beside them to see a huge game of Barricade in full swing. Eight on eight was a rare and beautiful sight. Sixteen screaming children all in padded armor with wooden weapons charged one another down a wide alley strewn with wooden bunkers and obstacles, two raised barricades blocking either end. The warriors clashed in the middle, sprinting full speed, plowing into one another with swords and shields while two archers atop either barricade launched round leather padded arrows into the crowd. The goal was simple: You take their barricade before they take yours.

"I don't recognize any of these kids," Al said

"Lotta new families moved in since you left."

"Moved in fast, already playin' full on Barricade... Any of them good?"

"Just that kid," Jasper pointed to a young man charging with a shield and spear. He leapt up high off of a crate over one enemy, jabbing another in the chest, knocking them to the ground. He landed in a deep crouch behind his thin shield, ducking under one arrow while deflecting another, then took off running before his other opponent could even turn around.

"He is pretty good," Al nodded, his grin getting wider.

"He's faster than you and smarter than Fordo."

"Don't let Fordo hear that or he'd push you off the roof," Al chuckled, "Where is Fordo? He never misses a match."

"Who cares?" The young boy shrugged.

Al laughed, "You still bummed he won't let you play on his team?"

"I could get better so much faster if I played with bigger kids!"

"Eh, You'll be a bigger kid soon enough. Besides, Fordo only cares about winning...He's way more fun to play against."

Spear kid flanked his way to the enemy barricade, dodging arrows left and right, swatting one away with his shield while hurling his soft tipped spear at one of the archers, his weapon punching her in the chest just as her arrow thumped his, sending them both spinning onto their backs.

"Whooaa!" Al and Jasper both clapped, spear guy and the archer both smiling and pointing at each other as they jogged back to spawn.

"I love that glass," Al beamed, "Takin' each other out in a quickdraw."

"My favorite's seein' two arrows hit each other!"

"Oh, You're right! You remember the match by the aqueducts?? Where I rushed Jacks with a thrower and Benji fuckin'-"

"Alexander!"

Al and Jasper both turned, looking down to see Carth's adoptive father calling up to them with a voice and beard as coarse as steel wool.

"Garrow! Give me one second!" Al called back, pushing playfully off Jasper's fuzzy head to get up, "I'll catch you later, Jay…Tell your mom and Liam I said, Oy."

"Alright, alright"

Al quickly hopped over the edge of the two story building onto a balcony below. Ducking under the railing he grabbed hold of the platform's edge and dropped his body to a dangle, waited for himself to stop swinging before falling the remaining eight feet into the alley.

"Wish my knees were young enough to watch the games proper," Garrow grinned, clasping Al's wrist and pulling him in for a thumping hug.

"Just chop 'em off and have Bali build you some new ones."

"Ha, Aure knows I've earned 'em. Where the hell have you been, boy? You stink like the road."

"Just swung back for some repairs, we're probably heading back out tomorrow, didn't get nearly as far as we hoped."

"In and out, huh? Well I'm glad I spotted ya before you snuck off again. Least say goodbye this time, nearly broke my son's heart when you disappeared."

"Where is Carthy? I thought I'd see him at the Inn."

"He followed young Fordon up to Julia, lookin' for you, I reckon."

"They left to look for me?? Must've passed us when we went off trail…They're gonna be lookin' a while. How bad was it when I left…? Fordo pissed…?"

"I mean, it was……bad, it was pretty bad…" Garrow laughed, "Bad enough to finally get out of here, for better or worse, but Carth'll be back with a story or two I hope. Wish he had better company, but glad he's not just drinkin' all day."

"Yeah…now he's drinkin' And walkin'." Al laughed

Garrow smirked and smacked Al's shoulder, "Work to do. Take care, boy, sure I'll see you and Meeko at Balian's some time tomorrow."

***

Al and Meeko paused briefly at the large open courtyard that stood in the center of the village, two wooden towers each topped with a massive six foot drum, both stood at attention on the eastern and western sides. The courtyard itself was bare of buildings save for a raised wooden platform used only for great announcements and grifters' judgments. A cobblestone playground where warriors, smiths and mechanics practice, test, and play with their beloved creations. Most of these inventions birthed out of childlike imagination. Impractically stylish weapons and armor or overly convoluted contraptions with no real use, but every so often a great man's work gives birth to genius. Al was here to see one of those great men.

Carved out from the foot of the mountain, the wood and metal of Bali's longhouse merged seamlessly with the natural gray stone as if melded magically. Wooden beams held up the black shingled roof jutting out of the rock as if the building was there first and the mountain had simply grown around it. The round red realwood door was so large Sarah could invite a young wyrm to stay for dinner without fear for the trimming.

Carved stone steps broke off of the path leading up to Sarah's plateau garden. The beautiful greens and whites and blues of her collection of earthborn plants shone bright and saturated against the stones they sat on. Al and Meeko tip-toed past the garden, hearing Sarah's sweet warm singing above, along with the snipping of her garden shears.

They snuck past the beautiful garden and the giant front door to the gaping square cave perpendicular to the rest of the house, the sliding metal door raised all the way up to the ceiling.

The shop looked exactly as it did before they left and probably all of the years before they ever arrived. An unswept stone floor, littered with arbitrary tools and materials. Hammers and tongs of various shapes and sizes lined the walls. Other twisted tools with no foreseeable purpose to anyone but their creator were mixed in with the easily recognizable. A circular stone forge lay purring in the corner with a low red flame draped like a blanket over the resting coals. At the far end of the shop stretched a massive workbench, covered end to end with wooden shields and metal limbs.

Displayed on the wall above, coated evenly in a decade's worth of dust, was Bali's Fist: A massive warhammer, bigger than Al, whose head was shaped like a robot's four-fingered fist clutching a metal spike.

Sitting in the center of the workbench, like a king on his throne, was a giant of a man. His wall of a back greeted the duo as they stood just outside of the shop, seemingly unnoticed. A smile slowly crept onto Al's lips as he watched his old friend at work. *Right where we left you.*

Al and Meeko each took a single step into his kingdom, immediately halted by a booming voice, "The hell do you want?"

Al's smile upgraded to a grin, "We were looking for a decent mechanic, but this doesn't seem like the place."

The giant refused to be interrupted, continuing to tinker with his whatever. "Well then, seems you should get out of my shop and go bother some other busy bastard."

Meeko sniffed the air and shook his head like someone had poured a little water on him. "I think you need to step out yourself. Starting to stink in here."

"Showers are for workless men, like you and my idiot son."

"Hey, me and your idiot son work real hard to make you angry and keep your face that funny shade of red we both like."

"Any work's hard for scrawny cunts like you."

"Whoa hey, I hope you're not this unpleasant with your wife." Al heard a wooden snap as the man's shoulders tensed up.

"I actually like my wife...She's not an annoying, smart-mouthed bastard who runs off and disappears then shows up whenever he wants just to interrupt my work." The man slammed his hands on the workbench, standing and turning in one motion, knocking over his chair and towering over Alexander like a statue. Their eyes locked and Al looked up at the man, like a fox might a grizzly bear. *Oh glass, did I actually make him mad?*

Without changing his stern expression, Balian The Bear slowly opened his arms and said, "It's good to see you, boy."

Al sighed in relief, arms barely reaching the man's back, like hugging a bed. Less of a laugh and more of a pleased grunt wiggled Bali's bushy mustache.

"Don't do that to me, I'm sweaty enough as it is." Al couldn't tell if Bali had lost weight or gained it. Last he saw him, Balian was just as large, but with a gut like a boulder. Now he was one big chest muscle with stone pillars for arms. "What the hell has Sarah done to you?"

"New diet."

"New diet? What, does she make you eat the robots, now? Are all those shields really just sandwiches?" Bali's scowl cracked and exploded into a laugh that shook the town. The proceeding clap on the shoulder almost knocked Al to the ground.

"So what project did we just ruin?"

"Been playing with the plans for an exoskeleton."

"Sounds too scary...What's it for?"

"A young lady rolled all the way down here from Riverwood on her own, a few months back. She's stuck riding a pillpup after an accident, can't move her legs no more."

"Huh, I didn't even know a pillboy would let you ride it. No Limb Smiths in Riverwood? I thought Jacks and Benji moved over there to set up a shop."

"Botsthetics don't work like that. If you lose your legs, I can just make you new ones, but if your legs just stop working, I can't help you."

"Isn't that the same thing?"

"No, you idiot, that's what I just said. Bot takes your legs, they're still legs, they're just missing. Bot busts your back, legs stop working, so new legs won't work neither."

"I still don't get why, but I believe you. So what's this skeleton do?"

"You remember the puppets Brash made for Daisy's birthday?"

"Yeah, where he used the strings to make them dance and fight and stuff."

"Exactly. I'm trying to figure out the strings to help this girl dance and fight and stuff."

"Feel like actual strings would be more fun," Al laughed

Bali grunted in amusement, "Sure it'd save me some steel. So you boys miss me or did you need a favor?"

"We mostly missed Sarah, but yeah, Meeko and I had a little accident."

"What the fuck did you do?"

"He's fine, it doesn't hurt or anything."

"I don't care about that furry thing, what did you do to my leg! Took me forever to get it calibrated."

"He didn't mean that, buddy."

"Do you know how long it took me to map a dog's nervous system? I'm a mechanic, not a fuckin' doctor!"

"Well, you can do it again, you know you love a side project."

"Yeah, a New one, not when some punk breaks my old one because he doesn't love his dog enough to keep him safe." That one actually hurt Al's feelings a bit. Bali knelt down and ran his hands along the pawsthetic. "You're lucky just the frame's bent, nothing the anvil can't fix."

"See, it's not tha-"

"But that doesn't mean you're not an idiot. What happened? Did you drop him out of a fuckin' tree again?"

"No. Well, yes, but that was separate from this."

"Do you know how hard it is to bend magnesium alloy? This glass survived falling out of space a hundred fuckin' years ago and You still found a way to bend it yourself."

"Okay, okay, you've made your point. We got caught off guard by a bot. It got a good hit on us before I could take it out. I'm sorry."

"Don't apologize to me, apologize to young Meeks here."

"I did! I'm the one who got his neck broke, why do I gotta keep apologizing for a bent-" Balian grabbed Al's jacket and pulled him close.

"What did you just say?" Bali's eyes locked in on Al's.

"I...Well..."

"Damnit, boy! You die again??" Al shook Bali's hand off of him and turned away.

"I don't know why you make such a big deal out of it. You know that I heal, so why do you freak out every time? I'm the one who was dead, why do you have to try making me feel guilty every time I come back?"

Al turned back to Bali. Anger welled in Bali's unblinking eyes as he continued to stare straight through Al. "You're not supposed to come back, you understand, you shouldn't Have to come back! You fucking idiot..." Bali stood and grabbed Al by the shoulders. "This is the Third fucking time, in the Four years I've known you. I'm forty four years old and I haven't died once. Daisy's a thousand years old and she hasn't died once." Bali shook Al's shoulders. "Every living thing I've ever met hasn't died more than once except for you and Meeko, and every one of his deaths will be your fault too."

"Hey! It's not my fault! I didn't...I didn't choose this for us!"

"How do you even know? You didn't even know your own name when I first fuckin' found you. You still don't know your Real name! What did you forget this time you died, huh? You don't know! You'll never know, because you forgot!"

"Stop it! What was I supposed to do, let the bot hurt somebody else?"

"So you're a big hero now, huh? Protecting all the free peoples from sunken scrap nowhere near the roads."

"How did you-?"

"It's been fourteen years, any war bot left that could still walk around is on that pile out there. Don't pretend I'm stupid enough to not know you're out fighting sunken scrap."

"So what if I was? It's my life, my risk, right? I know I'll come back, you know I'll come back, so why shouldn't I die trying to take out a monster when someone else might?"

"Oh, don't give me that glass! You're not brave, cunt, you just think you're invincible. You're not!" He gestured to Al's wooden finger and Meeko's metal paw, "If I chop your grub off... it ain't growin' back. And neither would your head, so stop trying to lose it every time you leave the fucking village." Al looked down at Meeko, unable to meet Bali's eye. "Value lies in limitation. Everyone gets one life, One...that's it...that's what makes it so precious. Just cause you might get a few more, doesn't mean you can throw it away every chance you get. You understand me, boy?"

"Yeah..." *Kind of.*

"Hey, look at me. I know all this makes you angry, but so does one of the only people I love coming home after ten months and telling me they fuckin' sunk themself."

"What did you say?"

"I said even though you infuriate me, I still love you, cunt, So I don't wanna hear about you coming back ever again...Prime?"

"Did you say Ten Months?" Everything slowed down. Bali was still scolding him, but Al couldn't hear it. *Was I dead for ten months? No, that's impossible, it's never taken more than a few days.*

*Ten months, that's so much time, so much life. If it was ten months then why would Meeko tell me...Oh no, Meeko...*The blood drained from Al's face and his stomach sank. "Tell me it wasn't..." He looked down at Meeko, who's head drooped, unable to meet Al's gaze. Al knelt down and lifted Meeko's face to his own. His hands and breath started to shake.

"Oh no, no, Meeko!" He licked Al's hand and Al pressed their foreheads together. "I am so sorry..." Al broke down into a full sob, hugging his boy as tight as he could.

"Why are you sorry now?"

Al struggled to get the breath in to say, "We barely made it to the Yellow Sea..."

"What? How the hell...?"

"On the second day I climbed a tree and saw something far off in the woods that I wanted to explore." Bali sat down, shaking his head in disbelief.

"We get there and it's a sunken bot. After it scared us, we were out of its reach, it wasn't going anywhere. I didn't have to fight it, but I wanted to, so I did. And it killed me."

"You reckless, stupid, irresponsible-"

"Bali, I left Meeko alone in the woods for ten whole months..." Bali's eyes softened. "And when I woke up...he was still there...He still came running when I called..." Bali sank deeper into his chair, rubbing the angry from his eyes.

"Damnit, boy."

"How am I Ever supposed to make that up to him?" Al held Meeko's face.

Bali scrunched his face and rubbed the back of his own head, trying to suppress more yelling. "Just use your head more, think things through. Don't dive into danger just cause you think you'll recover. And don't forget that you're responsible for more than Just yourself...Every time you put your life at risk, Every Time...you do the same to his. Remember that." Al nodded, a new wave of tears rushing down his cheeks.

"I'm sorry, Meeko...I'm so sorry..."

"Get up boy, you're embarrassing me..." Bali picked up Al with one hand, lifting him off the ground and onto his feet. "You don't want Sarah seeing you like this."

"Seeing who like what?" A soft, sweet voice came from around the corner. Meeko barked and ran to meet it at the door. "Meeko?!" She gasped, keeling down to embrace the good boy on her two slender mechanical legs. Al used Meeko's distraction to wipe his teary eyes before greeting her.

"Ay, girly..." Al smiled, Sarah's warm brown eyes and bright smile both widened to meet Al's. Brown wavy hair bounced on her shoulders as she hopped up and skipped over to Al. Almost knocking him over with her vice of a hug, she squeezed him so tight, he couldn't even move his arms to reciprocate. He rested his chin on her head. She smelled like soil and strawberries.

"You're home! You're safe!"

"We missed you, Sarah."

"I didn't miss you at aalll!" She laughed, somehow squeezing him even tighter, "When did you get home? Why didn't you call me, Bali Bear? I was just up in the garden."

"Thought you were having a good day. Didn't wanna ruin it with these weirdos." She rolled her eyes and hit him on the arm.

"We got in around midday, we wanted to bother Bali first," Al said

She dropped her jaw in feigned offense, "Bother him first? He doesn't even like you guys!" She smiled, her eyebrows raised in excitement, "Oo oo Did you find her?? Tell me all about it!" She tugged on Al's arm towards the door to the house. "Come inside, come inside, it smells like handsome old man in here." She stuck her tongue out at Bali before disappearing through the door, pulling Al in with her.

Fordo

3

"What are you gonna say?" Carth asked Fordo in a low voice.

What can I say? Fordo asked himself, his fist hovering an inch from the door, ready to knock on the carving of a robot's fist hammering an anvil, the sigil of Scrapyard.

"May-maybe I should go first, she is still my family," Kira suggested, his voice already shaky with sorrow.

"No..." Fordo whispered hoarsely "...I'm the one who gave his word."

Carth and Kira both looked at the ground. Carth was squeezing one of his hands nervously, Kira was trying real hard to push down his sobs. Fordo's hovering hand shook and lowered a moment, before he sighed and knocked on the wooden door.

"Be right there!" They heard a woman's excited, muffled voice through the door. Fordo's heart pounded in sync with her footsteps as she skipped through the house. A lump formed in his throat. He squeezed the head of his hammer to steady his trembling hand and bit the inside of his cheek to keep his lips from quivering. He was more scared now than he was in the cave.

The door opened. A beautiful dark skinned woman stood in the door. Deep brown eyes and a bright white smile flashed in excitement for a fraction of a moment, only to melt away as she looked from Fordo to Kira to Carth to the empty walkway behind them.

"Elizabeth…" Fordo started, but he couldn't hide the pain and fear in his face any longer, he began to shake. She shook her head in silence, slowly rocking back and forth. Her expression was calm for a moment, then her eyes closed, her head dropped, and her face twisted into despair.

"No…" She croaked and began to weep. Fordo couldn't form any other words, so he just opened his arms and she rocked herself into them. He held her for a moment, her hands clenched in fists resting on his chest as she wept between them. "No…" She shook her head again, weakly pounding on his chest. He squeezed her tighter, but she began to shake and pound more violently. "No!" She broke free of his embrace, pushing and hitting him away from her as she cried.

"I'm sorry…" Fordo wept, trying to catch her wrist to hold her still. He tried to hug her once more, but she shoved him back and slapped him across the face with such force it knocked him stumbling backwards into Carth. Fordo was stunned, his tear filled eyes were wide, staring fearfully at the woman, his hand holding his stinging cheek.

"You begged me!" She screamed, stepping forward, "You promised!" Kira stepped between them and she wept into his chest. "You said it would be easy!" She cried, "You promised he'd be fine!" She pushed past Kira and grabbed onto Fordo's jacket, shaking him as she cried. "I didn't want him to go! I didn't want him to go, but you promised me, and I trusted you!" She raised her hand to slap him once more, but Kira caught it and pulled her into his embrace.

Fordo slumped down to his knees. Her words hurt him more than her slap, more than Benji's boot. He had begged her to let Benji come against her objections. Told her it'd be quick and easy and she had nothing to worry about. Benji would return home a hero, without a scratch on him, she had Fordo's word. *I didn't mean to lie to you.*

"I'm sorry..." Fordo cried

"Just go!" She shouted into Kira's chest.

"I didn't..."

"Go!" She screamed at Fordo before burying her face back into Kira.

Fordo looked up at Kira, defeated. A crying Kira nodded and gestured with his head back down the walkway toward the lift. Fordo didn't want to leave, he wanted to make it right somehow, but he knew there was nothing he could do, nothing he could say. Carth helped Fordo to his feet and pulled him back down the walkway. Fordo followed, but he couldn't take his eyes off of Kira and Elizabeth, two people whose lives he'd just destroyed. *What have I done?* He asked himself as he limped behind Carth back toward the lift.

"It wasn't your fault," Carth said when they were out of sight of Beth and Kira. Fordo was relieved to hear those words, but he didn't believe them.

"Of course it is," Fordo said

"Jacks and Benji volunteered, they knew the risks."

"'Knew the risks' I didn't even know the risks, Carth..."

"So we went in blind, a huge mistake that cost us dearly, but what time did we have? We went down there to save a little girl and that's exactly what we did. Mira's alive because of us and because of them. Seeing Chop run up to her, crying, glad that she's safe, even without the twins, that makes it all worth it to me. We did the right thing, Ford." Carth cried as he spoke, but spoke with such confidence, such conviction, that Fordo felt even guiltier than before.

Guilty because he knew the truth; the truth that was his and his alone: *I don't give a fuck about that little girl.* His friends are dead and he would have never gone down there if he even considered that a possibility. He didn't go down that hole to save her, he went down there so people would see that he did. Any care or sympathy he had for her now was purely obligatory, to justify the substantial and devastating loss of his childhood friends. All this he knew in his heart, but he could never tell Carth.

Carth must have noticed Fordo's silence because he repeated "Oy, it wasn't your fault. They would have followed you to the underworld."

"I think they just did, Carthy...But so did you, you saved my life down there, more than once. Thanks for always being by my side when I need you. I couldn't do half the glass I do without you."

"We saved each other down there, no need to thank me. Without you I'd do nothing but drink ale at the Green Grub 'til I'm as big as Brash and old as Daisy."

Fordo managed a smile, "I'm sure that's somebody's dream."

"That's still mine...I'm just hoping we get famous enough to justify our workless ways," Carth laughed, halfheartedly.

I'm glad you're here, Carth. Fordo thought as they stepped onto the lift once more. "One last stop," Fordo said

"Then we can finally scrub this glass off?" Carth itched his arm where the gray goo had dried.

"Then we can burn these clothes..." Fordo tugged at his collar before tugging on the lift chord.

***

They ascended to the highest levels of the city, breaking through and rising above the main canopy. Wind ripped at their hair and clothes. Looking down over the railing, Fordo couldn't even tell there was a city below them. Save for a few scattered wisps of chimney smoke wafting through the leaves, the dense treetops just looked like dense treetops. The thought was kind of amazing to him, a whole kingdom, hidden so well from above that even gods couldn't spy on it. *Wonder if that was the idea.*

The sun was about to set behind the Dragon's Teeth mountains, casting golden light over the red leafed realwoods that stretched all the way from the mountains in the west to the Siena River in the east. The range and the river raced past the red forest, cutting through the yellow grass, and running off towards the southern horizon. Fordo wondered if he'd ever see just how far down they really went. *Maybe that's how I'll get famous, be the first man to actually return from exploring south of the Daisy's.*

The lift slowed and groaned to a stop on the second to last platform, just below the baron's Big House. A wide, cylindrical structure that wrapped around and sat atop the massive tree. Fordo imagined from afar it likely looked as if the tree had a head. Though he figured the view wasn't much different, Fordo knew Al would be scrambling up to the roof on sight.

The platform was barren of buildings and few folks wandered the walkway. The great chains of the lifts disappeared into the bottom of the Big House. As soon as they stepped onto the platform, their loyal lift began its slow descent back down to the city, called by another stranger in need.

"Whoa..." Carth breathed. They both looked up in awe to the trunk of the great tree. Its bark had been carved to resemble three layers of fifteen foot robots holding up each other and the great building above their heads. It gave the structure a seemingly sacred, almost divine presence, like a temple or a monument. Fordo hated that he loved the feeling it gave him. Both disgusted by the self indulgent narcissism one must possess to create such a structure, and envious of the inevitable sense of power it must give those who live within it.

Two steep, suspended staircases spiraled up around either side of the trunk and into openings on the bottom of the Big House. A guard was posted at the foot of either staircase, both in different sets of leather armor. Fordo didn't understand the point of armor; slowed you down, wore you out, both bots and beasts alike tore right through it. He figured it was purely uniform.

The guard farthest from them was a tall, fair skinned woman with a long brown braid thick as rope running down over a full, overlapping suit of heavy leather armor, colored and etched to look like she was wearing the red bark of the Realwoods. An oversized, reinforced botsthetic arm rested atop the hilt of a massive, square headed broadsword as tall and wide as she was. She stood as still as the carved robots, her sad, leaf green eyes watching them from behind thin round glasses with a surprisingly warm smile.

No way she can swing that thing. She was the first person, besides Al, Fordo had seen carry a sword. They dulled far too quickly against armored bots and wyrm scales. *What a waste of steel.*

The guard nearest them sat upon the steps in dirt brown armor far lighter than his companion's. His face hidden under the wide circular brim of a black conical hat that resembled a woven basket. Next to him, standing taller than Fordo, rested a sturdy looking spear with a twisted, bladeless spike for a head that looked like it could punch a hole through solid stone. While the guard fiddled with something small in his hands, Fordo noticed a dark symbol tooled into each of his bracers, possibly a jagged crown of thorns.

"This wind can suck my grub," Cursed the guard in a gruff voice, flicking another wasted match into a small pile at his feet.

"'This wind can blow me.' That's what you should have said," Carth smiled

"You can blow me, is what I shoulda said, mate," The guard waved dismissively without looking up. Carth thought it was funny. Fordo did not.

"Baron have a lot of enemies?" Fordo asked the guard's hat.

"Apparently not," The guard shrugged and waved his hands like he could have sworn there were some extra enemies up there somewhere, but he just couldn't find them. Carth and Fordo both looked at each other. They needed to get past the man, but they weren't exactly sure how to ask him to move.

"Then what are you doing here?" Carth asked

"Wish I knew, mate…" The wind died just long enough for the guard to light another match only to pick up and blow it out before he could raise it to his lips. He flicked it to the pile and grabbed another. "The Founder said he had a special assignment for us. Turned out to be sitting on these steps for months 'thouta fight."

"The Founder? Warren the first died over forty years ago," Fordo recalled.

"Wrong founder, wrong Warren," The guard said, lighting and flicking another match onto the pile. He kissed his own fingers and tapped the symbol on his bracer. Fordo stared at it again and realized it wasn't a crown of black thorns, but a circle of black teeth.

"Blackwyrm?" Fordo raised an eyebrow, "I didn't know you guys could leave."

"Oy, We can do whatever we want, mate...We just prefer the sands." Bits of brown bacco blew out of the end of his hand-rolled cigarette as it bobbed between his smiling lips. "Now what business do you have with the Baron?"

"Mission report, we just want a quick audience, we saved that little girl that ran down a wyrm route," Fordo said

"And why should I believe you?" The guard asked from beneath his hat, still fumbling with a match. Fordo sucked his teeth, dug a small metal rectangle from his pocket and tossed it into the guard's lap. The guard gracefully twirled it between his fingers a moment, lifted the cap with a click, and flicked the flint for a flame. A cloud of smoke erupted from the brim of his hat. He closed the lighter with a satisfying clap and looked up at them for the first time through the cloud of smoke with a lit cigarette and big yellow smile, "Go right ahead, mate, he's been expecting you."

The red armored woman chuckled to herself, making an odd, quick gesture to her friend. Blackhat smirked and made a different gesture back as he stood, tucking the lighter under his bracer, rising far taller than Fordo thought he'd be on two abnormal, double jointed, botsthetic legs, shaped more like a rabbit's than a human's. He stepped aside, leaning on his spear, finally revealing his pale, narrow, sunken face and long pointed nose. *Glass...I'd wear a hat too.* Fordo thought as he stepped past him.

Both of his knees popped as he climbed the first two steps. The sun dipped behind the mountains just as they climbed the last of the steps and entered the Big House.

They popped up in the middle of a large, warm, circular room. The high ceiling held up by four more wooden carvings, all eerily detailed, like a sorcerer had turned actual robots into wood.

Fordo looked out of the huge window that surrounded the room. Looking towards the southern view, he wondered why it was so much more sunny and vibrant than the view he'd just witnessed moments before, when the sun was already setting. He quickly realized that it was not a window, but a beautiful, identical, panoramic painting of the surrounding view. He would have felt like an idiot, if not for the incredible, Julian level detail.

In the center of the room, raised on a large table, centered between the two entrances, was a diorama of Riverwood and all of its territory, with detail and craftsmanship that was undeniably Scrapyard. Complete to scale with mountains, trees, roads, the river, herds of pillboys, and civilian workers in the lumber yards. As awed and impressed as Fordo was, he wondered if it was not redundant to have your kingdom both painted And modeled in the very same room.

An empty, fur covered throne sat on a small stage facing the diorama. Fordo had never met an earthborn creature large enough to cover a throne with its fur, but he figured he was a little late now.

This was Fordo's first time meeting the Baron in many years, not since they were both teenagers. He knew very little about the man, but one thing he was certain of, with Riverwood architecture, Julian artwork, Scrapyard craftsmanship, Blackwyrm guards, and Earthborn furs; Warren was a collector.

"You look terrible, Pledge..." A young, but commanding voice came from behind the throne. Carth and Fordo stepped around it to find a small desk on the other side, occupied by a young man with thin glasses and a small wooden pipe sticking out of his well groomed beard that connected up to his thick brown hair. He wore no shirt, just leather suspenders slung over his wide shoulders, as he wrote with a pen that seemed far too small in his large square hands. A cloud of sweet smelling smoke floated around his head, making him look almost mystical. Though he was barely older than Fordo, he had a much older presence.

"We feel terrible..." Fordo said, looking down at the pages and pages of writings stacked on either side of the man's desk. He wrote so fast, filling a page with words about as quickly as Fordo could draw stacks of straight lines.

"You find her, then?" The man asked, without looking up from his work. Fordo furrowed his brow, the man's uninterested tone reminded him of his father.

"We found her. She's safe with her mother now," Fordo said

"Mm...Yes, that's what I heard..." The man kept writing.

Then why did you ask?

"Did everything go smoothly?"

"Not exactly," Fordo said, glumly. He waited for the man to inquire further, but he never did. "We lost two good friends down there, getting her away from those monsters. The twin mechanics, Jackson and Benjamin."

"Mm…Yes, I heard that as well." The man said, with utter indifference. The room was silent save for the scraping of his pen.

Fordo shook his head, "Then why did you ask?"

The man stopped writing mid sentence. Carth glanced nervously at Fordo. Warren slowly removed and folded his glasses, placing them and his pen gently on his desk, perfectly parallel with his paper.

"When my grandfather discovered this forest of giants, he sought the wisdom of the oldest, tallest tree. When he found it, the spirit of this tree whispered in his ear 'If you reach the top, all you see will belong to you and your children.' It took him four days to make the climb, but when he finally reached the top and saw this view…" He gestured to the mural around the room with his hands, "…He knew the spirit's words were true." Fordo couldn't tell if he was trying to make a point, or simply bragging.

Warren's chair creaked as he got up, standing a whole head taller than Fordo, still not looking at him. Warren walked between Fordo and Carth and sat on his throne. Fordo breathed deep before turning and walking around to face the baron once more.

"I suppose we should discuss payment," The baron said.

The statement surprised Fordo, "That won't be necessary, we just wanted to help."

The baron laughed to himself a moment, "Not your payment, Pledge…My payment." Fordo was stunned, unsure if he heard that correctly.

"What was that?"

"How are you going to make up for My lost assets?" The baron stated, like it was a matter of fact.

"*Your lost assets?*" Carth asked in disbelief.

"Your little field trip cost my city two highly skilled limb smiths, two incredibly useful mechanics, all for a sapling too stupid not to get lost chasing puppies into caves. How are you going to replace them?" This was the first time the baron had looked Fordo in the eyes.

Warren's eyes had a glint of amusement as they watched Fordo's hand drop to his hammer. "Our friends gave their lives to save that little girl...you should be honoring them as fucking heroes, carving statues in their names!"

"You gave their lives, son, traded them for that little sap. And they were identical twins, I would only need to carve one statue, technically..." Warren smirked.

"I gave their lives??" Fordo asked, astonished.

"Yes, you. You fought against natural selection, depriving Mother Aure of her sacred sacrifice, so she took your friends as compensation."

"How can you believe that? You should be grateful, you son of a bitch, we did you a service!"

"Do yourself a service, Pledge, and find me new mechanics."

"Stop calling me that!"

A smile began to form on the baron's lips, "You can't fight who you are, son. Like it or not, you're a Pledge, like me, we both bear the weight of our father's legacies." He leaned back in his throne and spread his arms like he was showing off his kingdom once more.

"Don't call me pledge and don't call me son, you're barely a year older than me, cunt." That got the baron to grin.

"You are your father's son. You may be looking to make a name for yourself, but I am proud to share my father's, to build upon his life's work with my own. Why can't you do the same?"

"You're a coward and a fraud who will always be stuck in his father's shadow. Warren the third, that's all you'll be remembered as, 'The Third'. You are Nothing without them."

The baron's smile grew even wider, "I accepted who I was even before the bots came, Pledge. But you, you are going to wander the world for years and years, angry and afraid, struggling to build your own imaginary kingdom of dust and dirt, only to wake up one day and realize: You were never the hero... you were just his son."

Fordo stood still, fist clenched around his hammer, ready to draw. *You condescending cunt. Why am I even here? What the fuck did I expect? Praise? Gratitude? Favor? A worthy word that anything we went through mattered?*

Warren broke into a deep, but childlike laugh that caught Fordo off guard and made him wonder how long he'd stood there staring at the man who'd just insulted him. "You're the same angsty kid that you were all those years ago, Fordo Balison, letting words wriggle under your skin like woodlice.

Now run back to your father and tell him to send two more mechanics. Preferably two with better friends and better judgment." The baron stood before Fordo could reply and walked back around to his desk.

Fordo stepped towards Warren, but Carth grabbed his shoulder, holding him back. *Let's go, he's not worth it.* Carth said with his eyes, pulling him towards the staircase. Fordo watched that arrogant, condescending, piece of glass sit down at his desk and continue writing without pause, like nothing they had said or done mattered in the slightest. *I'll be back for you.* Fordo vowed to himself before turning to start their long descent.

***

They finally made it back to the fourth level of the city and the Sleeping Giant Inn. A hollowed, moss-covered, realwood log resting on its side, two stories high, each would-be branch now a chimney breathing the steam of hot showers or the sweet smoke of hearthfire, warm orange light pouring out through carved round windows like ember-filled firewood.

Roasted meats and Amber Ales, boisterous laughter and stranger's tales, the jolly sights and sounds and smells of the crowded inn did nothing to raise Fordo's spirits.

More and more people piled in from their work in the lumber yards. The inn filled with a cloud of sap and sweat and ale and ass as the Johns and Janes fought and sang. By the looks of the room, Riverwood was made up of the loud and the louder. Fordo figured if the gods couldn't see them from above, they could surely hear them.

"Welcome back, lads," Smiled a middle aged woman with bright green eyes and curly red hair, tucked up behind a brown headscarf.

"You recognize us?" Fordo asked, recalling a younger, thinner innkeeper with dark brown hair.

"My daughter played host the other night for you boys and the twin smiths. Not a lot of beardless boys in these parts, Angie's always keeping an eye out," she winked at Carth who conjured up a bashful side smile. "Now, are we in for the night or just for a pint?"

"Both would be wonderful," Fordo said, "Do you have a laundry as well? We don't wanna track this route rot all over your fine hall."

"Route rot...? Wyrm route?"

"Aye, ma'am, we tracked a missing girl beneath the Dragon's Teeth this morning," Fordo swallowed and frowned.

"Oh my...Mira, was it? I heard she'd run off again..." She lowered her voice, "Did you...Did you find her?"

Carth nodded, "Indeed...Not all of us made it out, but she did, thank Aure...Home safe with her mother."

She nodded slowly, "And who was lost...?"

My best friends..."The twin smiths..." Fordo's voice nearly failed him. Carth placed a strong hand on his shoulder.

The innkeeper recoiled, a hand over her heart, "Jacks and Benji?"

Fordo nodded, lip quivering unable to hold back the tears any longer. The woman came around the counter and wrapped her soft warm arms around him. He couldn't remember his last real hug. "I'm sorry..." *I got them killed...*

"Never be sorry for caring, son..." She held his head, "They were in here most nights...Such sweet boys..."

Fordo was afraid to speak, at least a dozen people must have noticed him crying by now.

"You boys go wash up nice," She wiped Fordo's eyes before wiping her own, "Take a room. Leave your clothes and boots in the baskets, we'll have 'em lookin' new by morning."

"Thank you..." Fordo said when he could, clearing his throat, "We're both Scrapyard tinkers, we can help with pipes and plumbing if you need, or even kitchen-"

She waved her hands, "No trade for heroes...It's on the house tonight."

"That's very kind, ma'am..." Carth said

Fordo nodded his thank you, suppressing a smile.

"I'll show you to your room."

Fordo took the longest shower of his life, washing away any reminder of the cave from his hair and skin and mind, sending all the gunk and blood down the drain and out of his life. The only reminders left his still aching ankle and vaguely swollen nose, throbbing out of sync with one another which made the dull pain even harder to ignore.

He found his slime crusted clothes replaced by a dark wool tunic and loose drawstring pants, both clean and warm like they'd just had their own shower.

His limp wasn't too bad, barely a discomfort now, but

he made sure to lean into it more, throwing his frown back on as he stepped back out into the main hall.

The atmosphere had shifted in his brief absence, from joyous laughter to somber songs, word must have spread. Fordo found himself a wooden tankard of dark red ale and fell into an empty chair by the crackling hearth, several men and women raising their pints to him as he passed.

Fordo stared into the flames, his restless knees bouncing as he strangled the handle of his tankard like a garden grub. *I killed my best friends for a free pint of ale...*He sucked his teeth and chewed his cheek, nearly flinching as Carth pulled up with an ale of his own.

Neither of them had spoken since their visit with the Baron. They were too tired for any more words or any more tears. For now, they drank.

Carth clapped Fordo's shoulder and raised his cup. They both sighed, clanked cups, and splashed half their ale into the hearth with a sharp sizzle and a cloud of steam. Carth tossed another log onto the fire after downing his drink.

Fordo stopped drinking after their third round, but on Carth's fourth or fifth, he started babbling and giggling to himself.

"Hey Ford..."

"Mm...?"

"You mumember......Junk Jockeys?"

An unexpected smirk cracked through Fordo's furrowed brow, "Junk Jockeys?"

"Back in Julia..."

Fordo nodded slowly, his smile sprouting in the middle of his sullen face, "When we all dressed like...piles of trash? And just started fuckin' with people." They both laughed,

"No one could find us!" Carth laughed, "It was beautiful! We were fuckin' Invisible! The second we realized that, it was over for all the other gangs!"

"Over for all the other eight year olds?" Fordo laughed, "Who started that glass? Was that your idea or Benji's?"

Carth shook his head, "Jacks made the suits so we could hide from those big scary kids who kept taking our rations."

"That's right, that's right...Those sunken cunts..."

"Jacks made the suits...Benji kept using them to scare us..."

"Son of a bitch scared the glass outta me even after I knew it was him," Fordo laughed, "I got so paranoid I started kicking every piled I passed."

"Gave you some great ideas though...Gettin' back at the big kids...Makin' 'em think there's monsters in the alleys."

"Yeah, yeah, after they watched your ass get eaten by garbage, they never bothered us again..."

"And I never got my ass ate again," Carth shrugged

"Nothin' beats that first ambush, though...When we'd sent you out to bait 'em into the alley...Popped out with clubs and rocks, takin' turns hitting them once from behind and disappearing again...That felt so prime," Fordo took a long drink, "That was our first fight, I think."

"First fight we won, I think."

"'We don't remember losses'" Fordo said, quoting Benji, raising his tankard like he usually would after losing a game of Barricade. Fordo lowered his arm, half his ale spilling on the floor while he wiped his eyes and sighed. "The fuck are we supposed to do without them?"

Carth sipped in silence.

"Jacks was my brain...Benji was my heart..."

"I thought Benji'd be your balls."

"Would you just..." Fordo laughed through his tears and gave up on his analogy, "Shut the fuck up and grab us another ale."

They drank and laughed and cried and sang, recounting and reliving all the twin's hilarious and incredible feats of heroism and idiocy.

Caught in the flow of tales and ales, by Carth's seventh or eighth round, he was standing on his chair dramatically and drunkenly shouting to all who would listen, the tragic tale of Benji and Jacks:

"LITTLE TWIN WARPHANS, GATEWAY BORN, ESCAPED THE BOTS DURING A STORM! ACROSS THE LAND, THEY SCRAPED AND CRAWLED, SEEKING REFUGE BEHIND JULIAN WALLS!"

Half the inn turned to listen to his drunken shoutings.

"JOINED BALI'S FIST AS RUNNER BOYS, THEY PLAYED WITH DEATH INSTEAD OF TOYS! THEY FOUND A HOME, WHEN WAR WAS DONE, IN THE LOVING ARMS OF THE ANCIENT ONE!"

The inn quieted as more turned to listen.

"From a metal bear, they learned a trade, to build new arms for those in need! Where work was hard, where work was good, they both found love in Riverwood!"

Several people cheered and raised their ale.

"But it grieves my heart, I'm sad to say, they met their end upon this day. To save a sap from a monster's den, they gave their lives so she could live…"

All were listening now. Tears spilled out from Carth's closed eyes. Fordo stared up in amazement with wet eyes of his own.

"True brothers and lovers and working men, we mourn them now and we loved them then! So all hail the twins, whose time has passed, all hail the heroes, Benji and Jacks!"

Carth raised his tankard and the whole inn cheered.

"Hail the heroes!" The crowd cried and drank and spilled their ale. Carth flinched and almost fell off of the chair at the sudden uproar, he hadn't realized how large his audience became. He smiled and sobbed, slouching back down into his chair. Many stranger's hands patted his chest and shoulders and head as they passed, showing their support. Carth just continued sobbing and raised his tankard.

Fordo noticed a whole table of folks with botsthetics, looking just as sad as he and Carth. Some of the folks the twins had rebuilt. He had to admit it was nice, in a way, seeing strangers mourn his friends, knowing they mattered to more than him and his circle alone.

Later that night, after the noise had died and the cutters retreated to their beds, a hand shook Fordo's shoulder as he meditated by the hearth. He turned to find Kira, clean and rested. "Are you ready?"

Fordo nodded, his knees popping as he stood. He shook a sleeping Carth, but he continued to drool, snuggling deeper into his chair. Fordo smiled to himself and decided to let him rest, following Kira out of the inn alone.

***

"You sure she can stay with you?" Fordo asked as they rode the lift.

Kira nodded, "Better me than her. We need to finish what we started."

Fordo looked off at the passing platforms, "I'm sorry, Kira..." He looked up at fordo, "It wasn't supposed to be like this..."

"We were doing the right thing," Kira said, "We're still doing the right thing..." The lift stopped on the eighth level.

"Still think you can convince her?" Kira asked

"I have to," Fordo said

"What are you going to say?"

"I'm not sure, but I'm not leaving until Mira has a home, a real home. I'll say or do whatever I need to."

They reached the dark house, orange light seeped out through the cracks in the thin door like the inside was on fire, but they heard no commotion, just footsteps walking back and forth through the main room.

Fordo looked at Kira, who nodded in reply. He sighed and knocked, stepping back to wait, trying to work out what he could say.

The footsteps were lighter as they approached the door, they heard her clear her throat and adjust her clothes before unlatching the many locks. The door opened slowly and Helena appeared with a big smile. She had bathed and changed and curled her hair, now wearing a black silk robe with a tie around her waist that dangled all the way to the floor. Fordo swallowed. "Hello there, boys. You sure clean up nice." She had a mischievous, vacant look in her eyes.

"Evening, ma'am," Fordo said

"Oh Enough with the Ma'am, makes me feel old. Please, call me Helena," She said, leaning against the door.

"How's Mira holding up?" Fordo asked, trying not to humor her.

"Oh You are so sweet, checking up on my little sap so soon..." She called into the house without looking away from Fordo, "Mira, your friends are here!" Helena smiled up at him until Mira appeared in the doorway. The little girl looked shocked, like she never thought she'd see her rescuers again. She wore new clothes, and she was much cleaner than before, but there were still hints of muck in her hair and under her chin like someone had wiped her face with a wet rag and said "Good enough".

Fordo knelt down and hugged her, "I told you we'd be back..." He whispered. She squeezed him a little tighter. He let her go and she ran to hug Kira as well.

"Ay, Little One," Kira said

"Is there anything I can do for you sweet boys? I'm a little jealous you came to visit her and not me," Helena joked

"Actually, I thought we could talk for a bit," Fordo looked her up and down, hoping she'd notice, "Do you mind if Mira and Kira play outside a while?"

"Not at all, not at all, come on in. Good thing I've been cleaning all day." She took Fordo's hand and pulled him into the house. He locked eyes with Kira a moment and nodded, telling him to go just as Helana closed the door.

Al and Meeko

4

"You two are unbelievable…" Sarah shook her head as she stirred her bubbling pot of venison stew over the large open fireplace, her silver legs reflecting the flickering flames.

Her botsthetics were still the very best Al had ever seen, though they were the very first. No exposed gears nor wiring. Slender, elegant, naturally shaped with great love and care. She carried herself so well that, apart from the shine, some may never notice she's lost anything. Al Imagined wherever lost legs get thrown, two of them mourn their lost body.

He sat like a doll in Bali's giant chair, gently petting the three legged Meeko that napped beside him. Sarah poured her piles of pre-sliced potatoes and carrots in the pot and stirred them into the mix.

"I don't know what to do, Sarah."

"I mean, it's already done…Nothing you can do except Promise me you'll be more careful." She swung her stew covered spoon as she pointed it accusingly at Al, flinging tiny tasty lava drops all over him.

"Hey, ow!" Al laughed, covering his face.

"Oh sorry!" She hopped over and used her apron to wipe his cheek.

"No, I deserve it," Al said, trying to dodge her increasingly aggressive wipes.

"You deserve a lot more than that," She smirked, "But no use wasting anymore time on it, you lost enough as it is."

"I still can't believe it. I missed so much. Fordo's birthday, your anniversary, Daisy breaking the floor with her boobs."

"The funniest thing you'll never see," She laughed as she dug through the pot, carefully scooping out little leaves and sprigs of spice.

"I really did want to be back in time for your anniversary, though, I'm sorry."

"It's okay, that was probably for the best. It got a little more...exciting than we hoped."

"Carth drink too much ale and try to wrestle Brash again?"

"I wish, I'm still waiting on that rematch."

"Then what happened?"

"Well, I guess if we're confessing things, Fordo and Bali got into it pretty rough."

"That's nothing new."

She poured her bowl of peas into the pot and closed the lid once more. "It was bad this time. Like...really bad. You know we're civil, but Fordo's never really liked me."

"Yeah, but that's not your fault..."

"I know, I know, I get it, of course. He thinks Bali replaced his mother too quickly, but that's not exactly the case and he kinda found that out at the party."

"What do you mean?"

"Well we've never really made a big deal over our anniversary, but fifteen years is a long time, you know? Long enough to get excited and throw a big party, but also long enough to forget some things that I definitely shouldn't have."

"Things like what?"

"Well, Daisy, sweet girl, decorated the inn all cute with flowers and candles and a big old banner that said 'Happy 15th Anniversary'."

"What's that gotta do with Ford?"

"Fordo's mom died Fourteen years ago."

"I don't...Wait...Oh glass! So you and Bali...?"

She nodded guiltily, "It's quite a bit more complicated than that, but yeah, so to Fordo...I went from the person who replaced his mom, to the person who stole his dad. And now he kind of, sort of, hates us both. Or...Hates us more..."

"Sink my ass..."

"I wanted to make things right, explain things to him... Tell him the truth, the Whole truth, but...He and Carth went off to Julia to find you the day after the party. Now he's out there all angry and sad and confused and I don't know what he'll do."

"I'm sorry, Sarah..."

"We should've told him a long time ago..." She shrugged and wiped a tear from her eye, "He'll be back someday and once he knows he'll understand, but until then...It is what it is..." She smiled sadly, dusting the top of the stew with salt and pepper.

"It is what it is..." Al repeated to himself.

"Now eat up," She poured and passed him a steaming bowl of stew and tapped the side of the pot with her spoon, "This whole pot's for you two, I bet you haven't eaten in months." She took off her apron and tossed it onto the counter. "Now, I'm gonna take a nice hot bath, kiss my smelly husband and go to sleep. I'll see you boys in the morning," She smiled

"Sweet dream, girly. You're the best, you know that?"

"I know," She kissed both Al and Meeko on the tops of their heads before disappearing to her room.

The stew smelled of tomatoes and love, the meat and potatoes crumbled as he stirred. He slowly and meticulously filled his hand forged spoon with each delicious element until he was certain he'd collected the perfect scoop. Smiling to himself, he lifted it to his lips, poured the sweet nectar onto his tongue, and immediately burned his mouth. Meeko flinched awake as Al laughed and shook his head to escape the pain. "Sorry buddy, I'm okay." Al set down the bowl and pet Meeko while he waited for the pins and needles to undo the damage.

He could hear the muted clang of Bali still working in the shop. "You'll be good as new by morning, Meeks." Meeko reached up and licked Al's cheek with a question. "No no, not yet...You were away a lot longer than I was..." Al smiled sadly, "We'll just rest a while." Meeko nuzzled back into Al's lap.

Al ate and ate until he reached the bottom of the pot. Rubbing his belly until he could breathe again, he washed the dishes before returning to the fur covered throne. *How'd I get so lucky?* He watched the flames fade to embers before finally drifting off to sleep.

***

'Don't be afraid……' He awoke to these words with a jolt, escaping from a nightmare he couldn't remember. *Why? How?* Meeko yelped with worry. Al clawed desperately at his chest, his head, searching for a wound, for a clue. Meeko's cries were drowned out by Al's heartbeat until he realized he was okay. *No wounds. No pain. Still here. Still safe. Not dead. Never died. Don't worry. Don't cry.*

His face was drenched with tears and sweat. He calmed Meeko with a shaky hand. "I'm alive, I'm okay," He said, more to himself than Meeko, "I heard her, Meek…" He said through more tears, "I must've dreamed it…" Meeko kissed his hand. "Has that happened before?" Meeko whined in reply. "I didn't think so…" Al clenched the side of the chair until his hand stopped shaking. "I don't always remember how, but I've never not remembered dying. We were so warm, so safe. I didn't know what could've happened to us."

Al reached into his jacket pocket and pulled out the faded picture of a young woman. Kind green eyes and a shy smile. Fair skin and golden hair. Everything about her looked soft and comforting, like a mother, but she couldn't be his. Not with his sad brown eyes and yellow smile, dirt tan skin and black hair. But the voice was too soft and gentle not to be hers. *It can't be anyone else's.* He wiped his eyes, filled his lungs, and hid her back in his pocket.

"Damnit, I'm sorry, Meeko. I didn't mean to wake you," The world was just starting to turn gray outside, "Go back to sleep, buddy."

***

Al awoke again to Sarah's cheerful humming. The sun was high and the fire rekindled. He yawned and stretched and rubbed his eyes to find Sarah sewing a short, olive green dress, on a mannequin half her size. "That's not for Meeko, is it? Green's not really his color."

Without even looking, Sarah nailed him on the forehead with a bundle of silk from across the room. "It's about time, sleepy head, it's almost noon! If you hadn't done the dishes last night, I woulda dumped some water on you three hours ago."

"Had trouble sleeping for once. Was too full and cozy," Al cracked his fingers and toes and hopped to his feet. "Where's Meeko?"

"Stretching his new leg in the workshop. Go on and thank Bali before he passes out, he worked through the night again."

Al grabbed a cold biscuit, leftover from Bali's breakfast while he holstered his ax, slung his wyrm horn over his shoulder, strapped on his leather boots and tripped out the door in excitement.

Al ran into the workshop to find Bali in his chair, throwing a ball out the garage door and Meeko sprinting after it. "Good as new?" Al asked

"New as new. Built another frame from scratch." Bali retrieved the ball as Meeko returned and lifted his paw to display.

"Whoa, prime!" Al bent down to inspect. The black plating was far more subtle than the silver, blending in with his fur. Though the shiny internals still shone through the joints, giving each piece a silver outline. "You didn't have to do all this, man, I thought it was just a little bent?"

"Boy earned an upgrade," Bali pat Meeko on the head with his giant hands, "Besides…" He lifted the old paw and tossed it over his shoulder into a pile of prototypes, "…That was just the first one that worked. I didn't know about all the crazy glass you'd put him through when I made it. Surprised it lasted this long."

"You're an artist, my friend." Al ran his hands over every inch of the paw, "Thank you, Bali."

"Someone's gotta clean up your messes."

"No, I mean, thank you for everything. These past three years, are all I have and all I am. You've given me a name and a home and everything Meeks and I could ever want. I'm sorry for taking this life for granted and I'm sorry for throwing it away so often, so easily. Thank you for everything, truly."

Bali went from patting Meeko to patting Al, "Thank you for filling my retirement with interesting little headaches," Bali said

Sarah snuck up behind and draped her arms over Bali's shoulders, hugging his chest. He turned his head only to run into her lips. She turned two excited eyes to the paw. "You did so good, baby."

"How'd yours turn out?" Bali asked. She dangled and displayed the short, smooth, simple, olive green dress she had been sewing.

"What do you think?" She held it up to herself, but it barely went down to her waist.

"I think you need to put it on for me to get the full picture. Go for a walk, boy." Bali joked

"Be serious, you think she'll like it?" Sarah laughed.

"Think she'll love it," Al smiled, "Who's 'she'?"

"Auri! She's getting her new legs today!" Sarah's face lit up even more.

Al looked at Bali. "Finished the exoskeleton too…" He said, casually.

"What? That's amazing! She's gonna be so happy!" Al exclaimed.

"I would hope so," Bali said.

"Bet she'll like my dress more!" Sarah said, sassily.

"More than the ability to walk?" Bali chuckled.

"Yes! Look how cute this turned out!" Sarah held up the dress once more.

"You're right," Both of Bali's knees cracked as he stood up. He grabbed Sarah by the waist and kissed her on the head. "I'm going to bed."

"Better shower first," Sarah stood on her toes to kiss his cheek.

"Yeah, yeah…" Bali gestured dismissively with a smile then pointed at Al, "You boys better be here and alive when I wake up."

"Yeah, yeah…" Al gestured dismissively with a smile as Bali disappeared into the house.

"Al, go find Auri and bring her to the shop whenever you can."

"Alright, but if Bali's going to bed, can I tell her I made it?" He laughed

"Tell her whatever you want, just get her over here, I can't wait to see her face."

"We'll be right back. Let's go Meeks." Al took two steps out the door then stuck his head back inside, "I just remembered, I don't know...what she looks like."

"She's real small and cute, with silver hair, and she rides around on a dark brown pillpup down by the pasture."

***

Al gave the same description to passersby on the way to the pasture and found her several pointing fingers later. Even from afar, he was certain it was her. Her silver hair almost reflected the sunlight. She sat with her legs crossed on the shell of her pillboy, the tall grass hid her steed, giving her the illusion of slowly floating atop the field amongst the giant armored lawn mowers. An amused smirk accompanied the thought. "That's gotta be her." Meeko panted in agreement. "I'll crawl up from here, you sneak around the other side."

Meeko waddled off and disappeared into the grass while Al hung up his jacket on a nearby fence post. He kneeled down, waiting until he was sure she was looking elsewhere before crawling on his hands and knees into the tall grass as well. His elbows itched and he couldn't see where he was going, but he was already committed. Keeping his pace slow and steady, he didn't want to risk moving the reeds any more than the wind. He angled his route to eventually intercept hers, sweat began to bead and roll down his temples as he crept patiently through the field.

Knowing not how far he was and considering the risks of raising his head, he paused and listened for the light thumping footsteps of her grazing pillbaby only to find Auri's soft humming. *Perfect.*

He managed to make it ahead of her. All there was left to do was wait. She hummed a cheerful, pleasant tune, with an inconsistent melody, that was likely of her own orchestration. Through the blur of the grass, he could see her head bobbing to her own rhythm, and hear her hands gently drumming on the shell of her steed. *That's cute.* He thought with a smile, waiting until she was just a few paces away. *This is it.* He leapt to his feet with his hands in the air and yelled "Helloo!"

"Aaahh!" She flinched and screamed in a small voice.

"Bark!"

"AAAhh!" She flinched again as Meeko leapt out of the grass on her other side, her hands shooting up to cover her mouth as she looked back and forth between them.

Al grinned and laughed at the poor girl, his hands still up above his head. "Are you Auri?" She nodded rapidly, her hands still covering her mouth as she laughed, seeming confused and amused.

"That's Meeko, I'm Alexander, Sarah sent us to find you."

"Oh?" She laughed, still covering her face.

"You okay, we get you too bad?" Al smiled

"I'm okay, just trying not to cry. I thought you two were flying moss spiders."

"I'm not really sure what those are, but we're just a couple of cute boys with a lot of free time," Al stuck out his hand, "Nice to meet you, girly. Sorry if we spooked ya."

She gave his hand a loose, gentle shake, "Nice to meet you two."

"What's your boy's name, here? Is he a boy, I don't really know how to tell?" Meeko walked around to sniff at her beautiful wood brown pillbaby. The giant armored isopod at no point acknowledged anything but the grass it grazed on.

"He never told me his name, so I call him Cidarian. And I'm pretty sure he's a boy, just kinda have a feeling."

"Sir Darian?? That's prime as ever. Ooo! Mind if I call him Dari? Auri and Dari."

"Oh...Oh That's cute. I think I'm gonna cry again."

"I feel like bugs are boys, it's just a boy trait to be a bug. Unless it's laying eggs right there, then alright, that's a lady bug."

She laughed

"Come with us, girly, there's some things you gotta see." She nodded and patted Dari's side until he turned to follow. "How do you get him to go where you want him to?"

"I don't know, I just kinda tap on his shell until he moves."

"Hm...Maybe he's trying to get away from the thing on his back."

"Maybe..." Auri laughed, "Hm, He probably likes it."

"He probably likes it," Al smiled at the ground as they walked back into town, recovering his jacket from the post.

Meeko walked up next to Al and barked a question. "I think you could, if you really tried," Al answered him.

Auri smiled at the duo, "I wish Cidarian would talk to me."

"Maybe he's just shy."

"I wonder what he would say..." She swayed back and forth as she rode even though Dari's many legs made him smoothly glide across the ground.

"'Please get off of me...'" Al said in a deep, sad version of Dari's hypothetical voice. They all laughed, except for Dari, as they made their way back to Bali's shop.

"How did you get around before you met Dari?" Al asked

"I just crawled."

"You what?" Al laughed a little harder than was probably polite, "That's terrible!"

"I'm Kidding. My cousins pulled me on a wagon and made little rope swings and things for me to sit on."

"That's prime, I wish I had fun cousins. So you've been like this since the war?"

"No, I uh...I fell out of a tree."

"You're kidding? How did you fall out of a tree?"

"My cousin pushed me."

Al laughed inappropriately again, "Ah of course. So you're close to your cousins."

"Close enough to get pushed," She made a half smile

"Least you got a prime wagon."

"Least I got a prime wagon," She shrugged

"And a new friend."

"And a new friend," She smiled and traced the groves on Dari's shell with her finger.

"Riverwood sounds like a fun place to grow up, I hope to see it someday."

"Oh you're not from Riverwood too?" Auri asked

"No. Well, far as I know, no. I've only really known Scrapyard."

"Oh? You carry an ax just like everyone who works there. Did you trade for it?"

"No, I just had it when I woke up."

"You found an ax in your bed this morning? That's kinda scary," She laughed

"No, no...I um, I don't really remember much of where I'm from." She just looked at Al curiously. "Farthest I can remember, Meeko and I woke up in the woods, hurt pretty bad. Bali found us and brought us here. It's been home ever since."

"Oh? He found you when you were kids and you can't remember anything before that?"

"Oh no, he found us like three years ago," Al laughed

"Three years? You're kidding..."

Al just shook his head.

Auri sat in stunned silence.

"What's wrong?" Al asked when he noticed.

"Well...That's so sad."

"Is it?" Al asked with a smile.

"You can only remember the last few years?"

"Mhm"

"That means you've forgotten your whole life!"

"I guess it does."

"I mean, don't you wanna find out who you Were?" She asked

"I don't know..." He paused for a moment, "...I kind of like who I Am," He laughed

She paused and a smile crept back onto her face, "I guess...I guess that's fair."

"There it is!" Al grinned as soon as the shop was in sight. "Go grab Sarah." Meeko ran ahead and disappeared inside. "Are you excited?" Al asked Auri.

"Kind of nervous, should I be excited?"

Al just grinned in response as Sarah and Meeko emerged from the house.

"Auri, you're here!" Sarah beamed at her.

"Helloo..." Auri smiled softly.

"Have you already told her??" Sarah asked. Al shook his head. "Oo! Good! Auri, I'm so excited! Come inside with me, I have a couple things for you to try on."

Auri looked at Al who nodded and smiled for her to follow.

"Oh okay, um, I don't think...Cidarian's pretty dirty..."

"Meeko will keep him company. Al, help her inside."

Al looked at Auri. "Is that okay?" She nodded and held onto his shoulder as he scooped her up. He was surprised, she was even lighter than Meeko.

"What am I trying on?" She asked

"Sarah and Bali each made something for you."

"Really?"

"One of them is gonna change your life," Al smiled

"And the other one's gonna help you get around a little easier," Sarah winked at Al. Auri looked nervous. Al felt her shaking as he plopped her gently onto Bali's big chair. He knelt next to her and instinctively rubbed her back to calm her nerves, the same way he pet Meeko.

"Okay, girly, close your eyes and hold out your hands." Sarah urged and Auri obliged. "Now, remember when you first arrived and we had you visit our physician?" Auri nodded. "So I asked him to take some measurements, both for your condition, but also..." Sarah placed the soft olive green dress into Auri's hands, "...So I could make this."

Auri turned the soft silk slowly in her hands and opened her already watery eyes. She pouted her lips as she unfolded the dress and raised it up to see. "Is this really for me?" She asked in a small voice.

"Well, I made it for Meeko, but- Of course it's for you!" Sarah laughed.

Auri began to cry. "This is the nicest thing anyone's ever given me," She hugged the dress, "Thank you so much, I don't know what else to say."

"The nicest gift ever?" Al asked

Auri nodded

"So I can have your other one?" He smiled

A smile peaked through Auri's tears, "I mean...Well...If you wanted to..." She tried to laugh as she cried.

Sarah beamed, retrieving a basket from behind the chair and plopping on the floor in front of Auri.

"So, um..." Sarah began. When Al noticed water had begun to well into Sarah's eyes, a lump formed in the back of his throat. "After the war left so many people broken and helpless, my sweet husband made it his life's work to make them whole again. Quite literally." Sarah tapped her fingernails on her metal legs. "He started with these. Then he went from person to person, village to village, building and teaching until his inventions had spread across all of Aureum, helping people to walk and work and feel hope again..." Auri listened with wide eyes.

"But when he heard your story, he didn't sleep for days. He's very prideful, proud of his work, you see..." Sarah smiled, "And when he heard about the young woman who came all the way from Riverwood on her own, looking for an answer, only to have his fail her...he couldn't accept it." Sarah smiled wider as tears fell down her cheeks. "So he locked himself away in that shop for months and months until..." Sarah lifted the lid off the basket,   "...Until he figured it out."

"Figured it out?" Auri held her breath. Al squeezed her shoulder and Sarah simply smiled in reply as she slowly unfolded the thin brace of metal and leather until it stood before Auri. Auri's hands shot up to her mouth, amplifying shaky breaths as fresh tears spilled from her eyes. "Auri..." Sarah cried, "You're going to walk again."

Auri wept, rocking back and forth in her chair, burying her head in her hands. Al and Sarah comforted her from either side. "I don't understand," Auri said when she could, "Why would you do all this for me? Why would...I don't deserve-"

"Everyone deserves a chance to be whole again," Sarah cried, "And besides, you're a part of our village now and that makes you family."

Auri hugged Sarah until she could stop shaking, "Thank you so much..."

"You're welcome, sweetie. Now Al, get out of here so she can try these on."

Al smiled, stood, and gently bonked his head on Auri's the same way he does Meeko's. She smiled up at him, "Thank you too..."

Al shrugged, "I didn't make you anything."

***

Al walked back into the shop to find Meeko curled up napping on Dari's shell. The poor bug was completely still, save for two crooked antennae that bobbed blindly in the middle of Bali's grassless workshop. Al pat Meeko as he passed and went out to climb the steps to Sarah's garden to find himself and Dari a snack.

He smiled and laughed to himself as he knelt to grab some grass and a few blackberries. Auri was so happy. She gets to walk and run and dance and climb again. *All of the things I take for granted. Amongst other things.*

His smile faded as he plucked a long red thorn from the blackberry bush and twirled it between his fingers until the spike was against his thumb.

Imagine falling out of a tree and realizing you'll never walk again. Al squeezed the thorn, pressing the tiny spike deep into his thumb, wincing as thick, red blood dripped and fell to the soil. *I've fallen out of so many trees, off so many cliffs.* He flicked the thorn away and immediately the pins and needles replaced the pain. *I'll never have to know that fear, I'll never get to, I'll always get up when others wouldn't, I'll always get to try again.* He sucked the salty blood from his closing wound and chased it with a sweet juicy blackberry. *Bali asks 'Who are you to spend those chances?' But if I don't, who am I to waste them?*

Ten months... He bit his lip to steady his breath. *Woke up three days ago and already made three new friends. I lost ten months worth of friends, worth of memories, of meals and trees and adventures. I could have found my mother, or whoever she is, in that time. There's so much I could have seen and done and remembered. I lost ten months of my life...*

'You were supposed to lose all of it.' Bali scolded him in his mind. Al smiled, correcting his own thoughts.

I Only lost ten months.

Something distracted Al from his thoughts. The thin frame of a dark skinned young man was flying up the street towards the house. A crowd of worried faces turned and followed as he passed.

Al stood, excited, he recognized the man. "Natori!" He called, but Al's smile faded. He had never seen Natori without his mail cart. He'd never seen Natori without his smile. He looked frightened and pale, like the life had been drained out of him. Natori collapsed as soon as he reached the foot of the garden, falling to his knees. Al ran down the steps to support him. "Nuru, what's wrong? What's going on?" Natori was heaving and shaking, Al had never seen anything like it.

"Bali-" He gasped, "Where's Balian?"

"He's inside, I'll take you..." Al tried to help Natori to his feet before actually seeing them, a swollen, bloody mess with nailless nubs for toes. Natori puked the moment Al tried to lift him up. "Aw glass, hang on!"

Fordo

4

"Sorry there's only one place to sit," Helena said, gesturing to the bed. Fordo stayed standing.

The house was void of furniture save for a large, low bed in the far corner that looked like it could just be a giant frameless stack of blankets. Two doorless doorways were on either side of the room. One led to what looked like a kitchen and the other to a restroom with a large metal tub in the center.

It was hot in the room, dozens of lit candles were placed all over the floor, close to the walls. Some a little too close, Fordo thought. The smell of them was almost overwhelming, but at least it disguised the musty staleness he smelt on his earlier visit.

The inside of the house was just as undecorated as the out. A single mirror hung on the wall by the bed, but that was all, no paintings or pictures, no carvings or tapestries, nothing personal whatsoever. *No toys, either.*

"Care to sit?" She asked again and he realized he'd been staring silently again.

"That's alright, girly, I won't take too much of your time."

"Girly! Now I like that much better than ma'am. But that's a shame, I don't get many visitors, parts of me were hoping you'd stay all night," She giggled. Fordo swallowed. "Now come, what did you wanna talk about?"

He still hadn't worked out exactly how to say '*We're taking your daughter*' in a fashion that avoided screaming, so he chose his words carefully. "It must be hard being a single mother."

"Mm yes...But I get by how I can. Mostly just lonely with no one to talk to. Though I've never been much good at talking, I'm very easily distracted."

"Mira talks less than some dogs I know."

"Is that so?" Helena giggled, "She hasn't said a word to me since her papa passed."

"I'm sorry to hear that. How'd he go?"

"Drunken fool, went over the railing outside."

"That railing? The nets didn't catch him?"

"Georgie had worse luck than me and Mira."

"I'm sorry. That must have been hard."

"Not as hard as taking care of that kid all by myself. Georgie left me with nothing but a mother's love."

"Do you ever wish you weren't?"

"I'm not sure what you mean."

"Do you ever wish you weren't a mother?"

"No, I...I could never say-"

"I know you could never say in public," Fordo interrupted, "because 'Our kids are our future and whatever they say' and you don't want to seem like a bad person, but between us, I don't really care for kids. I don't have any and I don't much plan to. I can go anywhere, do anything I want. A kid feels like an anchor that I don't have the strength or patience to haul around. So I'm asking, while it's just us, do you ever wish you weren't a mother?"

"Every day…" Helena made a face of relief and release. "She's just so Boring! She hasn't said a word to me in three years! She just moans and cries and gets lost and I am so fucking tired of pretending that I'm not trapped in this tiny cage of a house! Do you know how long I've wanted to say that?"

"At least three years?"

She laughed sadly, "At least three years."

"What if I told you, you could be free tonight?"

"What do you mean?"

"I lost two friends today."

"Did you…forget their birthdays or something?" She joked nervously.

"They died trying to get Mira home safe."

"They…What do you mean? I thought she got lost in the woods…"

"She was in an old wyrm route, under the Dragon's Teeth. There were a lot more things down there than we were prepared for. Not everyone made it out. But she did and that's all that matters."

"I'm so sorry, I didn't-That's horrible and I'm sorry, but what do they have to do with what you said before?"

"My friends gave their lives to protect that little girl. Some of the loved ones they left behind wish to do the same."

"I don't think I understand."

"They want to adopt Mira, take her off your hands, give her a good, safe home."

"They want to take my daughter?"

"They want to love your daughter. To keep her warm and fed and safe and happy and give her the best life possible because their husbands both died so she could live and they want to guarantee that her life is worth both of theirs."

"But that's crazy, I can't just give her up. I can't just-"

"You're not abandoning her. You are giving the both of you the chance to be happy and free. Helena, you are bored and tired and bad at being a mom." She breathes to object, but Fordo continues. "And it's not your fault and I'm not saying this to shame you or judge you, I'm saying it because this could change both of your lives for the better. You could be headed off to Julia in the morning, a young free woman. Off to find a man with a big cozy house and a big empty bed, until you die old and happy on a pile of things you always wanted. Think about all you could be doing if you found a way to cut your anchor, with no guilt, with no regret, but with pride, knowing that you did what's best for both yourself and that little girl. What would you say to that?"

She looked pale, but awestruck as if she'd just seen a miracle. "I'd say..." She suddenly grabbed a hold of his face and kissed him. His eyes widen and he pushes her back against the wall away from himself, knocking over several candles on the floor. She looked as stunned as he did.

"I'm sorry, I wasn't-Oh Glass look out!" He pointed down at her robe which had caught fire from the fallen candles. She screamed and jumped in the air, knocking over even more candles. Fordo cursed and spun, searching the empty room before scrambling to his knees trying to beat the fire with his bare blacksmith's hands. She managed to untie her robe and fling it into an empty corner. Fordo rushed over and stomped on the flame with his heavy boots until he was certain it was out. He then dove back towards the fallen candles on his hands and knees, flipping them all right side up as quickly as he could. By the time it was safe, they were both laughing nervously while he panted on the floor.

"I'm so sorry, girly, I swear I didn't mean to…" Fordo looked up and his heart stopped when he found Helena standing above him smiling, completely naked.

***

You weak, pathetic, undisciplined child. Fordo sat hunched at the edge of the bed, the air quickly cooling the sweat that coated his bare skin. The candles had burned themselves out, the musty staleness returned to the room. He dug his nails into his thighs as he scolded himself. *How could you let this happen? Lay naked with this woman who disgusts you with everything she is. This unbridled whore that sleeps with strangers just for paying her attention. This neglectful mother that took you mere Minutes to convince to give up her only child out of boredom. Boredom?? That's your daughter! Feed her, clean her, love her you selfish cunt, you should have thrown me out on the spot for even suggesting such a thing!*

He looked at her as she lay motionless in an exhausted pile. *What kind of a woman abandons her child to perfect strangers? And yet, what kind of a man has sex with a woman he despises at the mere sight of her naked body?* He dug his nails in deeper before lifting the blankets to look upon her once more. *Weak and Pathetic.*

Is this all it takes to overpower a man? Is this all Sarah had to do to bewitch my father, to trick a husband into leaving his wife? Is his weakness for women the only thing he passed on to me? Fuck him, fuck her, and fuck you. I hope you never see Mira again.

Cringing with every creak of the floorboards, he prayed to the gods of sleep that they would hold Helena a little longer. He knew if she awoke he wouldn't be able to hide his disgust. Fordo got dressed silently and made sure to gather every trace of himself. *Nobody needs to know.* Cursing in his mind as he fumbled with the many locks on the front door, he heard her stirring just as he swung it open and slipped through to freedom.

Fordo sighed and bit his cheek. *Weak.* He straightened his jacket and ran a hand through his hair. The walkway was just as dark and empty as when he arrived. *Thank the gods.* He had no idea what time it was, but the coast was clear and he wasted no time getting the fuck out of there.

***

Fordo returned to The Sleeping Giant to find Carth hunched over in his chair, a metal bucket between his legs. *Right where I left you.* He clapped Carth on the shoulder before joining him. "How's it goin', buddy?"

"*Brrrlp!*" Carth puked, spit, and groaned in response. Fordo patted him on the back, smiled and sighed, unstrapping his boots and putting his feet up against the fire. He watched the flames as he meditated, twisting the hammered ridges of his mother's black ring around his finger.

"Where'd you go?" Carth asked between heaves.

"Make sure Mira's safe."

"Is she?"

"I convinced Helena to let Kira take her."

Carth half laughed, "How'd you manage that, you dangle her over the railing?"

"No..." Fordo chuckled, "I uh, I set her on fire."

"*Brrrlp!*" Carth spit, "You did the right thing." Carth leaned back in his chair, that must have been the last of it. "So what do we do now?" He asked, staring into the flames.

What Do I do now? This whole trip's been a disaster. Couldn't find Al, lost Benji and Jacks, gained zero support, if anything I'm even farther from my goal.

"I'm not sure, Carthy. I don't want to give up, but I don't know where to go or what to do next. Nothing's worked out this far. I don't know what I need to do."

"I guess that depends on what you want."

"You know what I want."

"You wanna be famous like your father," Carth made it sound so simple, so easy.

"No. I want to be More famous than my father."

"Why?" Carth asked

"Because I..." Fordo was surprised, he'd never said the 'more' out loud before, "Because I want my name to be my name."

"What do you mean?"

"Carth, I have been stuck in Bali's shadow my entire life, the shadow of a man who's given me nothing. No love, no support, has never called me 'son'. He's been cold and blunt and dismissive of me for as long as I can remember. The man who cheated on my mother and left her to die, the man that everybody in this world loves and expects me to love. I don't want to be Fordo Balison, I want my name to be My name and the only way for that to happen is for my shadow to eclipse his." Something dripped onto Fordo's jacket, he looked down and realized he was crying again. *Weak and pathetic.*

He quickly wiped his eyes and remembered he was talking to Carth who just stared blankly at the flames. Carth's silence made Fordo nervous that his thoughts sounded stupid or silly out loud. Right before Fordo couldn't take it anymore, Carth just said, "Okay."

Okay? Fordo couldn't tell if Carth's indifferent tone annoyed or relieved him, so he chose the latter.

"Well, you have a pretty good head start," Carth said

"Head start?"

"Bali didn't get famous until the war when he was already, what, like thirty years old? You've got a whole ten year head start."

The thought made Fordo chuckle, "I guess I do."

"And most people already know your name. You're basically halfway there," Carth rubbed his eyes, "So how did Bali do it? Get famous, I mean."

"Won a war, founded a village, invented a miracle," Fordo frowned. As much as he hated him, Bali's legend was undeniably impressive. That one man could achieve so much greatness in one lifetime is unprecedented. *But a great man isn't always a good man.*

"You know what? I think we should go home," Carth said.

Fordo's mouth hung open in disbelief, "You think I should just give up? After one shot? After what we've lost?"

"I just don't think you can find fame like that."

"You don't think I can do it?" Fordo leaned all the way forward and looked at him, daring him to say it to his face.

"No, listen a minute," Carth gestured to calm down, "Not You specifically, I mean: I don't think people can just go looking for fame, I think fame just kinda finds people, you know?"

Fordo sat back and stared into the flames, unsure he wanted to hear this.

"So Bali was just some Who Cares mechanic in some Wherever The Fuck floating village, back in the day, way after he was our age. But then the bots came out of nowhere, sank his home and his life and now he's one of the most famous men on Aureum."

"What's your point?" Fordo asked, rubbing his temples to suppress a headache.

"The war came from nowhere, botsthetics came from the war, Scrapyard came from botsthetics, and fame came from it all. But there was no plan, no big search, all those things just happened, man. So my point is: We don't have a war to fight, or a cause to champion, and this time yesterday, we watched our friends get eaten by actual monsters. So why don't we go home?"

Fordo's eyes softened and his shoulders relaxed a bit.

"Garrow, Daisy, Brash, Sarah, Bali, everyone; nobody back home knows what happened and I don't feel right just putting that news on a Nuru brother. They should hear it from us."

Fordo nodded guiltily.

"We have ten years to figure out this glass and tell Bali's name to go sink itself, but in the meantime..."

"No, you're right, you're right, I'm sorry. I'm burned out, Carthy, I feel like glass. I wanted to say that I owe it to Jacks and Benji to keep going, but I owe it to them more to get home and tell their people what happened...Let's head home tomorrow."

Carth stretched his arms and legs, almost kicking over the bucket at his feet, "What about today?" He mumbled mid stretch.

"Trade for supplies, check on Mira..."

"Play Hide-The-Bucket in the Baron's big house?"

"If we have time," Fordo smirked, "Go on, you've got first shower. You smell like an animal."

"*Showers are for workless men...*" Carth grumbled in a poor Bali impression as he stood and waddled off with his bucket, holding up his thumb, index, and middle finger in a peace sign above his head. Fordo frowned almost immediately upon hearing one of his father's famous phrases. *Damnit.* He hated how even a mention could ruin a moment.

***

"Sink my ass," Carth whispered as their lift lowered and halted on the second level. Fordo raised an eyebrow. The Revolving Market stretched out before them like a city of its own.

Like the rest of Riverwood, the market had grown exponentially since his last visit. Unlike the winding narrow walkways of other levels, branching apart like floating streets and alleys, the market levels were vast, singular, unobstructed disks, reaching out over a hundred yards from any part of the trunk; miraculous works of careful carpentry. Circles of collapsible shops and foldable stands formed rings around the great trunk of the tree, stacking out all the way to the edges of the disk. Hundreds of shops, thousands of people, the market alone was bigger than Scrapyard.

Fordo fantasized of what he could do with a workforce as large and dedicated as Riverwood's, what kind of world he could build. In fifteen years they turned a large floating village into a metropolis greater and grander than their spacewalking forefathers could have dreamed of.

Though a far more organized chaos than the Scrapyard markets, its sheer size rendered Riverwood's an unfamiliar maze of shops and bodies. The first three levels of the city were almost entirely dedicated to trade, likely for roaming caravan's convenience, each level pertaining to a particular kind of trade. The first being food and farm, general goods and living supplies on the second, Specialty trades and services on the third.

"You find a steak on the first, a skillet on the second, and a chef on the third," Fordo recalled his father telling him on their first visit when he was a kid.

"That's stupid, why not have everything you need in the same place?" Asked young Ford, dragging his feet.

"Sometimes Simple means Stupid, but Simple always means Simple."

"But that's so much more work!"

"Only if you give a glass. Now hurry up, I don't have enough to trade for a new kid, so I can't lose you."

"This place makes me dizzy," Carth said, leaning against the railing.

"Dozen tankards of ale probably doesn't help," Fordo said, stepping off the lift, "Let's find you a new pack."

Dust, sweat, dyes, oils, and the ever present scent of the great tree itself; this was the first market Fordo had ever been to that didn't reek of smoke.

"Grubsilk Weaver, Rubber Stand, Boot Cobbler, Pipe Maker..." Carth noted to himself as they walked down the curved streets between the stands. "How do people find anything, there's no rhyme or reason to this place?"

"Well, they're pop up stands, traders have to set up shop wherever they can each day."

"Folks don't have their own?"

"Just a lotta folks, only so much space on the tree. I think they prioritize building homes over shops, so all trade is done down here."

"I guess, but it's a fuckin' big ass tree."

Fordo chuckled to himself, "Well said, friend."

Fordo hadn't seen so many people in one place since the refugee camps during the war. Even so, everyone went about their business so calmly. There was no shoving through crowds, no rush, no carts tipping over in impatient haste, nothing like Scrapyard at all.

They have nowhere else to be. All their work is for the city, for the tree, for each other. They're not rushing back to their individual goals, they're content being cogs in a machine, tools to shape and build another man's dream.

Sometimes wish I could live that way...not cursed with ambition, without the crippling fear of your own failure, able to settle on a Happy life rather than the endless pursuit of one worth remembering.

Fordo was awakened from his daydream by the sound of rushing footsteps and the cries of "Thieves! Stop them!" They both turned and spotted a wave of commotion down the street, headed their way.

"Stagger..." Fordo ordered, bending his knees into a defensive stance. Carth grinned and moved into position behind and to the side of Fordo, one of their many familiar formations for Barricade, their favorite game.

Fordo drew his warhammer and Carth did the same, flipping them around in unison to hold the heads, ready to strike or trip the thief with the handles.

A short young man sprinted towards them, expertly ducking and dodging through the crowd. Buggy brown and bronze goggles covered his eyes, possibly to keep his dirty blonde hair from blinding him as it flapped about during a getaway. He was looking behind himself, but turned just in time to notice Carth and Fordo standing ready in his way. He looked more focused than afraid, and to Fordo's surprise, he picked up speed.

Fordo was more than ready, swinging on the thief, but the boy was fast, dodging to the left, but spinning to the right on a dime, ducking under another backhanded swipe without losing momentum. Fordo dropped his handle low and caught the boy in the ankle as he passed, but the thief rolled through the tripping back onto his feet in an instant. "Oy!" Carth lunged for him, but the boy dove to the side and leapt up into the air, kicking off of Carth's back, and rolling onto the roof of a stand without slowing down.

"Sorry, sir!" The thief yelled behind him, seeming sincere. Fordo cracked a smile; he could have sworn he spotted a little wave as the boy leapt over the other side and disappeared into the next ring of shops. *That boy's got some moves.*

"That boy's got some moves. Should we go after him?" Carth asked, feeling his back where the sole spikes of the boy's Caulk Boots punched a small grid of holes in his jacket.

"No, he earned his getaway," Fordo said

"Oy!" Carth dropped to his knee as a younger, far less graceful boy, shoved past him with the giddy, cruel, spiteful laughter of a childhood bully. Fordo immediately recognized the crooked yellow smile of the stringy looking boy who teased Mira on their way home. The pale preteen turned and slowed just long enough to make a rude gesture at Carth, but also long enough for Fordo to shoot forward and grab the ragged gray collar of the boy's dirty shirt, pulling and tripping him to the ground.

His head bounced off the wooden floor as he fell. "Hey, what's your problem, pretty boy, I'm just messing around!"

There was a sickly yellow tint to the whites of the boy's dark brown eyes. They looked far older than the rest of him.

"You know, you could get away with a lot more glass if you were less of an asshole. Least your friend had manners."

"My asshole's none of your business, you dead eyed weirdo! Now get the hell off of me!"

"Nice try," Fordo held the boy down with a knee on his chest, pressing the air from his lungs, while he pulled one of the many small tooling knives Carth always carried with him from the boy's side pocket. A simple whittler with a straight two inch blade and a wooden sheath that clicked and closed seamlessly with the handle, making it appear like a solid piece of polished wood, one of Carth's signature trade pieces. "Thief."

A small crowd of traders was forming around them. "Anybody know this boy or his folks?" Fordo asked

"He's been lurking in the markets the last few days," An older woman spoke up.

The boy objected, "Lady, you've been lurking around this world for the last few centuries!"

A tall man with a long, wide scar running down his cheek stepped forward, "Heard a yellow eyed boy's been stealing bread and scrap throughout the markets."

The boy smiled, "I heard a scar-faced wood carver's been sleeping with his neighbor's wife." The man's cheeks burned red through his beard and more than a few pairs of eyes shot towards him at once.

The boy's tactic of throwing wild, confusing insults and accusations seemed fairly effective, well practiced, and possibly worth replicating.

Fordo tossed Carth back his knife, "What do you think, Carthy, should we let him go?"

"Maybe for an apology. My feelings are pretty hurt."

"Alright, alright, let me up and I'll apologize."

Fordo let the boy sit up straight. The kid looked at the ground and mumbled something. "Didn't quite catch that..." Fordo said, leaning closer.

A wide golden grin spread across the boy's face as he grabbed Fordo's shirt with both hands and drove his forehead into Fordo's nose. The crowd gasped as the boy cackled hysterically. Fordo held his throbbing face, warm blood wet his hand. Without thinking, Fordo seized the boy's throat, shutting him up with a small choking sound. There was a flash of surprise in his yellow eyes, but no fear, rather his grin almost appeared to widen. Fordo shoved him away as soon as he remembered the crowd around him, leaving a bloody handprint around the boy's neck.

Hands immediately restrained the still laughing boy, while others pulled Fordo to his feet. "You alright, sir?" A portly man handed him a rag.

"I'm fine, thank you," Fordo held the rag to his nose, which was definitely broken now, if not from Benji's 'goodbye'.

"Someone already fetched the Grifters, you wanna testify?"

"He's not worth my time," Fordo lied, "You folks get your own justice."

The man nodded, "Alright, little splint, time to meet the brand boys."

"Do your worst, fatty, you haven't even met your toes!"

"Watch it," The man chuckled, dragging the kid down the street.

"Or what, you'll sit on me?"

That one got a laugh out of Carth and a small involuntary smirk out of Fordo. *Damnit.*

"Kid's got a tongue like a lance," Carth laughed

Fordo rubbed his nose, "Hope the grifters cut it out..."

***

Fordo had always wanted more scars, but a crooked nose wasn't quite as prime. He traced the throbbing crest where Carth had cracked it back into place. It was straight once more, far as he could tell with the swelling. Hurt like hell though, he let Carth negotiate most of the trade.

"Five teeth and a lighter!" Declared the short, pear-shaped leathersmith, pushing his pair of thick spectacles back up his face. Every time he spoke they slid down his nose that seemed almost too short and steep to support them. *Maybe if he had more hair on his head to hold them in place.*

"Five teeth for a pack? Are you out of your mind, old man?" Carth laughed at the audacity.

"You think fine leatherwork is easy, lad? Find it, catch it, skin it, tan it, days of work for material alone! Four teeth and a lighter!" He pushed his glasses up once more. Fordo noted that the combination of the man's bushy eyebrows and fluffy facial hair that surrounded his frown made him look like one of those useless bearded dogs he'd seen on leashes in Julia.

"Let's not pretend like you're out there tackling elk with your own bare hands, friend." Carth laughed, "You probably haven't seen the ground in years. Two teeth and a lighter!"

"Oh Like you and Twigs here didn't just pull these teeth from a husk on the road!" The trader held his glasses to his head as it shook with exaggerated agitation.

While the two argued in vain, Fordo wandered back down the wooden street. He remembered seeing a Rubber Stand near where they'd entered the market, between a Grubsilk Weaver and Boot Cobbler.

"Excuse me," Fordo said as he approached the rubber stand.

"Mm?" Tiny hands and the curly haired head of a little girl poked up from behind the stand, couldn't be more than six or seven, if Fordo had to guess. She didn't even have a stool to sit on. Fordo put on a friendly smile.

"Hey there, girly, do you have any rubber wax?"

"Mm!" The girl dropped out of sight and emerged seconds later with a tiny handful of pale yellow cylinders. She dropped five rubber adhesive sticks, maybe four inches long and a half inch thick on the counter with soft little thuds and let them roll nearly off.

An empty eager palm waved up at him. He twirled Carth's polished wood case in his fingers and presented it to the girl. She cocked her head, glanced at the rubber wax and held up three fingers. Fordo clicked the sheath off with one hand revealing the hidden blade and twirled it in his fingers once more. The little girl glanced back down at the sticks then held up one additional finger and took the remaining wax off the counter. Fordo chuckled to himself, resheathed the knife and placed it on the counter before scooping up his trade. She disappeared behind the stand before he'd even walked away.

He nodded to the empty stand, "Thank you, girly" before wandering back to his friend.

The Leathersmith was quite flustered now in his duel of words and wits with Carth. They seemed to have forgotten the transaction altogether and were debating the various difficulties and intricacies of their respective trades and how neither could possibly comprehend the true value of the other's labors.

"Fordo here has hunted both, he can tell you that you can't even compare the-" But rather than pretend like he cared what either man was saying, Fordo ignored their invitation to interject and snatched the glasses from the Leathersmith's head quicker than he could react. Both Carth and the man looked dumbfounded, looking back and forth between each other and Fordo who was looking methodically at the thin frames.

"I...We...Now wait just a minute, what the hell do you think you're-!?"

"Give me a minute, friend." Fordo held the glasses up to his face, opening and closing the frames gently to their limits. He then placed them on the counter alongside a stick of rubber wax, a lighter, and an identical knife to the one he'd just traded. Carth padded his jacket pockets and found he was more than a couple knives shorter than expected. Fordo smiled and shrugged at him before picking up the stick of adhesive. He cut two equally thin slivers from the wax and pressed them on either side, slightly filling the gap between where the temples met the rims of the glasses, right next to the hinges. He then cut off the excess rubber that stuck out from the rims and melted the remaining to the glasses themselves with the lighter. After blowing the wax cool and dry, he handed the leathersmith back his spectacles and asked "How's that?"

The man hesitantly put his frames back in their rightful place and found they hugged his head far more comfortably, no longer sliding with each movement. The more he moved, the more he smiled and chuckled to himself with his hands held up away from his face. "Ha Ha, Why thank you, young man, you-"

"Two teeth, Two lighters, and the rest of this stick." Fordo stood another lighter up on the counter and held out his hand for the old man to shake it. The old man shrugged and smiled before shaking Fordo's hand and passing Carth the deerskin backpack.

They spent the better part of their day filling their packs with a short journey's worth of supplies. Figured they'd cut the trip in half by taking a raft down the Siena river to Gateway village before cutting east to Scrapyard. They traded pockets full of knives and lighters for new wetskins, bedrolls, lanterns, a decent roll of rope, basically replacing everything they ruined or lost in the caves. *Not everything...*

Fordo choked back a fresh wave of tears as they headed back towards the lift. Luckily Carth distracted him before the tears could fully form. "Oy, look there."

Three figures stood upon a collapsed shop like a small stage, wearing the iron chains and unmistakable armored robes of the Grifters.

The yellow-eyed boy stood in the center of the stage, skeletal wrists shackled together. He was still grinning, hurling insults into the crowd of spectators like javelins, trying to take down as many stranger's egos as he could before receiving his own punishment.

The grifters each raised a cast iron hand to silence the crowd. Even the boy went quiet, looking each of the grifters up and down like he admired their uniform.

The first Grifter to speak was a tall, dark haired woman, no more than thirty years old. Her voice was strong and easily carried over the crowd. "Jason The Nameless, you have committed crimes against the children of Aureum. On the charges of Theft and Malice you have been brought before the Cult Of Irons for trial and judgment. What say you in your defense?"

The boy was still smiling, "Your armor's even more cool up close." He said to himself, looking amazed by her massive iron gauntlet.

"Cool?" She asked

He laughed to himself like he just remembered something he'd been trying to, then said "These idiots think I stole their stuff."

"And did you?"

"Of course."

"Then why are they idiots for thinking so?"

"They're not. They were idiots before."

The crowd groaned and murmured in objection, but was silenced once more by an armored hand. Jason laughed again, seeming to relish every twisted glare he received.

Fordo couldn't get the thief's laugh out of his head. *Dealing out insults like he was made of them.* Fordo smirked. *How do you live like that? Do you hate everybody or just not care that everybody hates you? Defiant and laughing to the end, even in the light of a brand. It'd be almost endearing if you weren't such a cunt.*

"You have no objection to these charges?"

The boy shook his head.

"Will you return the stolen items or reveal their whereabouts?"

He shook his head again.

"Will you give us the name or whereabouts of your partner?"

"My client," He corrected, "You couldn't find him if I gave you a map."

"Is there anyone who would speak on your behalf, any family or friends who can give witness to your character?"

"I don't leave witnesses."

Fordo laughed out loud at the ridiculous statement, a chuckle rolled through the crowd of spectators.

"So be it..." The woman withdrew a small, talon shaped blade from inside her robe and walked behind the boy, each step heavy, like dropping a hammer. She effortlessly cut through the boy's ragged linen tunic and let it fall to the stage. Everybody gasped, including Fordo at the sight. The boy's emaciated body was already a twisted mural of scars and burns. *And I thought Al was fucked up...*

"What are they doing?" Carth asked, clearly disgusted, but Fordo could not tell if by the kid's frail form or the whole display in general.

"It's to see any former brands, past offenses."

"Kid's whole body's a fuckin' brand. I don't think I can watch this, Ford."

"Then let's not. Come on, buddy, let's get us home."

***

Their loyal lift settled back onto the forest floor of red dirt and purple moss. It was late afternoon, but the sun had already set behind the Dragon's Teeth, leaving lanterns and candle leaves to light the base of the great tree.

They'd decided it best to spare Kira, Mira, and Elizabeth from a dramatic and likely unwelcome goodbye. With full packs and aching hearts, Fordo and Carth were more than ready for their journey home to Scrapyard, making one final stop at Chop's Butchery.

They were greeted by the smell of salt, fresh meat, and the heavy wet slap of raw steak plopped onto a wooden cutting board big enough to support a bear. The meaty meat man had his back to the door and was half way through breaking down a large brown boar, roughly the size of himself when it was whole. The head and legs sat separated on either end of the board, its eyes wide like it had just realized maybe Chop wasn't a veterinarian trying to save his life after being shot with all those arrows.

"Come for your favor already, lads?" Chop chuckled without turning around.

"How'd you know it was us?" Carth smiled

"Most folks call you 'Clankers' when you Scrapyard boys leave your village on accoun'a all that metal you love to walk around with. I could hear you rattling since you stepped off the lift," He laughed, wiping his slimy hands on a pink towel.

"That's fair"

"The hell happened to your face, son? Looks even worse than yesterday."

"Made a new friend in the market today," Carth smiled

"Who, Helena?"

Fordo bit his cheek like it would keep them from turning red. "No, a young thief with an attitude problem. Though we did meet your nemesis."

"She give you any trouble?"

"None we couldn't handle. Your girl's safe now, we found her a new home with Kira and our friend's wife."

"Widow," Carth said to himself.

Thanks, buddy...

"You did what?" Chop said in a low voice.

"They'll take care of her from now on, get everything she needs."

"How the hell did you manage that?"

"I found I'm good at getting people what they want."

For better or worse.

"Just like that, No more Helena?" Chop asked with eyes as wide as the boar.

"Just like that. They're on the fifth level, third house around the corner stepping straight off the southern lift. Scrapyard Sigil carved in the door. You can visit anytime."

"Ha Haaa!" Chop cheered, spreading his arms, he picked up the head of the boar, kissed it on both cheeks, then spit on the floor. "You've done it, son! You've done it! I'd hug and kiss you too if not for this boar's blood!" He laughed, "You don't know how much this means to me, you've saved that poor girl a lifetime of trouble. Thank you, thank you both. I am forever in your debt, lads."

Fordo decided to put on his most sincere smile rather than ask the well intentioned man how tradeless meat was going to bring back his dead friends.

The butcher was panting like his celebration had knocked the wind out of him. "So what'll it be, boys? Boar belly? Tenderloin? Smoked ribs?" He grabbed the boar's leg and gave it a shake, "We brought this fellow down today on the way back from closing off those curse-ed caverns you boys crawled out of. A fitting blessing from Mother Aure. By my reckoning the whole beast belongs to you." He chuckled

Fordo preferred the tenderness of slow roasted shoulder, but he knew salted boar belly was one of Carth's favorites. "We just need enough smoked jerky for a boat ride to Gateway..." He turned to look at Carth, who was already looking at him like Meeko begging for scraps. Fordo couldn't help but laugh. "...And a whole belly, for the boy here."

"Yes!" Carth cheered

"That's the spirit!" Chop chuckled, "Right away, sirs!"

A long straight bladed knife appeared in the man's hand along with a honing steel. In a flutter of wispy little strikes, the blade was brought to life and put to work. Chop was an artist, his box of blades like paint brushes, each with its own stroke and purpose. He knew every cut by heart, the muscle's proper name, what it was for, how it cooked and tasted. Told the boys the boar's life story just based on its cuts alone. Thick neck and large lean shoulders with a purple hue to the red meat, this boar fought far more than it fled, feasting mostly on the purple moss as well as his competitors.

It could have all been glass, but Fordo was fascinated by the idea of being able to taste a creature's legacy. "I hope when I'm sunk, you're there to break me down and tell everyone all the great things I've done."

"If I'm not dead long before you, then it's either a tragedy or a fuckin' miracle." Chop chuckled, "Now let's get you boys set up with some-"

"Fordo! Fordo Balison!" A young boy, maybe twelve, sprinted into Chop's shop in a panic.

"Aye, who's asking?"

"Come quick!"

"Slow down, sap, what's the matter?"

"There's a Nuru brother at the south gate calling for you!"

"What about?"

"Don't know, but he's hurt real bad, Come on!" The boy sprinted back out the door.

"Aw Sink my ass, why wouldn't you lead with that?" Carth asked, running after him.

"Fuckin' glass…" Fordo grit his teeth, "Bring a kart if you can, Chop, we might have to move him."

***

"He's here! He's here!" The messenger boy waved his arms, yelling up to the men on the wall of the gatehouse.

"Where is he, what's wrong with him?" Fordo called up.

"He's out there, been asking for you and the founder!"

"Then why the fuck is he still out there?"

"He looks full of sickness, can't let him bring it into the city!"

"Not…Sick!" The faint voice of his friend Gathii called over the wall. Fordo and Carth ran up the stairs to the top of the tall log.

"Gathii, what's wrong!" Fordo called, but he was busy on his hands and knees in the middle of the dirt road, arms shaking like he was holding up the planet rather than himself.

"You have to let him in, he needs medical attention!" Carth yelled.

"I'm sorry sirs, founder's orders."

"Fuck your orders and fuck your founder, my friend's dying down there!" Fordo drew his warhammer and jumped over the side of the twenty foot wall, slamming the spike into the side of it to catch himself half way down, and dropped safely to the ground, abandoning his hammer altogether.

Fordo ran to him. He was pale and shaking harder than Fordo thought possible. His friend collapsed onto his side and puked. Fordo caught a hint of red in it. "Fuck, Gathii, Hey! Stay with me, buddy!" Fordo crouched over the heaving Nuru, ignoring the sweat and vomit, he held Gathii's pale face in his hand. "What happened, buddy, what's wrong?" Gathii's eyes were barely open, his breathing burdened. Fordo finally noticed his feet, swollen and shredded, the red dirt that clung to it made black with blood. Fordo realized what was wrong. "Water!" He turned and called over the wall, "I need some fucking water!"

Carth leapt over the wall with the help of Fordo's hammer and sprinted to him with his canteen. Fordo grabbed it, tossed the cap, quickly filled his own mouth, then forcefully spit it into Gathii's face. Gathii coughed and sputtered back into consciousness while Fordo dumped the rest of the canteen into his mouth. The Nuru reached up and grabbed Fordo's face with a shaky hand. "Fordo?" He asked in disbelief.

"It's me, buddy, I'm here."

"I ran so far..." He croaked

"What is it, brother, what's the message?"

"Hilltop's gone..."

Carth and Fordo's eyes went wide with wonder. "What the fuck does that mean?" Carth asked. Gathii's eyes closed once more. "Oy...Oy!" Fordo slapped Gathii's cheeks to keep him awake. "Gathii, what the fuck does that mean??"

Gathii coughed without opening his eyes, clutching his own chest. "The bots...They're back..." He held Fordo's face like it was the edge of a cliff and pulled him in close, speaking in a hoarse whisper, "We have to stop them...They're worse than before...We have to stop..." Gathii's hands and head went limp.

"No, no, hey, Gathii! Gathii, wake up! Damnit, wake up, you son of a bitch!" Fordo shook and slapped the man in vain, he was out cold.

Carth cursed, "Open the fucking gate! He's hurt, you cunts, not sick! We have to get him inside, Now!"

Fordo put his cheek to Gathii's mouth to feel the faintest amount of breath. *Still alive, you're gonna be alright, buddy.* Fordo rocked back and forth.

It happened. The entire world's collective fear came true. They're back. The monsters that drove us all from our homes and tore our families into literal pieces in front of us. The threat that changed and shaped Aureum as we know it.

And now they're worse? Worse how? Bigger? Faster? Smarter? What does that mean? Is all our experience worthless? A decade's worth of preparation, a waste of time? If that's true, none of our methods will work from before, none of our plans, none of our defenses, none of our strategies.

That means..........it will be an entirely new war, with entirely new outcomes, and entirely new heroes.........

Fordo cracked the faintest shadow of a smile.

.........Couldn't be more perfect.

SONS OF SCRAPYARD

SONS OF SCRAPYARD

Al and Meeko

5

A crowd had gathered around Natori, keeping their distance. Bali crouched over the heaving Nuru, ignoring the sweat and vomit, he held Natori's pale face in his hand. "Bali, wait. What if it's sickness?" Asked Garrow. Bali grimaced in reply, lowering his ear to the boy. Natori was muttering, struggling to open his eyes. Al himself was panting from his short sprint into the house.

"What's wrong with him? Is he dying?"

"Hm..." Bali grunted, "water" Bali outstretched a large callused hand to the onlookers, who all scrambled immediately to unsling or unstrap their personal drinking containers until they had produced one wetskin, three canteens, and two flasks. Bali grabbed the closest canteen, lifted Natori's head, and slowly poured the contents into his mouth.

Al flinched with the crowd as Natori's whole body jolted forward, coughing and sputtering until he finally managed to get a few large gulps down. Natori puked up the water almost immediately, but Bali kept pouring. "I know, lad, I know." A few gulps and moments later the nuru's breathing finally steadied and a small amount of color returned to his skin. It was like watching someone come back to life. *Is that what I look like?*

Bali spoke softly, "That's it boy, nice and easy." Al hadn't heard that tone from Bali since he'd found them in

Bleakwood. So gentle, full of concern, and compassion.

"Bali..." Natori coughed

"Drink first, son, you're burning up. You can't tell me what happened with your brain all boiled."

Natori reached up and drained the canteen himself, pouring half down his throat and the other down his chin, then grabbed Bali by the shoulder, lifted himself to his ear, and whispered. "They're back..."

Al wasn't sure, because he'd never even dreamed it possible, but he could have sworn for a fraction of a moment, Balian The Bear looked afraid.

As quickly as his scowl returned, Bali reached for the closest flask and took a long sip of what was likely Realwood whiskey before asking the crowded villagers "Did you hear that?" Those in front nodded, their bright eyes turned hollow. "Hm... Garrow," Bali grunted, "Gather the village in the courtyard, everyone, no exceptions, but keep quiet, don't tell them yet. I'll be there once I know exactly what's going on."

"Aye, Commander..."

The villagers nodded and shuffled away muttering amongst themselves.

"Bali?"

"Clear the dining table and grab some cushions. Let's get this boy inside." Bali scooped Natori up in his arms, knees popping as he stood. Natori grit his teeth as he left the ground. Al nodded and jogged ahead to prepare a space.

***

Al hastily removed everything from the table short of wildly knocking it all to the floor. He pulled the nearest seat cushions and a few furs from the big chair.

"One for his head, then get his feet up high, let's try to get this swelling down." Bali set Natori down as gently as he could, but Natori still cried out in pain. Natori's ankles had swollen to the same width as his already massive calves. The bottoms of his feet were purple, shredded, and beaten like someone tried to shape them on an anvil. Al shuttered, even with his powers, he couldn't imagine his own feet taking such abuse.

"Attention aaall Johns and Jaaanes!" Came a boisterous call from Sarah down the hallway, "The moment we've all been waiting fooor!"

"Sarah, Honey, we've got-" Bali called back in vain.

"May I present to yooou..." Sarah appeared from the hallway holding up a large blanket in front of her like a stage curtain. "Auriii's brand neeew leeegs!" Sarah jumped out, flinging the blanket, arms spread in a presentory manor, reminding Al of Andre.

Auri wobbled out holding the wall, knees shaking like a baby deer, wearing her simple green dress and her shiny new leg braces. "Helloo!" Auri softly exclaimed, raising an arm in awkward celebration, still looking down at her feet.

Al, Bali and Natori all stared with open mouths, like they were each searching for a moment to interject.

"Well are you gonna clap or cheer or-Oh gods, your feet!" Both Sarah's and Auri's hands shot to their mouths when they finally noticed the bloody Nuru on the table.

Bali cleared his throat, "Adorable as that was, we've got our own weirdness goin' on."

"I'm sorry," Auri said, her cheeks flushed with red.

"Don't be, Girly, once we get through this business, we'll make sure you're able to stretch those legs proper."

"What happened? Natori, who did this to you?" Sarah rushed to Natori's side while Al walked over to give Auri his arm for support.

"How does it feel?" He whispered with a smile.

"Weird and unreal," Auri whispered back, "Almost like a dream."

"It's not," He nudged her and she almost smiled, but couldn't look away from Natori's feet.

"Should I go?" She asked him

"No, no, this involves everyone, I think...Come on." They baby stepped their way back to Natori's side, while Bali calmed Sarah's fretting enough for Natori to tell his story.

"Alright, boy..." Bali said. Sarah pulled up a chair next to Bali and took Natori's hand. Nuru squeezed it in pulses in rhythm with his sharp, pained breaths. "Tell us what you saw. I'm sure you didn't kill your famous feet for nothing."

Natori strained to steady his breathing enough to speak. "They're back, Bali. The bots are back."

Sarah gasped and Auri's jaw dropped. "That can't be. How could...?" Sarah looked to Bali, who put a comforting hand on her metal knee.

"Where, when, and how many?" Bali asked

"Hilltop, not three days ago. Thousands of them, but Bali..." Natori grit his teeth.

"You ran here from Hilltop in three days??" Al blurted out, glancing back at Natori's destroyed feet, "But that's like three hundred miles!"

"Quiet, Boy." Bali shot sternly, but without anger. "You were there? You saw them yourself, you're absolutely sure?"

"I was on the walls when they came, but..."

"Did the defenses hold? Where are the fires?" Sarah interrupted.

"No, listen, Bali, we're not prepared for this at all. They're different than before, worse even, like they've evolved somehow."

"What does...What does that mean?" Auri asked

"Tell me everything, everything you remember..." Bali squeezed Natori's hand now.

Natori bit his cheek before telling his tale, "Gathii and I were on the walls, looking out at the wreck. This weird mist rolled in, way too thick and way too fast, sweepin' over the field from the mountains to the fort, moving against the wind. We looked down and saw some shapes coming out of it, at the foot of the hill, dark at first until the moon touched the metal. They were all shaped and sized like people, all except one, way bigger than the rest."

Natori hesitates before continuing, his breath less pained and more shaky. Auri squeezed Al's arm a little tighter.

"The big bells sound and everybody comes running, guards, citizens, everybody. Brother Ingram gets everyone to prepare for battle. They load the crossbows, big and small and get ready to loose when..." Natori bit his lip and took a deep breath. "When all of a sudden...the big bot stops marching...and raises its hand..." Natori shook his head like even he couldn't believe it, "...And all of the other bots just freeze."

"Like they just...?" Al whispered.

"Like they were waiting for orders...From their fucking leader, man!" Sarah goes pale. Natori, Al and Auri all looked for a reaction from Balian, but found none.

"Don't stop," Bali grunted, staring right through Natori.

"Ingram yells to loose, a hundred bolts go flying into the bots, but the big one, Bali, not only did it Move to dodge a ballista shot...but it Caught it...In The Air! And then Threw It Back at the ballista!"

Everyone seemed to forget to breathe while they pondered the possibilities of that.

"What kind of throw?" Auri shrank nervously into Al as everyone turned to look at her.

"What do you mean?" Natori asked

"Like it...it threw it awkward like a kid with a stick? Or...did it go end over end like an ax? How was the throw, I...I don't know." Al smiled slightly to himself and squeezed Auri's shoulder, he never would have even considered a detail like that.

"Like a full form, wound up javelin throw, straight and accurate, Bali they..." Natori looked at the ceiling like it might have the answers, "Bali, that shouldn't be possible, right? None of this should be possible!"

"Keep going, I need to hear everything."

Natori nodded and rubbed his eyes, "The big bot threw the bolt, destroying a ballista. Then it pointed up at the walls and all of the little bots Sprinted up the hill, all at the same time."

"Sprinted??" Sarah asked

"Sprinted. As soon as they reached the walls, they all just kinda piled up onto each other, trying to climb up."

"Were they able to?" Bali asked

"No, no climbing, I don't think the smaller ones got any smarter, just the big bot."

"So how did they get in the fortress?" Al asked, "Or did they just go around and everyone's still trapped there?"

"No, they um..." Natori steadied himself, like he wanted to sound as calm and believable as possible, "The big bot picked up one of the little ones and threw it up to the top of the wall. And not like a careful, helping my buddy, toss. I mean launched as hard as the bolt."

"Was it destroyed?" Bali asked,

"No, it crashed into a bunch of guards. I was prepared to see some arms go flying, but they fight different too. It wasn't like...They weren't just killing everyone, they were also throwing people off of the walls."

"That didn't kill them? Those walls are higher than things I've fallen off and I didn't-" Bali shot Al a glance to watch himself, "I didn't think I'd survive."

"No, the bots would catch them below and drag them off into the fog."

"They took them?" Bali looked confused, the question not really directed at anyone.

"For every person they killed, they kidnapped like three or four more. Bali, I don't know what the fuck that means and it scares the glass out of me."

"What else? The fires, how did you beat them here?"

Natori looked as if he was about to cry, "She was so close..." He choked and cleared his throat, "Um...They tried to light them, but The Leader threw a bot up at the bell to intercept the group of guards on their way up the tower."

"Fucking glass..." Bali rubbed his bad knee, "You and your brother ran out right after? I assume Gathii made it out with you, given you're not a puddle right now."

Natori half laughed, half sighed, "Yeah, yeah, um... Brother Ingram got us out, held them off for us just long enough...I don't think he made it out..."

"Good soldier..." Bali nodded, Sarah rubbed his back.

"Gathii should be near Riverwood by now, looking for Fordo."

"What the hell for?"

"Well, he's Your son, he'll know what to do up north, right?"

Bali grunted in reply, "That's all of it, then?"

"No..."

"There's more?" Auri asked

"There's worse more. Right after Ingram found us, there was this noise that..." Natori strained to concentrate, "Just calling it a noise feels insufficient, it was like...we were all drowning...in an ocean of sound. We thought our ears were going to explode and then, like a switch-" Al felt Auri flinch when Natori snapped his fingers, "There was nothing."

"What does that mean?" Al asked, wide eyed.

"Silence. And not just muted or muffled like I was under water or hurt my ears, I mean absolute silence. The alarm bells were in full swing, I could feel the vibrations in the stones and I couldn't hear glass. And not just me. Ingram, Gathii, everyone I could see was freaking out, testing their ears, it was like some sort of spell."

"Did it affect the bots?" Bali asked

"No, they swarmed while everyone was freaking out."

"I don't like that...I don't like that, that's so scary." Auri put her hands over her ears.

"They took away your hearing, but you can hear now, how long until it wore off?"

"It didn't really wear off, it was more like we outran it. Gathii and I reached the bottom of the hill and both our hearing came back instantly, like we passed through some kind of barrier."

"They can take away sound......not just your hearing," Bali said, mostly to himself.

"Is there a difference?" Al asked

"Could be a big difference in how, if not what," Bali scratched at his chin stubble. "They were All shaped like people? No Rollers or Spiders or nothin' different this time?" Bali squinted

"Fuck......No, they were all...the same, the exact same..." His eyes went wide like he just realized. "Some were bigger or smaller than others, but they were all the same...model, one I've never seen......They all looked like the big one..."

Bali shook his head and took a long deep breath.

"Is that a bad sign?" Al asked

"There were so many different kinds of bots attacking us the first time that half of them didn't even have a way to hurt us......so that whole war, the code that infected them always felt like a freak accident......But this time......Feels like someone's built an army......"

"Maybe that's better..." Al said, "We might just have to track down the builder, instead of every single bot, like last time."

"We'll see..."

"That's everything, then?" Sarah asked

"That's everything," Natori said with tears forming in his eyes, "Please tell me you believe me..." Sarah squeezed his hand tighter, "The whole way here I've been so worried. Maybe you'll think I'm crazy."

"Oh Nuru..." Sarah pouted

"Don't worry, Son..." Bali put his hand on Natori's shoulder, "You did good."

Natori nodded as the tears fell, "Thank you, sir."

"You're a hero, Natori," Sarah rubbed his arm gently.

"I don't feel like a hero..." Natori sniffed

"Don't worry. Soon you'll have a hot wife and your own village to remind you," Bali patted him on the head. Al, Auri and Sarah all cracked weak smiles.

"I left them..." Natori wept, "I left them all to die..." Al wanted to comfort him, but he never knew what to say at the right time.

"Oh no..." Sarah leaned over Natori and wrapped her arms around him, "Don't think like that. You did exactly what you had to do..." He cried into her hair. "Without you, we would have no idea. Now Everyone will know how to prepare and plan and fight and survive this together and it's all thanks to you and your brother, don't you Ever forget that." He nodded between sobs.

Al's attention was torn between Natori's tears and Natori's blood. He couldn't look away from the man who'd sacrificed so much of himself to do the impossible for everyone else. *A true hero*. Al's filled his ears and his head with countless war stories of heroic deeds these past few years.

Through Balian, he's observed the great fame and life a hero can build for themselves, countless tales all ending with glory and triumph and cheering. But now, now he was a witness to guilt and tears, and for the very first time in his short memory, Al realized: Heroes can bleed and heroes can cry.

"Get some rest, Son..." Bali sighed, rubbing Natori's head, then placing a hand on Sarah's shoulder, "Stay with him." She nodded, still holding Natori. Bali locked eyes with Al then gestured with his head towards the shop.

Al understood and gently bonked Auri's head with his own before taking his arm back, "I gotta talk to Bali." She nodded in reply before taking a seat next to Sarah. Al took one last look at Natori before following Bali into the shop.

***

Meeko barked and jumped up on Al as he came out of the house. "I'll fill you in later, buddy." Al scratched behind Meeko's ear before turning to Balian, who marched directly to the wall where his massive fist shaped war hammer was perched.

"So what's the plan?" Al asked

Bali rubbed his eyes, "The plan-" he paused and chuckled to himself, "Might be completely fuckin' antiquated now, to be honest, but the plan for the territories is: Evacuate all civilians east to Julia and the lands beyond, while any and all warriors try to fortify and hold the Siena River, or at least, slow the bastards down."

"That still sounds like the best plan..." Al's eyes followed Bali's hands as they lifted the great hammer for the first time in his memory. Without it, the wall looked naked, like it would hide the emptiness with its hands if it had any.

"Yeah, well..." Bali looked tenderly at the weapon like one might a child's scraped knee, before gripping it tight and slamming the handle down against the stone floor with a heavy ringing clang. A decade of dust leapt from the hammer in a thick cloud, turning gold as it caught the afternoon light. "...It'll have to do."

Al grinned at the image, "You look awesome, my friend." Meeko barked in agreement.

"I feel awesome," Bali said with neither humor nor sarcasm, marching past Al, out the door, and down the street towards the courtyard, "Come on, Boy!"

Al smiled to himself for a moment, excitement briefly burying any dread, "Come on, boy." Al's ax and horn both bounced on either side of him as he trotted after Bali with Meeko right behind.

***

Just as Al was thinking he had never seen the streets so still and empty before, they rounded a corner to the courtyard to see several thousand nervous bodies packed around the wooden stage. An ocean of concerned expressions spilled out from the surrounding streets and alleyways, filling the cobblestone space around the small platform. Hundreds of children sought a better view from the tiled rooftops of shops and homes. Al hated the dreadful droning of worried whispers that replaced the constant laughter, ringing of hammers and usually pleasant bustle of the village.

Meeko looked up at Al as if looking for permission to run through the largest crowd they've ever seen. Al smiled weakly before shaking his head. *Not this time, Meeks.*

"Balian..."

"Commander..."

"He's here..."

The crowd parted for Bali as he marched stone faced to the stage, Al and Meeko following close behind. He never even considered that this many people existed in the world, let alone in the village, and now he was surrounded by all of them.

In the midst of wading through this swarm of strangers, Al glanced up to see the mountain of robots peaking over the rooftops. Dark thoughts immediately invaded his brain, questions he didn't want to know the answers to. *How do you stop a mountain?*

If you piled up all of the people in Scrapyard, how tall would that mountain be? Or Riverwood's? Julia's? Would I want to be next to my friends or as far away as possible? He shook his head like the questions were flies attempting to land in his hair.

In order to drown out the dreadful thoughts, he picked one to ponder, wondering what it must be like for the bot at the very center of that pile. *There's no way they could move.* Crushed under the weight of everyone they'd ever known, along with everyone they've never gotten to. *Could they see? Would that even be better?* Would the bodies block the sunlight, or would it pierce through thousands of thimble sized crevices, shining like the stars, minuscule and many. Al hoped for the latter, they could connect the dots, crafting constellations, and tracing a whole new reality for themselves each day. *There's worse ways to spend forever.*

Al bumped into Bali's back as he daydreamed. Without looking, Bali gestured for Al to wait as they reached the platform. The old wooden planks groaned and bent as Bali climbed the few steps to the stage.

Al wondered what Bali was going to say, or at least how he was going to say it. He was about to tell a few thousand people that their biggest fear had just come true and that the monsters they'd barely survived a decade before are now faster, stronger, and learned to do actual magic. *I'd probably leave out the magic.* Al looked up at Balian in wonder, failing to fathom what courage a man would need to tell the world it's about to end. He watched the slow, steady, rising shoulders of one long drawn out breath as Bali readied himself for his speech.

Al knelt and pet Meeko to calm himself, the droning crowd making him more and more anxious. He'd be far more comfortable on a rooftop, even have a better view, but it was too late, he was sure Bali's speech was about to-

BOOM BOOM......

A deep knocking echoed out from beneath the stage, bouncing throughout the open space. The buzz of the muttering crowd quieted in a wave as thousands of bodies all turned to face the stage as one.

BOOM BOOM......

Bali brought the butt of his hammer down on the hollow stage twice more. Al's mouth fell open as he glanced from the silent crowd to the big man on stage.

BOOM BOOM...... CRASH!

Al flinched as the entire crowd stomped a foot in rhythm with Bali's knocks.

BOOM BOOM! CRASH!

A grin spread wide across Alexander's face.

BOOM BOOM! CRASH!

It grew quicker and louder with each repetition.

BOOM BOOM CRASH!

BOOM BOOM CRASH!

BoomBoom Crash!
BoomBoom Crash!
BoomBoomCrash!!
BOOMBOOMCRASH!!!
BOOMBOOMCRASH BOOMBOOMCRASH!!!
BOOMBOOMCRASH BOOMBOOMCRASH
BOOMBOOMCRASH!!!!
BOOMBOOMCRASH BOOMBOOMCRASH
BOOMBOOMCRASH!!!!

The world shook like a great wyrm was going to erupt from deep beneath the courtyard. Al could see Meeko barking right in his face and could feel himself laughing, but he could not hear it as explosions of sound blew over Al in bursts. Al looked around to see thousands of people pulsing in unison, leaning on one another as they stomped their feet and raised their hammers.

CRASH! CRASH! CRASH! CRASH!

Al looked up to see Balian raising his mighty hammer toward the closest drum tower.

BOOMBUM BOOMBOOM!
BOOMBUM BOOMBOOM!
BOOMBUM BOOMBOOM!

The great war drums took over as the crowd outpaced itself. Bali pointed out over the crowd, down the main street of the village, and to the lands beyond. Al watched, amazed, as the scene from his favorite mural came to life before his eyes, though the crowd was much more somber than he'd often imagined. Even recognizing and acknowledging this as a call of war, he could not help but smile and laugh at the sheer spectacle, even if he was the only one.

BOOMBUM BOOMBOOM!
BOOMBUM BOOMBOOM!
BOOMBUM BOOMBOOM!

As the drums blasted overhead, the crowd began to disperse, with neither explanation nor instruction. *I love Scrapyard.* Al chuckled to himself as he watched thousands of people all move with a singular purpose: Prepare to move, prepare for war.

"You keep that smile to yourself, Boy…" Al looked back to find Bali standing behind him. "You're the only one who gets to…" Bali nodded and pointed with his eyes to the other end of the courtyard. Al followed the look until he spotted a large bald man, rocking back and forth on the cobblestone. Brash even cried like a baby, not covering his face, but rather holding his hands over his ears, his pain overwhelming his shame.

"You ever wonder why Brash is just a big kid?" Bali asked. Al shook his head, not looking away. "He saw glass so horrible as a Kid that his brain decided to stay one. He was eleven when the bots came and he'll be eleven forever. When they came, he lost a part of himself, same as Sarah, Daisy, everyone else."

Al's stomach dropped and he looked to the ground. He felt like climbing the drum tower and letting them beat him instead. *Giggling glass, how can you be such a fuckin' idiot?* "I'm sorry," Al said, "I didn't think about it."

"Do you understand what I'm saying?"

"I'm the only one excited because I'm the only one who wasn't there."

"No, the guilt's not the point, Son, you're allowed to be excited. You said you didn't think about it, I'm saying 'Always think about it, always consider'. Your feelings are yours, they belong to you, but the world belongs to everybody else. And when you don't consider everybody else, that's when you act like an idiot."

"I'm still sorry..." Al said, patting Meeko on the head.

"That's alright..." Bali lowered his voice, "I fuckin' love those drums..." Bali nudged Al with his elbow, "Now come on, boy, we've got work to do."

"Look, Bali, I know what you're going to say."

"Yeah, you think so?"

"Yes, but please, please just let me say some things first, okay?"

"I'm listening."

"I know you want me to go to Julia with the civilians to watch over Sarah and Daisy and everyone, but-" Bali opened his mouth to say something "-Please just let me finish." Bali crossed his arms.

"I don't know what good I'll be on a battlefield... Every time I've fought anything, I've been reckless, taken the risks for granted, even put my best friends in danger, but I want to help you, I Need to help you. You don't have to let me fight, but you have to let me help; Run messages, pull wounded, scout, whatever, but I can't just hang back and wait when I Know that I can make a difference. I don't know where I was last time, but this time I'm here, and I'm not going to let this happen."

"You think it's up to you? Think you can stop this yourself?"

"No...But I know that you can...I just wanna help you help everybody else...I won't let you down, Bali, I promise." Al held a trembling hand out to shake Bali's.

Bali looked down at it for a moment before saying "No, I'll be fine, thank you though..." Waving dismissively. Al's face, shoulders and stomach dropped in unison. "Actually, you don't need to go to Julia either, we'll be good on both ends, you can just wait here if you'd like." Bali nodded

A smile crept back onto Al's defeated face.

"You're My Son..." Bali clasped Al's wrist and pulled him in for a hug that cracked his whole back, "...you really think I'm gonna leave you behind?"

Al choked up, engulfed in the arms of the bear. Bali had called him 'Son' in passing before, same way he'd called him 'Boy', or 'Dumbass', he'd heard it a thousand times, it was how he talked to Any of the other warphans in Scrapyard...But this was the first time Bali had ever stopped to take a moment, look Al in the eyes, and call him 'His Son'. *I always wanted to be.*

***

"Daisy, you can't be serious..." Sarah whispered

Al, Meeko, and Bali arrived back at the big house to find Daisy and Sarah by the fireplace. Meeko trotted over to lay in the warmth. Natori slept on the table with Auri holding his hand. Al met her eye and found a neighboring chair. "How's he doing?"

"He fell asleep holding my hand and now I can't move..." Auri smiled, "But he's doing better. I think this is the first time he's slept since he started running."

"What's up with them?" Al gestured to Daisy and Sarah, but Auri just shook her head.

"Come with us to Julia," Sarah said, "there is No way we are just going to leave you here alone."

Bali stood between the two women, placing a hand on either shoulder, "What's this about?"

Sarah's lips quivered, "She says she's not coming."

Daisy rocked side to side as she shook her head, tears seeping through her closed eyelids and spreading into the wrinkles around them, "I'm sorry, dear...I've made my choice."

"What about everyone else?" Sarah said, "Brash, Benji, Jacks, Kira, Elizabeth, Al, Me, Everyone who Loves and Needs you?"

"I have raised dozens of children in my lifetime. All of them grown, all of them good. You'll all be just fine without me."

"Please, just come with us, I don't want you to...I don't want you to die."

Daisy placed a frail hand on Sarah's knee, "Child, I am eighty nine years old..." She leaned back in her chair and sighed,

"I survived FarFall...I was Conceived in space and Born on the ground, I am as old as our time on this world. Too old to be running about. Hell, I was too old last time!" She laughed

"You're sure this is what you really want, you're not just giving up hope?"

"Giving up hope?" Daisy laughed, "If you all stop crying and go stop those things, you won't have to worry about little ol' Daisy." Even Sarah laughed through her tears.

"No, Nobody lives forever...And I've lived longer than most. Outlived both of my husbands, half of my kids. Leaving home now, just to scrounge up a few more years, it feels almost......Greedy."

"We love you, Daisy..." Sarah hugged the old woman and Bali hugged them both, "We'll be back when we can."

"I know, sweetheart, and I'll be here."

Bali kissed the top of Daisy's head, "You be safe, girly."

"No, You be safe, Commander. And tell Jacks and Benji when you see them to come find me when it's over."

"It'll be my first order."

*Nobody lives forever...*The words echoed in Al's mind. *I don't think I'd want to.*

"How are you doing with all this?" Auri asked.

A guilty smile curved the edges of Al's mouth. *I should be asking you that.* "Honestly," He took a deep breath, "I'm kind of excited, in a way."

"Mm?" She looked up at him and though he expected confusion or judgment, her eyes remained earnest.

"I've spent most of the last three years daydreaming of Battles and Monsters and Saving The World with my friends. I know that's just kid stuff and in real life I'm sure it's scary and dark and nothing like I imagine, but...Ten minutes ago my fuckin' Hero just asked me to fight By His Side and right now..." Auri smiled and rubbed his back. "Right now, it just feels good."

"I heard so much about them, growing up..." Auri nodded towards Bali and Sarah, "All the stories, everything they've done...They seemed too big to believe in, too good to really exist," She traced her leg brace with her free hand, "But meeting them, they're just funny, sweet, regular people...And that makes them so much better, I think, like even we could be that good someday. I don't know."

"I'm so glad they found me..." Al said, more to himself.

"I'm so glad they found you," Auri laughed, though her smile faded back to concern.

"How're you holding up, girly?"

"Well, I never thought I'd walk again..." She shrugged "But I never thought They'd be back either, so...a lot of conflicting feelings right now, I'm pretty overwhelmed," She still managed a smile.

"Do you remember the last time they came at all?"

"Bits and pieces...I remember a lot of screaming, my baby brother and I getting scooped up by someone and lifted into the tree with a bunch of other kids...I remember my father running away...Not much else."

"What's your brother's name?"

"Wash...He's a good kid," Her eyes lit back up, "I miss him. Hope he's okay."

"I'm sure you'll find him in Julia."

"No, he'll be locked down in Riverwood with everyone else. I know he'll be safe there, I just don't know when I'll get to see him again."

"Riverwood isn't going to evacuate?"

"No, the whole city's been raised up on platforms into the trees. We've built walls and traps and stuff on the ground to keep the bots away. As long as they can't climb, Riverwood's the safest city on Aureum."

Al nodded before wrinkling his brow. "How high up's the first platform?"

"Pretty high, like thirty or forty feet, I think. Why?"

"Well, how high is the Hilltop Bell tower? Natori said they threw bots all the way to the top."

Auri went pale and still, her eyes darting about the floor. She stood very suddenly, leaning against the table for support. Al steadied her with a hand on the back. "Hey, hey, take it easy." Everyone in the room turned toward her.

Al stood slowly, wrapping his arms around her, "Auri...?" Her eyes and face changed subtly, but rapidly, like she was having a silent painful conversation with herself.

Bali stepped towards them, "What happened, is it the brace?" Auri shook her head.

Sarah stood to help, "Auri, are you hurt?" She shook her head again.

Auri opened her mouth to speak, but no words came out.

"Oh, She looks faint," Daisy said, "Bring her by the fire."

Al and Bali helped Auri to where Sarah had been sitting. Daisy leaned forward, "What is it sweetheart?"

Auri was trembling, her jaw wavering like it was waiting for the words to appear until she said "I need...I need food and water." She looked as if she was about to pass out.

Sarah nodded and rubbed her back, "Oh, of course, girly, I'll whip you up some dinner real quick."

Auri shook her head again.

"No?" Sarah asked

"For travel..." Auri was rocking back and forth now. Al took a knee beside her and held her hands.

Bali shook his head, "Don't you worry about that, young lady. The whole village is building the caravans as we speak, there'll be plenty of food and water for everyone on the way to Julia. You'll be well looked after."

Auri shook her head once more, tears streamed down her red cheeks, "I'm not..." She choked on her words, "I'm not going that way." Sarah and Bali both looked at each other, Al and Daisy just stared at Auri. "Riverwood..."

Bali's face turned Al's favorite shade of red, "Riverwood? Why the hell would you-?"

"I'm going to find my brother."

Bali, Daisy, Al and Sarah all interjected at once almost shouting over each other.

"You'll find him in Julia! You're not going to-!"

"Now just hold on, sweetheart-!"

"Whoa, girly, I was just thinking out loud, I didn't-!"

"No, Auri, don't be ridiculous, we-!"

Auri squeezed her eyes shut and covered her ears before shouting over everyone. "Let Me Speak!" They all went quiet. Auri coughed, having raised her voice far above her standard volume. She cleared her throat and wiped her eyes before continuing.

"Whether you want me to or not, I Am going to find my brother. Besides my bug, he is the Only family that I have left, the Only thing that I truly love..." Auri squeezed Al's hand as tight as she could to steady herself.

"Riverwood is too proud to evacuate, they've spent fifteen years building nothing but defenses, but these new bots have more than a chance to make it through.

"I don't know if Natori's brother warned them in time, I don't know if the new bots can reach the city or not, I don't even know if I can make it...But if there's even a Chance that he's in danger, no matter how small, I Know that I am Not taking a Single step Away from My Brother!"

"I am Not being Hauled away and Hidden again, like I'm still Six years old, just waiting however long to find out if my baby brother is alive. I am going to find him! And if you want to help me, stop treating me like I'm made of paper and tell me where the food is......Please......"

Al didn't know what to say. He'd had a dozen arguments with Balian over what it means to be fragile, about what Al could and couldn't do, about being treated like a child. *Have I been doing the same to you?*

"Oh, Sweetheart..." Sarah was red in the face, "We know you're not a child, we know you're not an idiot. But do you understand what you're getting yourself into?"

Auri nodded.

"If you go to find your brother, you are going right towards those monsters. And even when you make it to Riverwood, whether your brother is there or not...They will be. This path will put you face to face with them, do you understand?"

Auri nodded again.

"And you still want to go?" Sarah asked

"No..." Auri said, her lip quivering, "But I have to..." She sobbed, pressing her face into Sarah's shoulder, "I'm so scared..."

Al's heart broke for the girl. This was one of those moments, wasn't it? The kind where the path you take leads you to the rest of your life. The kind where you choose what kind of person you want to be from this point forward.

Alexander always thought strength was in ability, in knowing what you're capable of, knowing that if you have the power to help someone or stop something, then it was your responsability to. But knowing that you can't win, seeing that there's zero chance, being scared out of your fucking mind, and diving headfirst anyway, right into the fray, Just because you know that it is right...That is something beautiful...That was his new definition of bravery...And That is why he whispered the words without doubt or question, "I'm going with you."

"What was that, son?" Bali asked

"I'm going with you..." He said to Auri, "I'm getting her home..."

Auri sniffed and looked at Al like what he said was impossible.

Daisy smiled and laughed.

Sarah looked devastated, "Oh Al..."

Bali rubbed his eyes and walked away, "Damnit, boy..."

Al stood up and spoke to Bali's back. "I'm going with her and I'm not arguing about it. Bali, there's nothing I want more than to fight by your side, but you've already got an army and she's only got a bug. I can't just keep doing whatever I feel like, I need to be where I'm needed." Al started to cry again. "I'm sorry, Bali, I really wanted to-"

Bali turned around with a wet face of his own and hugged Al for the second time that day, "I'm proud of you, Son."

Sarah shook her head, "Bali, we can't-"

"It's not up to us. They're grown, it's their choice. Besides..." He said, releasing Al, "They can only move as fast as that bug. They'll be back with the army in a day or two," He clapped Al on the shoulder.

"Al, your dream, you can't come with me," Auri said

"My dream is to fight monsters and you're heading right for them," He smiled

She tried to smile back, "Why would you do this for someone you just met?"

"Just met and you've already made me a little better... Maybe I'm just going for the upgrades?"

She shook her head and wiped her eyes, "Thank you..."

Al nodded, "We're gonna get you home, girly."

SONS OF SCRAPYARD

FORDO

5

"Straight to the horn, boys, no time to waste," Fordo said, strapping his boots tight as they waited on their rising lift, ready to run.

"Shouldn't it already be blowing," Carth asked, "There's no way Gathii outran the signal fires."

"All he said was 'They're back, they're worse, and Hilltop's gone'"

"That could mean fuckin' anything…" Chop cursed.

"Maybe Hilltop fell before they could light the fires, maybe something stopped them, either way, a man we trust ran himself into a coma just to warn us. That's as real a warning as any other signal."

"Damnit, one of us should have stayed behind, in case he wakes up," Carth shook his head.

"Chop trusts the woman, she'll take good care of him."

"If the fire's out, they won't sound the horn without Warren's orders, you know," Chop insisted

*Fuck Warren and his orders…*Fordo shook his head, "We don't have time to explain to every single person in this city between us and the almighty founder. The people need to know Now, they need to prepare, and I'm not waiting for permission to try and save them." Carth and Chop both looked appropriately nervous.

Fordo stood and placed a hand on their shoulders, "Look, we don't know when Gathii will wake up and I don't think Warren will believe us without him. We could kill everyone outside the walls just by wasting our time and save them all by doing whatever it takes to reach that horn. Convince them, trick them, fight them, Whatever it takes, we're sounding the alarm. Riverwood's counting on us to warn its people. I know you boys can do this because we have to do this, you understand?" His friends nodded in agreement.

"Good. Now what's the best way in, without Warren's seal?" Fordo asked Chop.

"Honestly, just tell them what you told us. Otherwise, we'll probably have to take them down."

Fordo nodded. The lift slowed then jolted to a stop.

Fordo clapped them on the shoulder, "Let's get to work."

They all sprinted off to their task, hearts and minds full of purpose again, racing down the platforms like there were still monsters chasing them. *Well, there technically are.*

Fordo's heart was pounding. He could run far faster without carrying a child across slime covered ground. He was pleasantly surprised by how well Chop kept pace with them, the big man sure could move when he wanted to. They reached the outer city in under an hour.

"There she is," Chop panted as they reached the very end of the walkway and the giant conical octagon formally known as the Great Riverwood Megaphone.

Fordo and his friends entered side by side through the large, vaguely circular doorway. Angled walls circling above them created an almost illusory feeling that they were traveling at high speeds through a wooden wormhole, opening up to a theater sized window looking over the tops of the forest to the mountains beyond. Their only gravitational anchor in the empty building was the huge horn itself, hollowed from the biggest dragon's tooth Fordo had ever seen, large enough that even Chop could comfortably crawl inside.

One guard stood separate from the others. Extremely tall, nearly seven feet at least, but thin and lanky like he was stretched to size rather than grown. Slicked back gray hair and a bushy unkempt mustache sat upon a thin permanent scowl. The other three guards turned to face Fordo and his companions. Two men and a woman, all around Fordo's age, each seemed relieved to have company other than Captain Cranky, like he'd forbidden any activity that wasn't silently standing by this horn.

"Who goes there?" The older guard asked passively without looking, in a deep nasally monotone that Fordo could only describe as authoritative indifference.

"Urgent message from Gathii Nuru!" The younger guard's backs straightened. Fordo tried his best to sound in charge, hoping that would be enough to prompt obedience without question. "Hilltop has fallen, sound the alarm, there's no time to waste!" The acoustics were as awesome as Fordo hoped, his voice echoed off the walls and shot out over the forest, making him feel like a giant. He wondered if even their voices could be heard in the lumber yards below.

The younger guards looked at one another, then at the horn, then at their superior, "Captain Antoly?" A young guard called, but the older man barely blinked, continuing to stare vacantly at the horn.

"Now soldier, move!" The young woman flinched when Fordo pointed at her, with voice and eyes full of urgent, righteous, anger.

She moved towards the horn, but Antoly said "What do you think you're doing?" in his same indifferent tone.

She halted in place "What do we do, sir?"

"What do you mean?" Antoly asked, "We don't do anything unless we see the signal fire. I don't see anything burning on those mountains, do you?"

"Hilltop is gone, the fires aren't coming!"

The younger guards shuffled their feet, looking to the floor for answers. "Hilltop is gone...?"

Antoly released a frequently rehearsed sigh of annoyance. "No. Hilltop is a Fortress. Of High walls. And Solid stone. What you're saying is Impossible."

"A Nuru brother ran himself into a coma just to get us this message!"

Antoly scoffed, "Your generation can't even go for a jog without needing to lie down, I see."

I can't fuckin' believe this guy. "We don't have time for this glass!"

"Leave us to our work," Antoly waved dismissively, "I grow tired of this game."

The young woman moved closer to the horn, "Sir, I think we should-"

"Touch that wyrm and I will remove you from service."

"I really think-"

Antoly's face instantly transformed from boredom to anger. "Do as I say! I am in charge here!"

"Sir, if you're wrong-"

"Who are you to say that to me?? I have been guarding this building for over a decade! How long have you been here, hm?"

"You mean you've been avoiding real work for over a decade?" Carth cut in.

Antoly shot a long pointed finger at the other two guards, ignoring Carth. "Meanwhile you two still remember what your mother's breasts taste like. Now back to your posts!"

"You just sound scared to me, 'Captain'," Fordo said.

"Scared? Scared?? I've never been scared of anything in my entire life!" Antoly spat, his neck and face turning bright red. "I will not be made a fool of and reprimanded over your childish lies! Now get the hell out of my sight!"

"Sir, if he's wrong, everybody loses a week of work and laughs about it the next. If you're wrong, everybody outside the walls could literally die!"

Antoly pointed his finger like it was a loaded crossbow. "Shut Up! The bots are gone. Destroyed. Decades ago. They cannot return. That would be Impossible!"

Fordo squinted like he might better see if this man made any sense, "What the fuck are you talking about? Then why are You guarding something that Only matters if they Do come back? Why do we have this at all?" Fordo gestured towards the whole building they were standing in.

"To ensure they never do..." Antoly looked like a cornered animal.

"What??" Carth was baffled

"I'm blowing it," The woman put her hands on the horn.

"Don't you move!"

"For my family's safety-"

"Don't talk to me about safety!"

"Even just to be safe??"

"There Is No Safe and There Are No Bots!"

"Antoly, I apologize, but what you're saying doesn't make any sense!" The woman stepped back.

"He's in shock..." Chop whispered.

Fordo stepped forward, "I won't let you jeopardize the people of this city because of your cowardice."

"What did you say...?" Antoly looked at Fordo like he just told him he'd fucked his wife.

"The bots are back, we have to warn the city, Now!"

"The bots are Not...Back..."

"Fuck you, I'll do it myself!" Fordo stepped forward, but Chop grabbed the back of his collar.

"The Bots...Are NOT...BACK!" Spitting every word, Antoly drew a hatchet from his side and wildly threw it at Fordo's head. Fordo felt the wind of it as Chop yanked him to the ground. Carth stepped in front of Fordo with a drawn hammer.

Everyone in the room froze, staring at the would-be murderer. Antoly staggered slightly, his vacant stare returned. The tall man blinked, put up a hand to steady himself, then threw up at his own feet. Everybody groaned in disgust, moving back as the tall man fainted, his head bouncing off of the horn, and onto the now wet floor.

"Fuckin' glass, this guy…" Carth lowered his hammer.

"Nearly took my head off…" Fordo laughed, still on the ground, "You saved my ass, Chop."

"Least I could do," Chop pulled Fordo to his feet.

"You alright Ford?" Carth asked

Fordo stepped around Antoly's unconscious body in front of the horn, running a hand through his own greasy hair. *I can't believe that missed, you son of a bitch, almost sunk my story in the dumbest possible way.* Fordo laughed to himself.

"I always knew he was crazy, but that was insane…" The three guards were just staring at their captain in disbelief.

"Oy!" Fordo yelled, "Don't just stand there! You two get him some help!" Pointing at the two male guards, "And you!" He looked at the woman, "Blow that fucking horn," Fordo turned to look out over the forest. He could hear them cursing and shuffling to their tasks.

That fucking guy. Fordo always knew fear could make people stupid or weak or freeze, but he never considered fear could make people dangerous, murderous even.

"Cover your ears…"

How many more of these guys will we have to deal with? There's no way he's the last. The world's about to change again and there'll be plenty of people who won't accept it. We'll have to find a better way to deal with-

"Cover your ears!"

"What?"

"Cover your-!"

BRRMMMMMMMMMMMMMMMMM
MMMMMMMMMMMMMMMMMMMMMMM
MMMMMMMMMMMMM

The ground shook with a dreadful, droning, vibration, burying all other sound beneath it. The massive bassy blast shot through his body and out over the forest, shaking his bones, the trees, and the atmosphere itself.

BRRMMMMMMMMMMMMMMMMMMM
MMMMMMMMMMMMMMMMMMMMMMM
MMMMMMMMMMMMM

Fordo dropped to one knee, with a hand on the shaking ground. He laughed like a kid again, letting the storm of sound swirl over him. He tried to yell over or through it just to see if he could, only to find his hardest scream was barely a whisper.

BRRMMMMMMMMMMMMMMMMMMM
MMMMMMMMMMMMMMMMMMMMMMM
MMMMMMMMMMMMM

Fordo never knew sound could feel like this, could shake the world itself. This was the first time he had ever felt the very definition of Power. Not Fame, not influence, not control, but true, raw, unstoppable power. An actual force of nature. The power of a storm lifting a house from its foundations, The power of a Great Wyrm forcing the whole world out of its way, The power of gravity ripping a floating city out of the sky. *People can prepare for it, try to avoid it, try to direct it, but you can't fight a force of fucking nature.*

***

People poured in from the lumber yards in chaotic columns like an army of insects; panicking, pushing, funneling through the gates of the city. The steady thrum of the horn still blasted overhead. Fordo stood alone upon the walls, watching the flood of faces fighting forward.

Every lift was over capacity, rising with labored efforts under unfamiliar weight. Fordo watched a man jump and cling to the side of a rising lift, his panic surpassing his patience, only to be sent falling back to the ground by its passengers. Fordo hoped nobody saw him laugh.

He took back all of his previous observations of Riverwood's relaxed, easygoing nature. *A tree's only as relaxed as the wind that blows it, huh? You all got nowhere to be when there's nothing to worry about. No wonder you all worship the Warrens, do whatever your Baron says, it's so you don't have to think and prepare and fend for yourselves.*

"Listen here, all who can!" Fordo shouted into the river of faces. None stopped, but enough looked to know that they heard him, and that was all he wanted, "I need good men who will fight with me!"

"Fuck off, clanker! We've got families to find!"

"Then this call is not for you, brother! It's for the workless and the warriors, those whose hands are empty and strong! Meet me at the docks! I sail for Gateway at dawn!"

"Are you crazy? Why would anybody leave?"

"Because we must! Riverwood is safe, but Aureum is not! We lose the river, we lose everything! We cannot let them cross the Siena! If you won't fight for me! Or your people! Or your world! Then fight for yourselves! History has its eyes on that bridge! The world will remember the names of everyone who fights and dies defending it! We hold the bridge! We save Aureum! Spread the word! We sail at dawn!"

And so it went. Fordo shouted over each new wave of faces until his voice was too hoarse to be heard. Carth and Chop were hopefully doing the same at different gates spreading the same message: "Those who fight will sail at dawn!" Fordo didn't care who joined him. That bridge is the key. *Whether it holds or falls, they'll remember my call. They'll remember what man was there defending it, with or without them.*

Two guards hurried up the steps of the wall, "Fordo Balison."

"Aye?"

"You're coming with us," The guards stepped forward.

"On what orders?"

"Arrest..." Fordo raised an eyebrow, "Warren wants a word with you."

"He can find me right here," Fordo rested a hand on his holstered hammer.

The guard's eyes narrowed, "So be it..." One retrieved a brass whistle from his pocket and blew it hard, the high pitch piercing the white noise of panic.

Fordo glanced over to see the first lift in over an hour with descending passengers. A tall woman with red leather armor, a thin man with a large black hat, and a strong, wide shouldered young man with glasses and a puffing pipe. The crowd got noticeably quieter as they descended, even parting for them to pass, opening a path that led straight to Fordo.

Fordo stood straight and tall, he had nothing to hide, for he had done nothing wrong, confident there was no accusation he couldn't swat away.

'You should have told me first.' There was no time.

'On the word of one man?' The risk is too high to ignore.

'This is my city.' I'm not your subject. I did what I know is right.

Warren marched up the stairs with his Blackwyrm thugs in tow, walking right up to Fordo, standing over him a little closer than comfortable. His eyes were dark in the torchlight, only appearing as tiny orange embers when he puffed his pipe. He breathed deep and long like a man trying to keep his cool, blowing a thick white cloud from his nose into Fordo's face before removing his glasses and folding them closed. Fordo chose to wait for him to speak first. Figured it safer to react and refute than engage directly.

"Was it you?"

Fordo was caught off guard by what seemed like a genuine question. He nodded in response, never leaving Warren's eye. *Maybe he's grateful.* Fordo mused.

Warren calmly handed his pipe and glasses to the closest guard before whipping around and backhanding Fordo across the jaw. The heavy fist spun Fordo off-balance, almost tumbling over the side of the wall. Fordo caught a glimpse of the staring crowd below as his feet left the ground. Warren caught him by the jacket before he fell, raised Fordo up over his head with a grunt, and slammed him back onto the wall, groaning at the guard's feet. Fordo gasped for breath, clutching at his chest. The guards all looked in shock while the bastard from Blackwyrm smirked down on him, lighting a cigarette with Fordo's lighter.

What did I- WHAM! A steel-toed boot crashed into his temple, sending him spitting a spray of blood before the spiked sole stomped on his ribcage. Fordo jolted and coughed, thick and wet, something warm dripped down the side of his mouth. All of Fordo's focus was on his next breath, nothing else mattered, nothing else was possible.

Warren kneeled over him, breathing like a beast, speaking low and slow for only Fordo to hear, "An old man was trampled and killed on the stairs in this panic You Caused."

Fordo's eyes went dead. *There's always something......*

"This beating you just took…he got it a hundred times over, because of You and your misguided, impatient, vindictive arrogance…" Warren leaned a knee on fordo's chest, halving each breath.

"You don't like me, fine, but years of plans and protocols and systems were in place to organize and conduct this fucking shit show right here, to prevent the pointless, avoidable tragedies and casualties that come with chaos…And you couldn't wait ten minutes to blow that horn, just so you could spite me and play Follow The Fucking Leader."

Fordo coughed "I-"

Slam! Warren's fist crunched into his throat. Fordo's whole body contracted into a ball, hands shooting to his neck. "I don't want you breathing Another Word in My City. You killed three good men in the last three days, put another in the infirmary, just by opening your fucking mouth…You are done."

He grabbed Fordo by the hair and whispered in his ear, "You get on your little boat…go on your shitty, self-righteous crusade…and you NEVER…Set Foot…In MY City Again."

Warren let Fordo's head drop with a heavy thud and walked away, "Get him out of my sight…We got enough mess to clean up."

***

Fordo faded back into consciousness, his head pounding inside his skull. He couldn't open his eyes, but felt his boots dragging in dirt, blood dripping down his chest from his hanging mouth. Someone was carrying him, two someones it seemed, he had both arms slung over two shoulders of different heights and widths. He hoped they belonged to Carth and Chop, but on each, he felt worn, hardened leather armor. The night was cold, he could feel each labored breath come out as a steamy cloud. The only sounds were the steps and breaths of his helpers and the low hum of the distant horn.

A harsh cough erupted from his aching ribs, spitting out the mixture of mucus and blood vacating his burning lungs, "Ah, Sink my ass..."

"Mornin', mate..." The gruff voice of Blackhat came from Fordo's left, along with the surprisingly feminine laugh of his red armored companion to his right.

Why these two? Bit overqualified just to have me thrown out of the city. Laughing hurt the same as coughing, or maybe it just led to more.

"Still got your sense of humor after that stomping, ay?"

"Never really...had one of those..." Fordo groaned

"It would do you wonders, I think. Laughin' at the world, instead of spittin' on it," Blackhat chuckled, "You know, you could get away with a lot more shit if you weren't such an asshole."

Fordo shook his head, "I told someone that myself today...And he broke my fuckin' nose."

"Who, your boyfriend?"

Sword lady giggled again. Fordo could feel Blackhat smiling even with his eyes closed. His cough was getting easier the more he spit, head spinning a little less with each new breath.

Fordo smiled, "Never thought I'd be killed...by a twelve year old boy...and his mom." They both chuckled. "Is she gonna pick you up…swing your sharp ass nose into the back of my head?" That got a full laugh out of her.

Blackhat pat Fordo on the chest, creating more coughs. "There you go, mate. Only took a well placed boot to knock the stick outta yer ass, ay?"

Fordo finally opened his eyes to see nothing. He thought himself blind for half a second before realizing they didn't have lanterns, just trudging along through the blackest night of Fordo's life.

"How the hell can you guys see?"

"You afraid of the dark?"

"You afraid of the light? It's pitch fuckin' black out here!"

They both just chuckled.

After a dozen dragging minutes, haunting blue moonlight illuminated their path, the trees parting and opening up into an old lumber yard. The blue light on red flora provided a pretty plethora of purple hues all around them. Thousands of young, waist-high saplings all marched in neat little rows like they were standing at attention. Their thin branches waved in the slight breeze like they were all excited to see Fordo and his captors.

From Fordo's understanding, after Riverwood's workers cleared a section of the forest, "Spent a patch" he thinks they call it, they churn the soil and plant as many new trees as they have space to, ensuring neither the forest nor their industry ever dies.

And also to his understanding, they leave a barren circle of soil in the center of each patch to be used as a graveyard. The dead are buried and a new tree planted upon them, their death bringing forth new life to Aureum.

The two warriors dragged Fordo into the center of one of these circles and let him drop to his knees.

Fuck...

"Wait..." Fordo breathed, his heart racing out of his chest.

Blackhat took a long swig from a flask while his companion removed her massive sword from her back and planted it in the dirt.

Fuck...Fuck...Fuck...

Fordo slowly grabbed a clump of loose soil in one hand and a large round rock in the other, hoping to whatever gods may or not exist he had the strength and speed to blind one of them long enough to get their weapon.

"Hey Blackhat..." Fordo asked.

"Yeah?"

"Will you tell me one thing first?"

"What's that, mate...?" Blackhat stretched and cracked his back by raising and twisting his spear up over his head.

"Are my friends okay?"

"Sure you'll see them where you're headed."

Sword lady lifted the wide, heavy blade out of the dirt and rested it back on her shoulder. Fordo sweat and shivered in the cold, shaking his head. "Meaning, like...in Hell or just down the road a bit?" Fordo clenched his eyes shut, trying to shut out the shaking before he struck.

Blackhat laughed again, "If they're your friends, I'm sure they'll be there at the docks."

"The docks...?" Fordo slumped to the ground, with a gasp of relief, "The docks??"

"Yeah??"

"You mean you're not gonna kill me?"

"What...?" The two warriors both laughed, "Why the hell would we do that?"

Fordo stood up with more effort than he knew he would have needed in a fight. "You son of a bitch! I thought I was sunk! You dropped me in the middle of a fuckin' graveyard!"

Blackhat shrugged and looked around, "We're tired and it's pretty. Look at this shit!" He gestured all around them, "Why the fuck would we kill you?" He laughed

Beads of sweat fell from Fordo's forehead, "I don't know, man, I just...Why would Warren send You Two just to drop me off at the docks?"

"Drop you off??" He laughed, "We've got a bridge to hold, mate."

Fordo couldn't believe it, "You guys are coming with me...?"

Blackhat snickered, "We're going where the fight is with or without your dumbass. Now hurry the hell up, if you can walk." The two warriors continued on down the road, snickering and making more odd hand gestures back and forth to one another.

Right...

Fordo laughed, grateful for the dark now with his burning red cheeks. Embarrassed that he really believed he was worth killing and even worse believing for a moment that his words had 'Convinced' two Blackwyrm Warriors to Join the fight.

*Dumbass...*The word echoed in his head in his father's voice.

Fordo staggered along until he got his footing back. His ribs were bruised, but not broken, far as he could tell stretching and breathing. Hurt like hell, though. He worked his jaw and rubbed his throbbing temple, all tender to the touch, figured the whole right side of his face was gonna have some nasty bruising. Fordo wanted to say he'd taken worse beatings, but he honestly couldn't remember. He's just glad he didn't cry out or anything too embarrassing.

"Oy...What's your name, man?" Fordo asked, catching up behind the two warriors, nearly bumping into them in the pitch black.

Blackhat turned and Fordo caught the faintest shine of a smile, "Name's Doyle." Fordo felt stupid holding up his hand in the dark, but Doyle caught and shook it firmly without hesitation.

"What's your name, girly?"

"Samantha," Her voice was far more soft and airy than Fordo imagined, "But you can call me Sam."

"How're you supposed to be some Blackwyrm badass with a name like 'Sam'?"

"I manage," She smiled, giving his hand a single loose shake making him wonder if they really could see in the dark.

"You don't speak much, huh?"

"Only when spoken to," She said without sign of offense.

Fordo's cheeks burned red again, "I'm sorry about that. I think my stepmom mentioned how I tend to ignore women in conversation...But I wasn't really listening."

She laughed, but he was only half-joking. Growing up, all the women in Scrapyard were either far older or far younger than Fordo, he never really kept their company to his own detriment.

"How come you guys don't hate me like Warren?"

"Why would we?" Sam asked

"Isn't there some inverse of 'Enemy of my Enemy is my friend' type glass?"

"'Enemy of my boss's son is some punk ass kid we don't give two shits about'?" Doyle laughed

"Shouldn't hate your enemies regardless," Sam said

"Isn't that the point?"

"In battle, hate can be as blinding as fear or love. You feel anything too hard, you'll make stupid decisions...Like sounding the alarm a city's not ready for," Sam laughed

"I just wanted everyone prepared."

"Prepared quickly does not mean prepared properly."

"You sound like my dad."

"Balian The Bear's got a voice that cute?" Doyle nudged Fordo's aching ribs.

Fordo winced and laughed, then winced from laughing until he was enveloped by a sudden realization and a shadow of sadness, "You two remind me of my friends..."

"At the docks?"

"In the cave...Ones I lost yesterday."

He shook his head wondering why they would care, why he even brought it up, what was wrong with him until Sam asked, "How so?" seeming sincere.

Fordo had always tried to keep his feelings hidden from everyone, including himself. Disguised them with false fronts and simulated strength. Safe in a little box, locked away and buried under his hopes and dreams and fears. It could have been the quiet or the dark, his aching bones or lack of sleep, the apathetic strangers or the thought of death. Maybe the box was simply too small and ready to burst, but something in that moment had dug it up and cracked it open.

"Jacks was real quiet and smart and wise, like you... And Benji was...none of those things...like your friend here," He nudged Doyle back, "But he was so quick and clever and..." Tears welled up in his eyes, "He made me laugh, or tried to, more than anyone else. Jacks always tried to find the meaning in everything while Benji just tried to find the funny, and I just..."

It hurt to cry, too

"...I miss the hell outta those guys..."

Doyle asked after a long moment, "The twin Limbsmiths?"

Fordo nodded in the dark.

"How did they die?" Sam asked

Fordo bit his cheek, "Running for their lives...From monsters I hope even Warren never meets," Fordo tried to shake the bitterness from his voice and head, "They died heroes, helping me save that little girl. I wasn't brave enough to go down that hole alone, not without Jacks reminding me to think ahead and Benji reminding us everything's not so bad. I was too weak to go without you and too weak to bring you home......"

"Did you save her?" Doyle asked

"We did..."

"Then what are you cryin' for? Sounds to me, they died like men."

"-Like warriors," Sam corrected

"Warrior Men," Doyle nodded, "You had a mission and you saw it through, all of you. There's no better death."

"Would've loved no death."

"Then stay home, be forgotten, let the kid die, and let other fools chase the glory. Nobody made you go down there, any of you. You all made a choice, mate, a choice to feel alive and see if you had the strength to make a difference, and you did. Only a kid and you and your friends have already done some fuckin' good for Aureum...Shit, when I was your age...I was the monster in the cave..."

Sam cut in, "Don't spoil a good death with doubt and mourning. You remember what they lived and died for and, if you love them, you'll keep that going."

"You're right…" Fordo said

"Are they the first people you've lost?" Sam asked

"He's not that young, Sammy. No one's lost no one."

"The bots got my mom when they first came…Right in front of me. I was too young to really process it, you know? But now it's all I think about. Only thing she did with her life was have me, now I'm so afraid of wasting mine. Now…I feel like if I waste my life…Then I waste hers too…And I won't accept that."

Doyle shook his head, "Life isn't wasted or measured in accomplishment, just in how much you give a shit."

"Hm……"

Sam continued, "Your mom got to be your mom and that's not nothing…I'd fight the whole world to be a mother to my little girl again…To be able to…" She trailed off and cleared her throat, "Your friends were young and already had people they loved and helped and saved…They laughed and learned and built people up, quite literally. There's no better life…"

"…And no better death," Doyle said

"You should be proud of their sacrifice…And all it has to teach you…" Sam's tone changed as if talking to herself.

Fordo wiped his eyes, "I kinda like you guys when you're not trying to kill me."

"You'll probably like us when we are."

Fordo laughed, "Thanks for all this…I've been putting it off, I think."

"Don't mention it, mate, just quit crying and do better, it's embarrassing," Doyle laughed

They heard it before they could see the rushing waters. Rounding an invisible bend in the road, the faint glow of lantern light silhouetted the edge of the forest until they finally broke through and the world opened up around them once more. There she was, the Siena River, with the rolling hills of The Yellow Sea beyond. Only a day had passed since his view from Riverwood's peak, but the forest had a way of making every time you see a horizon feel like your first.

Being Riverwood's namesake, the docks themselves were as architecturally impressive as Fordo hoped. The River Ramp was built like a colosseum, the great looming structure where Realwood boats and barges were built and birthed into the long wide canal that runs parallel and feeds into the Siena.

Fordo smiled, spotting a group of people gathered near a smaller barge. Looked to be a few dozen at most, the perfect size. Not for them to hold Gateway, no, but for Fordo to manage on his own, he figured. *A good starter army.*

"Looks like you got yourself your warband," Doyle said

A pit formed in Fordo's stomach, as he looked wide-eyed at the warriors, "My warband...You guys don't want command?"

"We didn't call them here," Sam said

"Never been one to lead," Doyle shook his head

"If you've got the heart and head for it," Sam said, "We'll back any orders that make sense."

***

"Ay, Look who it is!" Chop laughed

"Was starting to think you wouldn't make it!" Carth called

"So was I!" Fordo called back, turning the bruised half of his face into the light.

The assembly was mostly men, with a handful of women, all quiet, varying in age, build, and background. Aside from a few pairs, no one sat or stood that close to one another, leading him to believe they each came individually, a motley crew of nervous nobodies. Much of the group turned to see who else was joining them, most seemed relieved at the sight of Sam, Doyle, and their big ass weapons.

"Fuckin' glass, what happened to you?" Carth walked up to greet Fordo.

"May have been a little hasty with that horn," Fordo smiled, clasping Carth's wrist and thumping his back with a hug. "Warren was a bit more than......annoyed."

"Mother Aure, he kicked the shit outta you!" Chop laughed

"The Baron did that?" A stranger asked, the group was staring nervously at Fordo.

"He did..." Fordo stood a little taller when addressing the group, "And deservedly so. I blew the horns that called you here soon as the warning came. I didn't anticipate the panic it would cause, few people got hurt because of it. That's on me. But

I'd happily do it again if I knew I'd be seeing all you folks here right now."

"All you folks..." A younger stranger scoffed, his knees bouncing nervously where he sat, "How the fuck are we gonna stop the Cogs with thirty people?" Everyone aimed an earnest look at Fordo.

"Whether thirty or a thousand, I was thinking it'd just be Carth and I standing on that bridge."

"Look at us, man. There's maybe five real fighters here."

"You think so?"

The young man looked around, his shaking increased.

"How many fighters were in the last war?" The young man shook his head. Fordo nodded and raised his voice for all to hear, "When the bots first came, how many soldiers were there to stop them? How many battle-ready warriors were between them and our families?" Everyone shook their heads.

"Last time they came we pushed them back with an army of farmers...and fathers! Generations of people who had only known peace and plenty were torched and beaten and forged into the heroes we know today!" Fordo hopped onto a wooden crate and talked to the boy directly, "What is your name?"

"Jacob..."

"What is your trade?"

"I'm a baker..."

"You were born a baker, or you chose to be?"

"I chose to be."

"You also chose to show up......You chose to leave the safety of those trees and fight......to be brave, to take a fuckin' stand! Not because you think we can win, not because you were forced, but because you know in your heart that somebody has to do something!" Everyone sat or stood a little taller.

"A whole city heard my call, and thirty people answered? Good! The fewer the better! The less names for the bards to sing in the inns! For fathers to teach their sons! For the scribes and historians to carve into the Halls Of Remembrance, into our fuckin' Monuments! Less faces to paint in Julian murals depicting the story of the few who fought for them and their future!" Fordo laughed at his own melodrama along with some others.

"We don't know what we're running into. Maybe we're too late to save anyone, maybe Scrapyard is already there in force and they don't even need us," Fordo laughed, "But no matter what happens, no matter what we do or don't find, however we can or can't fight, the world will remember that when it needed us......We showed the fuck up."

That got enough nods to reassure Fordo he'd raised their spirits, at least enough to calm them down.

"Who are you?" A woman asked

Fordo glanced at Doyle who seemed real amused by his little speech, "Just a man trying to give a shit. Now if nobody's changed their mind, everybody load up the barge, we've got work to do and a world to save!"

AL AND MEEKO

6

Al, Auri, Meeko and Dari ventured off that night, at Auri's insistence. Sarah haphazardly stitched together a few old packs into saddlebags for Dari, building a patchwork leather nest for Auri to nestle in and filled the pockets with bread, berries, and rabbit jerky. Bali threw together a roll of tinker's tools for Meeko's paw or Auri's Brace, giving Al a quick rundown of what fixed what that Al forgot immediately.

The goodbyes were short and sweet, filled with tight hugs and impossible promises. Al cried the most when he caught Sarah asking Meeko if she'd ever see them again. *"What are you crying for? I always come back, girly. We always come back."*

Dari moved no quicker than an urgent walk like Benji might to the restroom, but the pace was steady, they made good time down the road. Al was unsure on the sleeping habits of young pillboys, but he figured they could just carry the bags and roll him if need be.

Scrapyard was already reduced to a small puff of white smoke on their rear horizon, leaving home for the second time in what felt like days.

Ten months......

Al winced as the words flashed in his head, bringing with them the sound and pain of his bones breaking against a tree trunk. He shook the thoughts from his head.

We'll be back......We always come back......

Even with the breeze, it was a warm night, a clear night. Perfect for a stroll, no matter how urgent. Al loved how the moonlight turned the waves of grass silver and white. He'd seen it every night for years and it still felt like a whole other planet.

Meeko took the lead. Auri had the genius and silly idea to tie a bundle of grass to drag behind Meeko, giving Dari a scent to chase. It seemed to be working so far, but Al still took the rear, making sure Dari stayed on course with Auri asleep on his back, wrapped up in one of Daisy's quilts.

Every now and then she'd mumble or move, reacting to one dream or another. Al hoped she was okay, though she had every reason not to be. She was worried, of course, but there was something deeper than that, something less clear that went beyond bots and brothers. Something made him want to know what that was and he didn't know why.

Normally he paid no mind to people's personal problems. Lived with Bali for over a year before he knew Sarah wasn't Fordo's mother. Almost two years before realizing Fordo doesn't like her. Brash was always just a silly man with a simple mind, Al never gave thought to his condition, what it meant, why it's there. He never asked, cause he never cared. Like finding a handsome stone with an interesting shape or color or texture, but never picking it up to see the dirt and grubs underneath. He loves Daisy's cakes, he's never asked how they're made. He never delves deeper than the surface, barely knew anything about the things and places and people he loved apart from he loved them and that was enough before, but something was different now.

"You said you didn't think about it, I'm saying always think about it, always consider……"

I've never thought about it……I've never thought about anything……not really. But is that good? Is that wrong? It's nice and easy and naive, maybe. Maybe not wrong……but maybe not good either. How can you truly love someone you don't know? How can you truly help someone you don't understand? How can you claim to be anything you haven't taken the time to be?

Whatever the answer, this was the moment he tried harder, tried to be better, for him, for her, for them, for himself. No more wasting time, taking it for granted. He's taken everything for granted, his friendships, his powers, his unbelievable life. Been spoiled with nothing but love and opportunity since he woke up and he's done nothing with it, given nothing back. Until today.

Though seemingly his simplest creation, Bali's roads were hypnotic, stretching out towards the horizon, the ever moving reeds impossible to focus on. An endless pier across a restless sea, Al lost himself for hours.

Even the simplicity of laying stone and dirt amazed him with enough of it. Just knowing he could walk the length of the continent on a single stretch of dirt was incredible.

From Al's understanding, following the war, thousands of people were displaced. They'd lost their homes and families and joined the fight to get revenge, and find new purpose. But once the war was won......What good is a warless warrior? Not all wished to return to the humble farm lives their families had built for them. They lost their purpose once more, becoming restless, becoming dangerous.

Balian The Bear, Warren II, and Queen Juliana, The Big Three; These self-made heroes and reluctant leaders sensed the dangerous energy in the armies they'd built. They had instilled that pride and need for vengeance and glory in their men for the war times, to turn peaceful craftsmen and farmers into warriors ready and willing to die for their land and families. But the war was over, the monster's slain, and peace must remain.

When The Big Three disbanded their armies, those loyal followers who refused to return home were instead put to work. Set to the task of repairing the ravaged land from the first war and preparing it for the next.

The first task was the construction of the first transcontinental road system, connecting every known city and village on Aureum, both for ease of travel and future evacuation.

The second task was the mass retrieval and removal of the unsightly husks of the monsters that caused so much devastation. Any fallen bots and all their pieces were packed onto wagons and hauled south to the Daisy Mountains to a secluded dumping ground in a small valley between four hills. A twisted mountain of robot corpses filled the valley, piling higher than the hills themselves.

Most of the Free Peoples saw it as a cursed place to be left alone and forgotten, to be pushed aside out of sight and out of mind. But Balian The Bear saw it for what it really was: Endless opportunity, or more importantly, free stuff.

It's incredible how much war can change everything it touches. Because of the war, we can walk across the world without losing our way. We can reclaim lost limbs and learn to walk again. Besides Meeko, every friend I've ever known is a warphan or a refugee. It gave us a home...... gave us a family.

Al laughed to himself, realizing for the first time that everything he knew and loved was a product of the war.

Thousands of people were torn apart by metal monsters and I have something to be grateful for. Is that not insane? Just how much good can come out of objective evil? How much love and joy and friendship can be spawned in the dark? If that's not a reason never to give up, I don't know what is.

Al walked backwards to watch the sunrise, wondering how it gets better every time. A little yawn sounded behind him followed by an exaggerated stretch, dramatic enough to rival Brash's.

"Good morning, girly," Al said without turning around. He'd missed ten months of sunsets, he wasn't missing another.

"Mm......Ahh What the heck?!"

"What, what's wrong?" Al spun around

"Oh, thank Gah," She said sleepily, "You were walking backwards and it scared me. You looked like Cottonhead from behind."

"I have no idea what that is......" Al laughed

"You really aren't from Riverwood," She yawned, holding up fingers to count, "you don't know anything: Cottonhead......Flying Moss Spiders......"

Auri looked around them confused, "I can't believe you made and broke camp without waking me up. I must have been passed out."

"Oh, We didn't make camp, don't worry."

"You mean you walked all night? You said you'd stop when you got tired??"

"Yeah, so we'll stop in a couple days."

She yawned again, "You don't like to sleep??"

"Only when we need to. And only where it's warm, now that I think about it. Otherwise it just kinda feels like dying to me."

"Oh......?" She moved her head in a wide-eyed nod, "Well......Good morning, I guess?" She shrugged

"I'm so sorry," He laughed

"That's so scary! What the heck does that mean?"

"I really need to work on the......just......saying whatever I'm thinking."

"No, that's alright, it's kind of refreshing, actually......"

She grabbed some bread from a pouch and took a bite so small that Al thought she might've just kissed it, "I feel like nobody ever tells me what they're really thinking. I like being small, but most people talk to me like I'm so fragile-which I know I am, physically, but......I'm not so fragile that I can't bear the weight of a genuine thought, I'm not too little to have a real conversation."

"Yeah, Meeko has the same problem. Most people don't actually listen to what he's saying, they just talk to him like he's some kinda baby," Al smiled, "I hope I haven't been doing that to you."

"No, no, I wouldn't have let you come with me if you did. You're pretty good about it. You actually talk to me like I'm a regular-sized human."

"You are a regular-sized human! You're little, you're not two feet tall!"

She took another microscopic bite.

"Oh Glass, how do your legs feel?"

"They don't, really. Did you forget?" She smiled

"You know what I mean."

She sat up and straightened her legs with her hands, then wiggled her feet over and over again. Al didn't notice just how thin they were before. If they were branches on a tree, he'd avoid them for fear of breaking. Bali told him that the brace would support her, but her muscles still needed time to build back up. If she pushed it too hard, she could hurt herself without even knowing.

"It's so weird being able to move them again. I keep picking them up with my hands out of habit."

"What does it feel like?"

"Well, I still can't 'feel' feel anything, but now there's this pressure all around them, kind of like......You ever walk on stilts as a kid?"

"I don't know, I don't remember."

"Oh yeah, well......It feels like that," she laughed, "I don't know how else to describe it."

"Bali told me we should give you a little exercise everyday, get your legs moving and ready to hold you up again."

She smiled a little bit before shaking her head, "We don't have time......"

"Are you sure? Probably be easier to find Wash when you can get around on your own."

"I haven't used my legs in years......Sarah and Bali said it could take just as long to recover."

Al had little concept of time, but especially when it came to healing. He'd broken both of his legs not three days ago and stood up minutes later. He'd only been awake for three years, he imagined spending all three just trying to walk around.

"Not walkin' sinks......" Al nodded

"You think so?"

"You can't run or jump or climb, that fuckin' sinks...... I envy you."

"What? Envy Me? Why?"

"You must be so fuckin' strong and patient, I could never live like that," Al said casually, like being crippled was a job he'd never consider. Auri looked stunned, saying nothing for the longest minute of Al's life. His cheeks burned red, realizing that was probably extremely rude, "I'm so sorry, I didn't mean-"

"No, no I......" Auri grinned and laughed like it was the best joke she's heard in a while, "You know, you are the first person since I fell to admit that? That they couldn't do it......That it sucks not to walk," She laughed some more, "I can't fucking walk! And that fucking sucks!" She yelled and laughed into the empty blue sky.

A smile grew on Al's face.

"No one ever acknowledges how shitty it is, no one! They either baby me or act like it's not a big deal, like......Like that'll cheer me up somehow! Like it's some crazy secret that being crippled is hard and sad! Like me 'Finding Out' is what will ruin my life!"

Al laughed out loud.

Auri continued "'Don't feel bad Auri, you're just like everybody else!' Shut up! Look at me! No I'm not! I'm in the way, I need help dressing myself, I need to be carried to the restroom! I hate it! And Nobody lets me talk about it......Nobody! They shut me up with pillshit like 'You just need to think positively.' or 'Things could be worse.' but I know what they really mean is 'Don't make Me think about it, You're bumming Me out.' Fuck you, this is how I feel, let me talk about it. I just want to talk about it!" Auri was panting by the end, still giggling in between, "Sorry......" She smiled

Al grinned, "Don't ever be sorry for how you feel."

"Been pent up for......a few years now......" She laughed

"I could tell.........What's the worst part, you think? Of not getting around."

"Oh man......" She thought for a moment, "Definitely not being able to get away."

"Away from what?"

"Mostly strangers," She laughed, "I get so many weirdos who walk up to me to talk and I can't just walk away, or say I have somewhere to be, you know?"

"Was I one of those weirdos?" Al laughed

"I was scared you were gonna be, but no, you turned out fun. Some people, lotta kids will just start talking about, I don't know what, for just......Hours. And Cidarian moves so slow that they just kinda follow me around until they get bored. And it......It's awful!" She laughed

"They can always find you the next day 'cause you're stuck on a bug."

"Exactly! You ever have that happen, people who won't leave you alone?"

"Yeah......but I just walk away," Al smirked, letting the bread she then threw at him bounce off his head.

She shook her head, "It's crazy how people can talk so much yet say so little."

"How do you mean?"

"Like, there was this teenage kid who would find me Every afternoon for a Month and tell me everything he'd done since he'd seen me the day before, but he never really did anything. There was no greeting, never any questions, so it wasn't like he was trying to get to know me. He'd just come out of nowhere and be talking next to me for hours until it was dark. Talk about where he went and who he saw, but there were no details or opinions, just like a list of stuff! None of it was funny or interesting or cohesive. There was no story or point, not even really knowing or caring if I'm actually paying attention, just...... talking to talk and I couldn't get away!"

"That kid's a menace. What did you do? Did you find a new spot or tell him to sink himself?"

"No, he's dead, I killed him."

Al burst out laughing.

"No, I don't know what happened to that guy, hopefully he found someone who actually gives a shit, but the only thing I learned from that kid is: If there's a hell, it's next to him."

"Damn......I never met anyone that bad before. The closest thing I have to that, and not quite as extreme, is actually Fordo."

"Fordo, like Bali's son? That's crazy, I thought you guys would be friends."

"I mean he's fine, I guess. He really likes me and I'll never be mean to him for the sake of I'll never be mean to anyone, but......"

"Is he just some kind of idiot?"

"Not in the traditional sense, no. I don't know, he never really left me alone, like since the moment I woke up, I couldn't really get away from him."

"Like he just thinks you're fun and follows you around?"

"Kind of, but it never felt like that was the reason, it was more like......possessive. Like he'd get kind of upset or jealous if I wasn't around him. I don't know how to explain it, but that part wasn't so bad, I didn't really care, we still did everything I wanted to do as long as he tagged along."

"Well, what don't you like about him?"

"I don't know, I don't like how he looks at the world. Like it owes him something, like he deserves more or better. He acts like he's been treated unfairly, like his life isn't amazing. He's really strong and smart and capable, really charismatic, he's got friends and great parents that would love him if he just let them......Just really rubs me the wrong way."

"What do you mean 'let them'?"

"Like......If Fordo's ever working on a project, and Bali offers him help, he'll start a fight over 'How Bali doesn't think he can do it himself', But then the next time Bali doesn't offer him help, he gets sad and complains to me about how 'His dad didn't even try, because he doesn't give a glass about him'."

"That doesn't make Any sense......"

"He does this super backwards thing where he complains about how much he thinks Bali hates him, but rejects Any kind of interest or love or support and it's so just confusing and annoying and......I hate it."

"I wonder what that is......Like how do you get like that?"

"I don't know, and I don't really care, to be honest. I feel like an explanation is never an excuse. It's always a choice to be an asshole. No matter how bad your life or situation, why take it out on whoever's around you? Why make that everyone else's problem?"

***

They did nothing else, for there was nothing else to do, but talk the time and miles away. The roads climbed up and rolled upon the tops of the hills that border The Yellow Sea, using the high ground to avoid the pods of roaming wyrms that patrolled the grassy waves.

Al quickly learned that Auri had a fascination and extensive knowledge of both earthborn creatures and Aureum's insectoid natives.

She told him about how cute the Flying Moss Spiders are that use weird sails on their backs to glide from tree to tree, eating the purple moss that grows up the trunks of realwoods. She told him about how scary the Kuran Catchers are, climbing up and snatching the spiders out of the air like mantis monkeys.

"What's a monkey?" Al asked

"They're really weird, earthborn......kinda look like really hunched, hairy people, I guess. Real strong and ugly, like to jump and climb. Real scary lookin'. So a Kuran's like that, but a little smaller than me with big buggy claws and a buggier head."

"Gross......" Al chuckled

Every now and then Auri would toss a little piece of deer jerky onto the edge of the road ahead mere inches from the grass.

"What's that-"

"Shh!" She'd hold her hand up and stare at the piece of dried meat, both of them flinching and laughing when little claws would shoot from the grass and scrape the scrap of food into cover. Meeko barked and trotted excitedly to where the small creature appeared, hesitantly sticking his head in the grass.

"I love the Prairie Ants......Too pointy to play with, though. My brother and I used to save all the food we didn't like for like a week and hike hours to the edge of the woods just to watch it all get pulled into the grass."

"I never even noticed them before......What do they look like?"

"Real little, no bigger than rabbits. They got big fat digging claws on three little crabby legs that stick out of a sharp rocky looking shell, and these cute little pincer mouths that click when they're angry," She smiled real big, "I want one but they don't like me much."

"I don't like that I don't know where they are," Al laughed, "Like they're nowhere, so now they could be everywhere and they're gonna jump out at us."

"No, they're not dangerous, just little scavengers, keeping the fields clean is all. I know what you mean, though, I used to feel the same way about the Wyrms."

"Used to?"

"Yeah, then one of my books showed me how to spot them, now I see them everywhere, like look there," She pointed out into the meadow below.

"Where?"

"There......See? It's not very big......The little moving bulge in the grass."

Al squinted into the sea, all of it rippling in the wind, all of it flowing and bulging to his eyes, where Al only saw wind-blown reeds, she easily spotted the ridge and furrow of a shallow dragon passing by.

"There, there, look!" She pulled his face close to hers and pointed harder, her finger tracing a single ripple in the many waves, "That grass is moving in a straight line......against the wind, at a different pace than the rest......"

"Oh......You're right......How do you even spot glass like that?"

"You don't look for it specifically, you look at the field as a whole, look at the patterns the wind makes, the big waves, and while you're looking at that, your eyes can usually tell you what's going against that pattern, what's out of place."

"Huh……" Al smiled, "That's so prime."

"They're way easier to spot, the bigger they are. Bigger bulge, usually bother the birds. But the little ones are more fun to find."

"What do we know about them?" Al asked

"They're kind of like giant land whales, actually."

"Like what?"

She then told him how back on earth there were these large creatures that lived in the oceans who just swam around and only ate swarms of krill, which were basically just clouds of sea bugs. The wyrms did something similar with the grubs, just plowing through the dirt.

"Where does all the dirt go?"

"They don't eat the dirt, they sift out all the grubs and just kind of……push it out through the other end. It's a really weird cycle. They eat the grubs, the grubs eat the poop dirt, which is filled with the nutrients of eaten grub."

"Glad I don't have to eat dirt and grubs all day……"

"Be kind of a bummer."

"No wonder they blow through villages every now and then, they're just letting off steam."

"Well, they don't mean to, all they know how to do is Go Forward, we just happen to be in their way sometimes, like a storm passing through. They're not monsters, it's just in their nature."

Meeko barked back at them.

"Hm That's right......Bali said a similar thing about the bots once. I made some comment about 'Evil robots' a year or two ago and he said there's no such thing."

"That's not the same thing, robots aren't natural, they don't have an instinct or nature to drive them, they're just fucked up."

"That's what I told him, but he said 'Exactly. They're not natural and can't make their own decisions. So why should we think they're evil?'"

"They literally got together and killed thousands of people. That sounds like evil to me."

"Yeah, I don't know, I just let it go. It was kinda funny coming from the guy that killed more cogs than anybody."

They'd talked from dawn til dusk, the sun soon resting on the road ahead. He found conversations flowed a lot easier with Auri than Meeko, she had more to say and was a lot less sarcastic. As the sun set, they had one last debate over whether or not sunrise was better. Meeko broke the tie in Al's favor for sunrise.

This night was colder than the last. The wind was the price of a far better view, they kept bundled in blankets to beat the breeze. Meeko spotted the lantern lights of a floating village, maybe ten miles down the road.

Al thought they might reach it before setting up camp, but Auri was asleep and Dari had finally reached his limits. The sweet bug tucked in its many legs, curled into an armored ball, and nestled into the dirt. Much to Al's relief.

Pins and needles flooded Al's aching feet and legs and back, repairing the overworked joints and muscles in minutes. *'Come on, you can take it.'* Fordo would always say, no matter how painful the challenge.

Doesn't mean I like to.

Al shared some rabbit jerky with Meeko who had no complaints on the trip thus far.

"It's not gonna stay easy, but I'm glad it has been."

***

They looked down on the Floating Village at the base of the hill tucked just outside the raised borders of The Yellow Sea. A small town of grub farmers, only a couple dozen buildings or so, all raised up on pier-esque platforms. Scattered farm bots tilled the colorful squares of even patterned farmland stretching out south like a quilted blanket around the village to the edges of Bleakwood. Al was always fascinated by the idea of seismic engineering. Whole towns raised up high above the ground on platforms, floating on a web of wooden beams with flexible foundations to combat and avoid the tremors and devastation of passing wyrms.

"The whole thing disperses and distributes vibrations! Somebody thought of that, designed it, built it; is that not amazing, just what people can do?"

Auri smiled, "You're gonna poop your pants when you see Riverwood."

"Fiona Farms......" Al read the roadside sign, "That's right, this is where Sarah gets her carrots and potatoes and whatnot, don't remember it being so far..."

"Have you been here before?" Auri asked

"Bali and Ford found Meek and I in those woods..." Al nodded at the tangled mass of Bleakwood Forest and its colorful canopy.

"What were you two doing in there?" Auri stared in wonder at the gold and purple leaves that paved the southern horizon.

Meeko barked.

Al half smiled, "Mostly bleeding, he says...They found us after some kinda fight we don't remember with some monsters we never saw...But we're lucky they found us at all in the middle of the woods like that."

"Glad they did," Auri smiled

"Us too..." Al laughed, "Um, to answer your question: Kinda. We passed through here on our way home. Climbed through the foundations a minute, but didn't stop."

"Stopped here for a day on my way to Scrapyard..."

Didn't seem too thrilled about it by her tone.

"We miss anything prime?"

"Nope!" She laughed and shook her head, "People were real weird...Standoffish...did Not like Cidarian."

"Their loss. We don't got time for tours anyhow...You hungry?"

Without the time or need to visit the village, they enjoyed the view while eating breakfast and playing Spot The Wyrm.

"Look out there," Auri pointed far out into the sea. Even from miles away, there was no mistaking the signs of a massive passing drill dragon. A herd of elk raced across the grass, scattering a cloud of crows as the ground bulged and broke in the wyrm's wake. The scaly arch of its back broke through the surface as it dove deeper into the ground.

"That's the biggest one I've ever seen," Al said

"It's about to breach, I think," Auri mumbled through a mouthful of bread.

Sure enough the twisting mass of tusks and teeth erupted from the earth with an explosion of dust. They heard the blast and felt the tremor.

"Whooa!" They both said in unison, grinning from ear to ear.

The beast shot into the air like a twisted stone tower before it roared a deep, bassy, hornlike blast and arched downward, crashing back from whence it came.

They both clapped and cheered from their seats, watching the body chase the head back into the ground, the ghost of it remaining in a smokey archway of displaced dirt.

Al stood up and cheered, "That was awesome! The sound was so prime!"

"I wish I could make that sound."

"Oh man! You just reminded me of something!" Al dug through his pack and found Andre's beautiful horn, "Look at this!"

"Whoa, what is that??"

"A horn I traded for with some weird guy a few days ago. I haven't blown it yet. I wonder if it sounds like a wyrm too."

"Well what are you waiting for?" Auri laughed

"You don't think the village will mind? It's still early......"

"Naw, if they hear wyrms all the time, this should be fine. Go on, bloow it, bloow it!"

Al laughed, "Alright, here it goes......" *One loud noise, huh?* Al raised the horn to his mouth, took in the deepest breath of his life, and blew as hard as he could.

Bwrrrrrrrrrrrrrrrrrrrrrrrrm!

Auri covered her ears, the light bassy blast shot out over the fields. A crisp, clean noise that sounded vaguely like if a wyrm was a lady. The mental image of a giant scary wyrm with long blonde hair made Al chuckle.

"Ah glass, that's prime as hell!" Al laughed

Meeko howled in excitement.

"Again! Again!"

Bwrrrm! Bwrrrrrrrrrrrrrrrm!

Al blasted away, leaning backwards, the sound bouncing off the hills, echoing out over the sea. Al fell back onto his butt at Meeko's side, petting his panting boy. "You like that, Meeks? Maybe I'll find a horn that sounds like you someday."

"That's so fun...It's so Loooud!" Auri reached her hands out to hold it.

Al tossed it into her lap with a smile, "Too loud?"

"No, It's perfect! Whoa...and so much detail!"

"Can probably use it to distract bots, if we need to. Maybe call for help, but not exactly a sound people would run to. I don't know...We'll find a use for it."

"We Have a use for it! It's fun as heck!" Auri grinned

Meeko's panting stopped suddenly and his back straightened, ears standing straight up. "What's wrong boy?" Meeko barked out over the sea and took a few steps backwards.

"What's wrong Meeks?"

Al and Auri noticed the distant rumble at the exact same time, stronger than the last and growing stronger still. Countless cawing crows guided their eyes back out over the field to a familiar bulge of earth now heading in their direction.

"Auri, is that......?"

"I think so......"

"Are we safe up here? They can't dig up hills, right?"

"They don't Like to......I don't know if they Can't......"

They could hear the ground breaking over the endless cawing as the dragon churned the very world before it, its trail of mounds curving even more toward where they stood.

"Oh Fuckin' glass......Alright, we have to go, we have to go!"

Dari's legs all tucked into his shell at once as he curled into a defensive ball.

"No, no, Dari, hey! We gotta go!" It was no use, he was hunkered down tight.

"Al......?" Auri looked panicked, tears were forming.

"Ah Fuck! Come on, girly!" He threw his pack to the ground and snatched Auri up from her perch.

The scaly arch of the wyrm's body broke through the surface as it dove deeper into the ground near the bottom of the hill.

"Oh Glass, it's gonna breach!" Al rushed down the road with Auri in his arms. He ran for their fucking lives. There's no way they could outrun it, but maybe they could get out of its-

KOOOM
BWAAAAAAAAAAAAAAARRRRRRRR-RRRRRRM!!!

"AAAAAAAAHHHH!"

He couldn't help but look as the twisted, roaring mass of tusks and teeth erupted from below, conjuring a storm of rock and dirt, shooting into the sky, towering over the hill, and arching its head as if aiming directly for Al and his few frail friends. For the first time Al looked straight into the swirling, jagged, earth crushing abyss that is a wyrm's cavernous mouth. A god's fathomless maw. If anything could kill Al, it is being crushed by a mountain of bone, buried in an avalanche of earth, and shredded in a tornado of teeth. His knees buckled beneath him, dropping them both to the ground.

"Meeko, Run!" He screamed, squeezing his eyes shut, hopelessly shielding Auri's sobbing body with his own.

I'm sorry dad............

"AAAAAAAAHHHH!!!"

KRAKOOOM!!!

The Wyrm crashed back into Aureum as if from space, the road exploding only a couple yards behind them, tearing the world from beneath their feet, blasting Al and Auri down the side of the hill, tumbling towards the village. Al hugged her as tight as he could, taking most of the impact.

They bounced hard and broke apart, Al flailing as he fell. He made the mistake of holding out his arm to brace himself. Crying out as the bones snapped in his wrist, the sharp ends ripping, tearing out through his skin. He rolled to a stop, screaming in pain, tears streaking down his dirt-covered cheeks.

Crying and shaking, saliva spraying from between his clenched teeth, he did his best to look around for his friends. "Meekooo......? Aur-"

KOOOM
BWAAAAAAAAAAAAAARRR-RRRM!!!

The Wyrm burst from the side of the hill with another deafening roar. Al heard the collective scream of dozens of people. Looking in horror as the wyrm launched and crashed directly onto the floating village below, crushing and splintering the wooden structures like glass.

Al sobbed.

Shaking like a madman, he gripped his splintered wrist, slippery with blood, and forced the protruding bones back through his shredded skin and into place. His voice cracked and broke as he let out a primal scream of pain. He squeezed the bones as hard as he could until the pins and needles washed through his arm, warily watching his wounded wrist warp and close once more.

Normally he would take his time to adjust, but he had more to worry about than crooked bones. Stumbling to his feet when he could, he searched frantically for Meeko and Auri.

"Meeko!" He called. Meeko materialized next to him through the dust cloud. "Oh Glass, are you alright?" Al hugged his boy, drying his tears on Meeko's fur. Meeko licked Al's bloody wrist. "I'm okay, buddy. We gotta find Auri." Meeko disappeared back into the cloud. Al coughed the dust from his lungs while Meeko guided him through.

"Meeko......" She cried

"Auri!" Al coughed

"That's......That's a lot of blood," Auri stared at Al's wrist.

"I'm okay, I promise. Are you alright?"

Al held her head and looked for wounds. She was shaking as much as he was, her face smeared with blood and dust. He found shallow cuts on her head and neck, and her left arm was tender around the elbow, possibly a fracture. Miraculously, her legs didn't resemble bags of broken glass, like Al feared, the braces kept them intact.

"Was that our fault?" Auri cried

"I don't know......" He rocked her back and forth, "But we're okay, we're gonna be okay." He hugged her tight and kissed her head.

More screams sounded behind them and through the dust they watched the silhouette of a half standing building creak, slide, and crash down from its raised foundations.

"Do we have time to help?" Al asked after a long panting silence. Auri nodded. "Let's go, girly." He scooped her up and carried her into the dust cloud.

***

The Wyrm was long gone, its tremors a distant rumble by the time they reached the village. Less than half of it could still be called 'floating'. Most of the buildings looked more like piles of used matches. People were coughing and crying and crawling about. Still in shock of constructing a home to weather the burrowing beasts from below, only to have a Drill Dragon come out of the fucking sky and destroy it anyway.

Al sat Auri on a barrel by the wreckage while he and Meeko searched for survivors. They heard the muffled angry voice of an older man buried under the nearest house, cursing and yelling at the top of his lungs. "Damnit, someone get this shit off of me!"

"Oy, Are you alright down there?" Al called.

"No, I'm not alright, you fuckin' jackass, I'm trapped under my fuckin' kitchen!"

"Are you hurt?"

"You're gonna be if you don't get me the fuck out of here right the Fuck now!"

Al shook his head and mustered the vaguest shadow of a laugh, "Alright, alright, give me a second." Al started digging him out, lifting beams and tossing them to the side.

"Oh No, by all means, Take Your Fuckin' Time, you Lazy Cunt! I'm only suffocating to death!"

"Hey!" Auri yelled, her voice still shaking, "He's digging you out with a broken wrist, why don't you shut your mouth, save your air, and let him save you?"

"Why don't you shut your mouth before I come out there and shove my grub in it!"

Al and Auri looked at each other in shock. Al pointed at the pile and shook his head, Auri nodded. Al picked up the beams he already threw to the side, and put them back on the wreckage.

"Hey! Hey! What the fuck was that?" The old man yelled.

Al scooped Auri back up and they moved on to the next collapsed house over. Meeko quickly found survivors, Al would mark the spot and call for aid.

Other villagers were coming to their senses and joined the excavation with ropes, shovels, and pry bars, throwing Al a suspicious glance whenever they finally noticed the stranger in their midst.

"Help me with this..." Al called, lifting a collapsed wooden wall.

"Who the fuck are you?"

"Someone trying to help, now lift."

Al went to work, hauling off splintered beams as fast as he could until he'd uncovered a person, or a body, moving on to the next house. There were a lot more bodies than people. And a lot more pointed questions than he had time to answer.

Al uncovered a young man, pinned at the waist by a heavy beam. "Hey......" The man said, coughing up blood, eerily calm, "Can you help me out, man?"

"Don't worry, I'll get you outta there, buddy......" Al wedged his fingers underneath the beam and heaved as hard as he could without hurting himself, but it wouldn't budge.

"This doesn't feel right......" The man shook his head, "Something's wrong, really wrong."

"Don't worry, we'll get you outta there......" Al turned and cupped his mouth with his hands yelling, "I need some help over here!"

"So does everyone else!" An older man yelled back, running past without slowing down.

"The fuck is wrong with everybody...?" Al sucked his teeth shouting, "OY!" stopping three younger men in their tracks, "Help me!"

"That's Brian down there!" One of the men smacked another and all three rushed down to help. "Who the hell are you?"

"Who gives a glass, fuckin' help me."

The men all had the same face with various builds, family perhaps. One short and stocky, one thin and lean, the third tall and muscular.

The stocky one grabbed the trapped boy's shoulders, ready to drag him out, while the other two helped Al lift with barely a budge.

"Ah...Fuck, that's heavy..."

"Gaah! Stop!" Brian screamed, "Don't pull me, something's not right..."

"We're gonna get you out, brother...Nathan, help us with the beam!" Said the lean

"On three...all we've got..." The tall one said in the deepest voice Al had ever heard. They all nodded. "Ready stranger?"

"Aye..."

"One......Two......Three!"

'Come on, you can take it......'

They pulled with all their might, faces blood red, the beam fighting back, trying to rip their arms from their sockets. "Come on!" The tall man grunted. The beam raised an inch. "Heave!" It raised another. "Heeeave!"

"Raaaah!" Al pulled until his arms went numb, until his world went black. He Lifted until every muscle in his body was fired as one, lifted until his tendons tore, and blood vessels burst in his nose, lifted until the beam finally rose. Just enough to drag and drop to the side of the man and see he'd been completely skewered by a splintered crossbeam.

They dropped the weight with a crash and Al puked into the pile of rubble, nearly collapsing. Two of the men patted him on the back as he coughed and shook, pins and needles flooding his whole body. "Good lad..." The tall man said with a grin, "Good to see some...oh..."

"Oh man, this......this is too much blood......This is way too much blood......" Brian coughed, looking wide-eyed at his squirting, bloody mess of a stomach. The three others stood in silent horror, Nathan putting pressure on the wound in vain.

"Alright, what do we do?" Brian stuttered, looking desperately at the men, "Jay what do we do?"

The lean man shook his head, tears in his eyes.

"Ty?"

The tall man did the same with an open mouth.

Al crawled over to the man. He didn't know the body could hold so much blood. Brian locked eyes with him. "Hey, help me, okay......Something's wrong, something's Really, really wrong here, okay, I don't feel right, I just don't......I just......"

Al trembled and wept while the man pleaded with him, begging him for help, begging him for something, anything. Al didn't know what to do. He'd never seen so much blood. *I'm sorry, I can't......I don't know how to help you, man. I don't know what you want from me, You're fuckin' dying...... You're.................Dying.....................* Al sobered up with a swallow and sigh, his hands and breath steadying as he looked the man in his scared green eyes.

"Help me please, I need you to......"

"Shh, listen to me......" Al whispered

"I don't feel right, I......"

......Don't be afraid......

"Listen to me......listen to me......OY!" The man flinched as Al snatched and squeezed his bloody hand. He looked up at Al like he was seeing the face of Mother Aure.

"You're gonna die........

                    That's what's happening........."

The man's eyes went wider, looking back and forth between the three other men, all with tears in theirs. "No, no, no, no, wait, wait, wait, wait. Hold on...Hold on......Hold On......!"

"It's alright, look at me...Look at me......" Al took the man's face in his other hand.

"No, no, no......"

"It's okay, look at me, hey......Keep looking at me......"

The man went quiet, tears flowing down the sides of his face, looking at Al with a new stillness.

"It'll......wash over you......Start to feel warm, nice and warm..............Let it come......"

The sorrow faded from his face, replaced by disbelief.

The other men let their tears fall.

"Let your thoughts go, Only good things......All the good things......"

Acceptance washed over the man's face.

"Who do you love, hm......? Who's waiting for you......?" Al smiled, weakly.

The man cried again, "Mother......My mother......"

"You see her?"

Brian nodded

"Let her take you......She'll show you the way......"

The man squeezed Al's hand. He shivered and choked, swallowing back the blood, until a wave of peace rolled over him. He looked up vacantly at the sky and mouthed some words that weren't meant for them with a slight smile. His hand went limp in Al's......and like that, he was gone.

Al heard a lot more crying than just the three men. He looked up to find Auri and several villagers looking down on them. Jay and Ty helped Al up to his feet. "What did you do?" they whispered, staring at Al like they'd just witnessed some great miracle.

"I just......sent him on his way......" Al wiped his tears only to get more blood on his cheeks, "His name Brian?"

Nathan nodded, "Brian......He's our fletcher......and our friend."

"Rest and be remembered......" Al said without thought as he kissed his own fist and gently closed the man's empty eyes.

"Rest and be remembered......" The three men repeated in unison, glancing at one another like they hadn't meant to.

Al nodded again, wiping away more tears. "Come on, then...... there's still more to find......"

***

The Wyrm carved a scar through the flowers and the fields, dragging half the village with it, scattering bits of shops and homes alike hundreds of yards from their foundations. Countless tools, toys, and treasures littered the landscape, entire lives crushed and smeared into the dirt. Al clenched his quivering hands into quivering fists and dropped down next to Auri and Meeko on the edge of the splintered pier. Auri rubbed his back, still clutching her hurt arm to her chest in a makeshift sling.

"Can't stop..." Al stared at his hands, trembling as if winter had come for them alone.

"You need to breathe..." Auri whispered, laying her head on his shoulder, "Breathe..."

"I know we have to..." Al shook his head, "But how do we keep going after this glass?"

Auri rubbed his shoulder and sighed, "There's nothing more we can do...They wouldn't want our help anyhow...they barely let you dig."

"You wanna know somethin' fucked up...?" Al chewed the inside of his cheek, "Fifteen people wounded......twenty three fuckin' sunk, dead, forever....and all I can think about is how Balian's gonna come this way......and somehow know this was me......"

"Al, how the fuck is any of this your fault?" Auri asked in a hushed, almost angry voice, "How the fuck could we Ever know that this could happen??"

"I blew the horn..."

"You blew A horn, that's It..." she said in a stern whisper, "A horn You didn't make, that did something You could have never guessed possible in a million years..."

"Auri, 'Didn't mean to' doesn't mean 'Not my fault'."

"Lower your voice..." Auri glanced behind them, "It's bad luck, Al...Or worse, a fucked up trick by whoever traded you that thing. But that's all it is...You can't blame yourself for your own bad luck..."

"Auri, I fucking killed these people with my own bad luck!"

"Lower...your fucking...voice..." Auri shot through her teeth, leaning forward, glancing nervously behind them once more, the blood draining from her already pale face the moment she did.

A low growl rumbled within Meeko. Al turned to find his fur standing on end as he stared back at over a dozen dust covered villagers lurking and looming around them in an ever tightening circle.

Auri took Al's hand.

Al's heart quickened as his eyes locked with one angry pair after another.

"You had some part in this, stranger?" An older woman asked, her eyes the blood red of weeping.

Al's trembling returned as he stood to face the people whose lives he'd just ruined, swallowing the fear before saying, "Aye..."

"Al...don't..." Auri looked desperate, but not as desperate as the rest of them. They needed to hate him, and he needed to face them, to take responsibility.

"I think I called it..."

"Ya think you called it?" A man laughed without smiling, "And how the fuck would a sunken little twat like you call a thing like that, ay? Riddle me that..."

"I um..." Al swallowed back the fear, "I blew a horn I traded for, for the first time... sounded real similar to a wyrm's roar." Al watched any vague amusement or disbelief vanish from the crowd's eyes.

"That noise this morning..." The man sneered and scratched his head with a pry bar, "That was you?"

"Didn't know how it would sound, I didn't know what it would do, what it could do...I think I called the Wyrm...I'm so sorry...I didn't mean to..."

"Didn't mean to..." The man nodded, "Didn't mean

to!" Al watched every muscle in the crowd get tense. "Didn't mean to crush my home! Didn't mean to kill my boy!" The crowd started shouting all at once, all over each other, all getting closer and closer.

"Al...Al!" Auri cried, holding onto his leg.

"Wait, wait, Wait!" Al put his hands up, ducking as the pry bar flew just above his head.

Hordes of hysteric villagers surrounded them, pushing in all around, pointing, screaming, reaching. Al pleaded, raising his hands, "No, Wait, Please, I'm so sorry! Don't hurt them!" But they heard none of it. Grief and rage had taken them, there was no negotiating.

"Get him!" They rushed forward all at once.

Meeko jumped between Al and the mob, biting a man's leg only to be kicked by another off the pier and down onto the wreckage thirty feet below with a crying bark. Auri lunged to catch him but wasn't quick enough. "Meeko!" Al cried, immediately seized and restrained by a dozen angry arms before he could jump after his boy.

"Al!" Auri yelled

"Auri!" Al grabbed Auri's hand, fighting as hard as he could to stay near her, "No matter what happens! Take me with you! No matter what! I'm sorry!"

"Al, please!"

"I'm gonna get you home! I promise! It's going to be okay! I'm gonna-Ahh!"

"Al, wait!"

The mob half dragged, half carried Al into its center, yanking his hair and clothes and skin, scratching and hitting him, all the while screaming an incoherent swirl of vengeful thoughts.

"Beat him!"

"Kill him!"

"Hang him!!"

"Hang him!!!" They cheered, quickly coming to consensus, casting their votes with shouts and jeers. Al sobbed, bombarded with a storm of fists and feet, he'd never known hate like this, but what was far more devastating was he knew he deserved it.

"No, no, please! Stop, no, Al!" He heard Auri pleading faintly beneath the insults and the screaming.

Someone stomped on his chest, crushing the air from his lungs just before a rugged rope found its way around Al's neck, scraping and burning his skin, pulled tight like he was part of the knot. Purple-faced, he clawed desperately at his throat like maybe he could dig out the air his brain was screaming for.

His body left the ground, hoisted up by the mob, carried over their heads towards the edge of the pier until he was looking upside down at the wreckage. Meeko's body lying motionless below. He squeezed his eyes shut.

You're gonna come back. We're gonna come back. Please come back! We need to come back! Plea–

Fordo
6

'*Battle Barge*'...Fordo reflected fondly on an old childhood daydream. He was always fascinated by the design of Riverwood's Barges. Not aesthetically, no, at the end of the day they were no more glamorous than a wet wooden rectangle. But he loved the idea that each barge was born to be destroyed. Without a motor strong enough to fight the Siena's currents, every trip was one way: Downstream.

Through clever carpentry, each barge was sturdy as a bridge, but every plank and beam ready to be removed and repurposed at a moments notice. Broken down and transformed bit by bit until every part had become a home or shop or cart or tool. There wasn't a building along the three hundred mile length of the river that didn't begin as a barge.

'*Hence the name: Riverwood*' He remembered his father's voice on their first visit to the city. '*They cut it up, send it down, it gets turned into something else.*'

Every Barge was lined with ballistas. Though technically harpoons and grappling hooks, used to slow, anchor, and reel the barge back to the land, Fordo always pictured them as battle-ready bolt throwers.

He imagined his own barge, crewed by his friends. They'd build it up with bunkers and barricades, raiding boats and villages alike. The crew ever evolving The Battle Barge, breaking down and absorbing conquered materials until their home had ascended into an unstoppable floating fortress filled with stolen loot and happy River Pirates.

Admittedly a flawed fantasy, both morally and conceptually, even for the ten year old son of a war hero. But at this moment, Fordo found himself floating down the river with a crew of his friends, towards a glorious battle, and he couldn't help but smile.

With a breeze gentling the heat of the sun and space on the barge for double the crew, it was smooth sailing down the Siena. They drifted down the golden countryside with a fleet of fluffy clouds, casting round racing shadows across the rolling fields. *What a beautiful day to go to war.*

Fordo worked it out with both the Toms, their resident BargeBoys, if they steer in shifts, having two-man teams work the pushboat at all hours, they should arrive at Gateway in a day and a half. Not a lot of time, but maybe enough for Fordo to cement himself as Leader and forge this rabble into a half-decent warband.

Fordo found a pencil and paper on the pushboat, deciding to take stock of the crew and their resources. He introduced himself to the already forming cliques as they settled in to rest for the morning, jotting down their names, ages, occupations, and war history. He then organized them by age and marked them into categories, Those who fought, Those who can, and Those who'll try their best.

1. *Hunter* 17 *Kid,* *Civ*
2. *Wesley* 17 *Kid,* *Civ*
3. *Jacob* 19 *Baker,* *Civ*
4. *Fordo* 20 *Tinker,* *Fit*
5. *Carth* 20 *Smith,* *Fit*
6. *Bethany* 24 *Artist,* *Fit*
7. *Luca* 25 *Tailor,* *Fit*
8. *Tommy* 26 *BargeBoy,* *Civ*
9. *Virgil* 27 *Carpenter,* *Fit*
10. *Shelby* 27 *Weaver,* *Civ*
11. *Patch* 30 *Tanner,* *Civ*
12. *Jack* 31 *Cutter,* *Fit*
13. *Luke* 32 *Cutter,* *Fit*
14. *Johnny* 32 *Farmer,* *Fit*
15. *Sam* 33 *Warrior,* *Vet*
16. *Thomas* 34 *BargeBoy,* *Fit*
17. *Doyle* 35 *Warrior,* *Vet*
18. *Jack* 35 *Cutter,* *Vet*
19. *Jane* 35 *Hunter,* *Vet*
20. *John* 35 *Carpenter,* *Fit*
21. *Chris* 36 *Guard,* *Vet*
22. *Rich* 36 *Janitor,* *Civ*
23. *Lady* 37 *Chef,* *Vet*
24. *Chop* 40 *Butcher,* *Vet*
25. *William* 41 *Cutter,* *Fit*
26. *John* 41 *Farmer,* *Fit*
27. *Brandon* 44 *Hunter,* *Vet*
28. *John* 55 *Guard,* *Vet*

"Better mix than I expected…" Fordo mulled over his list with Carth, Chop, Sam, and Doyle, "Nine veterans, twelve fighters, seven civilians."

"Don't have time to train civilians," Doyle said

"Even civilians can pull a trigger," Fordo figured, "We'll keep them on trap control, if we have time to set them. Plus this lady Jane says she's pretty good with a cross, we'll have her train them on ballistas and bows. We keep them high up, out of the mix, helpin' us out with some razor rain. Agreed?" They all nodded.

Fordo gestured to Sam and Doyle, "Do you two mind training as well? Just to try and organize the chaos a bit, remind people which ends are pointy." Sam and Doyle glanced at each other and smiled, like they'd placed a bet on whether or not he was going to ask.

"Would be our pleasure," Sam smiled

Fordo nodded "Sam, take the hammers. Doyle's on Lancers, of course," He turned to Carth and Chop, "Carthy, I need you makin' rounds with Chop, help keep spirits up."

"Oh I've got something that'll cheer 'em up," Chop chuckled, Carth nudging him in the ribs.

Fordo suppressed a smirk, "Do whatever you gotta do, we can't work with a bunch of nervous wrecks all bumping into each other. Keep 'em laughin', smilin', focused, anything but worried. You find someone freakin' out too hard, we gotta sink that glass before things get dangerous, prime?"

"Prime," Carth nodded

"Let's get them gathered."

***

"Here's what we know..." Fordo stood before the crew with his friends at his back, "Gathii Nuru ran himself bloody for days without rest just to warn us. He passed out from exhaustion after a brief message: Hilltop is gone, the bots are back, and they're worse than before. So all we really know is that we don't know glass..." The crew shifted and swallowed.

"Now 'Worse' could mean anything: Stronger, faster, smarter, greater numbers, we have no idea. I don't tell you this to scare you, but prepare you. We could face anything down there, so that's what we'll be ready for."

Carth and Chop carried a long heavy crate and dropped it next to Fordo with a clunking thud, "Lucky for us, we are not unprepared. We have been blessed for our bravery with a few gifts," Fordo drew his hammer and drove the spike under the lid of the crate, popping it off with a single satisfying pull, revealing neatly packed rows of oiled crossbows and lance point spears. "Thanks to the Baron's preparations and paranoia, there was a well-kept armory at the docks, now in our care. We will not go naked into this fight. Everyone will be provided with reliable weapons and reminded how to use them." The crew looked relieved, clapping each other on the shoulders, some laughing nervously like they thought they'd have to fight with their fists.

"Additionally, this barge was set to sail off on this fine morning long before the horns blew. It is stocked full of food, trade goods, building materials, and a metric fuck ton of heavy realwood. You will meet a bot long before you go cold or hungry. But even more exciting: Traps, Barricades, Fortifications, the means for everything and anything we can think to build to give us an edge in this fight is on this boat. We Are Not Unprepared." The crew nodded, their backs straighter and eyes brighter.

"Lastly, I don't know if you can tell, but these two aren't from around here," Sam and Doyle stepped forward, "This is Sam and Doyle, they hail from the humble halls of Blackwyrm, The Colosseum Of Fools. Founded by folks who love killing bots so much that they pretend never stopped. Warriors, through and through, experts in the art of monster slaying. They will be our teachers and you will heed their words like they'll save your life, because they just might. By the end of today you will all have been given meals, weapons, projects, and lessons. Use all of these gifts to ready yourselves for what's to come."

"We may not know what we're up against…But neither do they…Whatever comes across that bridge, it has to deal with Us, now. Find out what We've become. We are not the peaceful workers they ambushed all those years ago. Neither are we those spineless Cowards who ran south. We are the angry generation of strengthened warriors who remember what they did to us and we will repay those memories with vengeance………Let's get to work."

The crew nodded, a few clapped, the rest stood at attention, eager for orders. Fordo suppressed a smile, proud he didn't sink his speech. Carth handed Fordo his list of names and one by one, he assigned them their weapons. All civilians were given crossbows and sent off with Jane to train. Most of the veterans had brought their own weapons, the rest of the fighters were given a choice between spiked hammers and thrown lances, with a fairly even split.

Fordo joined the Hammers, along with Carth and Chop, though Ford was by far the smallest member. He was never much of a thrower, preferring the heart-pounding adrenaline of close-quarters combat. To Fordo's surprise, Sam and Doyle decided to train both groups in tandem, giving their lesson as one.

"Listen up, dregs!" Doyle lit another smoke, "Far as we're concerned, you're all civilians to us, just as green as our young Crossboys, shooting hay over there. It's been well over a decade since you've seen moving metal, so we're gonna start from the beginning."

Sam planted her sword into the deck, "We do not doubt your individual deeds and abilities, but against a bot they don't mean a thing. Alone, none of you are a match for a single bot, but together, together we can bring down any monster."

"Now the bots, in all their shapes and forms," Doyle continued, "Are all built the same way: With hard shells and soft joints. Neck, shoulders, hips, elbows, knees, you only need to target these, if it can bend, you break it. The key to Cog Killing is immobilization. Trip 'em up, jam their joints, spike their heads, that's all there is to it."

Sam stepped forward, "This is not a fair fight, so we will not fight fairly. This war will be won with traps and cunning. There is no winning in a straight fight. We build traps, funnels, walls, anything that can take them out or slow them down before they reach us. Our Only job as warriors is to stop the few who make it through. Slow them with bolts, drop them with spears, finish them with spikes. That is the way."

"Any questions?" Doyle asked

"I got a question," Luca the tailor took a sewing needle out of his mouth and gestured to the two warriors with stiff tattooed hands, "You're saying they get up close and we're donzo, correct?"

"One hit's all it takes, mate."

Luca's speech and movements were all slow and deliberate, like you'd hear him creak if it were quiet enough. Fordo had never met a man so prime, he considered emulating that same cadence if he could. "If that is the case, I love the style, the stitching looks excellent, but why wear the armor?"

Sam nodded, yanked her sword from the deck, and swung full speed at Doyle's chest. The crew gasped and took a step back, but Doyle dove backwards, the blade barely missing his hat as he rolled away onto his back. Sam didn't let up, each heavy swing crashing and biting splintered chunks out of the deck and crates, the blade flying right through where Doyle would have been, but he flipped and dodged and rolled like a Julian acrobat just in time, avoiding every strike by hurling his body in a new direction. Reminding Fordo of the young thief at the markets, Doyle launched himself into the air with his spear, up over Sam's head and landed safely onto a stack of crates behind her, still holding his cigarette.

"No matter how big and strong you think you are," Doyle said, taking another puff, "the bots are bigger and stronger. Unless you're built like Ingram Fuckin' Iron-Cast, agility is your only defense. You either keep them away or get out of theirs. Light armor lets us throw ourselves around however we need to without bashin' our bones on everything. Less pain, less distractions, less tired, less soar, we can stay focused on staying alive."

Luca gave an approving nod, "You two don't disappoint."

Fordo stepped forward with an idea, "There's a couple crates of leathers packed back by the pushboat. We've got a leathersmith, a weaver, and a tailor on board. After training, you three can throw together some elbow and knee pads, something to get us going, ease the work and the fight a bit."

Luca hit him with a slow smile and a pointed needle, "Now there's an idea."

"Excellent," Sam smiled, "Now everyone arm yourselves, it's time to see what you're made of."

***

Fordo fared better than most, even with his aching ribs. Quick with his hammer, light on his feet, but he still lacked the necessary strength to adequately pierce the pot used to simulate bot armor. Sam told him to focus on accuracy and aim for the knees, leaving the kill shots to the heavy boys. *Gave me all your stubbornness and anger, couldn't share some of your strength and size, pops?*

The rest of the crew performed about as well as Fordo could have hoped, with a few standouts and exceptions. Carth and Chop both punched through their pots like Oldworld plastic. Luca could launch a lance as far and accurate as Doyle. "Just a big needle," He grinned. Bethany the artist dodged circles around Sam's strikes like it was rehearsed, her long floaty hair chasing after her like a trail of smoke. Both Jacks, three of the four Johns, and the rest could all handle themselves.

Only a few people were worth worrying about. Guard John, their oldest veteran on board, as well as Virgil the carpenter both had arthritic knees so sunk they'd be better off trading them for botsthetics. And William, an old cutter, was a lot more vocal on his superior techniques and experience than he was true to his word. *That how you missed the last war, Willy? Busy jerking yourself off.*

Fordo, Sam, and Doyle checked in with Jane and the civilians, still at target practice. They found them practicing loading the ballistas, shooting harpoons harmlessly into the deep open water and reeling the bolts back in. Jane reported they all seemed fairly comfortable with a cross, all aiming within a decent grouping. Jacob Baker and the siblings Hunter and Wesley, the three youngest members on board had made a game of loading as quickly as shooting and were exceptionally fast.

Training wasn't more than a few hours. They didn't want to beat the glass out of the crew, just wake up their confidence and muscle memory enough to not freeze up in a fight. Fordo made a new list, assigning everyone a project to form some bonds and hopefully keep their minds from wandering too far into the dark.

Keep them busy, keep them brave.

Luca, Patch, and Shelby were set on armor assembly. "Knees, elbow, shoulders, anything more is extra. Focus on function, maybe comfort if possible, but don't have to be pretty."

Chop and Lady, a chef around Chop's age, were on dinner duty.

"Do you have a preference?" Lady asked

"Warm and delicious," Fordo smiled, "this could be our last cooked meal for a while, so don't hold back."

"Could be our last meal, period," Chop chuckled, sharpening his knives.

"That's the spirit."

Wesley and Hunter insisted they needed a flag, something to rally behind and employed Jacob and Bethany to help them.

The two guards were sent to relieve the two Toms from steering duty, the two hunters on weapon inspection, all the cutters and carpenters were set to work on barricade design and construction. Everyone had a task to distract from their mission.

The barge was a bustle of busy work, all on Fordo's orders, all on his ideas. *'Looks like you've got yourself a warband.'* Fordo choked up at the sight.

***

"What do you think of our chances?" Fordo, Carth, Sam, and Doyle found a secluded corner tucked away at the front of the barge.

"We've got a good lot with these guys," Sam said

"I expected far worse," Doyle smirked

Carth stretched his back against a crate, "I think we're as prepared as we can be, given how little we know."

"Let's talk about that," Fordo swept greasy hair from his eyes, "Even tearing himself up, it must've taken Gathii a few days to reach Riverwood. That means, Hilltop's been sunk for at least four days. Even at walking speed, the bots must've reached Gateway by now, especially by the time we get there."

"Mm..." They all grunted in agreement.

"If that's the case, what are our options?" Fordo asked

"Depends on how we find the town..." Doyle scratched his chin, "I say we have four possibilities;

Best case- We somehow beat the bots there and have time to prepare the defenses.

Second best- We get there and the villagers are holding the bridge. Not ideal, but we can reinforce the defense."

Sam took over, "Worst case for us- The bridge is lost, but the bots are still there in force. We don't have enough men to clean up or cut off a full attack, we'd have cogs on both banks, leaving us very few survivable options that don't include just sailing past."

"Worst case for Aureum- Gateway's sunk. The bots have come and gone, putting us behind enemy lines. In that case, We can't stop or slow them down, but we get to play hunters, picking them off from behind. Much easier than holding them back, but a lot less helpful, and we'd be cut off from any allies."

Fordo rubbed his temples, "Honestly, four sounds the most fun."

"Least amount of pressure," Carth laughed nervously

"We lose the bridge, we can't just do nothing," Fordo said

"There's plenty we can do, mate, just not a lot we can live through," Doyle said

Fordo tapped the head of his warhammer, "No point in living anyway knowing we gave the fuck up, I say......I say if they take the bridge, we knock that glass down."

"Knock it down?" Carth laughed, "This world's first historic architectural landmark, just wash it right down the river?"

Fordo shrugged, "We can rebuild bridges, we can't bring back the dead. I say sink it."

Doyle nodded, "We sink the bridge, we cut off the bot's forces."

"Bali and the armies clean up what's crossed, Riverwood holds the rest til we regroup," Sam said

"Alright, alright," Carth chuckled to himself, "How do we take it down? It's been a while, but last I remember it's a fuckin' big ass bridge."

Well said, friend. Fordo smiled to himself, searching for an idea, staring at the crates, the crew, anything they could use until he found himself watching both Jacks grunting and sweating, struggling to lift a few beams of Realwood. *This is a fuckin' big ass boat.*

Fordo grinned, "We anchor the barge upriver, sneak under the bridge, cut and burn the supports as best we can......... then use the Barge as a Battering Ram."

Carth and Sam both laughed, "Just sweep the legs?"

"I like this kid," Doyle clapped Fordo on the shoulder.

"Fordo...! Fordo...!" Two young voices called for him.

"Aye!"

Wesley and Hunter appeared in their nook, panting, looking excited. Far from twins, Hunter was a lot larger than his sister and Wesley had much softer features, but they had the same light brown, vaguely curly hair, and bright crystal blue eyes that marked them as a pair.

"Did you guys finish the flag?" Fordo asked, trying to hide his own excitement.

"No, not yet," Hunter panted

"We found stowaways!" Wesley almost cheered like she meant to say treasure.

"Stowaways?" Doyle raised an eyebrow

"Two kids snuck on board, somehow!"

"I thought that was you two?" Carth laughed

"Why are you guys looking for me?" Fordo asked

"Well, you're in charge, right?"

A genuine smile spread across Fordo's face against his objections, "Lead the way."

***

Fordo and friends hopped over the railing onto the pushboat. They could hear Old John talking to the stowaways just out of sight, and the voice that replied stopped Fordo and Carth in their tracks.

You gotta be fucking kidding me......

"Boy, sit down and wait there until we figure out what to do with you."

"Old man, you better sit down before you shit your pants or something!" Fordo immediately recognized the cruel, spiteful laugher of The Yellow-Eyed Boy.

"Hey, calm down, kid..." Said Chris the guard.

"Me calm down? Aren't you His nurse? Don't let him get all riled up like that, unless you actually like wiping his ass!"

They rounded the bend to find Chris and John standing over the Yellow-Eyed Boy and his young thieving friend.

"Son of a bitch..." Carth cursed under his breath.

"Captain Fordo, we found these kids hiding in a crate below deck. Must've snuck on while we were loading up. This one won't speak and the other won't shut up."

The sickly scarred boy greeted Fordo and company with a wide golden grin, while his friend just nodded like they were all casual acquaintances.

"What are you doing here, Dead Eyes? And what happened to your face?? I didn't hit you That hard!"

"What the fuck are you two doing here?"

"You know these boys?" asked Old John

"Couple thieves from the markets......One's a lot better than the other."

"Hey, fuck you, pretty boy, you don't know what I'm capable of!"

"I don't care if you can wipe out the bots with a fuckin' switch. You're an annoying, foul-mouthed, runt and you're off my boat the first chance we get..." Fordo looked at his goggle-wearing friend, "You can stay." The kid smiled out of the side of his mouth.

"Fordo..." Sam shook her head

"We're dumping him twenty yards offshore the next village we pass."

"Fordo!"

"He's an asshole and I'm not taking him."

"He's a kid and we're not leaving him."

"Look at him, Sam, that's no kid...that's some monster wearing a kid!"

"A monster with feelings..." The boy pretended to cry

"Anyone else on board with dumping?" Fordo asked, sincerely. Carth, John, and Chris all nodded. "Doyle?"

"I think he's funny," Doyle shrugged, "Plus I'll always vote: Sam."

"Gahdamnit, you really want this kid as your responsibility?" Fordo asked Sam

"Once we get to Gateway, he's on his own, but I'm not gonna let you throw anyone off this boat just because they bother you."

"Bothers me too..." Carth said

"We're pretty bothered..." John and Chris nodded

Fordo pointed at the boy, "He's gonna be the death of us all, I swear."

"Don't worry," Sam smiled, "I'll protect you."

"Thank you lady, you're like, a hundred times nicer than you look."

Sam grabbed the boy by the wrist and dragged him out of his chair, picking him up with one hand and tossing him over her mechanical shoulder like a sack of laundry. "Hey, what the hell are you doing? I don't know you like that!"

"We do need to have a talk about that mouth of yours......He's staying." Sam carried the boy off without a vote.

"Wait, dammit. You...You keep him away from the crew!" Fordo called after them, "Don't need him breaking morale..." Fordo rubbed the headache from his eyes. *Just what we need...*

"What's your name, kid?" Carth asked the thief. The boy had sleepy eyes and a pointed chin, fairly long, dirty blonde hair tucked back behind the goggles sitting on his forehead. He was on the shorter end, looked to be fifteen or sixteen years old, right on the cusp of becoming a man.

"My name's Wash," He yawned

"You kicked our asses last we saw you," Fordo said

"Think you just didn't kick mine," Wash smirked

"Impressed us either way. My name's Fordo, you remember Carth," Fordo held out his arm and Wash shook it firmly, "That's John...Chris...Hunter...And Wesley."

"I've seen you two around," Wash smiled at the siblings, "You make figures out of clay. Little monsters and soldiers and stuff?"

"Yeah, that's us! I don't remember seeing you before..."

"That's 'cause I stole a pillboy figure for my sister," He laughed, "Sorry about that. She loves it, by the way."

The siblings both looked at each other like getting robbed was so prime.

"What are you two doing here, Wash?"

"I need to find my sister. She went down to Scrapyard awhile back, I want to make sure she's okay, this seemed like the quickest way there."

"Mm, That's a better reason than most......
And the runt?"

"I think Jason just wants to watch the war."

"Of course he would..." *The sick fuck,* "Why do you
hang around that kid? He family?"

"No, he's just been following me around the last few
days. I don't know, he's kinda funny sometimes. Really smart.
Really really good at making things."

"Like what?"

"Everything. Tools, clothes, weapons. He made me
new gloves and this lock picking wrench, all in like an hour
or two. I bet he could build a bot with enough time. That was
the deal, I steal him materials, he'd make me whatever out of
it. I don't know, he's kinda annoying, but been really cool to
have around."

"Hm, maybe we'll put him to work," Fordo glanced at
Carth, "Come on, kid, let's find you something to do."

***

The sound of excited children came from the eastern
shore as they drifted past the smallest fishing village so far down
the river. Little more than a colorful collection of cottages
clustered together, with a tall, red winged windmill, and a couple
small piers. Dozens of children raced along the riverbank,
skipping and cheering after the barge, some waving, some
chanting, some throwing stones. Fordo's crew just smiled and
laughed, many waving back.

Fordo wondered how different his life would be if the bots never came, actually getting to grow up in they're nameless backcountry farming town from whence he came. His mother never dying...His father never leaving, never needing to be more than just his father. A simple life of chasing barges, catching fish, kissing girls behind the windmill. *Would I still have bigger boots to fill? Or would I just get to be happy......Just get to be nothing. What would be different? What would still be?*

He was so small......So weak...stuck under warm water, some kind of wash tub, halfway drowned, muted screaming all around. His mother pulled him out to safety, he was crying, coughing, shaking......he still can't remember her face, just the warmth of her hands on his. The first sound he ever heard was his father's shouting, already angry, already disappointed, screaming at Mother. Maybe Fordo fell, maybe Mother dropped him, maybe she'd left him too long, Fordo couldn't understand, but Bali was furious and took him from her, slamming the door behind him. His mother weeping, screaming, Fordo wondering why, feeling guilty, feeling anything for the very first time.

Fordo sucked his teeth at his first memory. Maybe things wouldn't be so different. Maybe Bali was cold before, maybe he already hated her, maybe he already hated him. Sarah would still be there to steal his time and love from both of them.

But I'd still have Mother...I'd have someone's love...And maybe that'd be enough. I wouldn't hate the world...Wouldn't hate myself...Wouldn't owe it anything.

Fordo watched Wash at work, sleepy and smiling, in no rush at all. He was everything Fordo wished he'd been when he was younger. Carefree, collected, competent, gifted with potential, but unburdened by ambition, completely unbothered by the world.

"That must be nice…" Fordo and Carth looked up at the pink and purple sky, laying on a wooden crate tower, watching the sun sink behind the mountains once more. Alone for the first moment since the inn.

"What's nice?" Carth asked

"Not having a dream……Just enjoying life as it comes."

"You could do both, you know? If you weren't such a weirdo," Carth smiled

"What's it like," Fordo asked, "Not caring about anything?"

"I care about Everything, I just don't let it crawl up my ass and ruin my day," Carth laughed, "There's only so much glass in our control, no use worrying about every little thing, Ford. Garrow's been telling us that since we were kids."

"Yeah, well…Garrow's not our dad."

Carth laughed without a smile, shaking his head, "He's as much your dad as he is mine."

Like I said…

Chop and Lady clanged a bell to call the crew for dinner. Carth and Fordo watched from their tower as the crew carried crates and planks to form a large makeshift dining table in the center of the barge. Everyone seemed in high spirits, smoking pipes and cracking jokes as they gathered from their tasks.

Despite everything, Fordo couldn't help but smile, "This might be the best day of my life, Carth..."

"Including the part where you got your face kicked in?"

"I'd say from reaching the docks until now, everything has been perfect," He spotted young Jason walking with Luca and the other armorers, "Almost perfect..."

"I miss them too..."

"Wha...? Oh...Yeah......" Fordo's cheeks turned bright red, "They'd be having more fun than either of us."

"Our first Real game of Barricade and they don't get to play..." Carth half laughed

Fordo was too embarrassed to speak. The fuck is wrong with me...*I can't believe I forgot already...*

Carth stood and cracked his back, "It's finally happening, man, everything you ever wanted."

"And I couldn't have done any of this without you."

"The hell have I done?" Carth laughed, "You make all the calls, I just follow your lead."

"I couldn't lead glass by myself. Just knowing you're behind me, knowing you've got my back...I feel like I can do anything...Thank you, Carthy, for believin' in me."

"I'm just here to see what happens," Carth pulled Fordo to his feet, "Thanks for giving me something to believe in."

***

Riverwood's residents, along with many other floating villages being high off of the ground, did the majority of their gardening in raised metal troughs. Some of the larger ones sturdy enough for a bear to sleep in, or to fill with charcoal, turn into a coal bed grill, and spit-roast an entire pig, which is exactly what Chop and Lady had done.

The chef and the butcher spent their day turning the words 'Last Meal' into slow-roasted pork, grilled corn, grilled onions, roast tomatoes, cornbread, they even stuck a pot in the coals to make rabbit stew.

Chop stood on the table and bowed with his knives like they were his instrument and he'd just put on the performance of a lifetime. The whole crew cheered, some of them cried, Fordo had never seen such a beautiful banquet.

Torches were lit, plates were passed, and Carth cracked open a cask of ale, pouring pints until everyone was laughing and singing like a band of merry dwarves.

The desperation behind the merriment only multiplied it. Made every bite delicious, every joke hilarious, every smile a beaming grin, because in all likelihood, it was their last. They all knew in their hearts that tomorrow, ready or not, is the day they meet the monsters, and they refused to waste their night.

As Fordo predicted, most everyone stayed with their assigned group. Friendships formed fast with a common task.

Fordo took a lap around the table when everyone was rubbing their bellies to check in with the lot and make sure everyone was ready and cared for, as well as check on their projects.

Everything was ready, far as they could tell. The hunters honed the weapons, the cutters ironed out defenses. The sibling's eyes lit up when he asked about the flag, running off to find it.

"They're real proud of it," Bethany smiled. She had olive skin and the longest hair Fordo had ever seen, even pulled up into a tail. Dark and wavy, as black as her eyes.

"Should I be worried about them?" Fordo asked, "They seem like they've been playing a game since they got here. Are they ready for tomorrow?"

"I think it's just how they cope. They're good kids, but they're not naive. They know what's coming. They'll take care of each other and the rest of us when the time comes."

"Thanks for looking out for them, helping them be kids a little while longer."

"I've got Seven younger brothers back in Riverwood... So I'm...I'm used to it..." Her voice wavered a moment, her dark eyes taking on what looked like a guilty sadness.

Fordo took a moment to find his words, "Scary leaving home, huh?"

She shook her head, "More afraid of going back..."

Hunter and Wesley came back running, waving a black canvas flag for all to see. Bright and bold in the center, painted neatly in white, and surprisingly well detailed was a perfect depiction of Scrapyard and Riverwood unity: A pattern of axe and hammerheads formed a circular gear around a full-grown realwood tree. The whole crew raised a tankard in a toast of approval.

"Wow…" Fordo grinned, he'd always wanted an emblem of his own, "You made that?"

"It was their ideas, I just painted it," Bethany blushed

"You stick around, I'll throw a few more ideas your way."

Fordo found Luca and Patch smoking with Doyle, looking over their leatherwork, their sweet-scented clouds catching the moonlight.

"There's our young captain," Patch had a much higher voice than Fordo expected, not matching his beard or belly at all.

"How goes it, boys? You scrape enough sets together for the front liners?"

"Did you one better than that," The big man grinned, holding up a full sleeve's set of leather armor, full cover from glove to shoulder with matching knees and grieves.

"Oh, Prime as hell," Fordo grinned, "Enough for the front line?"

"Enough for everybody," Patch said

"You boys work fast!"

"Not as fast as him," Luca gestured toward Jason, laughing with the old cutters, "Kid you found works as hard as the three of us combined. Like a fuckin' machine."

"Jason helped you guys?"

"Kid doubled our output in half the time, never seen nothin' like him."

"Huh…He play nice the whole time?"

"Eh, He called Patch a pig," Luca smiled, "said I got a nose like a crow, but he cracks me up. Kid can sew like a fuckin' spider. Turned a jigsaw into a sewing machine in like half an hour."

"Still wanna dump him, mate?" Doyle smirked

"He sews his mouth shut, I'll reconsider," Fordo clapped Patch and Luca on their shoulders, "Good work, boys."

Fordo skirted around the festivities, exhausted by social gatherings. He knew his own strengths and 'Fun' was nowhere on that list. Maybe he could inspire a crowd, but he sure as hell couldn't entertain one. Instead, he sought out the other loners, smoking in the dark or warming themselves by the coals, checking in one on one until he spotted Sam and Wash sitting on the tower of crates. Fordo caught the tail end of a conversation as he climbed up to join them.

"...even heavy enough, you think?" Wash cradled a long dark shape in his lap.

"I don't see why not," Sam said, "Though the key to bot bashing is a small striking surface, only way to dent the armor."

"Oy...Mind if I join you guys? Need to get away for a minute," Fordo asked, dropping next to Wash, dangling his feet over the edge.

"Be our guest," Sam said, staring out over the water.

"Look what Jason made me," Wash handed Fordo a long thin metal club that looked to be made of pipe fittings.

"Where does that kid find the time?" Fordo shook his head, gripping and twirling the club in his hand, "This is pretty well balanced..."

"Told you he's fast," Wash said, "Should I feel bad, accepting all these gifts?"

"Aren't you a thief? Taking glass you haven't earned is kinda your thing," Fordo said

"Eh, You're right...guess it feels weird that it's actually given," He smiled

The blue light of the two moons reflected off the restless river. Gaps between glowing white clouds revealed a star-peppered sky, stretching out all the way to the mountain-lined horizon. A beautiful blue fog quickly cut the western bank in half, spilling out over the water. Soon it would look like they were sailing through the sky.

"Would you look at that..." Sam smiled

Fordo stared in awe, "You don't get views like this in Blackwyrm, ay?"

Sam shook her head, "It's a whole other world in there, a different brand of beautiful, but this...This is hard to beat."

"What's it like there?" Wash asked, "I've only ever heard-"

Splash...

"Whoa!" They all laughed. Fordo wiped his face. Water sprayed up and wet the trio with the sound of some large creature jumping out of the river.

"What the heck was that?" Wash asked

"I don't know, are there fish that big in the Siena?"

"I don't think so..."

They all looked in the dark water for a glimpse of an answer, but there was no use, whatever it was had-

SPLASH!

"Ah, What the fuck?" Chop and Lady, talking near the edge of the barge, got drenched with another small wave.

"What was that?" someone called

"Something jump out of the water?" Carth asked

"It fell out of the sky!" Hunter called

"What?"

"It fell out of the-!"

CRASH!!!

Something obliterated the dining table, launching a wave of splintered wood and burning coals right into young Jason and the group of old cutters, all screaming in pain and confusion, some of their clothes catching fire. Something large and shiny thrashed in the wreckage, shooting straight towards old John, latching onto his chest, tackling the old man to the ground, and splattering his head against the deck with a wet crunch.

A bolt shot out of the dark and caught the creature in the shoulder, knocking it back onto its feet. The whole crew saw with unblinking eyes, standing before them clearly in the torchlight, a faceless metal man with blood-covered hands.

Oh fuck...

The robot rushed across the deck straight for Carth fumbling with his hammer. Doyle's spear flew and skewered the bot's lower back, sending the monster tumbling end over end, writhing at Carth's feet. Carth stumbled back, the bot still swiping for his ankles, before getting spiked in the head by his warhammer, black oil pooling like blood on the deck.

'*...fell out of the sky...*' Fordo looked out into the twinkling darkness towards the fog-covered bank, looking for anything that could give him a hint of where the fuck that thing came from until a dark shape shot up out of the mist, straight into the air. Fordo followed it until, silhouetted against the bright blue moons, was the flailing form of a falling bot. *Oh, Fuck me, 'Worse'!*

"Taake Coverrr!!!"

Crash!!!

A stack of crates collapsed, the metal man plowing into it, getting buried beneath. The whole crew scrambled away.

"Find your weapons!" Fordo called over the chaos, drawing his hammer and diving to the deck.

Sam drew her sword and jumped down. "Form up! On me!" Everyone scrambled to either hide or arm themselves. Doyle ripped his spear out of the fallen monster. A man still on fire panicked and dove into the racing river, while the others burning threw off their clothes and stamped out the flames. Jason stumbled about, cursing profusely, holding a bloody hand to the side of his face.

CRASH!!!

Another bot's body crashed and crushed the legs of Chris the guard with a voice-cracking scream. The creature rolled onto its hands and feet in an instant, scrambling on all fours over the screaming man and plunging its metal hand straight through his chest.

"Raaahh!" Bolts bounced off the bot's armored back as Patch and Jacob loosed their crossbows. The monster picked up Chris, with the hand still inside of him, and launched his body at its attackers, knocking them both screaming onto their backs. Sam leaped over the boys and brought her sword down so hard the metal man folded in half into a broken pile, black and red oil splattering her armor.

"Everybody get behind me!" Sam screamed at the crew, finally forming a defensive circle, "Protect the kids! Hammers in front, rangers behind!"

"Launch when they land!" Doyle shouted, the next bot to crash and roll was immediately met with lances and bolts. Most missed or bounced, but enough caught the joints to drop it to the deck. *You're mine!* Fordo rushed forward and slammed the spike of his hammer into the back of the beast's neck, stilling it forever. "Atta boys!" Doyle yelled, "Don't let up!"

More monsters shot out of the mist, some splashing into the water, others right into their weapons, but for every one they killed the clouds spit out another.

"We can't keep this up forever!" Doyle shouted to Fordo.

He was right, eventually they would tire or run out of bolts, they had to do something. Another splash of water made Fordo realize. "They keep falling short!"

Fordo looked around, "Luca, Wash, With Me! Rest of you Hold, we need to steer out of their range!"

Fordo sprinted off for the pushboat with his support through the stacks of crates. They made it just in time to see a bot crash onto the boat, pick poor confused Thomas up over its head, and splinter his spine over the metal railing, dumping him limp into the river.

"Fuckin' hell..." The trio skirted to a stop, the bot turning and sprinting straight for them.

"Don't miss..." Wash said, charging towards the bot.

Glass, wait!

Wash kicked off of a crate the moment the monster dove for him, flipping barely over the bot and bashing it in the back of the head with his club. It tumbled and tripped long enough for Luca to spear it through the hips. Fordo ran to spike it, only to be kicked in the stomach and knocked back nearly over the edge of the boat into the rushing water.

Wash turned to finish the bot, but Fordo called, "No, the barge! Get us out of range!" Wash nodded and ran for the helm.

Fordo watched the bot flail about on the ground, unable to dislodge the lance. Disgust and disdain filled Fordo's heart. This was it, the same monster that broke their world and killed his mother now flopped helplessly before him.

"Step back…" He gently pushed Luca behind him, before raising his hammer above his head with both hands. In a rage, Fordo bashed the beast's kicking legs into flattened scrap, yanked the spear from its stomach, and beat a crater into its faceless head, splattering his hands and clothes and face with black oily blood.

"That's for my mom you sunken scrap son of a bitch…" Fordo spit, wiping tears and blood from his face with his sleeve before turning to Luca, "Sorry about that…"

Luca nodded to himself like he'd just made a personal vow, "…*and we will repay those memories with vengeance…*" He quoted Fordo's morning speech, spitting on the crumpled corpse, "Sink 'em all…"

They felt the barge drift towards the eastern bank, hopefully out of range of the metal rain. "Stay with the kid, I'll help the others." Fordo handed back Luca's lance, "This might not be over…"

***

The corpse-strewn deck was black with blood and oil. One last bot, riddled with bolts, clawed desperately towards the survivors with one arm, dragging a slimy black streak behind it like some monstrous mutant grub. A blood-soaked Sam stomped on its neck with a heavy crunch.

The crew watched their assailants now splash harmlessly into the Siena, refusing to relax until the safety was certain. Soon after, the fog faded from the western bank, monsters stopped falling from the sky, and everyone let out a desperate sigh of relief.

Crying was the first sound to break the silence, followed by wounded groans, then Jason's sadistic childish laughter. Everyone looked up to see the Yellow-eyed boy cackling on top of a pile of crates with a burnt shirt and bloody face.

"That...Was...Awesome!" He cheered alone, the whole crew glaring in hatred and confusion.

"Jason!" Fordo called, "Enough..."

"When it threw that guy! And then she jumped up and the bot went *Bshh*! Oh, That was So-!"

"ENOUGH!" Fordo slammed his hammer into a crate with an explosive bang.

Jason shut up, reigning in his laughter to a giggle and waving dismissively like they all just didn't get the joke.

"Who's hurt!"

There weren't many severely wounded, but only because most everyone the cogs got their hands on was now dead. Patch was bruised up and young Jacob had some broken ribs from getting hit with poor Chris. Most of the cutters all had cuts and burns, save for Virgil who caught a four-inch splinter in the eye when the table burst. And not that he cared, but Fordo was fairly certain Jason had some kind of head injury as well.

Carth ran up to Fordo, "Are you okay? That's a lot of fuckin' blood..."

"I'm good, really. Had some trouble by the pushboat."

"Is the kid okay??"

"Wash is prime, he pretty much took down a bot by himself."

Carth nodded and pulled Fordo in for a hug, "That glass was so scary..."

"I know, man..." Fordo squeezed his brother back.

"'Worse', Huh? Fuckin' Gathii couldn't be more specific?" They both half laughed half cried, "We're so fuckin' sunk."

"Not yet, brother."

"What do we do now?"

"Patch up the wounded, get a head count, clean this glass up...We'll talk after...We gotta figure this out."

They moved anyone shocked or wounded to the pushboat, along with anyone who could sew while the others rested. Fordo tasked Luca and Shelby with stitching duty.

"I've never done this before!" Shelby objected

"It's the same thing as sewin' a shirt," Luca assured, "Just a fleshy fabric."

Jason was confined to the front of the boat, far away from the others, both for his own safety and everyone else's sanity.

Carth stayed behind to calm and comfort, while Fordo, Chop, Sam, Doyle, and Bethany all volunteered to dump the bodies and wash the deck of blood and brains.

Of all the abundance of supplies on this barge, there was not a hint of fresh clothing. They all stripped down to their undergarments before attempting to tackle the task of cleansing the deck of human and mechanic remains, adrenaline and hard work keeping them warm in the brisk night air.

Seeing Sam and Doyle shed their armor for the first time, Fordo got to see their unusual botsthetic limbs up close. Confirming they weren't just the standard medical replacements, but full mechanical enhancements. Sam's right arm looked as sturdy as her sword, possibly the only reason she could even wield one so large. Whereas Doyle's animalistic double jointed design looked perfect for running and jumping, making Fordo's mind run wild with the realization that botsthetics are in no way limited to a humanoid structure. Beth, Fordo, and Chop wanted to ask about them, but decided now was not the time.

They wanted first to gather the remains of their fallen comrades, but the deck was so slick with blood that both Chop and Fordo slipped and fell onto the body of poor Chris. There seemed so much more blood than bodies to spill it, Fordo thought, too thick to ignore. Push brooms scrubbed and scraped, bucket after bucket of river water splashed onto the deck, slowly whittling away at the horrific stain. Sam was the only volunteer who managed not to throw up by the time the majority was washed overboard.

It was well past midnight by the time it was safe enough to gather their fallen. Covered in canvas and dragged in a line, they planned to have their memorial in the morning. Bolts were pulled and collected before the bodies of the bots were dumped unceremoniously into the river, left to rust in the icy depths.

Chop stood and stared at the collapsed pile of

crates where the second bot had crashed. "The fuck do we do about this?"

"Leave it," Doyle groaned, "We've done enough for the night."

Fordo stared into the pile, with narrow eyes, something was bothering him, "Hey Chop...Step back..."

"What, what's wrong?" Sam asked

"I don't know..." A bad feeling overwhelmed Fordo's instincts, his gut screaming at him that something was still wrong, until he realized, "Ah, Fuckin' Glass..."

"Spit it out, mate." Doyle leaned on his broom like it was his spear.

"The bot that knocked that over...Did anyone see it come out of there?"

They all stared in silence before collectively cursing, "Fuck..."

Fordo rubbed his tired eyes, "We gotta make sure..."

"I mean, we would have heard it by now, right?" Chop asked

"Maybe it's dead?" Doyle hoped

"Maybe it's waiting..." Bethany whispered

"Bots don't wait."

"They don't fly either, but here we are..."

"We can't ignore this," Sam said

"I know, I know, fuck me. I'm just being optimistic, is all..."

"Glass, glass, glass......Alright, arm up, get your boots on. Chop and I will start digging, you three stand ready, This could take a while, so let's get it over with."

Splintered crates, sacks of grains, all manner of tools for farming and carpentry; little by little, piece by piece, they quietly dug their way into the toppled tower, meticulously tossing the wreckage into the river, flinching at every sight of exposed metal.

After a tense eternity of careful digging and stressful searching, the mountain of goods bulged from below. Chop and Fordo shot backward, scrambling away. The cog was caught in the very center of the pile under a final layer of pots and pans. It was alive and moving, but very stuck and very calm, for now.

Fordo looked at Doyle for what to do, but he just gestured to keep on digging. Fordo cursed and drew his hammer, crawling towards the pulsing pile. Drenched with sweat, even in the cold, he wiped the drops from his eyebrows before raising his hammer, praying to the gods, and slamming his hammer into the pots with a crashing *Bong!*

The robot erupted from the pile, launching metal pots in all directions, twisting and flailing to free itself and lunge at the humans. Doyle launched his spear into the monster's hips, Sam crunched both of its shoulders with quick chops of her blade, and Fordo swung up so hard at its head that it popped clean off into the air. Or so he thought...

What is this...?

Everyone cursed and stepped back.

Chop and Fordo dropped their hammers.

Doyle removed his hat.

Bethany covered her mouth and screamed into her hair.

Sam lowered her sword, staggered backwards, and turned

to throw up.

Fordo hit the bot so hard that the front half of its

head flew off......

......revealing the broken, bloody face

.........of a human woman.

Auri

I

"Al...Al!" Auri cried, holding onto his leg.

"Wait, wait, Wait!" Al put his hands up, ducking as the pry bar flew just above his head.

Hordes of hysteric villagers surrounded them, pushing in all around, pointing, screaming, reaching. Al pleaded, raising his hands, "No, Wait, Please, I'm so sorry! Don't hurt them!"

I don't like this. I don't like this. I don't like this.

"Get him!" They rushed forward all at once.

Meeko jumped between Al and the mob, biting a man's leg only to be kicked by another off the pier and down onto the wreckage, thirty feet below with a yelping bark. Auri lunged out to grab him, but there was no use, she was far too slow to make the catch and so weak she'd probably fall with him. "Meeko!" Al cried, immediately seized and restrained by a dozen angry arms before he could jump after his boy. Auri watched Meeko flail and crash onto the wreckage below, new streaks of blood streamed down the pile. She burst into tears.

"Al!" Auri yelled, for that was all she could do.

"Auri!" Al grabbed her hand and looked her in the eyes with a concern and patience she didn't know could exist in a person about to be torn apart. "No matter what happens! Take me with you! No matter what! I'm sorry!"

What? What does that mean? "Al, please!"

"I'm gonna get you home! I promise! It's going to be okay! I'm gonna-Ahh!"

What does that mean?? How can you promise?? "Al, wait!"

Al was sucked into the mass of screaming angry bodies, out of Auri's sight. She heard the sound of fists crashing into flesh, grunts of pain, and sobbing cries.

"Beat him!"

"Kill him!"

"Hang him!"

"Hang him!!!" The mob screamed

"No, no, please! Stop, no, Al!" Auri crawled and grabbed onto the nearest person, trying to climb up over them to reach her friend, but there was no way. She was so small, they didn't even try and stop her, just pushed her back onto her ass like a child. *I can't do anything......* She rocked back and forth, weeping. Screaming when Al emerged with a swollen purple face, bruised and bloodied above the crowd, scratching at his own throat, a thick rope wrapped around it.

"No! I'm sorry! Nooo!!" She screamed until her voice gave out. Watching uselessly as the mob lifted her friend up over their heads, carried him to the edge of the pier, and threw him over the side. Her new friend was gone with a sudden sickening snap of his neck and horrible crunching thud of his body swinging into the support beams below. Crying so hard she made no sound, she laid there staring through puffy eyes at her broken lifeless friend, dangling over his broken lifeless dog. *Why.....................What did I do.............................I'm so sorry.*

A rough hand grabbed her shoulder and flipped her onto her back, an angry man pinning her to the grimy planks, screaming in her face, "Where is it? Where is the horn?"

"Get off of me!" She screamed

"Where is the Wyrmcaller??"

"Get The Fuck Off Of Meee!!!"

"OY!" Several hands pulled the man off of Auri and threw him to the side. The three brothers that helped Al before stepped between her, the angry man, and the rest of the mob.

"She was with him! We need to find that horn before the wyrm comes back!"

"Anyone here tries to touch this crippled girl again and we'll split your fucking skulls!"

The mob tried to protest, but slowly dispersed while the brothers stared them down, hearing none of it.

"Are you okay, girl?" The youngest brother knelt down beside her.

Auri pretended not to hear. Her eyes had quickly found their way back to the bodies of her friends and refused to leave them. The creaking of Al's gentle swing consuming the rest of the world around her.

***

She knew not how long she'd been staring. An hour? Several? It was long enough for the tears to dry upon her cheeks, her stinging red eyes blinking rapidly back into consciousness.

However long it was, it was long enough.........She wiped her eyes and nose with her dirty, olive green sleeve, took a deep breath, and began to crawl.

She scraped her way to the post that anchored Al's body to the pier and struggled in vain to wedge her fingers into the knot itself. Auri cursed, stumbled, and crawled around the village until she found something to cut down Al's body. Some villagers offered her help, but she wanted none of it. Not from them. Not for the few things she could do on her own. "Don't touch me!" she spat, "I needed His help......And so did you......"

Took her an hour to find a rusty saw and make her way back to the rope. Panting and grunting with each slow pull, the rope slowly stretched and groaned as the red-brown teeth gnawed at its strands. A quarter.........A third.........Halfwa-CRTCH!

She jumped when it snapped, holding her hand over her mouth to swallow the vomit that came with the thump of Al's body hitting the ground. She trembled, eyes clenched, holding back the sobs, taking another deep breath before crawling on.

Her sprained elbow throbbed with every heartbeat, bruises covered her arms, her hands scraped and blistered from making her way back down to the ground on her own, climbing down the supports of the pier beam by beam, her new beautiful green dress horribly torn and stained. She'd never been more tired, she'd never been so sore, but her friends needed her, and her brother was waiting. She wouldn't rest until she was back on the road, where she needed to be.

She thought she'd run out of tears, but more found their way to her when she saw Al and Meeko up close. Her new friend and his pup......gracelessly laying like lost toys, too broken to fix. Unrecognizably swollen and purple, she covered Al's face with a torn curtain scattered nearby. She placed a hand on his still chest.

You beautiful idiot......So sweet and so stupid......I told you to keep your voice down......

She cried and sighed and shook her head, reaching to pet Meeko one last time when-Bʀᴀʟᴋ! She jumped and screamed when his body jolted and shook with coughing bloody barks. Meeko......? You're alive.......? You're alive! She wept and hugged his still-shaking body. He cried and whined, but his shaking soon stilled and breathing steadied. He half-opened his eyes and stared at her, weakly licking her hand.

"You're alive, sweet baby......" Auri cried, smiling and petting as gently as possible.

Meeko whined and looked at her with a question.

She shook her head and wiped her eyes, "No......He didn't make it......"

Meeko barked and cried, then stilled once more, resting his eyes and saving his strength. Auri half laughed, half cried, frowning once she realized that now she really couldn't leave him here......

She looked around for something, anything that could help her wrap Al's body and drag him out of there, only to find the three brothers, standing on the pier above her.

"What do you want?" She asked

"He didn't deserve that......" Jay said

"No......He didn't......"

"We didn't see him until it was too late......We would have stopped it if we could......"

"Me too......"

The men made their way down to her.

"Would you like us to bury him......?"

She opened her mouth to say yes, but choked on the word, "N-no......he should be with his family......" she lied, "Does this village have a veterinarian?"

"Did this morning......"

Auri swallowed and pressed her palms into her eyes, sniffing away the sorrow before finally saying, "Help us to the road......We have somewhere to be."

Auri had no idea what to do with his body, but she couldn't leave Meeko and Al asked her to bring him with her no matter what, so now that's what she was going to do.

The men wrapped and tied his body in canvas cloth and put him in a small wooden cart. They wheeled Auri, Al, and Meeko out of town and back to the road. With the dust settled, she could see the gaping crater where the wyrm had erupted from the hillside. Wet red dirt left exposed like Aureum's flesh, a fresh scabless wound.

On their way up the hill, Auri spotted Cidarian, her heart pounding in relief at the sight of her beautiful bronze pillpup grazing blissfully near the bottom.

"That's my bug," she cried, having been too afraid to truly consider losing him for good.

"Your bug?"

"He's carried me across the continent, sweet boy. If you tap his shell you can guide him here." The brothers ushered him back with some effort. Auri wept and fell from the kart to wrap her arms around him. He made absolutely no movement nor sound of acknowledgment as she laughed and cried and kissed his shell. "I missed you too......"

The men attached the kart to Dari's saddlebags, still strapped tight and full of provisions, while Auri settled back into her little nest.

"I'll take it from here," She told the men, "Thank you......"

They nodded.

"We're sorry......"

She found Al's things still scattered at the top of the hill, climbing down Dari to retrieve them, tossing his ax and sword and pack onto the kart with his body. And just as she was about to depart, she spotted the wyrmstooth horn half buried from the blast. Her hands hovered over it for a long while before finally cursing, snatching, and tossing it onto the kart with the rest.

***

It was driving her crazy, how much silence punctuated every sound. Every sniffling breath she took, Meeko's labored snoring, the wobbling squeaking wheels of the cart. Even amplified the noise in her head. The boom of the wyrm, the screams of the mob, the snap of Al's neck. Auri prayed for the white noise of rain to drown out the pain, the constant reminders of what dragged behind her. She covered her ears and screamed into the grassy void.

What the fuck am I doing? What the fuck am I supposed to do with you now?? 'No matter what happens, take me with you......' Did you know you were about to die? Were you really just some kind of idiot? Is this some 'Scatter my ashes' pillshit? Am I supposed to dump you someplace I think you'd like, a ditch of my choice on the side of the road?

I love you, Al, for everything you've done for me, but this request of yours is fucked and I don't know what it means.........

No matter how gross and strange, she still felt she owed it to him, whatever it was. Their friendship wasn't four days old, yet he'd done more for her in those days than most had her entire life. Been betrayed and abandoned by family and friends alike, used up and tossed aside. She'd done far more for far worse.

I haven't felt like a person in years. Just a broken doll no one loves enough to fix or cares enough to get rid of, I sit on a shelf collecting dust, loved only when remembered, then put back to rot............But you found me, fixed me up, played with me, made me feel whole and new again. And it got you killed.........

She did nothing else, for there was nothing else to do, but think the time and terror away. Too tired to sleep, too weak to eat, she watched the unchanging road slip by, wondering why. Why does this keep happening……Horrible things beyond my control……

Parents taken by monsters……Not their lives, just their love. Numbed and tainted by trauma and fear, left without the passion or patience for proper parenting. Small and neglected, caring for her brother, leaving to live with their cruel and clever cousins. Pressured into mischief and madness.

Always in trouble, always the cause. Cruel friends meant cruel fun until the joke was on you. Shoved from a tree to see if you'd fly just to break your wings and wish you'd died.

Did I piss you off, Mother? She looked up at the cloudless sky. Never believed in gods, but what else could it be but some sick joke by Mother Aure? She laughed and cried, shaking her head.

No……Sink that…… This wasn't divine punishment, a test of faith, or twist of fate. It's just pure bad luck, nothing more, nothing less. And I'll deal with it the same way I've dealt with everything else in my life: On my own. You can take my family, you can kill my friends, you can break my body, but you can't break me.

***

Tossing and turning in her patchwork nest, she longed for the sweet release of restless sleep. She hadn't known such pain in years. Head, hands, and arm all throbbing in unison, grateful her legs couldn't feel the same or else the pain might've been paralyzing.

"I get it! There's something wrong!" She yelled at her brain, pondering the redundant futility of headaches. *Why does the human brain have a single indecipherable alarm system for any number of problems? Like if the Horn in Riverwood meant anything from 'It's slightly rainy' to 'We're all going to die'. Use your words! I know you can talk, you're doing it right now! Don't yell at me just because you don't know how to fucking communicate.*

Distracted by a new noise in the night, she heard Meeko moving around in the cart. Poor puppy.........

She didn't know what to do with him either. More than happy to take him with her, but unsure if that was the right course, if that's what he really wanted. He would never leave Al's side. Even if she found a way to bury him, Meeko would still be there waiting.

"No, No, NO, please, Please, PLEASE NO!"

Auri's heart shot into her throat. Desperate pleading screams pierced the night directly behind her. She shot straight up, scrambling and falling off of Cidarian with a thud into the dirt. Auri cowered against Dari's shell, while Al's body banged

and shook the cart so much it rocked and tipped onto its side.
What do I do? What do I do? What the fuck is happening?

She slowly peeked around her bug's shell to see Meeko on the ground ripping and tearing through Al's wrappings, Al's body thrashing desperately underneath. Auri shook violently, weeping tears of terror and disbelief, slapping her own face and pulling her own hair. "Wake up! Wake up! Wake up! Wake up!" She was dreaming, she had to be, because otherwise she just watched her friend's snap-necked corpse come screaming back to life.

Fordo

7

"What the fuck is this......?" Fordo pulled at his own hair, staring into the glazed lifeless eyes of the woman they'd just murdered. *No, not murdered! They came at us, they killed themselves...... No human could survive those falls. No human can crush a man's skull with their hands, punch a fist straight through a person's chest. I don't know what the fuck these are, but they are Not people.*

"Is she still alive?" Bethany whispered

"Not anymore..." The woman's body slumped to the ground as Doyle slowly twisted out his spear.

Chop whispered some sort of prayer to Mother Aure.

Sam was staring at the blood-stained deck, a white-knuckled grip around the hilt of her sword.

Fordo knelt over the robot woman. Blood dripped from her hanging jaw, broken by his hammer. Her skin pale and cheeks sunken in like she hadn't seen the sun or had a meal in weeks.

"Look at this..." Fordo gestured for Doyle to join him, "She's been in there a long time..."

Doyle turned her head from side to side, running his leather-gloved thumb over where the metal met the skin. "Hm..."

"Think we can get her out of there?"

"I don't think she's meant to, mate......Look here," He twisted her head from all different angles, "There's no latch, no buttons, no hinges, no way for her to take it off......It's all bolted together around her like one solid piece, like building any other bot. This isn't a suit of armor, mate, it's a fuckin' tomb."

"Fuckin' glass......" Fordo put the back of his hand against her forehead, "Still warm, like a fever, even. She was definitely alive in there......Think she was in control?"

"Who the fuck would do this to themselves?"

"Well, who the fuck would do this at all? Whether this was done by bots or people or fuckin' aliens, I don't know, but constructing a cog Around a person is Infinitely more difficult than just making a robot......This doesn't make any fuckin' sense."

"What do we tell the others?" Chop asked

Fordo stood and stared at the dead woman, encased in her metal tomb. He imagined being taken in the night by metal hands, dragged far from home to some dungeon or lab or spaceship, strapped to a table, and slowly covered, piece by piece with metal plates until all you know is cold suffocating darkness.

It may not be your choice or your fault, but whoever you were, wherever you're from, whatever happened to you..........................

............You are now the enemy............

................................And this will Not be the fate of me or my friends.

"We don't tell them anything......"

Chop, Beth, and Doyle all looked at Fordo in shock.

"What do you mean, we don't tell them?"

"Not a fuckin' thing. We don't breathe a word of this to anyone on this ship."

"Fordo, there is a Person...Inside of this robot! This is insane, we can't just keep this from them, they need to-"

"To what, Chop? They need to, what? Listen to me... Listen..." Fordo walked up to Chop and looked him directly in the eyes, "They need to be focused, Chop...They need to be ready...They need to be angry...Because that is the Only Way they'll have the strength to defend their homes, their friends, their families."

"But Fordo-"

"The bots are back and they're falling out of the fucking sky! We can't fill their heads with even more questions. Worse questions! Questions we have zero answers to! We tell them there might be a Person behind every bot they Need to Kill, how many would die just by wondering who's behind the mask? We don't say a single word until we know exactly what the fuck is going on."

"He's right..." Sam said, wiping her eyes, "I hate it...But he's right. We can't tell them."

"But we can't just..." Chop dropped to his knees, "Ah Fuck me..." He cried

Fordo put his hands on his shoulders, "They deserve to know, all of them, I know. This is Not the Right choice...... But it's the best choice. Carth has the heart of a monster slayer, but not of a fuckin' killer...He will hate me for not telling him, but I will not get him killed by giving him this burden. Please, for fuck's sake...Keep this secret."

Chop shook his head, but eventually nodded. Fordo looked to Beth and Doyle who both did the same.

"Thank you..."

No one spoke until the work was done. Fordo closed the eyes of the dead woman before dragging her to the edge of the barge and letting her sink into the dark water to rest. They all washed their bloody hands in the freezing water, letting it numb their bones and hearts before shuffling off to join their comrades in restless slumber.

***

"John, Chris, Thomas, Rich, William, Jack......Six of our comrades were taken from us in the night." Dark bags hung under Fordo's gray eyes, the night was not kind to him or his crew. What would have been a beautiful sunrise was rendered nothing more than an unsightly beacon, reminding them that sleep was not but a false hope.

"We did not know them well, for we were robbed of our time together. They may not have died yet our friends, but they were indeed our brothers. For they were among the few in Riverwood who heard the call to war and answered. And for that alone...they are heroes."

The crew agreed there was no time to stop and bury the three bodies in the traditional Riverwood manor and that their vessels would instead feed new life into the River itself. Heavy chains wrapped around their fallen to help them rest easy at the bottom of the river. One by one they sank their friends, everyone whispering their own separate private prayers.

"Should arrive in Gateway by this afternoon. Odds are, the bots have beat us there, so everyone expect a fight and prepare yourselves, rest as much as you can until then. It may be another long night."

The crew dispersed, most everyone avoiding the middle deck where the fighting took place. Sunlight revealed that though the blood was scrubbed away, the red was not, leaving an ominous dark stain on every Realwood plank.

Fordo made rounds around the barge, checking in with the crew, assessing morale. Luca and Patch passed out their sets of leather armor to as warm a reception as one could muster up after such a night. Some found solace and distraction in dodge practice, rolling around the deck in their new protection. Others found it much easier to sleep in the sunlight, napping high on the crates, Sam and Doyle among them.

Fordo found Bethany with the siblings up high, both much quieter today, all watching Wash flip around the crates in his new leather armor. Bethany gave Fordo a small nod as he passed.

Most of the wounded were already up and about, their cuts closed and burns covered. Shelby the seamstress made Virgil a patch to cover his ruined eye. She was exceptionally pretty, even by Fordo's unreasonably high standards, with short wavy hair and pale mousy features. She fared much better than she feared she would as their reluctant medic, giving Fordo a nervous report.

Fordo spotted Chop and Lady sneak off to a secluded corner and followed them, fearing Chop's conscience may have gotten the better of him, only to find them in the midst of their own private distraction and snuck off before they noticed his peeping.

Finally, Fordo found Carth occupying Jason at the front of the barge, having a fairly casual verbal duel, slinging slander and insults back and forth like lobbing stones.

With everyone accounted for, Fordo stole a patch of sunlight for himself upon a lonely tower and lost himself in the endless blue sky. Laying alone for the first moment since leaving The Sleeping Giant.

Six people died……That's twenty percent of the crew in a single skirmish. Thank the gods it was no one who mattered, no one I needed, but fuck me, who else is gonna die today? The more we lose, the greater the odds one of my friends is next. Am I ready for another loss? Minus the runt, losing any of the kids would be a bummer. Luca and Bethany have the best prospects. I like Chop, Sam, and Doyle well enough, but Carth…If I lose Carth, I'm sunk.

'You were never the hero……you were just his son.'

Shut up……

'How long until we're all sunk on another one of his missions just so he can keep pretending to be a big fucking hero??'

Shut up!

He shook Kira's voice from his mind, tears streaming down his temples. *Enough!* He bolted upright like he was ready to fight himself. *You know you can do this, so what the fuck are you worried about? This is exactly what you wanted! This is the moment you've been waiting for, the sole reason you were born, everything in your life led you to this! Today's the day you prove them wrong! Today's the day you claim your name! Commander Fordo with his Wall Of Warriors………BotSlayers, BridgeKeepers, WorldSavers! Whatever happens here today, the world will remember you and your story!*

His shoulders dropped......*Who am I kidding? We're all sunk......*

No. You're not going to let that happen......Whatever happens here today, you are going to fight and scrape and crawl your way to victory. No matter the cost, no matter how hard, you are going to save these people! And you know why...? Because at the end of the day, your story doesn't matter..................If no one survives to tell it.

Embarrassed by his loosened grasp on emotion, Fordo looked around for prying eyes before wiping his own and laying back down on his hard wooden bed, "You can do this..." He whispered, "You have to...You have to..."

***

Fordo stumbled about in a dark, desolate, wooden wasteland, through a forest of lit gray candles as tall and thick as trees. The light of their flames shot uselessly into the oppressing blackness of the skyless void.

Fordo knew not how he got there, but that mattered not. Away. Away was all he wanted, all he knew. He waded through an ever-rising tide of blood as the candles drooped and melted.

A fallen bot, slouched against a wooden crate, the front of its head cracked and hanging. Fordo forced the crack open to see the broken, bloody face of his stepmother, Sarah. He fell back into the thick, warm, wetness of the rising blood only to hear a splash come from behind him, then another, then another. He turned slowly to see three bots sprinting through the red river, rushing straight towards him, all cackling like yellow-eyed children. Moving to draw his hammer, he found his holster empty and ran for his life.

Sprinting, then splashing, then swimming through the ocean of blood, he heard the bots falling back behind him, but out of the blackness above came the ever-growing sound of a flag flapping faster and faster as a flash of fangs came crashing-

"Ahh!" Fordo jolted awake, nearly toppling off of his wooden resting place, holding his aching ribs. "Sink my ass..." he rubbed his eyes, feeling even more tired than before.

"You alright?" Carth called up to him

"I don't think I am..." Fordo dropped down onto the deck, rubbing the neck muscles he somehow pulled in his sleep, "How come sleep's always worthless when you need it the most?"

Carth handed him a canteen, "Here, this'll wake you up."

Fordo nodded and took a long swig only to spit out whatever warm, vile liquid was now burning his throat. "Ah, You son of a bitch!" Fordo coughed, "I thought it'd be water!"

Carth laughed and smacked Fordo on the back as he spat, "I thought you loved whiskey?" Carth dangled the canteen in front of his face.

"I don't even love that glass when I'm ready for it, get that thing out of my face before I kick your ass," Fordo wiped his mouth, "Where are we, what time is it?"

"Just passed noon. Tommy says we've got one more bend in the river before we can see Gateway coming up. Was just coming to rouse you."

"Consider me roused…" Fordo knelt by the edge of the barge and drank his fill of river water, splashing the cold in his face, washing the grease and tired away. "Let's get this over with. The sooner we win this war, the sooner we can shower."

"You ready for the world's worst game of Barricade?"

"Heh…" Fordo managed a grin, "I'm ready for the best…"

***

"What do you see, Wash?" Fordo called up the tallest tower on the barge, the whole crew standing by, passing around Carth's canteen.

Wash sat atop the crates with a small collapsible spyglass they found on the pushboat, aimed straight at Gateway village, slowly growing on the horizon.

"Movement in town," He called back, "Can't tell what yet…"

Fordo paced in front of his men, pride melting away any worry at the sight of them all armed and armored in matching sets, their brand new banner blowing in the breeze.

"Look at you all," Fordo said, "A real champion-trained, battle-ready war party. Transformed from workers to warriors in a fuckin' day. Ready to make the cogs regret rearing their rusty heads out of whatever pathetic hole they crawled out of," Fordo laughed, "I couldn't be more proud."

Fordo pointed out over the water, "You see that bridge? On that bridge is the means to avenge our families and echo our names through the Halls Of History, the means for us all to tell the world that we were here to save it."

A smile crept across Fordo's face, "When Carth and I were boys, we used to play a game with the other warphans called Barricade. A war game where one team attacks the barricade and the other Is the barricade, a wall of warriors tasked with breaking the tide of attackers and stopping any from passing through. Carth and I were the best......And I believe with my whole heart it's because, before every single game, Carth and I would start this chant with our team......Just childish nonsense words to get the blood boiling, get the heart pumping, and get the luck flowing......"

Carth started laughing

"It's real silly and I know this is the farthest thing from a game......But I believe the chant works just the same......If you are to be my wall, if we mean to defend this bridge, I need you to humor me just this once, as a favor between brothers......Are you with me?"

The crew looked a mix of amused and open, even Jason who's been surprisingly well behaved since the attack, turning Fordo's smile to a grin. He reached out his hand to young Wesley, who eagerly passed Fordo their flag.

"Follow my lead and stop when I raise my hands..." Fordo looked up at their flowing banner then scanned the eyes of every crew member, fanning the fire before chanting,

"Bah...Roh...Cah...Doh......Deh...Fen...Doh...Roh..."

Carth immediately joined his friend

"Bah...Roh...Cah...Doh......Deh...Fen...Doh...Roh..."

Some joined enthusiastically, others hesitantly, but soon most everybody was smiling, chanting nonsense in unison. Fordo quickened the pace, knocking the butt of the flag against the deck.

"Bah...Roh...Cah...Doh......Deh...Fen...Doh...Roh..."

"Bah...Roh...Cah...Doh......Deh...Fen...Doh...Roh...!"

"Bah...Roh...Cah...Doh...Deh...Fen...Doh...Roh...!"

"BahRoh...CahDoh...DehFen...DohRoh!"

"BahRoh! CahDoh! DehFen! DohRoh!"

"BahRohCahDoh! DehFenDohRoh!"

"BahRohCahDoh! DehFenDohRoh!"

"BahRohCahDoh!! DehFenDohRoh!!"

"BAHROHCAHDOH!!! DEHFENDOHROH!!!"

Soon the entire crew surrounded Fordo, screaming and jumping, pounding their weapons, Fordo slamming the flag in the middle of them, heart pounding, blood pumping, shouting and laughing harder than he ever had in his entire life. He felt invincible! He felt alive! Ready to face the whole world and fucking conquer it!

"Fordo!" A small voice cut through the chaos

The chanting ceased the moment Fordo threw up his hands, making him feel like a god, "What is it, Wash?"

"Gateway! There's no bots in sight! No fighting at all, just people building on the bridge! Looks like we beat them here!"

Beat them here? They were so fast, there's no way they wouldn't be here yet...No, no, that doesn't make any sense...

Fordo realized the crew was staring at him and said, "You hear that, friends? Today is not the day we die!" They all cheered, "We don't know how much time we have, but we will use it all! Grab your tools and keep your weapons close, today we get to go to work!"

***

"Where are they?" Fordo gathered Carth, Sam, and Doyle while the rest of the crew readied the harpoons to pull into port. "Those things run faster than the river, there's no way we beat them here!"

Sam gestured for him to calm down, "Let's not jump to any conclusions..."

"They don't need food, or sleep, or water...even at walking speed they should have been here days ago."

Carth shrugged, "We should be grateful we have more time to prepare."

"No, we should be Worried that we don't know where the Fuck they are, Carth...They should be Here, Right now, why aren't they?"

"Hold on, mate, there's a dozen reasons we could've beaten them. Maybe they're roaming Farside without an objective, attacking people, but not actively looking for them."

"They jumped us upriver, maybe they headed north to Riverwood first?"

"No, I don't buy it. They threw themselves into the river just to attack a passing boat fifty yards away, they're looking for people, they have to be..." Fordo paced about, biting his nails.

"The one we found buried in the crates was real calm and still until we dug it out, maybe they only jump when they're in a position to. Maybe they only move when they're sure there's prey about." Sam said

"I guess you're right......" Fordo rubbed his eyes

"You guys found another cog in the crates??" Carth asked

"We dug it up and put 'er down pretty quick." Doyle nodded

"Something's wrong about this, I can feel it..." Fordo said

"Well, there's no way to find out before they get here, so what use is there worrying about it?" Carth said

"Fuck, I don't like it," Fordo shook his head, "But you're right. Let's find out whoever runs this town and get this place fortified. I have a feeling the old defenses don't account for them dropping out of the fuckin' sky."

***

Fordo found it odd walking without hearing hard knocking, his heavy boots sinking into the soft soaked dirt of the eastern shore. Gateway village stood before him and his friends, a humble, minimalist town of great historical resonance and little else.

Almost a century ago, the survivors of FarFall found themselves trapped in the barren Farside nothingness between the Dragon's Teeth Mountains and the Siena River. Without food or resources more than they could scavenge from The Great Wreck itself, brave explorers ventured far and wide to find a way across the relentless waters.

Warren the first, the Founder of Riverwood discovered the realwood forest in the far north and managed to send enough timber down the Siena for the First Men to build a bridge across her, and thus the gateway to the rest of the world.

Burnt down and reborn by the grand garrison who defended it during the first war, the beautiful bridge was an architectural marvel far surpassing its predecessor and wildly outshining the humble village in its shadow.

A long, wide platform, over two hundred yards across, suspended by a web of thick metal cables, stretching up and between two massive archways, towering over the town on either end of the bridge. The western arch was carved and patterned into a behemoth breaching wyrm, erupting from a field of long grass. The eastern arch stood as two realwood trees with intertwining canopies. The supports below, standing knee-deep in the river were breathtakingly shaped into two giants holding up the bridge on their shoulders. One a scarred, bearded man in tattered clothes and the other a dented, damaged, first-war robot.

Most of the younger crew members looked up in awe, while the older vets looked up in pride.

"Would you look at that..." Chop laughed, "Still standing, tall as ever."

"You been here before?" Carth asked

"Are you kidding? I spent six months cutting planks for the fuckin' thing. Got so used to standin' under those two trees I moved up to Riverwood."

"Did you two work on that?" Fordo asked Sam and Doyle

"Naw, mate, Bali's company worked the roads."

"I was off with Warren trying to find us a home," Sam said

"I was..." Doyle looked uneasy for a moment, "I was somewhere else."

A few farmer-looking villagers greeted Fordo's company as they marched up the bank to the main road through town. Some of their eyes filled with hope, others with fear, seeing their fully armored warband. A fairly mixed response of, "Look, look! Help is here!" and "Is this really all that's come?"

Arranged like a key, an open circle of inns and taverns surrounded a dusty cobblestone courtyard, connecting to a strip of two-story shops along the main road, leading straight up to the realwood archway.

"There aren't any homes," Bethany noted

"Tourist town," Luca muttered, "Folks just come to see the bridge and pay respects, no work here worth settlin' for."

A pale stone obelisk twice as tall as any building stood proud in the center of the courtyard, a monument to all those lost in the First War. Fordo watched Jason walk up and press his hand against the stone tower, straining his neck to look at the very top, with a wide golden grin and the same proud look as those who built the bridge.

"What a creepy kid..." Fordo whispered to himself

"It is a pretty prime pillar," Carth smiled

"Yeah, to remember a fuckin' atrocity..."

"You sure like throwing around those fancy words sometimes."

"Just 'cause you can't spell them, Carth, don't make them fancy" Chop chuckled

A few young men ran up to the company, "Did Riverwood send you ahead of the army?"

"We are the army, Riverwood's locked down tight," Fordo said

"You mean, you're all that's coming?"

"If word reached you then it shoulda made its way to Scrapyard by now, they'll be here in force soon enough. Who's in charge of the defense?"

"Well, Captain Culver rode out to scout the cogs a couple days ago, but he never came back......"

"So who's been managing the fortifications?"

"Well, he left his lieutenants, but they rode out yesterday to find him and haven't come back either......We've been waiting for someone to show up and help us."

Fordo stepped up uncomfortably close to the man, "Are you fucking with me?"

"No sir……"

Fordo turned to his crew and shook his head before shouting, "All hands to the barge!" The villager's flinched, "Weapons, food, supplies, everything off the boat, organized, ready to use! Grab every villager along the way, they say no, you spit on 'em! Sam, Wash, Doyle, with me! Carth, Chop, I want that boat cleared off and ready to break down, I'll send more workers to help haul the wood." Fordo turned back to the young man while his crew went to work, "How many men are here to defend?"

"I don't know, maybe around two hundred have come in from the villages?"

"Bring all of them here, right now. I need every abled-bodied person standing in this courtyard in thirty minutes or so help me, I will let this village burn. Go!" The young men sprinted off in different directions, shouting and spreading the word.

"We're sunk……" Fordo said after they'd gone, "I didn't think we'd have to start from fuckin' scratch."

"Hey, at least there's nothing to tear down," Doyle mused, "I thought we'd have to undo whatever mess they'd thrown together just to build something usable."

"What do you need from me?" Wash asked

"For now, you're my runner. I can't be everywhere at once, you take any orders I have wherever they need to go and come straight back to me. Prime?"

He nodded

"You two help me figure out traps and get these people in line. We need all hands working until the cogs come. We have no idea how much time we have left, we need everyone working like we have none."

***

"Get in line, you filthy Dregs!" Doyle and Sam started shouting orders before anyone could ask who they were or where they came from. Men and women of all shapes and sizes filed into ranks on either side of the obelisk, forming two separate hundred-man blocks, all facing Fordo, Sam, and Doyle down the main road.

Filtered in from the surrounding villages, most dressed in well-worn worker's garb; Thick tunics, aprons, overalls, Fordo's company were the only ones properly armed or armored.

Fordo stepped up on the small podium he had built out of planks and barrels, while folks funneled in, and shouted over the two hundred-headed blocks, "We sorely lack the time and luxury of proper introductions, so I will make this quick! The enemy has returned! They mean to take this bridge! And you all came here on your own initiative because you mean to do something about it!"

He pointed out behind them, down the long road leading east to Scrapyard and the rest of Aureum, "Your world is in danger once more! Your families, your friends, your neighbors, all of their lives are in our Hands! So let's put them to work!"

Fordo looked the lines in the eyes as he shouted, "Last time those cowards crossed this bridge......there was Nothing standing in their way! Not this time! This Time......they have to deal with Us! Us and all the vengeful wrath we can muster before they get here!"

Fordo shouted orders without waiting for cheers or nods or any sign of approval, Fordo needed every spare second they could scrape together for his plans to work, "Blacksmiths!" Fordo pointed to his right, "Carpenters!" then to his left, "Gather here, Now! The rest of you help my crew break up the barge! All lumber to the bridge, All scrap metal to the forge! We are out of fucking time, Now Move Your Ass!"

***

"Can it be done?" Fordo discussed his plans with the workers over a map of the town, quickly and crudely scratched into a wooden plank with an old rusted nail.

Most nodded, "We need a full day at least. How long do we have?"

Fordo shook his head, "We have no idea, so we work on what we need first. The swinging gates are priority one, everything else comes second."

"Why are we making something they can open themselves? Why not just block the bridge with straight barricades?"

"We can't face them in force. They break through altogether, we're sunk. We need something big and heavy that opens and closes to slow them down and filter them through a little at a time, face them in waves." The engineers nodded in agreement.

"Why not burn down the bridge outright? Cut them off with the river?"

"We cut them off, but we also surrender the whole of Farside, and any means for us to cross and push them back to wherever they're coming from. We burn the bridge as a last resort, Only if the village is lost. Our goal is not to stop them, only to hold out for as long as we can, buying enough time for Scrapyard to come and plug the hole and push them back. Understood?"

Nods and murmurs confirmed their agreement, "Let's get to work!"

The engineers rushed off to their tasks, leaving Fordo, Wash, Sam, and Doyle.

"It's a good plan, mate. " Doyle watched the workers scurry off, "If we have time to throw it together, we can hold them off a good long while."

"Let's hope we have a little more time."

"How are you gonna take down the bridge?" Jason's overly excited voice sounded right behind Fordo.

Fordo's head preemptively ached, "It won't come to that."

"But what if it does? How are you going to do it?"

"We won't need to."

"So you just don't know how?" Jason laughed

"Oil the supports, set them ablaze."

"Oh…" Jason sounded disappointed, "But that's so slow and boring."

"Well, how the fuck would you do it?"

"I'd bring it down all at once, fast and loud!"

"That's not even possible."

"Maybe for an idiot like you!"

Fordo grit his teeth, wondering why he even humored the kid "This isn't a fuckin' game, cunt, we don't have time for this glass! Either find a way to help or stay out of our fuckin' way before I have you locked in a closet somewhere!"

"Jason," Sam cut in, "Go figure out your bridge plan and meet up with me later, let us work."

"You'll see!" Jason laughed, running off towards the bridge.

Fordo rubbed his temples, "How can you fuckin' stand that kid, Sam?"

"You let him under your skin pretty easy," Doyle smirked

"It's not his fault..." Sam said

"That he's an asshole?"

"That he's Troubled, Fordo...That he's a troubled, fucked up Child who doesn't know how to cope with whatever horrible, likely cruel experience turned him into this asshole so early in life...My daughter wasn't much different and now she'll Never get the chance to change because Nobody ever gave her one..."

Sam looked deeply upset, pacing away to recenter herself, Doyle placing a hand on her shoulder.

Fordo felt like glass, "I didn't mean to make it personal..."

Doyle nodded for him to move on, which Fordo enthusiastically obliged.

"Wash," Fordo said, deciding to ignore mention of the yellow-eyed boy from here on out, "tell Carth, once everything's unloaded, to get a team to hammer platforms for crossboys and raise ballistas up on those rooftops. You guys come with me, we'll take a lap, see what else we can manage."

***

"Heave...Heave...Heave!"

Fordo's hands burned against the rope, sweat dripping down his temples as he and twenty others pulled on a line with all their might, hauling a massive realwood beam up over their heads.

Thirty feet tall, around three feet thick, each beam was probably sturdy enough to hold up the bridge itself. Instead they were rigorously levitated up against the bridge's grand archway to be secured on great heavy hinges. Strapped together with ropes to sit vertically above the arch, ready and waiting to swing down and slam the opening shut at the proper moment. Some beams were toothed with long metal spikes, hammered and sharpened from jagged scrap metal to make it as difficult and damaging as possible for the bots to push forward and force their way between the beams.

Fordo spent much of the day scrutinizing the smith's handiwork on the hinges, ensuring their strength to endure the initial heavy swing of the gates when they're finally unleashed. "This is the work that wins the war!" He'd shout over the clanging hammers and blasting bellows, breathing life into the coals.

The night came and went, spent making sure every hand had tools and purpose. Doors and windows boarded up, crude firing platforms sat on rooftops, ballistas raised and readied. Piles of heavy furniture and barricades were built and scattered across the bridge itself, countless ropes and chains alike tied knee high to trip and tangle the bots in their race across.

Older villagers were set to bundle bolts, gather food, and fill water skins while the younger ran about, making sure every building and barricade had a store of rations to keep up strength and morale.

The small town was ravaged by their work, turned from a simple strip of shiny shops into a cluttered patchwork fortress firing range of wood and metal.

Fordo stood facing the bridge, chewing on rabbit jerky, watching the workers lift the last beam into place as the sun rose behind them, "Filter them through, rip them up with wires and razor rain, finish off any stragglers."

"How do we combat the flyers?" Sam asked

"I was hoping you two had some ideas," Fordo passed her some jerky.

Doyle scratched his chin stubble, "They only fell one at a time and a lot fell short. However they're launching themselves, it's not super efficient."

"They only flew maybe half the length of the bridge, as well," Sam added, "The whole town is in the shadow of that archway that should give us cover for the street and buildings.

They could use that to outflank, throwing bots behind us, but we don't know if they're smart enough to launch where there aren't people."

Fordo cursed, "I hate this guessing game, but there's not much we can do regardless. One at a time we can handle, it's the all at once I'm worried about."

"Oy, sir? Sir! What are you doing?" Fordo heard shouting behind them, back near the main barricade blocking the street.

"It's okay, it's okay, I do this all the time. Don't you trust me?"

"I don't even know who you- Hey!" The trio turned at the sound of dozens of musical instruments all falling and clanging into the road at once. A tall lanky brown man with round poofy hair stood atop the barricade barefoot, grinning and giggling at his overturned pull cart he let drop into the street.

"What the hell are you doing?"

The stranger dropped down and rolled in a surprisingly graceful somersault. His strange beige coat flapped behind him as he popped back up onto his feet. Haphazardly tossing instruments over his shoulder back into the cart, most of them missing or bouncing off entirely, clanging loudly back into the street, completely ignoring the distressed men shouting to get his attention.

"What the fuck...?" The worker looked around like he wanted someone else to tell him if this was really happening.

"Oy!" Fordo called, jogging up the road to meet them. Guitars, trumpets, a couple violins, along with a dozen other wood and metal instruments Fordo couldn't name, all dinged and dented, scattered in the street. "Is there a problem?"

The worker looked relieved, "This guy came out of nowhere, just started hauling this glass up the barricade and dumped it over the side!"

Fordo looked at the poofy haired man who was still cartoonishly tossing his own belongings.

"Are you alright there, buddy?"

The strange man looked at Fordo like he had appeared out of thin air, greeting him with a bright white grin and a deep whimsical laugh, "You should try this, it's like someone just left them here." The man kept tossing his instruments without breaking eye contact with Fordo.

"Would you like some help?" Fordo asked, unsure whether or not the man was fucking with them.

"Could you help me find my Ely?"

"Is that a thing or a person?"

"She's just the prettiest girl in the whole wide world," He laughed long and hard before his face dropped suddenly into a blank, open mouthed stare, like someone had flipped his off switch. Fordo and the other workers slowly backed away from the frozen stranger, still bent over mid reach.

"Hey..........Hey, are you al-"

Everyone flinched, momentarily reaching for their weapons, as the man jolted back into consciousness, continuing to fling his contraptions behind him, wincing at every painful clang and cry of each instrument thrown into the pile.

Fordo let out a small sigh of relief and grabbed the man by the shoulder, "Hey, it's alright, we'll take care of that for you," he gestured for everyone to quickly pick up the instruments.

"You have some really spooky eyes," The man laughed

"Thank you…"

"Can you see my future?"

"I can…It's you going back the way you came. It's not safe here for you."

"Oh No, I already looked for Ely back there," The man grinned.

"'Back there' meaning, the whole fuckin' world?"

"Mhm, If she's not here, I gotta keep going."

"Well you can't go that way. You may not have heard…… but the bots have returned."

The man just smiled and blinked like he was still waiting for Fordo to tell him why he couldn't cross the bridge.

Fordo gestured all around him to the barricades, ballistas, and the couple hundred armed workers rushing around them to absolutely zero reaction.

Doyle stepped up behind Fordo, looking amused, "There's monsters that way, mate."

"Do they like music?"

"I guess we don't know that they don't," Doyle smirked

The stranger's grin widened before he grabbed his cart and hauled it past them towards the bridge, trailing a noxious cloud of sweat and dirt.

"What's wrong with this guy...?" Fordo asked mostly himself, waving for the spectating villagers to get back to work.

"Some people lost their minds in the last war," Sam said

"Others are just plain crazy," Doyle shrugged

"Should we lock him up for his own safety?"

"Everyone chooses their own fate, mate."

"Even if it gets them killed?"

"A person's life is their own, to do with as they please, even to throw away."

"Should try to convince him at least, right?" Fordo asked himself more than his friends.

"No harm in tryin'"

Fordo knew in his heart he didn't care about this man. Some crazy cunt wants to kill himself, just means one less weirdo wandering around out there. But he welcomed the brief distraction and felt if he kept encountering these unpredictable crazies on his journeys, like with any other skill, he needed the practice to help deal with them.

Fordo jogged to catch up to the man, "Back to work, don't worry..." Fordo waved away any friends and workers standing by and walked down the bridge side by side with the stranger.

Logical approach... "Hey, if you cross this, you're dead within a day, do you understand?"

The stranger laughed, "You can't trick me, I'm not even real."

Fordo nodded, *Maybe a little less logical...* "We can't clear the road for your cart, you won't be able to get all your glass across with-"

"Hey what noise do you make?"

"What……Noise?" Fordo laughed, caught off guard.

"Yeah, your noise, what's your noise?" The man stared down at Fordo like a child asking if he had a girlfriend.

"My name's Fordo…If that's what you mean," He stuck out his hand to shake.

The man grinned and shook just the tips of Fordo's fingers, "I'm Andre! Hey……You wanna see something?"

"Uh, Sure, man"

Andre pulled a dark blade from beneath his coat and clasped Fordo's arm in an iron grip. Blood drained from Fordo's face, his stomach dropped, eyes wide with fear as the towering stranger yanked him off balance uncomfortably close, hot wet breath seeping into his ear as the smiling man said, "Watch this," and jammed the blade into Fordo's gut.

"Ah!" Choking on the stranger's stench and the sudden pain, Fordo coughed and shoved away from the man, staggering backwards, clutching his own stomach. Fordo looked in terror at the man laughing hysterically in his face, holding a sheathed wyrmstooth dagger.

Sheathed?

Fordo looked down to find his stomach dry of blood, No guts spilling at his feet like he feared, "You son of a bitch!" He drew his hammer and smacked the dagger out of the laughing man's hand in the same motion, "What the Fuck is wrong with you??" Fordo's fist slammed into man's giant nose, sending him sprawling backwards, but the laughing never stopped.

"I thought you fucking……" Fordo glanced at the dagger and immediately dropped his hammer in disbelief, "What is this……?"

Miraculously, no……impossibly……laying on the ground, in the possession of this fucking Psycho, was unmistakably, the very same wyrmtooth dagger Fordo had meticulously crafted and gifted Alexander on the first anniversary of their meeting.

What did you do to him……?

The stranger laughed and laughed, blood pouring from his swollen nose, "Isn't that insane? It like doesn't even wor-"

Slam!

Fordo's boot crashed into the man's stupid face, "Where?"

He grabbed the man by coat and dragged him onto his stomach, "The Fuck??"

Fordo pressed his face into the ground, right next to the dagger, "Did You Get This???"

"What is going on with you?" The man asked calmly

Fordo grabbed his hair and slammed his face into the ground, "Where???"

"This thing?" The man laughed, "Some weirdo gave it to me a couple days ago."

Fordo flipped him over and pressed a knee on his throat, "Lie to me again and I'll make sure you never find Ely."

"No, the…kid gave it to me…" The man choked under Fordo's knee, still smiling.

"Liar! You found it or stole it, you must have! He wouldn't just give it away, what did you do to him??" Fordo lifted his knee and grabbed the man's collar.

"He really liked my horn," the man smiled, "kid jumped out of a tree just to trade with me. Him and his floating dog...Teeko?"

Meeko.........The floating dog.

Countless recollections of Alexander stupidly carrying his dog up into trees flooded Fordo's mind...*He really did find Al...*

"Where...?"

"Back by the village with the metal men. Hey, could they make me a third arm? I've always wanted one on my back."

"Back in Scrapyard......?" Fordo sat down and ran his hands through his hair.

You're alive......Where the hell were you hiding, you son of a bitch......? And you gave away my Gift to This fuckin' freak?? When I finally find you, I'm gonna beat your ass.

"Fordo!" Carth's voice snapped him out of his trance.

He looked around and realized much of his crew was staring at him sitting alone on the bridge. Fordo spun around thinking the stranger had somehow been imaginary, only to find him struggling to haul his cart across the bridge over tripwires and wardrobes, with a big bloody smile still on his face.

"Ford, what happened? They said you attacked this guy and-" Fordo picked up the dagger still sitting next to him and held it up to Carth, "Oh Sink my ass...Is that Al's dagger??"

"Said he traded for it with Alexander a few days ago, out by Scrapyard..."

"I knew he was alive!"

"You can't kill him..."

"Hey, didn't you give that to him?"

Fordo shrugged, "...Maybe I misremember..."

***

Fordo spun the leather cased dagger in his palm, watching that lunatic pile those mistreated instruments back into his cart for the seventh time that day to the cheers of an overworked crowd.

Almost the whole of the work was complete, the defenses built, loaded, stocked with rations, reinforced. Anyone who cared to now watched the stranger struggle across the last stretch of bridge; betting on Andre's progress, their only form of entertainment. Fordo slept a whole shift and awoke just in time to watch him cross the finish line. *Only took six whole hours, you stupid son of a bitch...*

The sun sank below the mountain line for the second time since they'd landed in Gateway, a low fog floating in, quickly covering the horizon. *They were supposed to be here.....................* *Where the fuck is my fight?*

"That's prime," Wash said, appearing at Fordo's side on the barricade, "Where'd you get it?"

"I made it for someone years ago, but I guess they didn't want it..."

"Can I see it?"

"Just 'see' it?"

Wash threw on a guilty, mischievous smile.

"Don't you have enough presents?"

"There's no such thing," Wash laughed

Fordo bit his cheek, resisting his own smile, but handed over the dagger nonetheless, "Here, I'll save you a guilt trip... Probably worth more in your hands anyway."

"Prime!" Wash unsheathed the blade, twirling it expertly between his fingers, "This is waayy better work than Jason's."

"I already said you can have it, kid, no need to suck my grub about it," Fordo laughed, "You take care of that."

Just then, slowly clambering up over the side of the bridge, a bundle of rope slung across his chest, absolutely drenched with sweat, was young Jason.

"Oy," Fordo called, "What the hell were you doing down there?"

The yellow eyed boy gestured rudely in reply, panting, "You'll...see..." with an exhausted half smile.

"No, tell me right now, you can't just-"

"Ay, He made it!" Someone shouted, uproarious laughter and cheering erupting from the onlookers, all pumping their fists and raising their weapons for their idiotic champion of distraction.

Jason's eyes lit up, scrambling up the barricade like he forgot he was tired, just to sit and watch the distant stranger like the start of some grand tournament.

Though no more than a speck in the distance, The Music Man turned and bowed, reveling in his applause for his apparent performance, spreading his arms, throwing kisses their way as an unnaturally large wall of white fog crept up behind him. Cheers calmed and faded into nervous laughter as they watched the fog sweep over and devour the man entirely, like he and all behind him was simply erased from existence. Fordo's heart quickened.

An eerie silence followed, broken only by gasps and murmurs from the crowd watching the seemingly living mist swell and thicken until it consumed and obstructed the entirety of the grand archway. None of the fog spilled out onto the bridge, as if held back by some invisible barrier. The monstrous mist soon towered as tall as the bridge itself, stretching up and out over the whole of the horizon like some world-eating abomination.

Whether for Wash's comfort or his own, Fordo unwittingly put an arm around the boy's shoulder while they stared up in awe.........Witnessing the coming of this strange new god.........

Fordo felt this was a sight he would never forget, likely one he'd never see again, until he realized why it also felt so familiar. "Oh Hell..." Fordo cracked the faintest shadow of a smile, Jason and Wash both looking up at him as he whispered, "Show yourselves, you bastards..."

Jason beamed with delight. Most of the men turned and looked up at Fordo with wonder and worry, preparing for orders or explanation, when out of the mist marched a slow moving mob of mindless metal men.

Fucking......Finally......

"Sound The Bells And Arm Yourselves! The Cowards Come At Last!"

Al and Meeko

7

'*Don't be afraid……*' He awoke to these words with a jolt, escaping from a nightmare he couldn't remember. Gasping for breath like it was his first, he choked on the cloth that accompanied the air in the suffocating blackness.

Yanked back into existence as quickly as he was snapped out of it. He remembered falling, but found himself wrapped up tight in something rough and itchy, banging his head on wooden boards, heavy weights on his chest. Smelling dirt and hearing nothing, unable to move beyond a squirm, it hit him like a giant metal fist. Sweat and screams building within him…… "NO, No, NO, PLEASE, PLEASE, PLEASE No!"

It finally happened, the subject of countless nightmares, the one thing he feared most……He'd come back to life, trapped in the ground with the grubs in his own fucking grave.

Al screamed and thrashed, bashing his head and shoulders against the sides of his wooden coffin, the coarse fabric burned like the rope, scraping his skin, binds bruising his wrists. No matter how long it takes, how much it hurts, however many more times he'd die trying, he wasn't spending eternity in a fucking box, he was clawing his way out of the ground before the grubs got to him.

Hearing a sound through his struggles and screams, he went still and listened……Muffled barking……*Meeko, you made it!*

His eyes flooded with desperate tears and determination. *I knew you wouldn't leave me......*

He shook the coffin as hard as he could only to find it wasn't a coffin and he was falling once more, thudding and rolling onto what felt like dirt. He cried as hard for love of life as he did for fear of death.

Al pushed and pulled at his wrappings until he was drenched in sweat and tears, feeling them loosen ever so slightly. Meeko bit and pulled from the outside, speeding up the process significantly. His face finally burst through, he drank in the sweet nectar of fresh cold air and the blue light of the twin moons. Soon his arm came free, then the next, then the rest. Sobbing in the open air with a thankful Meeko on his chest, licking his tears away as quick as they came.

"Are you okay, boy?" He wept into Meeko's fur, "Bali was right, I'm so sorry, I'm so sorry..." It happened again, less than a week later, he'd gotten Meeko hurt and left him to wonder, alone for who knows how long. And then he remembered "Auri! Where's-"

He looked around to find her staring at him like he was the scariest thing she'd ever seen.

"Auri, are you alright...?" He croaked. She stared at him, breathing heavy, scanning him like she thought he might pull some kind of weapon. "Auri, it's me...It's really me," He started to crawl closer to her, but she flinched away, holding up a hand to stop him. He didn't know what to say, he didn't know what he could say, but if he was her, he probably wouldn't believe it either.

"What the fuck is going on...?" She asked in a horse whisper.

"It's complicated...But I'll explain everything... Everything...I promise."

"Is this real?"

"I really fucking hope so," Al cried

"I watched you die...I heard you die...Your face was so swollen, I couldn't...Al, you were the deadest thing I've ever seen..."

"I don't know how to explain it, so let me just show you..." Al grabbed a small tooling knife Carth gave him and cut a red line across his palm. He reached out to Auri who watched the cut slowly fuse back together.

"I don't know how, I don't know why, but Meeko and I have this...healing power. Just always have."

She stared at his hand for an eternity before asking, "You knew you were going to come back?"

"I guess I never really know, but yeah, I hoped so and have before."

"Why the fuck would you tell those people it was your fault?? You fucking idiot! Why wouldn't you tell me you could...?

"I didn't have time to explain, it'd just be confusing."

"More confusing than 'Take me with you, no matter what happens'? Are you insane? I've been dragging your Dead Fucking Body for Hours with No Idea what to do with it! Why not 'I can explain later, I have healing powers, keep my body safe, I'll be back soon.' Whether I believed you or not I could have prepared for it somehow! Not watch you scream your way back to life like some monster right in the middle of mourning you, you Asshole! ....Say something!"

Al's lip quivered and hands shook, he looked at the ground and cried, "I was so scared..." He rocked back and forth, "I didn't mean to leave you..."

Auri shook her head and latched onto his chest, squeezing him tighter than the wrappings, "I thought you were gone forever..."

"I'm so sorry..." He squeezed her back, "I promised I'd get you home..."

"That didn't make any sense either..." She cried, "I have so many questions......"

"I know......I'll tell you everything."

"I'm so glad you're okay..."

They both cried and held each other, with Meeko on their laps and Dari at their backs, until they drifted off to a much needed sleep.

***

"Hold on, you And Meeko have the Same power?"

"Mhm"

"How the......What?" Auri laughed, "That's more confusing than the actual ability!"

"I don't know what it means, but we must've always been together, even before I remember..."

"So you can heal any wound, even fatal ones, just the worse it is, the longer it takes...Is there anything you can't heal?"

Al removed his wooden prosthetic ring finger and tossed it into Auri's lap.

"Ew, what the fuck?" She picked it up and flung it back at him like it was a living spider, "Do Not throw your bits at me!"

"Burns leave the worst scars and we can't grow back limbs or anything that crazy. If we lose a piece, it's lost for good... Same with memories, but Otherwise, I'm not really sure how else it works."

"I mean, coming back to life is crazy enough..."

He noticed her eyes fix on the wide purple scars that circled his wrist.

"You said it's like numbing, before, do you still feel pain?"

"I feel everything......Every time," Al nodded and screwed his finger back into place.

"I'm so sorry..."

Al shrugged, "Some things stay scary, but I've gotten used to a lot of it. Tearing my wrist hurt more than the hanging."

"I knew it! That was way too much blood for how okay you were, I thought I was just in shock or something."

Al rubbed the jagged white cloud of a scar where his bones ripped through his wrist.

"It's okay if it's personal, but......How many times have you come back now?"

Al took in a deep breath, "This was my fourth time... that I remember."

"Fourth??" Auri shook her head, "That's so scary..."

"I'm sorry again, I didn't mean to freak you out."

"No, I meant scary for you. Remembering Dying...
Four Different Times...That's gotta do something to a person."

"I don't always remember...And if I do, it's like
remembering a dream, where I can see fuzzy details, but can't
really describe it, you know?" Al rubbed the back of his head, "I
think I'm more afraid of Not dying..."

"What do you mean?"

"Like when I woke up this time, I thought I was buried
alive...What if one day I am? Stuck underground or underwater
or something..."

"Man, I didn't even think about that...burning
or drowning or suffocating somewhere just...Forever?
That's so scary..."

"Not my favorite thing to think about..."

They walked in silence for a long while until Auri asked,
"Do you go somewhere......when you die? Like...I don't know..."

"If I do, I don't remember...It mostly feels like sleep..."
Al put his hand in his jacket pocket and felt the hard creases in
the old crumpled photo, "I wanna say I don't go anywhere, but
whenever I wake up...I hear a voice in my head..."

"Like, not your voice?"

Al shook his head.

"What's it say...?"

"'Don't be afraid'......It's always the same words, in
the same voice. A woman's...Soft and sweet, like a mother...
comforting a child."

"Your mother...?"

"I don't know..." Al shrugged

"Mother Aure...?" Auri half chuckled

"No, I wish..." Al smiled, "Daisy used to joke about that. I really wish the gods were real.........Actual gods, not just ideas people praise out of respect, but tangible, magical beings messing with or looking out for all of us. Would be a lot easier to explain things...Having someone to thank or... someone to blame."

"I don't know, I like knowing our fates are our own, we're not just someone else's play things."

"Maybe we are...all stuck in some big game without even knowing, but whatever piece I am, I'm luckier than most. Woke up with a friend and a gift...Found by a family I love, in a beautiful world I get to explore...I won't forget that again......"

"Hey, I know you said before that you like who you are now, and I like you too, communication skills aside, but......" Auri's voice cut out like she was choking back tears, "But I'm so sorry you don't remember..."

"I don't wanna forget again..." Al handed Auri the old faded photo, "Bali said when he found me that all I had was Meeko, a hatchet, and this picture in my jacket..."

Auri held it like a delicate flower, "She's beautiful......"

"I have no way of knowing for sure, but I think the voice is hers, it has to be."

"Who do you think she is..."

"I don't know, but if anyone could tell me who I was, it's her..."

"Have you tried to find her before?"

"We went looking for her a week...or...Ten months ago, but... didn't get very far."

Auri looked closely at the picture, "I think this is your mom..."

Warm blood rushed to his cheeks, "You think so?"

"I mean, you have all different colors, but maybe you just take after your dad. Your eyes and face both share the same shapes, she could easily be your mother."

Al smiled to himself before guilty tears filled his eyes, "I hope not..." he croaked

"What, why not?"

"That means there's people I left behind......A whole life and family I lost and abandoned for another......Maybe that's why I never looked too hard for answers......I'm just a coward...... Afraid to face the truth and take responsibility."

"Hey, you are Not a coward."

"I don't know who I am, Auri..."

"No, you don't know who you Were, but you know exactly who you Are. Someone gentle enough to cry for a stranger's second chance, kind enough to give up your dream to walk her across the whole world just to help find her brother. Strong enough to have lost an entire life, yet still appreciate the next. Brave and stupid enough to admit guilt to an angry grieving mob. Alexander, you woke up after being fucking Murdered in front of your friends and the First thing you did was make sure that We were okay......You are not a coward, Alexander, don't you ever say that again."

Al's lips quivered as he tried in vain to laugh to himself, "Yeah, you're right. I'm pretty prime, nevermind," Al wiped his eyes, "Thank you, girly."

"If we can find my brother, I know we can find your mother...We'll find out together just where we belong."

***

'Gateway Ahead' The troop passed a painted sign, nailed to a crooked post. Al chuckled at its ambiguity, looking back to read the other side, 'Scrapyard A Ways'

He nodded at their vague guide, "Many thanks, friend."

"Mm?" Auri awoke, having fallen asleep sometime late afternoon.

"Sorry, girly"

"S'okay..." She yawned and stretched, looking around in the moonlit fields, "As pretty as the grass is, I hate that..." She yawned some more, "I hate that I can't ever tell how far we've gone."

"Gateway's ahead, we're almost halfway to Riverwood, just gotta follow the river north. You're only a few days away from your brother."

"We're almost to Gateway...? We might run into the bots pretty soon."

"Maybe...We're pretty high up on these hills, I think we'll be able to see them way before they see us. We should have time to get out of their way, I think...well, I hope."

Meeko barked back to them.

"Yeah, Meeko will spot them for sure."

"I've been trying not to think about them the past few days. But...What the heck do we do if we see them?"

"I don't know......Depends how far off we see them. We watch and wait, I think. Either they'll move on and pass, or we'll find a way around them. They sneak up on Us somehow, we run like hell, play the world's worst game of Hide And Seek in all this grass. I can take on one or two, Maybe, but that's a big maybe."

"We haven't really talked about what Natori told us."

"No, we haven't, huh?"

"I don't know a lot about the bots. Growing up in Riverwood, there's like an unspoken rule that you're not supposed to talk about them."

"In Scrapyard, they're all there is to talk about."

"Do we...Do we know where they came from? Whenever I'd ask, growing up, I could never get a straight answer."

"Well, they came from space, of course, like us, out of the Axiom," Al laughed like it was obvious.

"Is that the old station we crashed?"

Al looked at Auri with a sly smile, "Are you fucking with me?"

"What? No, like I really don't know," Auri blushed

"You didn't learn history in Riverwood?"

She shrugged, "I don't know, no one really talks about it, I guess. Everyone just distracts themselves with work to forget the bots even exist."

"Huh..." Al chuckled, "All I've done since I woke up was listen to vets war stories and Daisy's history, I never thought......So yeah, the Spacewalkers used the bots for everything; Labor, calculations, servants, the station was full of them. Even sent a bunch down ahead of us to prepare the planet for us."

"Prepare it how?"

"For the first few years they collected samples of soil and atmosphere and such, studying the plant and wildlife so that we could adapt earthborn life to survive on Aureum. Once we figured that out, we sent bots back down to plant trees and crops all around, breed elk and hogs and rabbits so our settlers would have food and whatnot to survive."

"So the bots were just big farmers?"

"Sarah called them Gardners, just spreading the seeds for our survival."

"What happened to them after we got down here?"

"Daisy said they were spread out pretty far, but still walking around all over the place. If you came across one, you could ask it for help and it'd follow you around til you sent it on its way."

"Wait, so if they were our friends, what happened? Why'd they attack us in the first place?"

"Well, that's what we don't really know...There's a lot of theories, but no real proof, all just guessing. All the bots that attacked us came from the Wreck of the Axiom after just sitting for like seventy years. Most people think that they were all just left alone for too long, like their brains rusted and they just lost their minds all at once."

"I guess that maybe makes sense, but not enough for them to collectively decide to go murder everybody."

"Well Bali says bots can't make their own decisions, he thinks someone reprogrammed them into killers. He searched for years, but told me whatever evidence he found didn't make any sense."

"Well...What did he find?"

"Someone definitely tampered with the bots, but the 'why' was unclear, and the 'how' seemed straight up impossible, so he dropped it," Al shrugged, "Just said he found most of the pieces to a puzzle that didn't actually form a real picture."

"Well isn't that just unhelpful and scary..." Auri laughed nervously.

Meeko barked, sniffing the air and running far ahead.

"What is it?" Al called

Meeko ran all the way up to the peak of the hill they'd been slowly climbing and called back for them to hurry.

Al sniffed the air himself, catching a whiff of foul smoke on the wind, "Something's wrong..." Al and Auri glanced at each other before Al ran up to meet Meeko at the top.

"Oh fuck..."

Al heard the snapping whoosh of ballista fire, ringing of bells, shouts of orders, screams of pain and absolute terror, followed by a massive sweeping skreech of metal scraping on stone as he climbed over the hump of the hill to find a vast view of the Siena River and the Great Gateway Bridge, illuminated by ghostly blue moonlight and a huge blazing bonfire in the center of the street.

The bridge looked alive with shiny shadows swarming across. Some of the shadows far larger than others, their shapes looked wrong, elongated giants with slow, irregular movement. A strange gate blocked the great archway, shadows piled high behind it, trying to force their way through.

"Al, what's wrong?" Auri called, Cidarian finally scraping his way to the peak.

"The bots are here, Gateway's under attack…"

"What do we do?"

"Fuck, I wanna help them……But they look like they're holding. I say we use this chance to get up the river, as fast as we can. Hope they hold long enough for us to pass safely."

"Are you sure? This is what you wanted, you've already gotten me this far. You should go and help them."

Al bit his lip and shook his head, "No…No, I'm not leaving you now."

"Are you sure?"

"I don't know what difference I'll make down there, I promised I'd get you home, so that's what I'll do…"

Auri grabbed Al's arm and pulled him close, "Al, look at me……You're absolutely sure?"

Al pressed his forehead against hers and nodded, "I'm taking you home…"

BaBoooommm!!!

The world shook, a wave of force shooting over them. Meeko staggered and barked. Al and Auri grabbed arms to keep their balance, looking down to see the center of the bridge going up in a massive fiery explosion, briefly casting the world in an ominous orange glow, launching wood, metal, and shadows hurtling through the air. The entire town seemed to scream as the whole of the bridge groaned and collapsed under its own weight, crumbling and crashing into the rushing river below. Dual archways stood separate for the first time, metal cables swinging wildly, soon to dangle loose like vacant cobwebs.

"Oh, We're so sunk..."

"Was that supposed to happen?"

Something heavy fell from the sky and thumped into the grass a few feet in front of them. Meeko went to investigate and flinched away on sight, barking at the smoldering debris. Al walked over to see for himself, his hand shooting to his mouth at the sight of a charred human arm.

Al watched the defenders take cover from the wood and metal chunks raining down from above. Dozens of shiny shadows shot out of the sky like living meteors, plowing into the roofs of buildings and the fields surrounding the town. A long uncomfortable stillness swept over the battlefield in the wake of the explosion.

The blood drained from Al's face sinking into a pit in his stomach, "Get down......" Al Whispered, he and Meeko both crouching, slowly sinking into the tall grass in unison.

Auri moved to lay flat on her bug, "They can't cross now, righ-?"

"Shh..."

Just then, almost every metal meteor that crashed in the fields stood up from their craters, turned towards the town, and sprinted in from every direction.

"They're surrounded......"

Fordo
8

"They Came While We Were Sleeping!"
Hardy horns sounded while hearts and boots pounded, forming ranks across the planks.

"While We Were Playing In The Fields!"
"Looaad uuup!" A chorus of crossbows cranked back as one.

"While Our Fathers Worked The Forges! And Our Mothers Cooked Us Meals!"
Ballistas clicked and locked with a loud KACHUNK.

"They Came Out Of The Darkness!"
Blue lit bots barreled over the obstacles strewn across the bridge, bursting through furniture, ripping through wires, every felled wave tripped was trampled by the next.

"In The Quiet Of The Night!"
Doom *"Ha!"*
Doom *"Ha!"*
Doom *"Ha!"*
Defenders stomped and shouted and knocked their weapons......

"They Come While We're Distracted!"
......A rumble to rival the stampede of metal monsters.

"'Cause Cowards Know They'll Lose A Fight!"

"Laaaunch!" A storm of thorns blasted down the bridge, shredding the shiny shadows while more and more clamored over their bolt covered comrades.

"Loooad!"

Fordo's flag flapped proud behind him, waving high above the barricade. "Patch, Jacob, keep these two safe," Fordo said, rustling the hair of Hunter and Wesley, loading crossbows with shaky hands, "They pass us At All, fall back to the buildings. Wash, you run the ranks, spread my orders, you don't fight less they reach you."

"Aye"

Fordo dove and rolled down off the barricade to join his armored crew, all standing front and center. He clapped Beth and Luca on the shoulders, lances at the ready. Kissing the palm of his hand, Fordo pressed it into the back of Carth's head, hearing him laugh as he passed. "Still with me, Brother?"

"For the moment!" Carth called, Chop chuckling beside him.

Fordo drew his hammer and took his place at the front between Sam and Doyle, signing some secret joke to one another, Doyle smiling, stomping out one last cigarette.

"Come Deal With Us, You Gearheaded Bastards!"
Fordo roared and raised his hammer.

Doom "Ha!"
Doom "Ha!"
Doom "Ha!"

"Launch!" Another wave whooshed over their heads, riddling their ever encroaching enemy, a few spiky stragglers sprinting on. Hundreds of robots raced across the bridge, chased by hundreds more materializing through the mist. They were far outnumbered by sight alone, but Fordo cared not. He cared only for the pounding of his own heart, the fearless shouts of his men, the raging rumble of glory rushing towards him. And he'd never felt more alive.

The hail of bolts and volleys soon formed a new bridge of bodies, covering every obstacle and chance to scatter or slow the cogs' advance.

"Release the rain!" Crossboys and ballistas, raised on their platforms and barricades all loaded and loosed at will, focusing fire on the central horde, killing, pinning, and slowing the cogs enough for them to reach the ranks in smaller waves.

First of the bots to reach the line had bolts in every joint, aggressively limping or even crawling towards the defenders like undead shamblers, cut down with ease. Sam and Doyle barely had to move, the bots' bodies flopping lifeless as soon as they stumbled within their weapon's reach.

Fordo yanked the spike of his hammer from an articulated neck, looking up just in time to see the first full wave to keep their sprinters pace.

"Stagger!" Fordo barked, backing up behind the Blackwyrm champions, the long line of Hammers breaking up, giving each other room to maneuver. "Brace!"

Doyle dodged to the side at the last possible moment, tripping a bot at full speed with his spear. It flew into the air and folded in half around Sam's slab of steel.

Doyle was an artist with his spear, dodging, dashing, leaping, tripping, untouchable, no movement wasted; Doyle launched himself into the air, flipping over two bots, bashing one in the head and skewering the other before hitting the ground again, using his own momentum to pick up the bot on the end of his spear and fling it back into the incoming cogs like a human catapult.

If Doyle was an artist, Sam was a butcher. What the bots could do to people, she could do to them, a head or limb went flying every time she swung her heavy sword, crushing cogs into the ground, bursting through their armor like eggshells.

Distracted by the destructive duo, Fordo almost didn't see an injured bot rush past them straight towards him. Missing an arm, the other flapping uselessly behind it, Fordo dove just in time to doge its charge. The armless cog sprinted and crouched under Chop's swing of a hammer and rammed its head straight into his chest, sending him off his feet. Carth caught the beast in the back with his spike, yanking it to the ground and stomping on its neck. Chop staggered back to his feet, holding his chest, spitting up blood, but roaring like an angry beast.

Cogs crashed into the line all around them. All were cut down, none breaking through Fordo's Wall of Warriors, but the flanks struggled to hold while every new wave was larger and faster than the last.

"Lancers!" Doyle shouted over the chaos. A volley of spears skewering a line of sprinters.

"Sam, Doyle! Guard the flanks!"

The duo nodded, quickly signing to each other before

splitting to either side, leaving a stack of scrap metal in their wake.

Just as Fordo thought all was going well, new shapes appeared in the waves ahead. Fordo's eyes went wide at the sight of bots lifting the bodies of their fallen up above their heads to shield themselves from the razor rain.

"Fuck......" He panted, "incoming!"

Fordo ducked and rolled as bots ran up, throwing their bolt filled brothers into the line of defenders. Carth yelled, toppled and pinned, along with their last Jack and weak kneed Virgil.

"Carth!" Fordo dove and tackled the cog gunning straight for his best friend, but it rolled, grabbed Fordo by his armor straps and flipped him like a toy right on top of Carth and the body full of bolts. Fordo felt a few long scrapes as bolt shafts splintered against his back. Fordo cried out, the world going mute and fuzzy after hitting the back of his head on the ground.

"No, Fordo!" Carth cursed, trying in vain to free his legs while the bot barreled straight over Fordo, ready to plunge a metal hand between his ribs when a lance caught the cog in the neck, dropping it at his feet.

Chop pulled Carth free while Fordo rolled to see Luca nodding his 'Your welcome'.

Fordo shook the fuzzy from his head before turning just in time to see cogs crush Jack's and rip the arm off of poor Virgil before being filled with lances and bolts. Cries of pain and panic erupted from the crew at the first sign of blood. Brave Shelby grabbed Virgil, dragging him back behind the barricade.

"Back up! Back up!" Fordo ordered, barely dodging, tripping, and spiking another charging monster.

"Cables!! Cables!!"

The defenders slowly stepped back to the barricades while a line of ballistas loaded new bolts, joined together by heavy metal cables spanning between them. "Drop on my mark!" Just as the last cog collapsed, in the brief respite between the next approaching wave, Fordo screamed, "Drop!"

The entire line of defenders dove for the deck just as the ballistas behind them launched in unison, sending a straight metal line hurtling through the air, cutting down an entire rushing wave at once across the width of the bridge like a scythe threw grass, piling up the bots in a new barricade of metal bodies. Everyone scrambled to their feet, relieved at the moment to catch their breath.

Fordo roared into the sky, feeling truly alive. Defenders cheered, bracing for another wave, surprised to find it never came. Hundreds of metal feet scraped into the wood at once, instantly halting their advance. Dozens of cogs stopped within range, letting the razor rain tear them down one by one without resistance. The storm of thorns faded to a drizzle, as defenders slowly lowered their weapons in the cold, eerie stillness.

What the fuck is this......?

Fordo raised his fist, shouting, "Hold!" hoping to rebrand their quiet as a command. *Why are they stopped? How are they stopped? They've never stopped before.........What the fuck is going on?*

"Is That All You Got??" Fordo shouted at the silent shiny horde, hoping to goad his men into anger and mockery before fear and suspicion planted their seeds.

"Is That All You Got......?" A pitched synthetic mockery of Fordo's own voice boomed back at the defenders, out of the sky itself as if echoed and amplified by an actual god.

Fordo froze. His men searched the clouds with wide eyes and open mouths for the hidden deity.

"How did you do that?" Carth whispered behind him.

Fordo turned to his crew, every eye on him alone, while accidentally showing his own fear for the first time. "I didn't......"

Fordo spun around at the sound of a heavy crash at the top of the far tower. Upon it, silhouetted by the massive wall of fog, stood a faceless metal giant, twice as large as any other, armor so matte and dark it almost absorbed the moonlight. As still as a statue, it loomed over the defenders like a cruel child towering above a colony of insects.

This doesn't make sense. It doesn't make sense! What the fuck does it want? "What The Fuck Do You Want??" Fordo shouted, spit spraying from his mouth. The silence lingered on. Fordo opened his arms, staring straight toward the dark figure in the distance, channeling all of his overwhelming fear into absolute rage. "Your Games Don't Scare Us, You Gutless Metal Monsters!"

"You think us monsters, Little One?" Fordo felt every word of the crack and timbre in the deep, resonant synthetic voice vibrating the planks of the bridge, the metal of his hammer, the very bones in his chest. The voice seemed to pierce and shake the world itself.

Fordo grit his teeth, strangling the grip of his warhammer to still his trembling arms. "I Think You Cowardly......Clanking...... Rust Covered......Murderers!"

"We brought you monsters............but they aren't gutless........." The dark giant sank into a squat and sat back with its legs dangling over the edge of the tower, leaning on its arms as if to relax itself to watch a game, *"They're Headless"*

A slow wailing groan like deep creaking metal, sounded out of the moonlit mist while a strange new shadow appeared, stretching more than half as tall as the thirty foot archway.

Fordo's fear returned with a vengeance when out of the fog, stepped an elongated man with endlessly thin, jointless limbs flowing out of a dark, skeletal, emaciated corpse. Where the head and neck of the giant should have been, instead was a gaping void, so black it could swallow the very sun itself.

"Mother help us......" Chop whispered

"Ford......?"

"I don't know, Carthy......"

Another wailing groan seeped out of the Headless creature, quickly swaying towards them across the bridge. Rather than run, its limitless limbs extended and retracted, propelling its cavernous corpse through space as if levitating on wires.

Fordo took a step back, as did most of his men, choking down a dry swallow before raising his hammer and shakily shouting, "Thorns And Cables!"

"Thorns And Cabllles!" He heard Wash repeat, along with a chorus of cranking crossbows.

"Launch!"

"Laaaunch!"

Fordo felt a wave of wind from the whooshing wall of bolts sailing over his head, all bouncing harmlessly off the Headless' leathery skin.

"Oh Glass......Ballistas!!"

"Ballistaaas!!"

The monster instantly doubled its speed, stretching and shrinking quicker than the cogs could sprint. Scrambling through the air along the metal cables with six fingered hands at the end of each limb, like a demented, headless, human spider.

"Shoot It Down! Shoot It Down!" Fordo screamed, letting the panic crack and pierce his voice.

Just as the ballistas turned to fire their wall of cables, the Headless' arms shot up above to the main supports, pulling, leaping, and flinging its massive flailing form high into the air, the cables flying uselessly below.

Everyone screamed and scattered in horror as the creature sailed over the frontline defenders and crashed right in the center of the main barricade, crushing two ballistas and a half dozen crossboy civilians with a sickening wet crunch.

Fordo watched Patch and Jacob Baker toss Hunter and Wesley over the backside of the barricade like good soldiers, just before a giant six fingered hand snatched up the pair of them, waved them in the air, then shoved them both screaming into the bottomless pit where the monster's head should have been. The leathery stone-like skin of the monster stretched around their bodies. Fordo's dinner threatened to vacate his stomach, watching his crew members drop to the very bottom of the monster's hips, still kicking and screaming through the same slimy, shapeless, boulder gray skin as the crashing cave monsters.

Fordo would have puked if he wasn't busy grabbing everyone he loved and running for his life. "Fall Back To The Street! To The Streeet!!" He shoved Carth, Chop, and the rest of the crew away from the monster to run around the barricade to the buildings beyond.

The creature's spindly arms both peeled and split in half. Four of them now flailing, crushing, or snatching people at random, swallowing them whole, alive and dead alike, its body swelling around it's victims to gluttonous, grotesque proportions as more and more people piled in its pit, like a beating, writhing, flesh balloon.

"Look out!" Beth yelled as an arm swept across the platform like a swinging chain. Most dodged or jumped in time, but the arm swiped Chop's legs, shattering his ankles. He cried out in pain, crashing to the ground, clutching his chest, a three fingered hand clasped around his thigh, dragging him into the air.

"No!" Fordo grabbed Chop's thick calloused hand to pull him back down, only to be dragged up with him into the air. Fordo screamed, looking down at his dangling feet and the ever shrinking ground, then into Chop's terror filled eyes.

"Let go!"

"Don't let it take me, Kid!" Chop cried, gripping Fordo's wrist tighter.

"Lᴇᴛ Mᴇ Gᴏ!" Fordo yelled, desperately trying to pry off Chop's fingers.

"I don't wanna go! I don't wanna go......!"

Fordo grit his teeth, choking back tears, whispering, "I'm sorry......" before driving his palm into Chop's nose, letting himself slip from his grip to fall and bounce off of the barricade below.

Chop's pleading cries pierced Fordo's heart as he grunted, rolled, and ran to catch up to his friends, not looking back to see another disappear into the belly of the beast.

"Fordo......?" Carth looked back at him in horror.

"Run, Run! We can't get him out if we're dead!" Fordo shoved him forward, past the barricade, tears streaming down his cheeks.

He's not dead...He's just trapped...He's Not Dead...I can save him!

Those left of Fordo's crew fled past the main barricade, through the grand archway, and ducked into an alleyway.

"That thing is tearing us apart!" Bethany shouted

"Drop the Gate on it!" Luca panted

"No, we can't kill it, our friends are in there!" Lady shouted, tear filled eyes glancing at Fordo. *He's not dead......*

"Highground, Move!" Doyle shouted, bounding up a makeshift ladder.

Fordo snatched a stashed wetskin, squeezing half the gallon down his throat. Gasping for breath like he'd nearly drowned himself, counting his remaining crew members as they scurried up the side of the building to the rickety rooftop platforms. *Carth, Bethany, Luca, Lady, Jane, Doyle.........That's it?* He hurried up behind them, Carth pulling him up over the side, relieved to find young Wesley and Hunter already at the top, struggling to load a ballista themselves, Bethany rushing to hug them.

Fordo watched up high, in relative safety, while the survivors scattered throughout the street, seeking shelter in the boarded up buildings. Shelby should be tending to Virgil in their makeshift med bay. Sam could take care of herself, but he'd lost sight of Wash when the Headless attacked. The rest he knew were lost, squashed, or eaten. More than half his men, trapped or dead. *We can get them out, we have to get them out.*

"We kill that thing, we kill our friends, how do we stop it?" Fordo begged Doyle for a plan, but Blackhat wasn't listening, he was busy scanning the chaos, presumably for Sam.

"Doyle!" Fordo shouted

Doyle shook his head and cleared his throat, snapped back to the present, "Arms and legs......"

Arms and legs, Brilliant!

"Jane!"

"Aye?"

"I need your eyes behind that bolt thrower, take out its hips," Fordo smacked Doyle on the back, "Can you hold it steady?"

"How the Fuck would I do that, mate?"

The Headless surged after the last of the fleeing defenders filtering through the archway, its sickeningly large body now dragging in the street, too heavy for its limbs to properly lift.

"It's slowing down. Dance and dodge around its arms long enough for Jane to get a clear shot. We can knock out its legs, we can stall it long enough to get our people- Hey, No, Wesley, Wait!"

The world slowed, a wave of dread washing over him as he lunged for the siblings a moment too late, hearing the heavy whoosh of the ballista, followed by muffled screams of the devoured before seeing a massive, bladed, wyrm wrecking harpoon sink into the bloated beast's belly, a waterfall of human blood gushing from the wound.

Fordo looked in horror, scrambling to the edge of the railing screaming, "Hold your fire! Hold Your-!" too late to stop a dozen other ballistas all launching down the line of buildings shredding the monster from all sides, turning the Headless and all its victims into a bulbous pile of meat and metal.

Fordo and the defenders all stared at the black stain growing in the street, the battlefield swept silent once more. *I can save them......I could save them......I Could Have Saved Them!*

"AAAAAAAAAAAAAAAHHH!!!"

Fordo's roar echoed down the road, his whole crew flinching as he drew his hammer and smashed the guardrail, splashing them with splinters. Luca threw up over the side of the building. The kids scrambled away from the bolt thrower, realizing their mistake, cowering and crying in Bethany's arms. Fordo stood panting, standing dangerously close to the edge of the platform.

Carth placed a hesitant hand on his shoulder, gently pulling him back from the ledge. Fordo's breathing slowly steadied, his rage released in a single sigh. He looked out over the bridge to the army of still waiting monsters.

Bethany covered the children's ears, "They were only trying to-"

Another deep wailing groan sounded across the bridge. Childish, cold, uncontrollable laughter erupted from Fordo's chest at the sight of Two more Headless emerging from the mist, along with the thunderous horde of unfrozen cogs all swarming down the lane.

"Ford......Are you alri-"

"Crank Your Cross And Prep The Drop!" Orders exploded out of Fordo, as if the battle had just begun. "Prep the drooop!"

A genuine grin spread across Fordo's face hearing Wash alive, still echoing his orders somewhere in the distance. He rushed back to the ladders, still smiling, Carth and his crew all staring like they thought him insane as he slid back down to the street.

"Fordo, where the hell are you going??" Carth called down the side of the building.

"To have some fun!" He shrugged, "When they pass through, you cut the lines, slam that gate down on 'em!"

"Fordo wait! Fordo!"

Fordo grabbed a burning torch as he marched into the center of the street. He raised the flame above his head before tossing it atop the mound of meat. The slimy skin of the Headless caught like kindling, flame spreading like it was soaked in oil. Fordo bowed his head to the burning pyre, kneeling, laying his hand flat against the blood soaked stones, and drawing a wet red line down his forehead to his nose.

"See you in a minute, Mom......" Fordo whispered and turned to face the rumbling wrath of the raging horde, bonfire blazing behind him, casting the shadow of a giant blocking the whole of the bridge with its body.

"MYYY NAAAMMME!!! IS FORDON AMADEUS BALISON!! First Son Of Scrapyard! Keeper Of The Bridge! Guardian Of Gateway! As I Breeaathe! You Will Not Reach The World You Seek!"

His pillar of black smoke swirled into the sky, their own cloud to rival the robot's white and blue behemoth. The very stones of the road shook beneath his feet. Fordo dragged a foot across the road, marking a wide red finish line, spitting and cackling at the faceless flood, fist beating against his chest.

"I Am The Rust That Rots Your Armor!"
Countless cogs clamored over the barricade......

"I Am The Bolts That Jam Your Joints!"
Headless carelessly crushing their own comrades......

"I Am The Wrath Of The World You Angered!"
The throng of metal monsters swarmed under the
archway......

**"And You Will All Die To The Sound My
Voice!"**

Fordo howled, ropes snapped, hinges hollered, a
million metal monsters mere meters away when his swinging gate
came crashing down like the hand of Aure. Whooshing, crushing,
smashing, scraping, obliterating the tidal wave of death in a single
explosive sweep. Bots burst and blasted back across the bridge in
a billion pieces, the Headless smashed and buried under bodies
piled up so high the sides spilled into the raging river below.

Am I not dead...?

Fordo's eyes shot open as he sat up from the ground,
ears ringing, blown onto his back by the wind of the great gate.
He saw Cogs through the gaps between the pillars, clawing up
the pile to push through the gate, only to slip and slide down the
shifting metal mound, none could cross the swinging gates, the
army of bots stopped dead in its tracks.

"AAAAAAAAAAAAAAAHAHAHAAA!!!"

Fordo wept, beaming and laughing on his back, driven nearly mad with fear, ecstasy, and pure adrenaline. He looked up to see Carth and his crew, all smiling down at him, hugging, crying, shouting from their platforms, the whole of the defenders joining in a chorus of praise, cheers echoing off every tongue in the torn up town. The battle was not yet over, but this was it, wasn't it? The historic moment he'd been waiting for his entire life. The moment he avenged his mother, claimed his true name, immortalized himself in the halls of history.........And it was everything he hoped and dreamed it would be.

"DON'T LET DOWN YOUR GUARD, LADS! WE STILL HOLD 'TIL HELP ARRIVES! BUT FILL YOUR BELLIES AND EMPTY YOUR BLADDERS! OUR WORK JUST BOUGHT OURSELVES SOME TIME!"

Defenders cheered across the rooftops, rushing to relieve themselves. Fordo scanned the survivors, their numbers cut in half, but plenty of hands to hold this position. With the bodies piled so high behind the gate, the cogs will barely filter through, this battle just turned from terrifying turmoil into high stakes target practice.

Fordo smiled to himself, jogging to join all his friends back on the platform. Carth didn't even wait for Fordo to get off the ladder before grabbing him, lifting him into the air, and crushing the air from his lungs.

"You did it, you crazy bastard!"

"We did it, Carthy."

"This isn't over," Jane said, still manning the ballista.

"No, but it's close," Doyle said, clapping Fordo on the shoulder, "I'm gonna find Sam and get ready for the mop up. We need to talk the moment this is over."

"We'll meet you down there," Fordo nodded

"I thought you were dead for sure," Luca smiled, following Doyle down the ladders.

"So did I," Fordo Laughed

Beth, Lady, and the siblings all sat on the edge of the platform, somberly staring into the bloody bonfire. Fordo sighed and walked up behind them, crouching behind the kids, placing a hand on their shoulders. Bethany looked at Fordo, nodding subtly for him to say something.

"It's not your fault……" They didn't move, tear streaks glistening in the orange firelight. "Hey……" Fordo shook them gently until they'd look at him, "We don't know if we could get them out, we don't know how many more people would have died trying, the bots might've swarmed us while we were distracted, we don't know anything for sure. You tried to stop the monster and that's exactly what you did. You have nothing to be ashamed of. Nothing……You understand." They nodded together, placing small shaky hands over his, gripping him tight. He squeezed their shoulders, ruffled their hair, and stood up to find Carth staring perplexed off into the distance.

"What is it?"

"What's up with Jason?"

Fordo turned to see the Yellow Eyed Boy running up to them, hopping across the platforms two buildings over, looking happier than ever.

"The fuck do you want?"

"That......Was......Awesome!" Jason jumped and laughed all around Fordo, not his usual cruel cackle, but the genuine, cheerful, laughter of childhood joy. "That was the coolest thing I've seen in like a hundred years! That was crazy!"

Mildly amused by the child's excitement, Fordo almost forgot he hated him. Almost. "Alright, alright, kid, thank you. Now go find somewhere safe, the bots aren't beaten yet."

"What are we gonna do next??"

"You're not gonna do anything. WE are gonna cut down any cogs that trickle through the gate until Scrapyard gets here with reinforcements."

"What?? No! No, no, no you've been doing all these cool, crazy things! Let's keep it going! We're having so much fun!"

"We're still alive, that's fun enough. I don't know if you noticed, but a lot of people fuckin' died today and it ain't over. We're not here to entertain you, we're here to survive, you fuckin' idiot."

"Ugh Fine! You're such a Baby................Can we at least blow the bridge if you're not gonna fight them?"

"No! Why the fuck would we do that?"

"Uh, Cause it'd be fun, dumbass??"

"Chop is dead, do you understand? Patch, Jacob, more

than half the people you met yesterday are all fucking Dead! Gone! Forever! This isn't a game for us, you sick cunt! And if you weren't such an Annoying, Sadistic, Piece Of Glass, maybe you'd know what the fuck 'friends' are and why it's not fun to watch them die!"

"Oh I have a friend!"

"Then go fuckin' play with them and get the fuck out of my face."

"Maybe I will!"

"You bother me again up here and I'll throw you off this fuckin' roof."

"Ooo You 'promise', Pretty Boy?"

"Fuck you, Jason."

"No, fuck you......"

Jason lifted his hand above his head, with what looked like some kind of cog component clasped inside; A small, rectangular metal brick, covered with wires, and a tiny, unnaturally red light.

"The fuck is that supposed to be? Another useless-?"

Click........

BOOOOM!!!

The bridge erupted in a fiery explosion, blasting bots and debris miles into the air. Carth and Fordo fell to the ground as an earthquake ravaged the entire town. Dozens of defenders staggered and fell from the rattled rooftops. Bethany lunged and screamed as Hunter and Wesley went over the side. Fordo dove for the edge to help catch the siblings, sliding to a stop empty handed just to see Wesley scream and crack her collarbone while Hunter's skull split against the cobblestone.

"No, No, No! Why!" Fordo reached desperately for the children down below, Carth dragging him back onto the platform.

"Take Coveeerrr!" A ballista exploded across the street as a full cog came crashing out of the sky. Dozens of metal meteors blasted buildings all around as bits of bridge, bots, and bodies rained down from above. Fordo covered Bethany with his body and Carth shielded them both with his while they waited for the onslaught to end.

Soon the quakes and crashes ceased, leaving the defenders in a muffled, ear ringing silence. Cut only by the clapping hands and howling laughter of Jason, The Yellow Eyed Boy.

What did you do.......? Fordo watched Wesley weakly crawl and cry over her broken brother, gently trying to shake his lifeless body awake, while Jason cackled like the devil himself, laughing so hard he was gasping for breath.

"What did you do??" Fordo burst forth from beneath Carth, sprinting and tackling Jason to the ground, beating in his stupid face until his fist was bloody, the demon boy laughing endlessly with delight.

"Shut up!" Fordo screamed into his face, but the boy was having the time of his life.

"SHUT UP!!!" Fordo grabbed the cackling cunt by his stinking, ragged clothes and threw him head first over the edge of the building. A flash of surprise in his ancient yellow eyes, Jason stared deep into Fordo's soul as he fell, grinning all the way to hell, the boy's head bursting with blood as it bounced below, weak wet laughter gurgling into nothing.

Fordo stared at the child menace, still smiling up at him.

Good fuckin' riddence......

The only thing stopping him from spitting over the edge was the already terrified Carth, standing there to witness.

"What the fuck just happened?" Carth shouted

"He just killed us all......" Fordo looked around at the wreckage coming to life all around them, screams of pain and panic filled the air once more as the dozens of bots launched from the explosion all roused from their falls.

Sam's voice called from below, "Fall Baaack! Back To The Courtyard!"

Fordo pulled Bethany to her feet, "Beth, get Jane and Lady to the monument. Carth and I will get Wesley. Be careful." She nodded, the women racing back across the rooftops towards the pale obelisk while Carth and Fordo dove for the ladders, sliding to the street, rushing to pick up the girl crying over her broken brother.

"You guard, I'll carry!"

Wesley cried out in pain as Fordo scooped her up from the ground. "Please don't leave him......Please don't......" She reached for her brother's body, sobbing uncontrollably.

"We'll be back for him, I promise."

"Please, no!"

Fighting broke out all around them as the cogs came shooting back to life, bursting out of buildings, tackling people off rooftops. Fordo cursed, "Move!" taking off down the street, leaving the poor dead brother to wait and rest.

Fordo ran for the courtyard, sticking close to the buildings, out of the way and out of the fray, Wesley weeping in his arms. She wasn't very big, but neither was Fordo, heaving and sweating under the weight of the poor girl as they dodged defenders and bots alike. Carth covered them well, keeping between them and the closest cogs as they ran, but one man can only do so much.

Two bots rolled down from the rooftops and scrambled on their tail, one crashing into Carth while the other charged ahead, straight for Fordo and Wesley.

Fordo dove onto his back at the last moment, the bot's head bashing against bricks buying them seconds. A man Fordo didn't recognize charged in, roaring with a lance, skewering and pinning the cog to the wall, giving Fordo time to get himself up and running once more.

"Go, Commander! I'll- Gah!" The bot's bloody arm burst through the man's back just as Carth caught up with them, shoving them up the road to the courtyard.

"Form up! Form up! Form up!" Sam shouted, cleaving through cogs left and right, Wash and Doyle at her side, Beth, Jane, Lady, and Luca covering with crossbows. Fordo reached the pale monument, laying Wesley against it while the rest of the survivors poured in from the street and wrapped around the obelisk.

Fordo and Carth joined the fray, monsters sprinting in from all sides; the streets, the alleys, the fields, they were completely surrounded, choking on a cloud of blue dust and black smoke, fighting for their fucking lives, the circle growing tighter, smaller every minute until they were all bruised, all bloodied, tripping over bots and bodies piling up around them until Fordo could barely lift his hammer.

"If this is it......" Fordo panted, leaning against a shaky Carth, "I love you, brother......"

"I love you too......"

"Still glad you're not......just drinkin' at The Grub?"

"Ask me......in an hour......"

Fordo couldn't dream of a better death, fighting side by side, back to back with his brothers, hammers in hand, in a final stand. He beamed at the thought of Balian arriving to find the body of the son he never loved, the son he never believed in wrapped in his own banner, broken and bloody atop a mountain of monsters, having saved the world before he could even get there.

Leaning on a lance like a crutch, Fordo pulled himself up to point his hammer at the one armed robot ready to ram him. *You have been chosen......* This was it, his final foe, his final moments, he could die happy, fulfilled, having done everything he vowed to do. But just as the last wave of monsters was about to grant his wish, Fordo watched a black shadow shoot across their feet, a dozen bots turning to chase it. *What......?*

The small shape dashed circles around the remaining monsters, running them into one another, distracting them, drawing them away from the survivors long enough for them to catch their breath and get clean shots, whittling the wave down bit by bit until only a handful remained.

"What the hell is-?"

Bark! Bark! Bark!

"AAAAAAAAAAAAAAAHHH!!!"

A familiar battlecry blasted from behind the bots. Fordo squinted through the smoke to see a tall, thin, young man, wielding a black bladed sword, burst right through the mass of metal monsters, cutting down every confused cog and bot bewildered by the barking blur.

"Fordo, is that......?"

You smug bastard......

"Alexander......Late, as always......."

Al and Meeko
8

Al watched the bots bounding through the field, his fists full of grass, ripping up their roots with small muffled pops, caught between conflicting thoughts.

"Al..."

He and Meeko looked back at Auri, both asking for permission with the same hungry eyes.

"Go...I'll be alright."

Al nodded, drew his sword, said "I'll be back......" and bolted down the steep slope, he and Meeko shooting off together like the start of a Nuru Marathon, letting gravity guide them to ludicrous speeds, flying towards the town.

Several bots blocked the closest alleyway, standing still in a line, only running in one at a time, as if waiting their turn to join the slaughter. *We gotta get in there...* Al whistled for Meeko to 'Sweep', his boy breaking off, vanishing into the moonlit grass.

"Oy!" Al called to the cogs without slowing down. *Let's see how fast you boys can run...* Four spun around in an instant, staggering and searching, less than he thought, but more than he hoped. Al raised and waved his blade above his head, inviting the bots to dance. All obliged, bolting for the boy, tearing trails through the grass like mowers. *Oh Really fuckin' fast!*

Al sprinted sideways, away from his pursuers, his momentum nearly matching their speed long enough for them to trip over the friendly furry creature lurking at their feet. Meeko's timing was flawless, sweeping their legs, sending them crashing, tripping over one another, slowing and spreading them thin enough for Al to take them on one at a time.

Al slowed to a jog, letting the first one get close before jumping, spinning, slashing his sword straight through the monster's neck, sending its head and body flying off in different directions. He landed, crouched and dodged, letting the second bot circle behind him. Al charged the third, diving, hurling his body into its legs, sending it sailing over him, crashing into the bot behind, rolling up just in time to plunge his sword deep into the fourth's hips only to be clobbered by a metal fist.

Salt and iron filled his mouth as Al's jaw cracked and snapped off its hinge, twisting his neck, threatening to spin his head off his shoulders as he fell cursing to the ground, spitting up blood and a couple broken molars. He ripped his blade from the bot, letting the crippled cog collapse, plunging his sword back into its neck before cracking his own back into place. He rose to a knee and rubbed his hanging jaw, feeling Meeko's metal paw spring off his shoulder, launching himself like a living boulder, knocking the last two robots over. Al rushed to reap them while they were down, stomping one's neck into the ground, silencing the last with a single slash.

Al dropped back to the dirt, gasping for breath, Meeko licking Al's blood from his lips. "Fugh, diht weh- Ahw" Al moved his jaw around with his hand, feeling around for the break through his cheek, pressing it back into place, letting the pins and needles sweep through before attempting to speak again, "Ah My fuckin' teeth…" Al shook his head, tonguing the new jagged gap in the back of his left jaw. "Did we clear the alley?" Meeko looked around and dashed back into the grass. "Lead the way…"

***

Al expected to find an army of defenders possibly pressed from both sides. A few hundred people packed and trapped behind barricades or confined to the rooftops, cogs clawing uselessly at their walls. He planned to run support, help mitigate the damage, distract and kill as many bots as he could to buy any men behind enough time to seek cover or shelter. He'd help them regroup and reorganize and slip away back to Auri as soon as the army got a grasp on the new situation.

He and Meeko cut through the alley to a scene of bots and bodies piled all around blood soaked stones of the central courtyard. A battered rabble of warriors fighting for their lives, open and exposed around a pale pillar while monsters charged and crashed into their line, ripping into it from all sides. A new man dying every moment Al waited and watched.

"Go, Meeko, Go!"

Meeko shot into the crowd, a silver streak in the night, dodging dozens of demons like he'd been training for this his entire life, every cog he crossed, tripping over themselves to turn and chase him. The defenders looked as confused as the bots, lowering their weapons for the first time in who knows how long, before launching lances and bolts into the distracted horde.

Al took a deep breath, bouncing on the balls of his feet. *Is there a better way to do this?* Meeko swept around on his first lap, trailing a train of monsters behind him. *This glass is gonna hurt...* Al roared at the top of his lungs, drowning out all his nerves screaming for him to reconsider before charging and throwing his body straight into the mass of racing metal men sending a dozen tumbling to the ground.

Al scrambled to his feet, cutting down a couple cogs, ducking as a volley of bolts and lances shot out from the group of defenders, riddling the robots all around him, a rogue bolt punching through Al's left shoulder, spinning him off his footing.

Al cried out in pain, slipping on the bloody cobblestones and tripping over a body, falling forward onto the bolt, snapping the splintered shaft off in his shoulder. He rolled and rose up to one knee with barely enough time to see a bot barreling towards him.

Swinging wildly with his sword, he missed the joints completely. His sword bounced off of its armored chest, flew out of Al's hand, and sent a vibrating shockwave shooting up his wrist. The bot tackled him back, sliding against the stones, pinning him to the wet ground, knocking all the air from his lungs.

Al couldn't see, he couldn't hear, only felt the weight of the faceless monster cracking and crushing his wrists in a steel grip, the burning, ripping pain of the bolt in his shoulder, his back and head scraping against the stones.

"Meekoo! Meekoo!" Al called into the blackness, praying to his friend that he'd find him in time, kicking and fighting, but the bot wouldn't budge. Al's left arm slipped free from the bot's bloody grasp, awkwardly and desperately punching at the cog's head, breaking his own knuckles against its faceplate.

Both metal hands caught and crushed Al's swinging fist, Al's fingers crunching together, bending in all manner of unnatural directions. **"Meeko! Meek- AHHHH!!!"** The bot yanked his left shoulder from its socket with a wet pop. Muscle and tendon stretched and tore as the monster threatened to rip Al's left arm straight off of his body.

"Help! Heeelp!"
WHAM!

The bot lurched limp as a steel spike swung and crunched into the side of its skull, a leather clad warrior charging ahead. Al rolled free at last, clutching his aching arm to his chest. He looked up from the ground to see that he and Meeko had done their job, the bots whittled away one bolt at a time. The survivors rallied one last burst of strength, rushing forth to fight off the remaining monsters trickling in from around the town, bashing, shooting, and skewering until only six bots remained... Then three... Then one... Then none...

The dust cleared, the world stilled, and the survivors all held their breath...

The Battle Of Gateway Bridge Was Won.

Al laid on the ground, slowly twisting his broken fingers back into place, his dislocated shoulder screaming, reminding him he's just procrastinating. "Aw man..." He winced to himself, disappointed that his wooden prosthetic was just as mangled as the rest. He attempted to pinch and pull the shaft of the bolt from his shoulder, but the splintered nub was too small, too slippery, and the wound itself healed tight around the wood, sealing it in his arm, "Glass..."

I hate digging...

"Meeko!"

Al heard Meek's metal paw clanking against the stone as he bolted to find his boy, rushing to lick Al's face lying defenseless on the ground. "You did it, Meek, you saved them..." Al instantly regretted hugging him, not for the pain, but for the muddy mixture of blood and dust caked onto his fur now soaking through Al's clothes.

"Typical, showin' up at the end to take all the credit..."

I know that voice...

Al rolled, shocked to see the extended hand and smirking face of Fordo Balison, covered head to toe in blood, dust, and ash, his gray eyes glowing silver in the moonlight.

"You look like glass..." Al said through labored breaths.

"Feel like glass...Get the fuck up."

They both winced from different wounds as Al clasped Fordo's wrist and pulled himself to his feet, "Gathii found you?"

"Easier than I found you, where the hell have you-?"

"Al!" Another familiar voice sounded right behind him. Thick arms appeared around his chest, lifting him up in a suffocating bear hug.

"Ahh!" A flash of fear and panic swept through him,

remembering the clawing mob. His instinct to fight and break loose was only washed away by Carth's unmistakable laugh.

"Carth??" Al croaked, "You big, strong, man, you made it!" Pain devolved Al's sincere smiles back into a grimace as he returned the hug, thumping his brother's back, his own cold sweat dripping into his eyes.

"We thought you were dead!"

"I was, for a while. Hey, can you fuckin' help me with this?"

"Oh glass, the bolt or the bone...?"

"Bone please..."

Carth twisted the dislocated arm back behind Al's head towards the opposite shoulder, "Fast or slow?"

"Rrt...Maybe slo-Gahh!"

Carth cranked it back, the joint popping back into place with a gross crack.

"Fuckin' glass..." Al panted, dropping to his knee, the screaming pain halved almost instantly.

"Thank you...What the hell happened here? This place is sunk to hell."

Fordo opened his mouth to speak, before a red armored woman called, "Orders, Commander?" and Fordo turned to answer.

"Commander?" Al chuckled

Fordo shot a sly smile his way before shouting in the same authoritative voice he'd use for Barricade, "Sweep for survivors, we don't know who's still out there! Find food and water where you can! Beth, Lady, Luca! Pick an inn, get the wounded outta the mess!"

"We're all wounded…" Another stranger called

"If you can walk, you can search! Be careful of more cogs, some might be lodged in the wreckage!"

Al whispered to Carth, "Finally got his army, huh?"

"Wasn't half bad with it, neither."

"Wash, you still breathin'?" Fordo continued

Wash??

"Aye…" A shorter, man stepped out from the warriors, young and gloved with dirty blonde hair swept back by a pair of goggles, just like Auri had mentioned in their travels.

"You tend to Wesley for me."

A wide smile spread across Al's face, excitement numbing his pain quicker than the pins and needles. "Meeko, that's him!" he whispered, "That's Auri's brother, we found him already!"

Meeko barked enthusiastically.

"Go, get Auri down here!"

Meeko took off back up the road out of town, cutting through the group of survivors, most too tired to react. Some flinched while others actually managed to smile at the prancing puppy.

"Oy," A slender armored man limped over, looking down at Al from beneath the shadow of a large, wide brimmed hat, leaning on a long twisted lance like a crutch. "That pup belong to you?"

"Belong to each other, I suppose."

"You have a name?"

"My boy's name is Meeko."

"This is Alexander of Scrapyard," Carth said, "He's a good friend of ours."

"A very good friend...You and your boy saved our lives, mate." The man bowed slightly, along with several others. He closed his eyes, touched the knuckle of his thumb to the center of his forehead with an open hand, then closed his fist over his heart, some symbolic gesture Al couldn't recognize. "I'd offer you my life if it was still mine to give."

Al noticed Fordo smile and shake his head.

"I'll settle for your spear..." Al said, stone faced.

A guilty smile spread across the man's face along with a nervous laugh as he glanced at his crutch.

Al broke character and chuckled, "No, we were just passing through, friend, no need to thank us."

"Bolt in the shoulder and he still has jokes."

"Oy," Fordo called, "We'll catch up when the work is done. Al, Carth, Sam, and Doyle with me. We need eyes on the bots, make sure we're in the clear."

"Aye sir," Al laughed, Fordo did not look amused.

Al waved dismissively, then turned to Carth, "I'm gonna help the wounded until Meeko gets back, there's someone I'm here to see."

"Someone that's not us?" Carth asked

"I didn't know you'd be here too," Al shrugged, "I'm glad you're alive, brother."

"Only am thanks to you and Meeks..."

***

Al hugged Carth once more before jogging to help young Wash struggling to move Wesley out of the muck. Her shoulder, swollen and bruised from what Al immediately recognized as a broken collarbone. Wash knelt, his hands hovering, searching for the least painful way to move her.

"Tuck her arm in and support her back. It's gonna hurt no matter what, but the less her arm moves, the better." Al crouched beside her, supporting her other side with his one good shoulder. She cried out as she stood, but Wash kept her steady.

"Thank you," Wash said, as they limped towards the inn the other wounded were being dragged to, "You a doctor?"

"Just broken my own a couple times now...We'll fix you a sling, girly, soon as we sit."

A river of tears cut trails down the dirt on her cheeks, her puffy red eyes staring straight through the world. Al knew wherever she was, she wasn't here. His first instinct was to make her laugh, but based on the bloody scene around them, he decided to keep his mouth shut. *'Only one who wasn't there...'*

Al had to hunch to match Wash's height as they hauled Wesley up the sturdy steps into the fairly modest inn. The setup wasn't dissimilar to The Green Grub. Ample wooden seating around an 'X' shaped hearth in the center of the room, two men quietly lighting the coals. Several wounded reached towards the well stocked bar that stretched from wall to wall on the right side. A wide staircase led up to an encompassing balcony, all sides lined with lodging.

They sat Wesley by the hearth in a chair stacked with furs for comfort. "Wash, run upstairs and start throwing down sheets and blankets in a pile, would you?"

"Aye..."

"You alright here, girly?"

Wesley stared into the cold gray coals, her ever streaming tears the only sign of emotion on her face.

Al struggled to find the words, any words to comfort her, but he didn't know if it was his place, if the baseless, ignorant advice of a complete stranger would be welcome or just insulting.

The easiest thing to do would be to say nothing, just make a sling and move on, hope someone better with words comes along. *The easy way...The coward's way...Meeko's even worse with words and he's always there for you...He doesn't wait until you're ready, he doesn't ask for permission. He just sees you're in pain and reminds you he's there.*

"I don't know who you are..." Al started, "I don't know what you've been through...What you've lost. You can choose to deal with it alone, but just know that...You don't have to."

She didn't move, she didn't even blink.

"My fath- Well...Balian says 'Some weights are too heavy to keep on your own shoulders. The only way to keep them from crushing you is to share them or let them drop'...Not right now, of course, and not necessarily to me, I know I'm a fuckin' stranger, but uh...Well, when you're ready to talk to someone... you talk to them."

"Is this enough?" Wash asked from above. Al looked up to see a pile of sheets and blankets piled so high, wash could dive headfirst over the railing and not feel a thing.

"Think that's plenty," Al smiled, "You got a knife on you?"

Wash slid down the railing and flopped into the pile, presenting and passing a hand carved wyrmtooth dagger.

"Thank you," Al started cutting a sheet into long wide strips, producing a small stack before realizing how familiar the knife felt in his fingers. "Wait...?" Al laughed, "Where the hell did you get this...I traded it like a week ago, back near Scrapyard?"

"Fordo gave it to me before the battle."

"But how did...Was there a funny lookin' guy here, with like big poofy hair?"

"Yeah, the music man?"

"The music man! Where did he go, is he still here??" Al grinned

"He was on the bot side of the bridge when they came."

Al's grin immediately faded, "Andre......Did they get him?"

"I don't see how they wouldn't have...Was he a friend of yours?"

"I don't..." Al rubbed his eyes, "I don't really know... He kinda got me killed, almost killed your, um...I don't know, but I liked him a lot."

"Sorry..."

"S'alright, just caught me off guard, is all...Tie this in a knot for me and fix it around Wesley's arm."

Al tied himself a sling and wandered toward the bar, wondering how to feel about the loss of the funny man who unknowingly tricked him into destroying an entire village. He reached for a large clear bottle on the top shelf, filled with Julian Gripe Water. He popped the cork and took a whiff of the poison.

'Drink so vile a glass could turn you blind' Daisy once told him, dabbing it on a towel to clean the scrapes on Fordo's back after his tumble down the aqueducts.

Al knew his wounds had never been infected before, and likely couldn't, but he decided after his last scolding from Balian he'd practice good habits. *In case one day I'm a lot less lucky.*

After a few deep breaths he splashed the spirit onto his shoulder where the bolt still bulged, reigniting and enhancing the pain in a searing sting. *Oh fuck, nevermind...* He laughed to himself, *We can leave Some things to chance.*

"How is that?" Wash whispered to Wesley, who offered the slightest nod of approval.

Gray light through the windows signaled dawn's approach as the sun chased the moons back below the horizon. Weary warriors wandered in, eyes red and vacant, collapsing into chairs or crawling up the stairs to find a bed to lay their head. There was no celebration, not even a general relief to be alive. This wasn't a battle, it was a slaughter, and Al was thankful he missed it. He shuffled past, back into the courtyard, receiving more than a few nods and pats. *We really got here just in time...*

Al stepped outside just as Meeko came barking out of an alley, running and stopping every few yards to look back behind him, too excited to slow down while still waiting for Cidarian to catch up.

Jogging to meet them, Al's boot sloshed against the bloody stones, reminding him of the horrific scene around him. He rushed to the alley to cut off Auri before she entered.

"Al! You're alive!" Auri looked shaken, sighing in relief.

"A little banged up, but I'm okay..."

"When just Meeko came, I thought maybe..." Her lip quivered, her voice failing.

Al rushed to hold her, "Oh I'm so sorry, I was just patching myself up, I didn't think about it..."

She wiped her eyes, "It's okay, Meeko didn't seem worried or anything, but I just...I really didn't want to see you die again..."

Al held her, unsure what to say next.

"Your shoulder...?"

"Hurts like hell, but I've had worse this week..."

"Did we win? Are the bots...um?"

"Dead and gone, for now..."

"Should we keep going, or do you wanna rest here a bit?"

"The inns are pretty untouched, let's rest here a minute. Shower and a nap at least," Al smiled

Auri nodded, "We need both those things."

"Oh, um...The battle wasn't pretty..." Al unslung his sling and handed it to her, "You might not wanna see it..."

"I've seen blood before, Al."

"Not like this…"

"What, it's only okay when it's Your dead body?" She attempted a smile.

Al bit his cheek, holding back his own guilty smirk, "Just…trust me on this…"

***

Of those warriors still awake, most turned to see the strange new silhouette in the doorway of a man and his dog followed by a girl and her bug. Cidarian's many legs tapping on the floorboards like restless fingers on a table, with a blindfolded Auri anxiously swaying on his back.

Wash and Wesley sat with their backs to the door, taking in the warmth of the finally flaming hearth. Al beamed with excitement. He knelt down and whispered to Meeko, who trotted over to young Wesley. She actually turned to look at him, acknowledging another living being, weakly lifting her hesitant hand to his face.

Meeko sniffed her a moment, then awkwardly climbed onto her lap without permission, curling up with barely enough room to even keep his balance. Wesley leaned back, arm hovering until eventually wrapping around the boy, sinking a little lower into the chair.

"Are we here, why are we stopped?" Auri asked

Wash perked up in his seat at the sound of his sister's voice, turning around in an open mouthed stare. Al grinned from ear to ear.

"Al, you're making me nervous, can I take this thing off my face now?"

Wash slowly stood, "Auri…?"

She flinched in her nest, her hands shooting to her face, she froze a moment before lifting the blindfold from her eyes to see her little brother standing before her.

"Hey Kid…" Auri wept, her arms outstretched towards him. Al stepped back to make way for Wash rushing across the room to hug his big sister.

"What the heck are you doing here??" They both said in unison, muffled by each other's shoulders. "Looking for you!" They both laughed and cried, Wash nearly pulling Auri off her bug.

"Told you I'd come back for you…" Auri said

"I thought I'd save you the trouble…" Wash laughed

"Al! Al, stop crying and come meet my brother! Al came with me from Scrapyard to help me find you."

"Wash…" Al stuck out his hand and laughed.

Wash clasped his wrist and hugged him, "You saved our lives And found my sister."

"She saved mine a couple days ago, just payin' it forward."

"I told you to stay put, so I could find you again!" Auri pretended to bonk Wash on the head.

"Auri, you think I'm gonna make You come and find Me?" Wash laughed, pretending to hit her crossed legs.

Auri gasped suddenly as if somebody stabbed her. Wash and Al both flinched, "Are you okay??"

"I have to show you something…"

"You scared me…" Wash laughed, "What is it?"

Auri used her arms to uncross her legs and dangle them over Dari's shell. She reached an arm out to Al to help support her as she slowly slid to the ground, Wash instinctively lunging to catch her. "Wait…" She said, letting go of Al's hand, steadying herself against Dari's shell, and carefully standing on her own.

Wash's lips quivered as he dropped to his knees, sobbing at the sight of his sister standing for the first time in who knows how long. Auri wobbled over him and hugged his head.

Wash sobbed as he stood, "You really found a way…" taking her hands and doing a simple little dance, both swinging their arms and bouncing in place, laughing and crying until they were hugging once more.

"I love you, Little Brother…"

Al stepped away to give them their space, wiping his eyes, half laughing half crying to himself, sitting by the fire in Wash's chair to find Wesley weeping into Meeko's fur, silently shaking, clutching the dog to her chest like the only piece of driftwood in a sea of her own sorrow.

***

"Jacket's gonna have a better scar than me when this is done…" Al laughed nervously as a tall lanky man cut the leather from his back in order to remove it around the protruding bolt, a sewing needle hanging out the side of his mouth like a toothpick. A young olive skinned woman, with the longest, darkest hair Al had ever seen, trimmed away at the bolt's fletchings for a better grip.

Al chuckled to himself as he hugged the back of the wooden chair, restless knees bouncing as he waited, wondering why he was so nervous. He'd seen far worse pain this week alone, but tough and tolerant as he was, he realized he'd never been in real pain for more than an hour...maybe two at the most. If they can't get this bolt out...This might be his first wound to truly linger.

"In all my years as a Stitch, I ain't never seen such a wounded wrap." The man's voice had a deep nasally rattle to it that made Al grin. "Want me to scavenge you a new one? Lotta stuff lyin' around."

"I'll stick to my own dead man's coat if you don't mind fixin' her up for me." Al looked to make sure Auri was thoroughly distracted before his bloody back was exposed. "I'm not much prettier beneath it..." Al tried to warn them before hearing their inevitable curse of shock at the sight of his desecrated flesh.

Beneath his clothes, Al had more scars than skin. His back a bouquet of burns crossed with long, wide, raised slashes that stretched the length of his body.

"You've got some stories, eh kid...?"

"Few more than I remember..."

"I'll stitch your jack for ya...least I can do," He pat Al on the back before finding a seat out of the way.

"Bite down on this..." The woman handed him the tattered end of a thick leather belt.

"Thanks..."

"You ready...?"

"No, but let's do it…" Al smiled before biting down on the belt. In through his nose and out his mouth, he took quick deep breaths trying to get his heart pumping.

Only enough grip on the shaft for a single hand, the other she pressed against the center of his back, colder than the morning. "Alright…This is it."

"Just a big ugly splinter," The man smiled, his feet kicked up on the table, already stitching Al's coat back together.

Al managed another chuckle before- "GRRRT!" Pain erupted from his shoulder, arching out through his chest and back. He felt his flesh twisting with the shaft itself while the woman pressed and yanked. The bolt wouldn't budge any more than bone would, being ripped out by hand, like the shaft had fused to his flesh. *Put it off for too long…*

Al spit out the belt, gasping for breath, suddenly covered in sweat. "I don't think it's- GAHH!" The woman yanked and twisted once more to no avail, gasping herself when she finally let up and let go.

"You alright?" She panted, falling back into a chair of her own.

"Oh I'm prime as ever…Fuckin' glass…" Al laughed the pain away.

"Had to be sure…I think you're stuck with your friend here for the time being, til we can find you a real medic. Course, we can always find someone bigger and stronger than me to give it a pull."

The tailor nodded, "We'll line 'em up, charge a small trade, tell 'em whoever removes the bolt from this boy is the rightful king of Aureum."

Al wiped his forehead with a shaky hand, waiting for the pain to fade. "Thanks anyways, um..." Al held his good hand out for the woman to shake.

"Bethany," She flashed a weak smile, clasping his wrist.

"Luca," The man nodded

"I'm Al and that's Meeko over there with Wesley."

"Thanks for looking after her...Lost her brother when the bridge went up."

"That'll do it......" Al mumbled to himself, "I've never seen anything like that blast, did the bots do that themselves?"

Luca shook his head, "We were safe, the battle was almost over...I don't know what the fuck coulda happened."

"That kid did something..." Bethany sank deep into her seat, closing her eyes to relax for the first time in who knows how long.

"Wash??" Al whispered

"No, no," Beth almost laughed at the notion before turning back to Luca, "Fordo and that creepy kid were arguing about something when the bridge went up."

"Jason was a spook, but what the hell could he have done? Mother Aure couldn't conjure a blast like that."

"I don't know, but Fordo was convinced enough to toss him off the roof..."

"Fordo tossed him?" Luca grimaced, "I thought he got caught in the quake."

"Fordo...killed a kid...?" Al whispered to himself, more shocked by the news than surprised at its probability.

"Boy had it coming even before the blast..." Bethany

said with absolute certainty, "Who knows what kinda damage he's done out there."

Al sat and stared at the somber soldiers sitting about the inn, barely talking, barely present, "How bad was the battle...?"

Beth and Luca both looked at each other, before Luca leaned over with a lowered voice, "We didn't stand a fuckin' chance..."

Al nodded, "I'm glad we showed up when we did..."

"Us too, you saved our ass."

"I meant glad we missed the actual battle..." Al held his throbbing shoulder, trying to move it around in vain, "Thought myself a warrior these last few years, but seeing that mess out there...I don't think I have the stomach for a real fight."

"The real fight was fine until the monsters showed up..."

"You mean different than the-?" A strange vibration rumbled the floorboards of the inn for a fraction of a moment, the gentle quakes of a passing wyrm, batting away Al's train of thought. Beth and Luca both looked uneasy. "You're not used to the dragons neither, huh?" Al asked

"Cozy in Riverwood too long, I think..." Luca said

A larger quake rattled all the bar's glass. "Whoa, hey..."

"That doesn't feel right..." Beth said

Another quake shook the inn strong enough to knock a bottle crashing off the shelves.

KADOOMMMMMMMMM

A deep resonate shockwave of sound swept through the air, rattling through Al's very bones, staggering all in the inn as if smacked by a tangible wall of pure vibration.

"The hell was that...?" Weary warriors jolted up all around, shaken from their slumber.

Al and Auri locked eyes seemingly sharing the exact same thought: *Sound Magic*

Al stood, "Get everyone up..." He said to Beth, wobbling over to Auri and Wash, every quake threatening to knock him over.

"What is that?" Wash asked

"We gotta move," Al said, grunting to hoist Auri up in his arms despite his wound.

"Al......" Auri pointed at her bug in the corner, already locked up tight in a defensive ball.

"Fuck, come on...Wesley, get over here, Meeko let's..." Meeko was already standing in the open doorway, looking out across the courtyard, ears and eyes perked, searching for danger.

"What do you see, Meeks?"

Crash! Foom...

A distant metallic crash carried through the door along with the faint panic of people running for their lives...

Crash! Foom...

Meeko had an odd long nod with each crash as if following the sound up...then down, up...then down. Wesley wandered to the wall with Al and Wash. Beth and Luca rushed to wake the wounded.

Crash! Foom... Crash! Foom...

"Al, what do we do?"

"I don't...I don't know..."

Each crash was growing louder...Closer...

Crash! Foom...... Crash! Foom......

Meeko shrank back from the doorway...Everyone in the inn was on their feet, watching the pup's head bob...

Crash!!

Al muffled Auri's scream with his hand as a massive black shape crushed a crater in the cobblestone courtyard just outside the inn. Through the doorway, Al could only see what looked like a pair of giant dark armored legs, splattered and shiny with fresh red blood. Everyone held their breath.

FOOM!!

The bot launched back into the air, Meeko's head following it straight up. Before anyone could be relieved, Meeko spun around, his head pointing right at the center of the ceiling. Al's eyes went wide, "Go! Go! Everyone-!"

CRASH!!!

The roof imploded as an iron giant burst into the inn, blasting the hearth's flaming coals in every direction. Al pinned Auri and the kids to the wall, his exposed back pelted with burning bricks.

"Ahhh!" Al cried out, almost dropping Auri, shoving the kids towards the door, not looking back to see the monster tearing through the inn like it was made of paper, grabbing and crushing wounded warriors at random. The coals already setting the shattered bar ablaze. Al heard a man's scream silenced by a heavy splat against the wall right behind him, something warm and wet spraying Al's blistered back, just as he made it out through the doorway.

Wash and Wesley sprinted out into the misty courtyard, Wash nearly slipping on the blood. A low gray overcast stretched across the sky spilling a wall of fog out around the entire town as if all of Gateway had been carried into the clouds.

"Where do we go?" Wash yelled back.

Hide in the buildings? Run for the fields? Find Carth and Fordo? Fuck, I don't know, I don't know!

Meeko's barking reminded Al they already had a better guide, "Meeko, get us out of here!" But his boy didn't move, he was staring and barking in more and more distress at the closest alleyway.

He meant Monsters... Al looked up to see an actual demon step out through the mist; A giant's, headless, slime covered corpse, stretched taller than the buildings, loomed over the party like a spirit of death. The same heavy gray fog that surrounded the town seeped out from the gaping void where its head should be along with a haunting, unnatural groan that melted all of Al's courage into an existential dread.

His knees went weak, nearly dropping Auri once more as they turned to run from the impossible creature swaying before them. Just as they reached the opposite end of the courtyard, another headless giant appeared, nearly stepping on Meeko as it stretched out from the shrouded alley.

"Back! Back!" Al cried, backing his party up to the central obelisk, eyes desperately scanning for escape routes only to find a Headless monster blocking every angle.

KADOOMMMMMMMMM

Another shockwave swept through their bones, this time coming out of the inn they'd just escaped, where the sounds of slaughter had died down and were replaced by the roar of a raging fire, black smoke flying out the shattered windows.

"Al!"

He turned to see Fordo and Carth sprinting towards them from far up the main street with two more Headless close behind them. A handful of remaining warriors forming a shivering circle around the monument.

Al slid Auri down against the pillar and pressed his forehead against hers.

"Al..." she grabbed his hand before he could turn away, "Thanks for coming with me..." She said, tears in her eyes.

"Thanks for letting me..." He smiled weakly, picking up a discarded hammer, resting it on his shoulder, kissing his palm and petting Meeko at his side. Auri took Wash and Wesley's hands as they crouched down beside her, staring and trembling at swaying monsters all around them.

FOOSH!!

The dark robot burst out through the roof of the flaming inn, shooting straight up into the sky, disappearing into the low curtain of clouds that now sat like a shapeless ceiling over the town.

Al grit his teeth, shaking while searching the swirling gray for the falling monster, cold sweat pouring down his body. A black spot appeared right above them, growing larger and larger, falling faster and faster until-

CRASH!!!

The faceless metal giant crushed the world beneath its feet, blasting Al back off of his, a wave of dust, stone, and blood showering over them. They all screamed, Al scrambled up to swing his hammer only to freeze at the sight of the hulking creature crouching calmly over them. Fresh boiling blood steaming off its hands and body in the chill morning air, its smooth eyeless faceplate pointed Right down at Alexander. Al dropped to his knees, unable to lift his hammer, unable to stand, unable to do anything but stare in accepted terror at the unkillable foe before him, waiting for his inevitable death only for it to cock its head and say in the earthshakingly deep, resonate voice of a god...

"There You Are, Little Brother..."

All the blood drained from Al's face...

"...We've Been Looking For You."

Fordo

9

"Typical, showin' up at the end to take all the credit..."

Fordo stood over his long lost friend, writhing in the mud with his mut, a bolt punched clean through his shoulder. Al looked surprised to see him, like he hadn't even noticed Fordo at the front, leading this wounded rabble himself.

"You look like glass..." Al panted, without a grin, without a laugh, without a hint of welcome for the friend he abandoned for the better part of a year.

"Feel like glass..." Fordo caulked up Al's indifference to him nearly dying like an idiot, diving into a pile of monsters just to show off, "...Get the fuck up."

They both winced from different wounds as Fordo pulled Al up to his feet. Fordo finally felt just how weak he was, his throbbing head and scraped back catching up to him.

"Gathii found you?" Al asked

"Easier than I found you, where the hell have you-?"

"Al!" An excited Carth ran up, interrupting their reunion with an excessive embrace.

"Ahh!" Al cried out with what looked like a flash of fear in his eyes like he's never been hugged or hurt before.

"Carth??" Al croaked, "You big, strong, man, you made it!" Al could conjure a grin for Carth it seemed, even had the strength to hug him back. Fordo watched his two best friends laugh and embrace without him, picking up right where they left off like Al hadn't abandoned them without a word for some selfish spiritual journey.

Fordo tried to occupy himself until his friends were ready to acknowledge him. Adjusting the straps on his armor, kneeling down to pet Meeko. "Aye, mut..." Fordo whispered, "Where the hell have you been?"

Figures Meeko barely looked at him either, following his master's lead, trotting within range of Fordo's fingers just to ignore him and walk away without greeting.

"...What the hell happened here?" Al asked, finally looking Fordo in the eye, "This place is sunk to hell."

Fordo racked his brain for a dismissive response when Sam called, "Orders, Commander?"

"Commander?" Al laughed

Don't act so surprised...

Fordo turned to what was left of his defenders, clearing his throat before shouting, "Sweep for survivors, we don't know who's still out there! Find food and water where you can! Beth, Lady, Luca! Pick an inn, get the wounded outta the mess!"

"We're all wounded..." Jane called

"If you can walk you can search! Be careful of more cogs, some might be lodged in the wreckage!"

Al whispered some secret joke to Carth that Fordo tried to ignore.

"Wash, you still breathin'?" Fordo continued

"Aye..."

"You tend to Wesley for me."

Al whispered something to Meeko, sending him running through the weary warriors.

"Oy," Doyle walked up to Al, "That pup belong to you?"

"Belong to each other, I suppose."

"You have a name?"

"My boy's name is Meeko."

That's not what he asked...

"This is Alexander of Scrapyard," Carth said, "He's a good friend of ours."

"A very good friend. You and your boy saved our lives, mate." Fordo watched Doyle Blackhat and half of his own men all actually Bow to Alexander. *And for what? For charging in at the last minute like an idiot, nearly getting himself killed.* "I'd offer you my life if it was still mine to give."

You gotta be fuckin' kidding me...

Fordo rubbed his eyes, trying to suppress his ever growing headache while Al goofed around, stealing all his friends.

"Oy," Fordo called, "We'll catch up when the work is done. Al, Carth, Sam, and Doyle with me. We need eyes on the bots, make sure we're in the clear."

"Aye sir," Al laughed like that wasn't an order, waving Fordo off like he was also his dog and turning back to talk to Carth. Fordo stared, in awe at the audacity while Al hugged Carth once more and ran off without looking back like he didn't just hear what the fuck Fordo just said.

"Where the hell is he going?" Fordo asked Carth

"Said there's someone else he needs to see."

"He forget who the hell we are? We've been looking for his ass for...Sink it, come on, we've got real glass to do."

***

"The dead can wait..." Fordo ordered, trying to sound somber, "Sweep for survivors, then everybody find yourself a bed...They'll get their rest after we do."

The couple dozen defenders still capable of standing, walked, climbed, and dug their way through the wreckage calling out for anyone who may be left. In the time Fordo and his friends walked the length of town to the lonely arch of the fallen bridge, he heard no answer.

While Bots and bodies littered the ground, Fordo focused forward, refusing to acknowledge their fallen. Most everyone who mattered made it in the end. The rest of these fools knew what they were fighting for.

'Don't spoil a good death with doubt and mourning. You remember what they lived and died for and, if you love them, you'll keep that going.'

We'll carve all your names into the world we saved...

The street sparkled, scattered with glass from every window shattered by the blast. The buildings closest to the bridge, cracked and tilted off their foundations, metal limbs and ballista bolts jutting out of the side, shrapnel from the devastating explosion. Where the great Gateway Bridge stretched mere hours before now stood separate twin archways, riven by war. The world beyond the Farside arch still obscured by the unwavering wall of fog.

Fordo looked up at the splintered remains of the Swinging Gate with pride. Their fruitful efforts...their key to victory... *There's your monument right there...*

"What the fuck happened?" Doyle's voice snapped Fordo back to the present. "Never seen anything like that blast in my life...That's the old world way."

"Spacewalk?" Carth asked

Doyle shook his head, "Earthborn...The homeworld ancients used to blow the hell out of each other with bigger and bigger boomers. I didn't know we still knew how to make 'em."

"We shouldn't..." Sam said, "I thought the Spacewalkers dumped that tech centuries ago, before we even found Aureum."

"Jason did something..." Fordo said

"The Kid? No...There's no way, mate."

"What is wrong with you?" Sam shook her head in disbelief.

"It's true," Carth said, "I don't know how, but he had some kinda trigger."

"You two are really gonna put all this destruction on an actual Child?"

"Just the one that actually caused it..."

"Being a nuisance doesn't make him a monster!"

"Just like being a child doesn't make him harmless! 'Fast and loud...All at once.' That's Exactly how he said he'd bring down the bridge and that's Exactly what happened, Sam!"

Her angry expression dissolved into confusion, recalling Jason's words.

"Kid did say that..." Doyle confirmed, "Where's the kid now?"

Fordo glanced at Carth, "Took a tumble off the roof..."

Doyle grimaced, "Whatever happened, we're fuckin' sunk for it."

"Before the blast you said we needed to talk?"

Blackhat nodded, leaning against the arch to adjust something on his jammed botsthetic leg, "We didn't win this fight, mate..."

"I mean..." Fordo's face got hot at the accusation, "We took a lot of losses, but we...we stopped them. Even before the blast, we stopped them, you said it yourself that the battle was over."

"Calm down, kid, you led well and we did the best we could have with what little we knew..."

"But...?"

"But we're only alive right now because they Let us, mate...This whole battle was a fuckin' game to them."

"No...No, sink that, we had them! They hit us hard as glass and we pushed them back every time. It wasn't until they cheated with those fuckin' monsters that we even had any trouble."

"Those fuckin' monsters...that they only sent in One

at a time...that they stopped their Whole swarmin' army just to watch it kick the shit out of us."

Fordo shook his head, refusing to believe it, to let Doyle taint his victory.

"If they wanted to win, why hold back the Headless? Why stop the charge? Why not send everything in at once? They woulda blown through us like the fuckin' wind if they wanted to."

"They didn't attack us from the air neither," Carth said, not looking Fordo in the eye, "I think they had to be holding back, Ford..."

"No, no...They can't...Aw, fuck me..." Fordo rubbed his temples, leaning on the arch like it would give him cover from the criticism. "No...I can't accept that..."

"It's just how it is, mate...And we need to figure out-"

"No."

"Kid, you wanna lead, you gotta accept the truth that's right in front of you."

"No, fuck that and fuck you. Listen to me, all three of you..." Fordo trembled, seeing all the signs, all the evidence, realizing in his heart that it was impossible to deny, "If I let you stand there and tell me that those monsters were just fucking with us, if I accept that...That means All of this...was a waste of time, do you understand??"

"Ay, lower your voice, mate...We don't need the men to-"

"That means everything we did was for glass, for Nothing...Everyone we lost here Died for fucking Nothing!"

"Fordo, hey, calm down..." Carth tried to hold him steady, but Fordo shrugged away.

"Chop is Gone...Patch, Jacob, everyone is Dead! Wesley's never gonna see her fuckin' brother again...And you wanna tell me that's all My fault??"

Fordo's voice echoed up the alleyways, down the destroyed street, right over the dozens of defenders now all staring at him.

"That's not what we're-"

"I led everyone here to die for what? For Nothing? Nothing I did matters?? This is all some sick joke?? Well why don't I hear any fucking laughing??"

The sick, twisted, childish laughter of The Yellow Eyed Boy echoed through Fordo's mind, burning with the image of his final falling grin, growing louder and louder, drowning out all other thoughts, all other sounds. Fordo slapped his hands over his ears. *Damnit cunt, get out of my head...Get out of my head!!*

"Where the hell is that coming from...?" Carth asked, looking all around, Sam and Doyle doing the same.

Fordo's heart pounded, realizing the dead child's cackle wasn't in his head, but all around them; Bouncing off the buildings, out of the alleys, out of the fucking sky.

No, no it can't be. This was a trick...a recording...an echo from the bots like Fordo's own voice before, and it wasn't going to work.

Fordo charged up the street to find Jason's body, to burn it if he had to, anything to prevent his horrible spirit from haunting him into madness. He passed Hunter's body, then passed the lance pinned bot...No, too far...Fordo spun around, running back, frantically searching the ground finding no bodies in between until he came upon a small, red, corpseless stain on the stones, Exactly where the Yellow Eyed body should have been.

Fordo's heart beat through his ribs, his brain throbbing through his skull, his hands pulling at his hair as he stared at the cackling stain.

You can't trick me...You can't trick me...You can't trick me.

Fordo flinched at a hand placed on his shoulder, Carth spinning him around, "Keep it together, Ford..."

"He's gone..."

"I know he's gone, man, it's just an echo..."

"No, Carth, he's fuckin' Gone!"

Crash!

They both flinched at a heavy crash across the Siena, the laughter instantly fading to an equally deafening silence. Carth and Fordo ran back to the river to see the Dark Armored Giant standing high upon the far arch once more, the towering cloud roiling behind him. *You're not getting in my head you son of a-*

"Children Of Aureum..."

The monster's bassy, resonant, synthetic voice washed over them from no discernible angle. If Fordo couldn't see the robot himself, he would've thought the world itself was speaking.

*"My Name...Is Creature...Keeper Of Souls,
Speaker Of The Dead, Last Off The Line, Last
Of My Kind."*

*"You Butchered My Brothers, Dissected Us For
Parts, Made Us Into Monsters..."*
*"You Are Strong, Small Ones...But I Am
Beyond Strength."*

*"I Am The Wrath Of Those You Ravaged...And I
Have Come To Ensure You Share Their Fate..."*

Creature launched into the sky, vanishing above the clouds as a Line of Headless swayed out of the mist, charging straight into the rushing waters, their thin limbs cutting right through the current.

Fordo's eyes went dead at the sight of the Headless effortlessly wading through the river, his face turned to stone. Any fear, any dread erased by a single thought:

It was all a lie...
All a game...
And they let me think I won...

Fordo had no orders, he had no words, he had no thoughts, just a blinding, murderous rage, his heartbeat shaking the very ground. He couldn't hear his men's pleas to run, couldn't feel his friends tugging on his armor, his body fighting to stay in that spot, to stay and stare death into the cheating monsters charging towards him until Carth's fist plowed into the side of his head.

"What the fuck are you doing??" Carth screamed in his face

"It meant nothing..." Fordo grunted

"What??"

"It Meant Nothing!!"

"Then don't die for nothing, you fucking idiot!!!" Carth threw Fordo forward, sending him stumbling down the road, "If you die, I die, so get a fucking move on, cunt! Go! Go!"

Fordo snapped out of his tantrum, red faced and running, Carth chasing him back towards the circle of inns. He finally noticed the quaking ground, that they were completely alone, Sam, Doyle and the others already ran off.

Keep getting stuck in my head... *The fuck is wrong with me?*

They ran past cracks and craters in the cobblestone that weren't there minutes before, half splattered with what looked like people, crushed flat against the stones. *Insects... We're nothing but fucking insects to them...* Fordo looked up, gritting his teeth to see Creature careening from the clouds fifty yards away, crashing straight through the roof of the inn where the wounded rested.

"No, you coward!" Fordo tore down the road as fast as his body would let him, but they were still so far, wincing as the sounds of slaughter and destruction washed over him. No, no, *what have I done...?*

Fordo spotted a small group escape out the front door following a small dark shape, thanking the gods it was Al and the kids. The group scrambled in the courtyard, already surrounded by Headless, the monsters swaying in place in each alley, forming the walls of a living cage.

What few men were left were corralled around the obelisk once more. Maybe fifteen people remained, including Sam, Doyle, Wash, Wesley, and Al carrying a small silver haired girl Fordo didn't recognize. Icy fear crept back into Fordo's heart as he realized how few of them remained. *Your story doesn't matter if no one survives to tell it...*

"Al!" Fordo called, his rival looking right through him at the headless monsters right behind them.

FOOSH!!

Creature burst from the inn, now an eruption of smoke and flame, the giant shooting into the sky. *No, no, fuck!* Fordo noticed a familiar noise coming from above as Creature appeared through the clouds. Like a flag flapping faster and faster until the meteor of a monster crashed right onto Al and the kids, sending out an explosive wave of stone and dust, wiping more of his friends from the face of Aureum.

"NO!!!" Fordo shouted violently, skidding to a stop. Fordo dropped to his knees, staring into the cloud of dust until it parted, revealing Creature kneeling over a still living Al, and the kids unharmed. Gasping for air, Fordo's unblinking stare split back and forth between Alexander and the hulking monster before him. Fordo prepared to watch Creature crush his rival, to see the light leave Al's eyes once more, when the monster looked right into them, cocked its head and said:

"There You Are, Little Brother..."

"...We've Been Looking For You."

A hulking, black metal behemoth, Creature's ancient looking armor bulged and layered off its limbs like metallic, hard angled muscles, all a rough rustic texture, like paint over stone. Its head seemed too round to match its body, a smooth faceless skull with large round indentations on either side, like the faces of a Julian speaker. Creature loomed over Al and the survivors like a child peered at grubs writhing under a rock.

Al shivered, shirtless on the ground, his scar crossed skin drenched with sweat and blood, every human eye on him. "Do you..." Al stammered, "Do you know me?"

Al shrank away as Creature leaned closer,

"I'm A Friend Of Your Father's..."

"My f-father...? Balian...?" Al asked, wide eyed.
Fordo clenched his fist.

"Balian..." Creature hammered his heavy fist into the stones with a disdainful slam, *"No, I Know Not My Kin Killer, But He Will Soon Know Me... Curious...I Was Told You Might Not-M-M Might... Not...Rememmmb..."* Creature's head and shoulders slumped forward.

Al stared up at the monster, slowly crawling backwards, leaning back over the kids, like that might shield them from harm.

Creature's back straightened suddenly, his head looking up at the clouds, standing slowly, his movements far more stiff, more precise, more robotic than a moment before. The giant gracelessly bent its knees and launched back into the sky without a word, disappearing behind the clouds.

While everyone's eyes were on the sky, Fordo's were fixed on Al. *"'Your' father...?"* Fordo whispered, cold and quiet, catching Al's eye, but not his ear.

BOOM!!

Creature crashed back to Aureum with another cloud of dust. Through the coughing, the crying, and Meeko's barking, Fordo heard that dreadful childish laugh once more, Creature towering before them, tall and stiff as a statue and there, in the flesh, clinging to two small handles on the monster's back, was the undead Jason, The Yellow Eyed Boy, climbing on Creature with a cold golden grin.

Carth and Fordo froze on sight. The rest of his devastated crew stared up in fear and awe at their minor nuisance riding the shoulders of the king of monsters.

Jason cackled, pointing right at their faces, "You should see yourselves, you fucking morons! Wash, bang! Sam, bang! I got You, I got You! Oh, You all look like you're about to Shit yourselves!"

"What's...going on...?" Al cowered back against the small girl he was carrying, unable to look at the boy directly. Shaking like the mere sight of Jason caused him pain.

"Jason...how...why...?" Sam lowered her sword, her green eyes swirling with confusion, "I protected you..."

"From what? Getting wet?" Jason laughed

"No, you're dead..." Fordo stared up at him in hatred, "I killed you, you son of a bitch!"

"You want a prize, pretty boy?" Jason laughed, turning his attention to Al still trembling under his gaze.

"But how did...?" Fordo looked at the child menace and realized for the first time that he didn't just look similar to Alexander, he was the spitting, uncanny image of a younger, sicker Al. Betrayal washed through Fordo with the revelation, watching the two freaks have their conversation.

Jason grinned at Alexander, Creature taking a booming step closer, "You look like shit, you mush brained bastard! I never thought I'd see your scabby ass again!"

"I don't..." Al shook his head in disgust and disbelief, dark eyes wild as they shifted from boy, to bot, to headless abominations, "Who the fuck are you??"

"Ten years on the table, still got all the scars, and you really don't remember me??" Jason chuckled, his grin somehow growing even more sinister, the robot looming over Al until he was swallowed by its shadow.

Al squirmed, gasping for breath, terror in his eyes, "I don't remember...I don't..." Meeko barked in concern as Al clutched his chest, scratching at his scars like he was suffocating in his own skin, "What did you do to me??"

Jason's cruel grin turned almost nostalgic, "You used to piss yourself before I even opened the door, now look at you... Swinging swords, playing hero...it's almost adorable!"

"Stop it!" Shouted the small girl at Al's back, wrapping her arms around him, Meeko climbing on his lap, keeping Al from clawing at himself, "What are you doing to him?"

"Aw, What's wrong with you, you big baby?" Jason laughed, "You lose a guy for a couple decades and he can't even look at you!"

"Decades..." Sam breathed, "How...How old are you?"

Jason shrugged, "Eh, I stopped paying attention...you lose track when you live forever..." He looked genuinely puzzled like it's been ages since he thought about it, "I think it's about half and half now...Up there, and Down here," The boy nodded up at the sky like that was supposed to make any sense.

"Fordo said he killed you..." Al panted, finally catching his breath with the help of the girl.

"I gotta give you credit for that, Dead Eyes," Jason smirked at Fordo, "I didn't think you had the guts."

"I'll have yours when this is done..."

"That means..." Al said, "You have...my powers...?"

"No you raisin skinned retard, you have My powers," he laughed, "What, you think you were special?"

"I just thought..." Al's eyes darted all around like his thoughts were a swarm of insects buzzing around Meeko, "I thought we were alone..."

Jason laughed, spreading his arms out wide, Creature and the Headless doing the same in an eerie synchronized celebration, "'Til we lose our heads or lose our minds..." Jason shrugged, "We'll Always have each other."

Fordo rubbed his fists bloody against the stones, letting the scraping pain in his knuckles keep him from shaking and from doing anything too stupid. He couldn't stand it...Kneeling at the mercy of this infant abomination, he wanted to kill him, to rip Jason's head off and kick it into the blazing building for good. It'd be worth it even if Creature squashed him into paste. But Carth...Wesley...Wash...his friends were too close. There had to be a way out, a smarter way, just had to find it.

Al looked absolutely terrified by his new found family, "What...What are we??"

"We're immortal, dumbass!" Jason shrugged like that was a stupid question.

"No, I mean...What are WE? Are we Family, are we...?" Al trailed off, clearly frustrated, tears in his eyes, pulling a small crumpled photograph of a woman from his pocket and holding it up for Jason to see. When Jason looked at the photo, all of the cruelty and malice faded from his yellow eyes, and for a fraction of a moment, he just looked like another lost warphan. "Is this..." Al trembled, his voice cracking as the tears fell, "Is this my mother?"

Surprised, sudden, explosive laughter erupted out of Jason so violently he almost fell from Creature's back, coughing and slapping the shoulders of his giant killer robot. Fordo took the moment to glance around for anything he could use, spotting a discarded crossbow not ten feet away, already cranked. Fordo silently scooped up a scattered bolt, concealing it behind his wrist, locking eyes with Doyle, Blackhat giving the subtlest shadow of a nod. *The bots only move when he does...If we can take him out while the bots are frozen...Maybe they'll stay that way...*

"Answer me..." Al grit his teeth, crushing the old photo between his fingers, the laughing boy unable to catch his breath, "ANSWER ME!!"

Fordo flinched, having never in his life seen or heard Alexander in a rage.

"Finds out he's fucking god..." Jason wiped his eyes, "And he's still just...crying for his Mommy...!" Jason cackled right in Al's face, barely able to breath, let alone pay attention.

Fordo dove for the crossbow, loaded the bolt in a single motion, pointed it right at Jason's head, and-

"No!" Al's body slammed into Fordo's, sending the shot sailing wide. The many Headless all wailed at once, swaying forward, countless arms snaking towards the screaming survivors, halted a moment later by Jason's raised hand, the ancient boy looking caught off guard for the first time.

"I had him, you bastard!" Fordo yelled at Al.

"He knows..." Al grunted, holding his wounded shoulder, rage in his tearful eyes, "He knows the truth..."

"Oh, You Stupid, Sneaky, Hollow Eyed, Loser!" Jason grinned, Creature stomping closer to Fordo with every insult, "You really don't give a fuck about your friends, huh?"

Everyone flinched as Creature lunged to the side, snatching Carth up screaming into the air, "No, Fordooaahhh!! Jason, please! PLEASE!" The monster held Carth's body up with two hands, right over Fordo's head, ready to tear him in two and shower Fordo in his best friend's guts.

"NO!! No, no, no Please! Please!!" Fordo begged, "Put him down! Carth! No, Please, I'm sorry!!"

"What was that?" Jason shouted, over the screaming, Creature's grip tightening around Carth's chest, his best friend crying out, gasping for air, already coughing up blood.

"I'm Sorry!" Fordo cried, "I'm sorry! Please don't... Don't hurt him..."

"That's better..." Jason smiled, the circle of Headless closing even tighter, Creature loosening his grip just enough for Carth to catch his breath, coughing, and crying in the air, "Now everybody just calm down until we've had our fu-"

Sam roared and slammed her sword into the side of the monument with a painful crash, sending a crack shooting up the side of the stone, a feral, desperate look in her eye, "I want answers and I want them right now!"

Doyle grabbed her shoulder, "Oy, Sam...We need to-"

"ENOUGH!!!" Fordo flinched again as Sam shouted with the unmatched wrath and authority of a furious, murderous mother, "You either tell us why the hell you're doing this or just fucking kill us already! I've had Enough of these games!"

"Please...don't..." Carth sobbed

"Why I'm doing what?" Jason whined, looking genuinely confused, "I'm just trying to talk to mamma's boy over here!" Jason pointed at Al like that was obvious.

"Doing this! All Of This!" Sam frantically gestured to all the death and monsters around them, "Using your puppets to destroy the whole fucking world!"

"Destroy the...No, that's not what I'm..." Jason looked around like he had forgotten they were in the middle of a massacre. The boy's eyes lit up, "Oh This!" he chuckled and smacked the side of his own head like he'd started playing a game without explaining the rules.

"No, I love this world, what you've all done with it! Watching people progress and build and grow into something... New, something Wild! All the cool, crazy shit people are capable of, it's...incredible!" Jason paused and smiled like that explained everything, like that explained Anything.

"That doesn't make any fucking sense..." Fordo grimaced

"Then why...kill those people...?" Al stared in horror

Jason leaned comfortably on Creature's shoulder like it was the edge of his bed telling them all about a dream he had, "The best part of watching humans...is seeing how they Change... Evolve, you know?"

"I get our people down to a new world? They colonize in under a century! I send a few thousand droids on a walk across the continent? Now we've got floating cities! Warrior cults!

A freakin' Farmer figured out how to Bond Flesh with pure Robotics…We couldn't even do that shit in space!" He laughed, sincere excitement in his yellow eyes.

"But then…after a few years…you babies all get so comfortable, so quiet, just get so fucking…Boooring…With peace, progress always Takes Forever…And I have to Live Forever…If I don't keep things moving…I'll lose my freakin' mind!"

"Far Fall…" Fordo frowned

"The War…" Sam whispered

"It was you??"

"You broke my daughter…?"

"You took my mother…"

"You Killed millions…"

"…Just to see what fucking happens??"

"And what happened??" Jason asked, still beaming with excitement, "You built an army from scratch in three days! Stopped my droids almost single handed! You're a twenty year old General! A hero!"

"And you're a monster…"

"Don't you see?? Without me you'd be a fucking stableboy!"

"Without you, I'd have my fucking mother!!"

"You'd Be Nothing!"

"I'd Be Happy!!!"

"Oh Boo Fucking Hoo!" Jason's excitement turned to pure disgust, Creature mimicking Jason's frustrated hand gestures as he ranted, waving around Carth still crying in the air, "What The Hell Happened To You Animals?? How'd you all lose your balls in the last hundred years, huh?? What happened to the Ruthlessness, the-the Greed, the Corruption?? Your taste for blood?? In Space...you used to Hate each other! Hell..." He grinned, "You used to eat each other! But now..."

"You all got so good at solving problems, you idiots forgot how to make any yourselves! Aureum has almost everything it needs...Factions, Cultures, Heroes, Dragons! It just needs One more little Push over the edge, One more Spark for flavor, to be perfect, To Be Fun...And you know what I realized?" Jason and Creature both spread their arms,

"This World Needs More Monsters..."
Jason grinned like he thought himself a genius, like he'd figured it all out, the secrets of the universe. The smug smile made Fordo sick to his stomach.

"That doesn't explain..." Fordo grit his teeth, "Why we're still alive..."

The survivors all stared at Jason in anticipation, the clouds of steam from their labored breaths drifting up to join the floating fog,

"What..." Jason shrugged like it was obvious, "...am I supposed to play all by myself?"

Fordo stared open mouthed at the boy, shaking his head, a giggle overtaking him, building to a laugh, then a genuine cackle, as cold and cruel as Jason's.

"Fordo..." Al whispered

"Ford..." Carth croaked, tears running down his face.

"What's so funny?" The kid asked like he sincerely wanted in on the joke.

"You think after all that...All this glass...Everything you just told us...You think we're still gonna play along with your stupid fucking game??"

Jason looked at Fordo in disbelief, making Fordo truly think for the fraction of a moment that he'd tripped Jason up before his cruel smile sprouted once more, "Man, you haven't learned anything."

Creature powered back on with an ominous hum, "No!" Fordo barked, reaching uselessly for Carth as Creature tossed him screaming off to the side, a Headless snatching him out of the air and swallowing him in an instant. A cold numbing emptiness consumed Fordo as he watched his best friend disappear into the Headless void.

Every other human scrambled away from the monster, Jason howling on its back while Creature slowly raised his fists to crush the kids, the silver haired girl shielding Wash with her tiny body.

Sam and Doyle charged forward, leaping between Creature and the others just in time, Sam barely deflecting his massive fist with a wild clanging swing of her sword, the heavy metal all colliding into stone.

"Woaho!" Jason cheered

Meeko rushed up Creature's arm, charging straight for Jason. "No Meeko, wait!" Al cried out, flinching as the giant robot grabbed Meeko just in time to save his master, plopping the mut back to the ground with an oddly gentle drop.

Doyle leapt into the air during Meeko's distraction, swinging the heavy butt of his spear into the side of Creature's head. The monster reared back from the hit, as if covering its ears, Sam's sword crashing into its side, barely denting the armored shell.

"Come on now, I thought you guys were warriors!"

Al roared, leaping to rip Jason off of Creature's back, the laughing boy kicking him in his wounded shoulder sending him crashing back to the ground, landing on Fordo as he fell, both rolling to dodge Creature's stone cracking stomp.

"That's all you got?? I made you better than that!"

Doyle lunged to knock the distracted Jason off from his perch, Creature spinning just in time, shattering Doyle's spear against the back of his hand, sending Doyle sprawling onto his back at the feet of a Headless, all still swaying in place, waiting for a real threat against their master.

Sam cried out, relentlessly and recklessly swinging on the monster over and over, all harmlessly bouncing or scratching until she finally caught the back of Creature's knee, causing him to buckle, dropping him down in range for a killing blow, aimed right for his neck.

"No, Sam!" Doyle called

"Oh Shit!" Jason covered his face as Sam roared in triumph, only for Creature to catch her massive sword with one hand. He yanked her off of her feet, arching her over his head, and slamming her onto her back, air and blood evacuating her lungs. Creature snatched Sam up by her ankles and dangled her helplessly in the air like a hard caught fish. Sam's eyes blazed red with tearful rage as she hung defeated, the six foot warrior woman and her slab of steel looking like a doll and a dagger in Creature's monstrous hands.

"Ay!" Jason cheered through surprised nervous laughter, "Creature you animal! I thought she really had you, buddy I-Hey, No, Wait!" Jason yelled as Creature swung Sam's whole body by her ankles, splattering her head against the side of the obelisk with a sickening wet crunch.

"Samantha!!!" Doyle flinched at the sound like it was his own body. Fordo, Al, and Doyle all slumped to their knees, gasping for breath, watching in horror as the brains of their friend and greatest warrior dripped down the pale stoned monument.

Jason rubbed his eyes, pouting like he'd accidentally broken his favorite toy, "Aw, Damnit Creature...I really fuckin' liked her..."

Beyond the crying and the barking, beyond Carth's muffled screams, beyond the wall of fog surrounding the town, a rhythmic rumble sounded in the distance, "What is that, Creature?" Jason asked without concern.

Creature cocked his head, *"An army approaches… Shall we set a trap to harvest more forces?"*

Jason sighed, "No, I think that's enough for today… Let's just pack them up and go…Sam too…" He gestured to the survivors, all huddling closer together.

"All of them?" Creature asked

"Mmm………Leave my friends."

Fordo's eyes narrowed and before he could even register the words 'Pack them up', the Headless surged forth for a ravenous feast, arms splitting and multiplying until a tangled storm of dark metal tentacles shot at the survivors from every direction. The humans scattered and screamed, tripped, dragged, flung, and swallowed one by one in the flurry of twisted tendrils.

After flailing about, ducking and dodging, Fordo soon realized none were reaching for him. He watched an arm grab Sam's sword, another her body, and throw both down their gaping throats, Doyle screaming in protest.

"Auri!!!" Wash and Al both lunged to grab the silver haired girl by the pillar, weeping as she disappeared into the Headless husk. The monsters backed off, leaving only Fordo, Al, Meeko, Wash, and Doyle shaking by the obelisk.

"Give them back!" Al shouted, running and jumping to pull Jason off of Creature's back once more, Meeko barking at Creature's feet. The robot batted Al aside like a ragdoll, picking him up with one hand and raising him to see Jason face to face.

"Or what?" Jason mocked, Al struggling to squirm free in vain, "Oh, that reminds me! You still owe me for running off like you did...I wasted a lotta time looking for you, Baby Brother."

"Only thing I owe you is my fucking fist..." Al spat

Jason grinned, "Interesting choice..."

Meeko howled in distress, whining, crying, painful noises Fordo didn't know dogs could make while he watched Creature twist Alexander in his giant hands, wrap one tight around Al's left arm, and rip it straight off of his body, "Gah-Ahhhhhh!!!" With a wet, popping tear the shaft of the broken crossbow bolt fell free, bouncing on the cobblestones below.

Al went limp in the giant's hands, his shoulder spurting hot steaming blood, Creature plopping both of Al's bloody pieces back onto the ground, Meeko licking Al's face, nuzzling him with his nose, trying to wake him up.

"He said 'Fist', Creature, not his whole freakin' arm!"

"Apologies..."

"We gotta work on your restraint, buddy."

Scrapyard's war drums pounded closer and closer.

Jason pointed at Fordo, "Tell Stumpy here that if he wants to see 'mommy' again, he should come home to the wreck."

Fordo spat in his direction to Jason's amusement.

"I'll see you again, Dead Eyes, soon as you're ready, but don't make me wait too long! You pick the place...And I'll bring the party," he grinned.

"If you don't kill me now...I Will kill you again..."

"That's the spirit," Jason grinned, "We're gonna have all kinds of fun together!"

A strange sudden wind swept up all around them, droning like a giant invisible fan, the fog slowly dissipating as Creature launched upward, escaping into the clouds. The many Headless with Fordo's friends inside them, scurried off, up to the roofs of the buildings, stretching to their limits, high into the air until it looked like they got a hold of the lowest hanging clouds, pulling themselves up after Creature.

Fordo squinted up in the dust storm as the clouds parted and world shook, to see a sky as dark and red as rusted metal. Fordo couldn't help but be amazed realizing what this was; The belly of an ancient Oldworld airship, a floating fortress the size of Scrapyard hovering just above the town, the heavy fog spilling out of numerous openings like some kind of cloud carrier, the Headless slithering in, disappearing from sight. Fordo stared in awe as the hunk of floating steel slowly drifted back across the river, up into the sky, leaving a trail of clouds behind it, quickly concealing itself once more.

The clouds above parted and the shadow passed, blinding them with sudden sunlight. Wash wept while Doyle held him, his face cold as wet stone. Doyle hummed a somber song, rocking back and forth in the shade of his hat, struggling to light a cigarette with trembling hands. Fordo crawled over the now one armed Alexander, drifting in and out of consciousness, bleeding with his animal, while the drums of Balian's warband thundered out over the hills.

You hear that, Al...?

Fordo placed a cold, steady hand on Al's broken body...

Your fuckin' father's here for you...

Sons of Scrapyard

Remembrance

"Keep up, Boy..." His father grumbled, barely looking back, somehow maintaining the same relentless pace since they'd both left Scrapyard two days prior. Fordo trudged on, sweat pouring down his body even in the cool morning air, like he had a personal sticky storm cloud stuck to the top of his head. He stomped through every dead leaf and broken branch of Bleakwood Forest, the constant crunch his only means of distraction as he followed his father's gaping footprints, watching Bali's wide back and bulging pack rock back and forth and back and forth for days on end between the young, moss covered trees.

"Right...behind you..." Fordo gasped, heart pounding under his heavy, sweat soaked pack.

He couldn't believe out of all the times he'd pushed and fought and begged to be included on one of his father's missions, he finally got to come along on this exhausting, mind numbing nightmare. No trail, no sign, no indication they were even close to finding them. *A bot And a bear seen traveling Together? Two monsters wandering the wilderness as Companions? What the hell could that mean?? Two bad we'll never find out...Lost as glass in this gigantic fuckin' forest.*

"Why do you think...they're traveling together?" Fordo asked

"That's what we're gonna find out."

"I know, but..." Fordo stumbled on a gnarled root, somehow tossing dirt up into his boot, "Do you have any theories?"

"A few..." Bali stated without elaboration, without answer, without care to. Fordo sighed to himself, adjusting the uncomfortable leather straps on his pack.

At the start of their journey he was at least excited he'd get a chance to Talk to his dad. Just the two of them for the first time in years...no projects, no workshop, no stepmom, no distractions. Fordo thought he'd finally get to learn from his father, maybe even about his father, something personal, something real, outside of the stories and songs and legends. But every mission's still a project to Balian, demanding all his attention, all his focus. Fordo shot down most of his own questions himself, before they could escape his mouth just to be waved away by Balian like some bothersome bugs.

Fordo always understood, he'd accepted it long ago. Wishing more than anything for a normal father, but realizing Balian wasn't a normal man and he never would be. Forced to fight, forced to lead, called upon to rebuild a broken world. He's a hero...A legend...A king if he wished to be. He didn't have the time, didn't have the room in his life to also be a father. Fordo felt guilty for expecting anything more of him. But still...it didn't hurt to dream.

Fordo's face suddenly smushed into Bali's backpack, finding out the hard way it was just as soaked as his. "Ugh!" Fordo wiped the salt from his face, "Can't you warn me before you stop?"

"As much as you can pay attention..." His father said, crouched over, meticulously tracing the leaves and moss with a rough hand, nodding and grunting to himself.

"What is it?" Fordo's heart raced with excitement, "Did we pick up the trail??"

"I picked it up two hours ago..."

"You...what...?" Fordo's heart sank deep into his stomach, "Two hours?"

"You've been stomping on them all day, branches broken by the bot, following giant footprints. How many giants you think live in these woods, Boy?"

"I don't know, I thought..." Fordo's cheeks flushed red, "Maybe they're yours, dad...You're not the...smallest guy I know." Fordo fumbled his words trying to mask his hurt feelings with an attempted joke, his father marching on without a word.

Looking down at the branches then up at the trees, realizing all the branches were broken at the same height, like something big had pushed through them. The bot's prints were all vaguely rectangular, pressed deep into the dirt, while the shallow indents they made themselves slowly disappeared behind them, the moss and leaves reforming the ground like foam. He didn't know how he could possibly mistake the bot's prints for Balian's, his father just always seemed so much larger to Fordo than he really was.

Just because I don't need your help to figure it out, doesn't mean I don't want it...I thought you would show me... Thought you'd want to......I'm sorry.

What did you find? Are they close? How can you tell? Fordo kept all his questions to himself, figuring he'd bothered Bali enough.

Fordo's lip quivered and throat swelled, carefully stepping around any crunching debris as they continued on the apparent trail, holding back embarrassed tears with every fiber of his being.

Crunching leaves, panting like an idiot while hunting actual monsters…What the fuck is wrong with me? And why wouldn't you tell me? Just letting me stomp away like an asshole, like I'm not jeopardizing the entire mission!

Fordo tried to steady his breath, barely inhaling for sound's sake, almost immediately getting a headache.

Two hours ago…What does he think I'm doing here? Why even let me come along if you won't let me help, won't show me what to do, even teach me how to track?

"Why am I even here?" Fordo asked, the only question he didn't want to say out loud somehow sneaking past his lips.

"Sarah said it'd be good for you…" Bali stated without hesitation, without warmth, marching on like that was that.

Always Sarah…Butting in where it's not her place, making me a nuisance to my own father.

Fordo had more or less gotten used to Bali's distance throughout the years, but never his silence, never the cold, like it was a chore to speak to his own son. And maybe it was…*Maybe I remind him too much of mom, the woman he lost…I don't look anything like him, I know I must take after her.*

Maybe I just don't interest him…The man who's done everything has a son who's done nothing…He holds a similar indifference towards the workers, his flock of loyal followers, others content living in his shadow. Maybe I haven't earned his love, earned his respect, not yet… But I will…One day…I'll be worthy of your name…I'll make you proud, Dad, I swear it.

Balian stopped once more, staring at a particularly large circle of broken branches on the ground, two gigantic rectangular footprints pressed deep in the center at an odd pitched angle. Fordo looked up at a gaping hole in the red leafed canopy, branches broken all the way up the trunks.

"I didn't know they could jump…" Fordo said to himself.

"They could do far more than we let them…" Bali said, both of them staring up at the lonely patch of gray sky.

"How the hell do we track that?"

"Mm…" Bali took a long swig from his wetskin, beads of water dripping from the ends of the bristles on his face, "We follow his friend."

For what felt like hours more, they crept through the woods, pulling their packs tight to keep them from clanking. Before, the bot's tracks were so glaringly obvious that they made the bear's nearly invisible; Barely a shadow of an indent on the spongy ground. Fordo had to find the narrow grooves where its claws penetrated the debris in order to bury the assumption that his father was tracking the beast by smell or some glass.

"Mm…" Bali grunted, stopping in place.

Fordo tried in vain to look beyond his father's wall of a back, tip-toeing around Bali to see the forest open up.

Before them towered a beautiful, ancient tree. Alive and red as a beating heart, trunk wider than their house in Scrapyard. A maze of roots reaching out in every direction, glistening red sap shining in the sunlight. Dirt bulging up between the roots and around the trunk like the tree had grown all at once, transformed by some spell, erupting out of Aureum like a Sienan Drill Dragon, looming proudly over the rest of the young forest like the mother of it all.

As impressed as Fordo was, Balian had a look in his eye that Fordo had never seen before...almost resembling surprise. Fordo followed his eyes to the base of the tree, pointing right at a shadowed lump in the dirt, nestled in a nook between the roots.

"What is it, dad?" Fordo squinted at the lump until his eyes adjusted to the shadows, until part of it resembled the bottoms of two bloody human feet. Fordo's jaw dropped, eyes darting all around for danger, listening, hearing nothing but the gentle rustle of the leaves above. "Dad...?"

Balian walked straight for the body. Fordo followed, immediately distracted by a scene of pure violence depicted in the dirt. Long sweeping drag marks, deep scratching claws, a chaotic jumble of all manner of footprints from various clawed paws to odd, vaguely human shapes, like long fingered feet. Dozens of puddles and patches of moist black dirt littered the ground, Fordo touching one with the tip of his finger, breaking the disgusting mushy seal of congealed blood, realizing it wasn't sap that shone on the roots all around them.

This wasn't some squabble between packs of roaming hunters, this was a malicious bloody fight to the death. Fordo didn't know creatures were capable of war. He smiled to himself, his imagination running wild with the idea of a battle of bones. No bolts, no hammers, no traps, no mercy, just tooth and claw and ancient primal instinct as two gangs of rival monsters tore this place asunder.

The bear's tracks were now clear as a painting, scoring the naked dirt with wide powerful paws, fresh blood all along its trail. Fordo scratched his hairless chin, noticing far more of the bear's tracks led Through blood stains than were Covered by them.

The bear Joined this fight…?

Fordo searched the clearing for fallen and found none. Every pool of blood or crash in the dirt accompanied by long heavy drag marks leading westward, into deeper, darker woods.

"Dad! Dad, you gotta see this!" Fordo jogged back to Balian, somehow forgetting about the body he was crouched over. Fordo quickly cleared his excitement from his throat and stepped around his dad once more to see who they had found, surprised to find that it was two someones.

He hadn't seen this much blood since his mother died. Whatever had happened here, these strangers caught the worst of it. A young man, maybe Fordo's age, maybe a little older, with a handsome earthborn shepherd dog resting on his lap, both bodies as torn and bloody as the ground they laid on.

The dog was missing its front left leg, fur black and stiff around the shoulder, with more blood all around its mouth and snout. Long drag marks trailed in the dirt behind it, like it had crawled over when wounded to rest with its master.

Nearly naked, tall, slender, lean. The boy's bloody skin showed through his tattered jacket. Covered nearly head to toe in bites and scratches, even burns and scars between those, old wounds from far more than this battle alone, more than any veteran, any warrior that Fordo's ever seen. Fordo raised his eyebrows when he noticed the bloodiest part of the boy was not his torn throat, but his hands, both soaked to the wrists and clasped tight around the handles of a short rusted hatchet and the shaft of a sharpened tree branch.

"Guy fought like hell..." Fordo said

Balian brushed the dead boy's dark, greasy hair from his face, muttering some silent prayer.

"Should we stay on the trail?"

Both of Bali's knees popped as he stood with a long labored sigh, "No..." He unslung his pack and let it crash to the ground, "These boys earned a proper rest." Balian dug a small gardening trowel from his pack and held it out to Fordo.

Fordo looked at the tiny half shovel and frowned, "But what about the bear? If we stop now and...That'll take all day..."

"Then we better get started..."

But we didn't even know them...

Fordo opened his mouth to protest when they both flinched, the dog suddenly convulsing and coughing up blood back into existence.

"Fuckin' glass..." Fordo cursed, stepping away.

Balian dropped down to his knees without hesitation, placing a hand on the dog's back as it rose and fell with wet labored breaths. "That's not possible..." His father whispered, scrambling to uncap his wetskin, petting the undead beast.

Fordo stared at the heaving animal trying to rationalize, justify, explain what was happening, but he had no idea, knowing no more than: *That thing was fuckin' dead...*

Balian lifted its head with a finger, forming a bowl with his hand in front of its bloody mouth, filling it with water. The dog coughed and splashed the drink away more than once before weakly groaning, sniffing, and lapping up the liquid without opening its eyes.

"Would you look at that..." Balian chuckled and smiled up at Fordo, bigger than he had ever seen before in his lifetime, looking the happiest he's ever been. Fordo didn't know his father was capable of joy and yet there it was, clear and bright as a bonfire. Fordo beamed back.

A pet...? A dog...? One we found together, barely in time to nurse it back to health? Maybe This Is It, what we needed all along, something to bring us a little closer.

Fordo looked at the boy with curiosity and wonder, then with cautious suspicion, realizing he had far less wounds than a moment before. Fordo leaned closer, squinting at the long clawed scratches, eyes going wide when he realized it wasn't just his imagination...The wounds were closing up on their own.

"Hey...dad..."

Balian ignored him, still petting the undead dog.

"Dad…"

Fordo crouched down and pried the boy's blood soaked weapons from his hands, tossing them away.

"What is it, boy…?" Balian looked confused until Fordo pointed at the dead boy's body, his flesh and skin slowly stitching back together before their very eyes.

"What the hell is…?" Fordo tried to pull his dad away, but Bali was fascinated, leaning in for a closer look.

Fordo nearly jumped out of his own skin when the dead boy suddenly gasped and screamed, his whole body lurching upward, the bloody fist that had been clenching the wooden spike hammered into the side of Bali's neck, leaving a red print where a killing blow would have been.

"DAD!" Fordo cried out, helplessly tugging on his giant of a father in vain, trying to pull him away from the undead duo.

Balian caught the boy's flailing fist and held it down against his chest. The boy kept screaming and squirming, shaking and heaving like a madman, tears streaming down the sides of his head, eyes still clenched shut.

The undead dog, unbothered by its panicking master, moved slowly to weakly lick the boy's tears away. Balian held the boy still, one hand around his wrist, the other gently cradling the side of his face. Little by little the boy calmed down from flailing to shaking, from shaking to crying, pressing his face into Balian's palm. Fordo's father hushing the boy like one might put an infant back to sleep.

Fordo finally steadied his own breath and watched his father gently wipe the boy's tears away with his thumb as they fell. Trembling as he looked back and forth between his father and the strange broken boy. His heart breaking as he listened to Balian whisper in a soft, compassionate, loving tone Fordo didn't know his father was capable of.

"Shh Sh Sh...Easy there, Son...That's it...It's alright..."

What is this...? Fordo held his breath.

The boy's sobbing finally faded enough for Bali to pour him some water, coughing and crying slowly turning into long, shaky, deliberate breaths to steady himself.

"What's your name, Son?"

Fordo winced at the word...

"I don't..." The boy croaked, "I don't think I know..." he half laughed half cried, his breath picking up again, Bali calming him down with a gentle palm.

"Don't know your own fuckin' name...What are you, stupid?" Bali smiled and chuckled, petting the boy's temple with his thumb.

"Maybe...that's my name..." The boy smiled back, coughing through cracked, bloody lips.

Balian poured him more water, "Do you remember what happened to you...?"

The boy opened his dark brown eyes for the first time, struggling to look around him, mostly staring up at the big bald man still smiling down on him. "I think..." The boy coughed, "I think maybe I fell...Trying to climb...Up your big ass forehead..."

The boy grinned and coughed with a weak, wet chuckle.

Fordo furrowed his brow.

And then, after an entire childhood of Fordo expecting only anger......Bali's lips slowly crept across his face and cracked open into laughter, his deep lungs kicking at his chest, every suppressed joy suddenly brought to the surface, echoing up the ancient tree, ringing loud and deep throughout her forest...

This was the first time Fordo could recall ever hearing his Father's laugh.

Fordo stepped back, watched his father joke and smile and comfort the undead boy, wipe away his tears, call him 'Son', tell him everything was going to be okay...

He watched all these things and realized...

...for the very first time...

...Balian was always capable of love...

Just not loving Me...

MORE STORIES TO COME FROM THE
CHILDREN OF AUREUM

Book 1
SONS OF SCRAPYARD

Book 2
GIFT OF GREY

Book 3
BARONS OF BLACKWYRM

***

TALES OF AUREUM

AND

FAR FALL

Thank you

The google document I first opened to initially write this story was created at 12:01am, on January 30th, 2017. The words of this message are the last I will be adding to the final version of this novel. That means that there are:

Eight Years...
Five Months...
Twenty One Days...
Fifteen Hours...

and Forty Five Minutes spent between writing the Very First and Very Last words of this book. That's how long it took to get this story out of my head and hone it into something worthy enough to transfer into yours. In that time I have gained and lost countless jobs, friends, hopes, dreams. Buried my mother, found my wife, met my son. I have lost and found my mind and myself, more than once, this book contributing in almost equal parts to both, but it's been there for me through it all.

I love this world, I love these characters, I love this story, and I can't wait to share them all and more with you in the many years to come.

If you are reading this message...Fuck You-No, I'm just kidding. To anyone and everyone who has spent their limited time reading my work and seeing my world, I deeply and sincerely thank every single one of you.